CAROLINE ANDERSON
SHIRLEY JUMP
LINDA GOODNIGHT

MILLS
BOON

Published in Great Britain 2013
by Mills & Boon, an imprint of Harlequin (UK) Limited,
Eton House, 18-24 Paradise Road, Richmond, Surrey TW9 1SR

CHRISTMAS MIRACLE © by Harlequin Enterprises II B.V./S.à.r.l 2013

Their Christmas Family Miracle, *A Princess for Christmas* and *Jingle-Bell Baby* were first published in Great Britain by Harlequin (UK) Limited.

Their Christmas Family Miracle © Caroline Anderson 2009
A Princess for Christmas © Shirley Kawa-Jump, LLC 2009
Jingle-Bell Baby © Linda Goodnight 2009

ISBN: 978 0 263 91038 4
eBook ISBN: 978 1 472 01618 8

05-1213

Harlequin (UK) policy is to use papers that are natural, renewable and recyclable products and made from wood grown in sustainable forests. The logging and manufacturing processes conform to the legal environmental regulations of the country of origin.

Printed and bound in Spain
by Blackprint CPI, Barcelona

THEIR CHRISTMAS FAMILY MIRACLE

BY
CAROLINE ANDERSON

Caroline Anderson has the mind of a butterfly. She's been a nurse, a secretary, a teacher, run her own soft-furnishing business and now she's settled on writing. She says, "I was looking for that elusive something. I finally realized it was variety, and now I have it in abundance. Every book brings new horizons and new friends, and in between books I have learned to be a juggler. My teacher husband, John, and I have two beautiful and talented daughters, Sarah and Hannah, umpteen pets and several acres of Suffolk that nature tries to reclaim every time we turn our backs!"

CHAPTER ONE

'WE NEED to talk.'

Amelia sat back on her heels and looked up at her sister with a sinking heart. She'd heard them arguing, heard her brother-in-law's harsh, bitter tone, heard the slamming of the doors, then her sister's approaching footsteps on the stairs. And she knew what was coming.

What she didn't know was how to deal with it.

'This isn't working,' she said calmly.

'No.' Laura looked awkward and acutely uncomfortable, but she also looked a little relieved that Amelia had made it easy for her. Again. Her hands clenched and unclenched nervously. 'It's not me—it's Andy. Well, and me, really, I suppose. It's the kids. They just—run around all the time, and the baby cries all night, and Andy's tired. He's supposed to be having a rest over Christmas, and instead—it's not their fault, Millie, but having the children here is difficult, we're just not used to it. And the dog, really, is the last straw. So—yes, I'm sorry, but—if you could find somewhere as soon as possible after Christmas—'

Amelia set aside the washing she was folding and got up, shaking her head, the thought of staying where she—

no, where her *children* were not wanted, anathema to her. 'It's OK. Don't apologise. It's a terrible imposition. Don't worry about it, we'll go now. I'll just pack their things and we'll get out of your hair—'

'I thought you didn't have anywhere to go?'

She didn't. Or money to pay for it, but that was hardly her sister's fault, was it? 'Don't worry,' she said again. 'We'll go to Kate's.'

But crossing her fingers behind her back was pointless. Kate lived in a tiny cottage, one up one down, with hardly room for her and her own daughter. There was no way the four of them and the dog could squeeze in, too. But her sister didn't know that, and her shoulders dropped in relief.

'I'll help you get their things together,' she said quickly, and disappeared, presumably to comb the house for any trace of their presence while Amelia sagged against the wall, shutting her eyes hard against the bitter sting of tears and fighting down the sob of desperation that was rising in her throat. Two and a half days to Christmas.

Short, dark, chaotic days in which she had no hope of finding anywhere for them to go or another job to pay for it. And, just to make it worse, they were in the grip of an unseasonably cold snap, so even if they were driven to it, there was no way they could sleep in the car. Not without running the engine, and that wasn't an option, since she probably only had just enough fuel to get away from her sister's house with her pride intact.

And, as it was the only thing she had left, that was a priority.

Sucking in a good, deep breath, she gathered up the baby's clothes and started packing them haphazardly, then stopped herself. She had to prioritise. Things for the next twenty-four hours in one little bag, then everything else she could sort out later once they'd arrived at wherever they were going. She sorted, shuffled, packed the baby's clothes, then her own, then finally went into the bedroom Kitty and Edward were sharing and packed their clothes and toys, with her mind firmly shut down and her thoughts banished for now.

She could think later. There'd be time to think once they were out of here. In the meantime, she needed to gather up the children and any other bits and pieces she'd overlooked and get them out before she totally lost it. She went down with the bags hanging like bunches of grapes from her fingers, dumped them in the hall and went into the euphemistically entitled family room, where her children were lying on their tummies watching the TV with the dog between them.

Not on the sofa again, mercifully.

'Kitty? Edward? Come and help me look for all your things, because we're going to go and see Kate and Megan.'

'What—now?' Edward asked, twisting round, his face sceptical. 'It's nearly lunch time.'

'Are we going to Kate's for lunch?' Kitty asked brightly.

'Yes. It's a surprise.' A surprise for Kate, at least, she thought, hustling them through the house and gathering up the last few traces of their brief but eventful stay.

'Why do we need all our things to go and see Kate and Megan for lunch?' Kitty asked, but Edward got there first and shushed her. Bless his heart. Eight years old and she'd be lost without him.

They met up with Laura in the kitchen, her face strained, a bag in her hand.

'I found these,' she said, giving it to Amelia. 'The baby's bottles. There was one in the dishwasher, too.'

'Thanks. Right, well, I just need to get the baby up and fold his cot, and we'll be out of your hair.'

She retreated upstairs to get him. Poor Thomas. He whimpered and snuggled into her as she picked him up, and she collapsed his travel cot one-handed and bumped it down the stairs. Their stuff was piled by the door, and she wondered if Andy might come out of his study and give them a hand to load it into her car, but the door stayed resolutely shut throughout.

It was just as well. It would save her the bother of being civil.

She put the baby in his seat, the cold air bringing him wide awake and protesting, threw their things into the boot and buckled the other two in, with Rufus on the floor in the front, before turning to her sister with her last remnant of pride and meeting her eyes.

'Thank you for having us. I'm sorry it was so difficult.'

Laura's face creased in a mixture of distress and embarrassment. 'Oh, don't. I'm so sorry, Millie. I hope you get sorted out. Here, these are for the children.' She handed over a bag of presents, all beautifully wrapped. Of course. They would be. Also expensive and impossible to compete with. And that wasn't what it was supposed to be about, but she took them, her arm working on autopilot.

'Thank you. I'm afraid I haven't got round to getting yours yet—'

'It doesn't matter. I hope you find somewhere nice soon. And—take this, please. I know money's tight for you at the moment, but it might give you the first month's rent or deposit—'

She stared at the cheque. 'Laura, I can't—'

'Yes, you can. Please. Owe me, if you have to, but take it. It's the least I can do.'

So she took it, stuffing it into her pocket without looking at it. 'I'll pay you back as soon as I can.'

'Whenever. Have a good Christmas.'

How she found that smile she'd never know. 'And you,' she said, unable to bring herself to say the actual words, and getting behind the wheel and dropping the presents into the passenger footwell next to Rufus, she shut the door before her sister could lean in and hug her, started the engine and drove away.

'Mummy, why *are* we taking all our Christmas presents and Rufus and the cot and everything to Kate and Megan's for lunch?' Kitty asked, still obviously troubled and confused, as well she might be.

Damn Laura. Damn Andy. And especially damn David. She schooled her expression and threw a smile over her shoulder at her little daughter. 'Well, we aren't going to stay with Auntie Laura and Uncle Andy any more, so after we've had lunch we're going to go somewhere else to stay,' she said.

'Why? Don't they like us?'

Ouch. 'Of course they do,' she lied, 'but they just need a bit of space.'

'So where *are* we going?'

It was a very good question, but one Millie didn't have a hope of answering right now...

* * *

It was an ominous sound.

He'd heard it before, knew instantly what it was, and Jake felt his mouth dry and his heart begin to pound. He glanced up over his shoulder, swore softly and turned, skiing sideways straight across and down the mountain, pushing off on his sticks and plunging down and away from the path of the avalanche that was threatening to wipe him out, his legs driving him forward out of its reach.

The choking powder cloud it threw up engulfed him, blinding him as the raging, roaring monster shot past behind him. The snow was shaking under his skis, the air almost solid with the fine snow thrown up as the snowfield covering the side of the ridge collapsed and thundered down towards the valley floor below.

He was skiing blind, praying that he was still heading in the right direction, hoping that the little stand of trees down to his left was now above him and not still in front of him, because at the speed he was travelling to hit one could be fatal.

It wasn't fatal, he discovered. It was just unbelievably, immensely painful. He bounced off a tree, then felt himself lifted up and carried on by the snow—down towards the scattered tumble of rocks at the bottom of the snowfield.

Hell.

With his last vestige of self-preservation, he triggered the airbags of his avalanche pack, and then he hit the rocks…

'Can you squeeze in a few more for lunch?'

Kate took one look at them all, opened the door wide

and ushered them inside. 'What on earth is going on?' she asked, her concerned eyes seeking out the truth from Millie's face.

'We've come for lunch,' Kitty said, still sounding puzzled. 'And then we're going to find somewhere to live. Auntie Laura and Uncle Andy don't want us. Mummy says they need space, but I don't think they like us.'

'Of course they do, darling. They're just very busy, that's all.'

Kate's eyes flicked down to Kitty with the dog at her side, to Edward, standing silently and saying nothing, and back to Millie. 'Nice timing,' she said flatly, reading between the lines.

'Tell me about it,' she muttered. 'Got any good ideas?'

Kate laughed slightly hysterically and handed the three older children a bag of chocolate coins off the tree. 'Here, guys, go and get stuck into these while Mummy and I have a chat. Megan, share nicely and don't give any chocolate to Rufus.'

'I *always* share nicely! Come on, we can share them out—and Rufus, you're not having *any*!'

Rolling her eyes, Kate towed Amelia down to the other end of the narrow room that was the entire living space in her little cottage, put the kettle on and raised an eyebrow. 'Well?'

She shifted Thomas into a more comfortable position in her arms. 'They aren't really child-orientated. They don't have any, and I'm not sure if it's because they haven't got round to it or because they really don't like them,' Millie said softly.

'And your lot were too much of a dose of reality?'

She smiled a little tightly. 'The dog got on the sofa, and Thomas is teething.'

'Ah.' Kate looked down at the tired, grizzling baby in his mother's arms and her kind face crumpled. 'Oh, Amelia, I'm so sorry,' she murmured under her breath. 'I can't believe they kicked you out just before Christmas!'

'They didn't. They wanted me to look for somewhere afterwards, but...'

'But—?'

She shrugged. 'My pride got in the way,' she said, hating the little catch in her voice. 'And now my kids have nowhere to go for Christmas. And convincing a landlord to give me a house before I can get another job is going to be tricky, and that's not going to happen any time soon if the response to my CV continues to be as resoundingly successful as it's being at the moment, and anyway the letting agents aren't going to be able to find us anything this close to Christmas. I could *kill* David for cutting off the maintenance,' she added under her breath, a little catch in her voice.

'Go ahead—I'll be a character witness for you in court,' Kate growled, then she leant back, folded her arms and chewed her lip thoughtfully. 'I wonder...?'

'What?'

'You could have Jake's house,' she said softly. 'My boss. I would say stay here, but I've got my parents and my sister coming for Christmas Day and I can hardly fit us all in as it is, but there's tons of room at Jake's. He's away until the middle of January. He always goes away at Christmas for a month—he shuts the office, gives everyone three weeks off on full pay and leaves the country before the office party, and I have the keys to keep an eye on it. And it's just sitting there, the most fabulous house, and it's just made for Christmas.'

'Won't he mind?'

'What, Jake? No. He wouldn't give a damn. You won't do it any harm, after all, will you? It's hundreds of years old and it's survived. What harm can you do it?'

What harm? She felt rising panic just thinking about it. 'I couldn't—'

'Don't be daft. Where else are you going to go? Besides, with the weather so cold it'll be much better for the house to have the heating on full and the fire lit. He'll be grateful when he finds out, and besides, Jake's generous to a fault. He'd want you to have it. Truly.'

Amelia hesitated. Kate seemed so convinced he wouldn't mind. 'You'd better ring him, then,' she said in the end. 'But tell him I'll give him money for rent just as soon as I can—'

Kate shook her head. 'No. I can't. I don't have the number, but I know he'd say yes,' she said, and Amelia's heart sank.

'Well, then, we can't stay there. Not without asking—'

'Millie, really. It'll be all right. He'd die before he'd let you be homeless over Christmas and there's no way he'd take money off you. Believe me, he'd want you to have the house.'

Still she hesitated, searching Kate's face for any sign of uncertainty, but if she felt any, Kate was keeping it to herself, and besides, Amelia was so out of options she couldn't afford the luxury of scruples, and in the end she gave in.

'Are you sure?'

'Absolutely. There won't be any food there, his house-keeper will have emptied the fridge, but I've got some basics I can let you have and bread and stuff, and there's bound to be something in the freezer and the cupboards to tide you over until you can replace it. We'll go over there the minute we've had lunch and settle you in. It'll be great—fantastic! You'll love it.'

'Love what?' Kitty asked, sidling up with chocolate all round her mouth and a doubtful expression on her face.

'My boss's house. He's gone away, and he's going to let you borrow it.'

'Let?' Millie said softly under her breath, but Kate just flashed her a smile and shrugged.

'Well, he would if he knew… OK, lunch first, and then let's go!'

It was, as Kate had said, the most fabulous house.

A beautiful old Tudor manor house, it had been in its time a farm and then a small hotel and country club, she explained, and then Jake had bought it and moved his offices out here into the Berkshire countryside. He lived in the house, and there was an office suite housing Jake's centre of operations in the former country club buildings on the far side of the old walled kitchen garden. There was a swimming pool, a sauna and steam room and a squash court over there, Kate told her as they pulled up outside on the broad gravel sweep, and all the facilities were available to the staff and their families.

Further evidence of his apparent generosity.

But it was the house which drew Amelia—old mellow

red brick, with a beautiful Dutch gabled porch set in the centre, and as Kate opened the huge, heavy oak door that bore the scars of countless generations and ushered them into the great entrance hall, even the children fell silent.

'Wow,' Edward said after a long, breathless moment.

Wow, indeed. Amelia stared around her, dumbstruck. There was a beautiful, ancient oak staircase on her left, and across the wide hall which ran from side to side were several lovely old doors which must lead to the principal rooms.

She ran her hand over the top of the newel post, once heavily carved, the carving now almost worn away by the passage of generations of hands. She could feel them all, stretching back four hundred years, the young, the old, the children who'd been born and grown old and died here, sheltered and protected by this beautiful, magnificent old house, and ridiculous though it was, as the front door closed behind them, she felt as if the house was gathering them up into its heart.

'Come on, I'll give you a quick tour,' Kate said, going down the corridor to the left, and they all trooped after her, the children still in a state of awe. The carpet under her feet must be a good inch thick, she thought numbly. Just how rich *was* this guy?

As Kate opened the door in front of her and they went into a vast and beautifully furnished sitting room with a huge bay window at the side overlooking what must surely be acres of parkland, she got her answer, and she felt her jaw drop.

Very rich. Fabulously, spectacularly rich, without a shadow of a doubt.

And yet he was gone, abandoning this beautiful house in which he lived alone to spend Christmas on a ski slope.

She felt tears prick her eyes, strangely sorry for a man she'd never met, who'd furnished his house with such love and attention to detail, and yet didn't apparently want to stay in it at the time of year when it must surely be at its most welcoming.

'Why?' she asked, turning to Kate in confusion. 'Why does he go?'

Kate shrugged. 'Nobody really knows. Or nobody talks about it. There aren't very many people who've worked for him that long. I've been his PA for a little over three years, since he moved the business here from London, and he doesn't talk about himself.'

'How sad.'

'Sad? No. Not Jake. He's not sad. He's crazy, he has some pretty wacky ideas and they nearly always work, and he's an amazingly thoughtful boss, but he's intensely private. Nobody knows anything about him, really, although he always makes a point of asking about Megan, for instance. But I don't think he's sad. I think he's just a loner and he likes to ski. Come and see the rest.'

They went back down the hall, along the squishy pile carpet that absorbed all the sound of their feet, past all the lovely old doors while Kate opened them one by one and showed them the rooms in turn.

A dining room with a huge table and oak-panelled walls; another sitting room, much smaller than the first, with a plasma TV in the corner, book-lined walls, battered leather sofas and all the evidence that this was his very personal retreat. There was a study at the front of the house which they didn't enter; and then finally the room Kate called the breakfast room—huge again, but with the same informality as the little sitting room, with foot-wide oak boards on the floor and a great big old refectory table covered in the scars of generations and just made for family living.

And the kitchen off it was, as she might have expected, also designed for a family—or entertaining on an epic scale. Vast, with duck-egg blue painted cabinets under thick, oiled wood worktops, a gleaming white four-oven Aga in the inglenook, and in the middle a granite-topped island with stools pulled up to it. It was a kitchen to die for, the kitchen of her dreams and fantasies, and it took her breath away. It took all their breaths away.

The children stared round it in stunned silence, Edward motionless, Kitty running her fingers reverently over the highly polished black granite, lingering over the tiny gold sparkles trapped deep inside the stone. Edward was the first to recover.

'Are we really going to stay here?' he asked, finally finding his voice, and she shook her head in disbelief.

'I don't think so.'

'Of course you are!'

'Kate, we can't—'

'Rubbish! Of course you can. It's only for a week or two. Come and see the bedrooms.'

Amelia shifted Thomas to her other hip and followed Kate up the gently creaking stairs, the children trailing awestruck in her wake, listening to Megan chattering about when they'd stayed there earlier in the year.

'That's Jake's room,' Kate said, turning away from it,

and Amelia felt a prickle of curiosity. What would his room be like? Opulent? Austere? Monastic?

No, not monastic. This man was a sensualist, she realised, fingering the curtains in the bedroom Kate led them into. Pure silk, lined with padding for warmth and that feeling of luxury that pervaded the entire house. Definitely not monastic.

'All the rooms are like this—except for some in the attic, which are a bit simpler,' Kate told her. 'You could take your pick but I'd have the ones upstairs. They're nicer.'

'How many are there?' she asked, amazed.

'Ten. Seven en suite, five on this floor and two above, and three more in the attic which share a bathroom. Those are the simpler ones. He entertains business clients here quite often, and they love it. So many people have offered to buy it, but he just laughs and says no.'

'I should think so. Oh, Kate—what if we ruin something?'

'You won't ruin it. The last person to stay here knocked a pot of coffee over on the bedroom carpet. He just had it cleaned.'

Millie didn't bother to point out that the last person to stay here had been invited—not to mention an adult who presumably was either a friend or of some commercial interest to their unknowing host.

'Can we see the attic? The simple rooms? It sounds more like our thing.'

'Sure. Megan, why don't you show Kitty and Edward your favourite room?'

The children ran upstairs after Megan, freed from their trance now and getting excited as the reality of it began to sink in, and she turned to Kate and took her arm. 'Kate, we can't possibly stay here without asking him,' she said urgently, her voice low. 'It would be so rude—and I just know something'll get damaged.'

'Don't be silly. Come on, I'll show you *my* favourite room. It's lovely, you'll adore it. Megan and I stayed here when my pipes froze last February, and it was bliss. It's got a gorgeous bed.'

'They've all got gorgeous beds.'

They had. Four-posters, with great heavy carved posts and silk canopies, or half testers with just the head end of the bed clothed in sumptuous drapes.

Except for the three Kate showed her now. In the first one, instead of a four-poster there was a great big old brass and iron bedstead, the whole style of the room much simpler and somehow less terrifying, even though the quality of the furnishings was every bit as good, and in the adjoining room was an antique child-sized sleigh bed that looked safe and inviting.

It was clearly intended to be a nursery, and would be perfect for Thomas, she thought wistfully, and beside it was a twin room with two black iron beds, again decorated more simply, and Megan and Kitty were sitting on the beds and bouncing, while giggles rose from their throats and Edward pretended to be too old for such nonsense and looked on longingly.

'We could sleep up here,' she agreed at last. 'And we could spend the days in the breakfast room.' Even the children couldn't hurt that old table...

'There's a playroom—come and see,' Megan said, pelting out of the room with the other children in hot pursuit, and Amelia followed them to where the landing widened and there were big sofas and another TV and lots and lots of books and toys.

'He said he had this area done for people who came with children, so they'd have somewhere to go where they could let their hair down a bit,' Kate explained, and then smiled. 'You see—he doesn't mind children being in the house. If he did, why would he have done this?'

Why, indeed? There was even a stair gate, she noticed, made of oak and folded back against the banisters. And somehow she didn't mind the idea of tucking them away in what amounted to the servants' quarters nearly as much.

'I'll help you bring everything up,' Kate said. 'Kids, come and help. You can carry some of your stuff.'

It only took one journey because most of their possessions were in storage, packed away in a unit on the edge of town, waiting for the time when she could find a way to house them in a place of their own again. Hopefully, this time with a landlord who wouldn't take the first opportunity to get them out.

And then, with everything installed, she let Rufus out of the car and took him for a little run on the grass at the side of the drive. Poor little dog. He was so confused but, so long as he was with her and the children, he was as good as gold, and she felt her eyes fill with tears.

If David had had his way, the dog would have been put down because of his health problems, but she'd struggled to keep up the insurance premiums to maintain his veterinary cover, knowing that the moment they lapsed, her funding for the dog's health and well-being would come to a grinding halt.

And that would be the end of Rufus.

She couldn't allow that to happen. The little Cavalier King Charles spaniel that she'd rescued as a puppy had been a lifeline for the children in the last few dreadful years, and she owed him more than she could ever say. So his premiums were paid, even if it meant she couldn't eat.

'Mummy, it's lovely here,' Kitty said, coming up to her and snuggling her tiny, chilly hand into Millie's. 'Can we stay for ever?'

Oh, I wish, she thought, but she ruffled Kitty's hair and smiled. 'No, darling—but we can stay until after Christmas, and then we'll find another house.'

'Promise?'

She crossed her fingers behind her back. 'Promise,' she said, and hoped that fate wouldn't make her a liar.

He couldn't breathe.

For a moment he thought he was buried despite his avalanche pack, and for that fleeting moment in time he felt fear swamp him, but then he realised he was lying face down in the snow.

His legs were buried in the solidified aftermath of the avalanche, but near the surface, and his body was mostly on the top. He tipped his head awkwardly, and a searing pain shot through his shoulder and down his left arm. Damn. He tried again, more cautiously this time, and the snow on his goggles slid off, showering his face with ice crystals that stung his skin in the cold, sharp air. He breathed deeply and opened his eyes and saw daylight. The last traces of it, the shadows long as night approached.

He managed to clear the snow from around his arms, and

shook his head to clear his goggles better and regretted it instantly. He gave the pain a moment, and then began to yell into the silence of the fading light.

He yelled for what seemed like hours, and then, like a miracle, he heard voices.

'Help!' he bellowed again, and waved, blanking out the pain.

And help came, in the form of big, burly lads who broke away the snow surrounding him, dug his legs out and helped him struggle free. Dear God, he hurt. Everywhere, but most particularly his left arm and his left knee, he realised. Where he'd hit the tree. Or the rocks. No, he'd hurt them on the tree, he remembered, but the rocks certainly hadn't helped and he was going to have a million bruises.

'Can you ski back down?' they asked, and he realised he was still wearing his skis. The bindings had held, even through that. He got up and tested his left leg and winced, but it was holding his weight, and the right one was fine. He nodded and, cradling his left arm against his chest, he picked his way off the rock field to the edge, then followed them slowly down the mountain to the village.

He was shipped off to hospital the moment they arrived back, and he was prodded and poked and tutted over for what seemed like an age. And then, finally, they put his arm in a temporary cast, gave him a nice fat shot of something blissful and he escaped into the blessed oblivion of sleep…

CHAPTER TWO

SHE refused to let Kate turn up the heating.

'We'll be fine,' she protested. 'Believe me, this isn't cold.'

'It's only on frost protection!'

'It's fine. We're used to it. Please, I really don't want to argue about this. We have jumpers.'

'Well, at least light the woodburner,' Kate said, relenting with a sigh. 'There's a huge stack of logs outside the back door.'

'I can't use his logs! Logs are expensive!'

Kate just laughed. 'Not if you own several acres of woodland. He has more logs than he knows what to do with. We all use them. I throw some into the boot of my car every day and take them home to burn overnight, and so does everyone else. Really, you can't let the kids be cold, Millie. Just use the wood.'

So she did. She lit the fire, stood the heavy black mesh guard in front of it and the children settled down on the rug with Rufus and watched the television while she made them something quick and simple for supper. Even Thomas was good, managing to eat his supper without spitting it out all over the room or screaming the place down, and Amelia felt herself start to relax.

And when the wind picked up in the night and the old house creaked and groaned, it was just as if it was settling down, turning up its collar against the wind and wrapping its arms around them all to keep them warm.

Fanciful nonsense.

But it felt real, and when she got up in the morning and tiptoed downstairs to check the fire before the children woke, she found Rufus fast asleep on the rug in front of the woodburner, and he lifted his head and wagged his tail. She picked him up and hugged him, tears of relief prickling her eyes because finally, for the first time in months, she felt—even if it would only be for a few days—as if they were safe.

She filled up the fire, amazed that it had stayed alight, and made herself a cup of tea while Rufus went out in the garden for a moment. Then she took advantage of the quiet time and sat with him by the fire to drink her tea and contemplate her next move.

Rattling the cage of the job agencies, of course. What choice was there? Without a job, she couldn't hope to get a house. And she needed to get some food in. Maybe a small chicken? She could roast it, and put a few sausages round it, and it would be much cheaper than a turkey. Just as well, as she was trying to stretch the small amount of money she had left for as long as possible.

She thought of the extravagant Christmases she'd had with David in the past, the lavish presents, the wasted food, and wondered if the children felt cheated. Probably, but Christmas was just one of the many ways in which he'd let them down on a regular basis, so she was sure they'd just take it all in their stride.

Unlike being homeless, she thought, getting to her feet and washing out her mug before going upstairs to start the day. They were finding that really difficult and confusing, and all the chopping and changing was making them feel insecure. And she hated that. But there was Laura's cheque, which meant she might be able to find somewhere sooner—even if she would have to pay her back, just for the sake of her pride.

So, bearing the cheque in mind, she spent part of the morning on the phone trying to find somewhere to live, but the next day would be Christmas Eve and realistically nobody wanted to show her anything until after the Christmas period was over, and the job agencies were no more helpful. Nobody, apparently, was looking for a trans- lator at the moment, so abandoning her search until after Christmas, she took the kids out for a long walk around the grounds, with Thomas in his stroller and Rufus sniffing the ground and having a wonderful time while Kitty and Edward ran around shrieking and giggling.

And there was nobody to hear, nobody to complain, nobody to stifle the sound of their childish laughter, and gradually she relaxed and let herself enjoy the day.

'Mummy, can we have a Christmas tree?' Edward asked as they trudged back for lunch.

More money—not only for the tree, but also for deco- rations. And she couldn't let herself touch Laura's money except for a house. 'I don't know if we should,' she said, blaming it on the unknown Jake and burying her guilt because she was sick of telling her children that they couldn't have things when it was all because their unprincipled and disinterested father refused to pay up. 'It's not our house, and you know how they drop needles. He might mind.'

'He won't mind! Of course he won't! *Everyone* has a Christmas tree!' Kitty explained patiently to her obviously dense mother.

'But we haven't got the decorations, and anyway, I don't know where we could get one this late,' she said, wondering if she'd get away with it and hating the fact that she had to disappoint them yet again.

They walked on in silence for a moment, then Edward stopped. 'We could make one!' he said, his eyes lighting up at the challenge and finding a solution, as he always did. 'And we could put fir cones on it! There were lots in the wood—and there were some branches there that looked like Christmas tree branches, a bit. Can we get them after lunch and tie them together and pretend they're a tree, and then we can put fir cones on it, and berries—I saw some berries, and I'm sure he won't mind if we only pick a few—'

'Well, he might—'

'No, he won't! Mummy, he's lent us his *house*!' Kitty said earnestly and, not for the first time, Millie felt a stab of unease.

But the children were right, everybody had a tree, and what harm could a few cut branches and some fir cones do? And maybe even the odd sprig of berries...

'All right,' she agreed, 'just a little tree.' So after lunch they trooped back, leaving the exhausted little Rufus snoozing by the fire, and Amelia and Edward loaded themselves up with branches and they set off, Kitty dragging Thomas in the stroller backwards all the way from the woods to the house.

'There!' Edward said in satisfaction, dropping his pile of branches by the back door. 'Now we can make our tree!'

The only thing that kept him going on that hellish journey was the thought of home.

The blissful comfort of his favourite old leather sofa, a bottle of fifteen-year-old single malt and—equally importantly—the painkillers in his flight bag.

Getting upstairs to bed would be beyond him at this point. His knee was killing him—not like last time, when he'd done the ligaments in his other leg, but badly enough to mean that staying would have been pointless, even if he hadn't broken his wrist. And now all he could think about was lying down, and the sooner the better. He'd been stupid to travel so soon; his body was black and blue from end to end, but somehow, with Christmas what felt like seconds away and everyone down in the village getting so damned excited about it, leaving had become imperative now that he could no longer ski to outrun his demons.

Not that he ever really managed to outrun them, although he always gave it a damn good try, but this time he'd come too close to losing everything, and deep down he'd realised that maybe it was time to stop running, time to go home and just get on with life—and at least here he could find plenty to occupy himself.

He heard the car tyres crunch on gravel and cracked open his eyes. Home. Thank God for that. Lights blazed in the dusk, triggered by the taxi pulling up at the door, and handing over what was probably an excessive amount of money, he got out of the car with a grunt of pain and walked slowly to the door.

And stopped.

There was a car on the drive, not one he recognised, and there were lights on inside.

One in the attic, and one on the landing.

'Where d'you want these, guv?' the taxi driver asked, and he glanced down at the cases.

'Just in here would be good,' he said, opening the door and sniffing. Woodsmoke. And there was light coming from the breakfast room, and the sound of—laughter? A child's laughter?

Pain squeezed his chest. Dear God, no. Not today, of all days, when he just needed to crawl into a corner and forget—

'There you go then, guv. Have a good Christmas.'

'And you,' he said, closing the door quietly behind the man and staring numbly towards the breakfast room. What the hell was going on? It must be Kate—no one else had a key, and the place was like Fort Knox. She must have dropped in with Megan and a friend to check on the house—but it didn't sound as if they were checking anything. It sounded as if they were having fun.

Oh, Lord, please, not today...

He limped over to the door and pushed it gently open, and then stood transfixed.

Chaos. Complete, utter chaos.

Two children were sitting on the floor by the fire in a welter of greenery, carefully tying berries to some rather battered branches that looked as if they had come off the conifer hedge at the back of the country club, but it was the woman standing on the table who held his attention.

Tall, slender, with rather wild fair hair escaping from a ponytail and jeans that had definitely seen better days, she was reaching up and twisting another of the branches into the heavy iron hoop over the refectory table, festooning the light fitting with a makeshift attempt at a Christmas decoration which did nothing to improve it.

He'd never seen her before. He would have recognised her, he was sure, if he had. So who the hell—?

His mouth tightened, but then she bent over, giving him an unrestricted view of her neat, shapely bottom as the old jeans pulled across it, and he felt a sudden, unwelcome and utterly unexpected tug of need.

'It's such a shame Jake isn't going to be here, because we're making it so pretty,' the little girl was saying.

'Why *does* he go away?' the boy asked.

'I don't know,' the woman replied, her voice soft and melodious. 'I can't imagine.'

'Didn't Kate say?'

Kate. Of course, she'd be at the bottom of this, he thought, and he could have wrung her neck for her abysmal timing.

Well, if he had two good hands...which at the moment, of course, he didn't.

'He goes skiing.'

'I hate skiing,' the boy said. 'That woman in the kindergarten was horrible. She smelt funny. Here, I've finished this one.'

And he scrambled to his feet and turned round, then caught sight of Jake and froze.

'Well, come on then, give it to me,' the woman said, waving her hand behind her to try and locate it.

'Um…Mum…'

'Darling, give me the branch, I can't stand here for ever—'

She turned towards her son, followed the direction of his gaze and her eyes flew wide. 'Oh—!'

'Mummy, do I need more berries or is that enough?' the little girl asked, but Jake hardly heard her because the woman's eyes were locked on his and the shock and desperation in them blinded his senses to anything else.

'Kitty, hush, darling,' she said softly and, dropping down, she slid off the edge of the table and came towards him with a haphazard attempt at a smile. 'Um…I imagine you're Jake Forrester?' she asked, her voice a little uneven, and he hardened himself against her undoubted appeal and the desperate eyes.

'Well, there you have the advantage over me,' he murmured drily, 'because I have no idea who you are, or why I should come home and find you smothering my house in bits of dead vegetation in my absence—'

Her eyes fluttered briefly closed and colour flooded her cheeks. 'I can explain—'

'Don't bother. I'm not interested. Just get all that—*tat* out of here, clear the place up and then leave.'

He turned on his heel—not a good idea, with his knee screaming in protest, but the pain just fuelled the fire of his anger and he stalked into the study, picked up the phone and rang Kate.

'Millie?'

'So that's her name.'

'*Jake*?' Kate shrieked, and he could hear her collecting herself at the other end of the line. 'What are you doing home?'

'There was an avalanche. I got in the way. And I seem to have guests. Would you care to elaborate?'

'Oh, Jake, I'm so sorry, I can explain—'

'Excellent. Feel free. You've got ten seconds, so make it good.' He settled back in the chair with a wince, listening as Kate sucked in her breath and gave her pitch her best shot.

'She's a friend. Her ex has gone to Thailand, he won't pay the maintenance and she lost her job so she lost her house and her sister kicked her out yesterday.'

'Tough. She's packing now, so I suggest you find some other sucker to put her and her kids up so I can lie and be sore in peace. And don't imagine for a moment that you've heard the end of this.'

He stabbed the off button and threw the phone down on his desk, then glanced up to see the woman—Millie, apparently—transfixed in the doorway, her face still flaming.

'Please don't take it out on Kate. She was only trying to help us.'

He stifled a contemptuous snort and met her eyes challengingly, too sore in every way to moderate his sarcasm. 'You're not doing so well, are you? You don't seem to be able to keep anything. Your husband, your job, your house—even your sister doesn't want you. I wonder why? I wonder what it is about you that makes everyone want to get rid of you?'

She stepped back as if she'd been struck, the colour

draining from her face, and he felt a twinge of guilt but suppressed it ruthlessly.

'We'll be out of here in half an hour. I just need to pack our things. What do you want me to do with the sheets?'

Sheets? He was throwing her out and she was worrying about the *sheets*?

'Just leave them. I wouldn't want to hold you up.'

She straightened her spine and took another step back, and he could see her legs shaking. 'Right. Um…fine.'

And she spun round and walked briskly away in the direction of the breakfast room, leaving him to his guilt. He sighed and sagged back against the chair, a wave of pain swamping him for a moment. When he opened his eyes, the boy was there.

'I'm really sorry,' he said, his little chin up, just like his mother's, his eyes huge in a thin, pale face. 'Please don't be angry with Mummy. She was just trying to make a nice Christmas for us. She thought we were going to stay with Auntie Laura, but Uncle Andy didn't want us there because he said the baby kept him awake—'

There was a baby, too? Dear God, it went from bad to worse, but that wasn't the end of it.

'—and the dog smells and he got on the sofa, and that made him really mad. I heard them fighting. And then Mummy said we were going to see Kate, and she said we ought to come here because you were a nice man and you wouldn't mind and what harm could we do because the house was hundreds of years old and had survived and anyway you liked children or you wouldn't have done the playroom in the attic.'

He finally ran out of breath and Jake stared at him.

Kate thought he was that nice? Kate was dreaming.

But the boy's wounded eyes called to something deep inside him, and Jake couldn't ignore it. Couldn't kick them all out into the cold just before Christmas. Even he wasn't that much of a bastard.

But it wasn't just old Ebenezer Scrooge who had ghosts, and the last thing he needed was a houseful of children over Christmas, Jake thought with a touch of panic. And a baby, of all things, and—a dog?

Not much of a dog. It hadn't barked, and there was no sign of it, so it was obviously a very odd breed of dog. Or old and deaf?

No. Not old and deaf, and not much of a dog at all, he realised, his eyes flicking to the dimly lit hallway behind the boy and focusing on a small red and white bundle of fluff with an anxiously wriggling tail and big soulful eyes that were watching him hopefully.

A little spaniel, like the one his grandmother had had. He'd always liked it—and he wasn't going to be suckered because of the damn dog!

But the boy was still there, one sock-clad foot on top of the other, squirming slightly but holding his ground, and if his ribs hadn't hurt so much he would have screamed with frustration.

'What's your name?'

'Edward. Edward Jones.'

Nice, honest name. Like the child, he thought inconsequentially. Oh, damn. He gave an inward sigh as he felt his defences crumble. After all, it was hardly the boy's fault that he couldn't cope with the memories... 'Where's your mother, Edward?'

'Um...packing. I'm supposed to be clearing up the branches, but I can't reach the ones in the light so I've got to wait for her to come down.'

'Could you go and get her for me, and then look after the others while we have a chat?'

He nodded, but stood there another moment, chewing his lip.

Jake sighed softly. 'What is it?'

'You won't be mean to her, will you? She was only trying to look after us, and she feels so guilty because Dad won't give us any money so we can't have anything nice ever, but it's really not her fault—'

'Just get her, Edward,' he said gently. 'I won't be mean to her.'

'Promise?'

Oh, what was he doing? He needed to get rid of them before he lost his mind! 'I promise.'

The boy vanished, but the dog stayed there, whining softly and wagging his tail, and Jake held out his hand and called the dog over. He came, a little warily, and sat down just a few feet away, tail waving but not yet really ready to trust.

Very wise, Jake thought. He really, really wasn't in a very nice mood, but it was hardly the dog's fault. And he'd promised the boy he wouldn't be mean to his mother.

Well, any more mean than he already had been. He pressed his lips together and sighed. He was going to have to apologise to her, he realised—to the woman who'd moved into his house without a by-your-leave and completely trashed his plans for crawling back into his cave to lick his wounds.

Oh, damn.

'Mummy, he wants to talk to you.'

Millie lifted her head from the bag she was stuffing clothes into and stared at her son. 'I think he's said everything he has to say,' she said crisply. 'Have you finished clearing up downstairs?'

'I couldn't reach the light, but I've put everything else outside and picked up all the bits off the floor. Well, most of them. Mummy, he really does want to talk to you. He asked me to tell you and to look after the others while you have a chat.'

Well, that sounded like a quote, she thought, and her heart sank. It was bad enough enduring the humiliation of one verbal battering. The last thing she needed was to go back down there now he'd drawn breath and had time to think about it and give him the opportunity to have a more concerted attack.

'Please, Mummy. He asked—and he promised he wouldn't be mean to you.'

Her eyes widened, then she shut them fast and counted to ten. What on *earth* had Edward been saying to him? She got to her feet and held out her arms to him, and he ran into them and hugged her hard.

'It'll be all right, Mummy,' he said into her side. 'It will.'

If only she could be so sure.

She let him go and made her way downstairs, down the beautiful old oak staircase she'd fallen so in love with, along the hall on the inches-thick carpet, and tapped on the open study door, her heart pounding out a tattoo against her ribs.

He was sitting with his back to her, and at her knock he swivelled the chair round and met her eyes. He'd taken off the coat that had been slung round his shoulders, and she could see now that he was wearing a cast on his left wrist. And, with the light now shining on his face, she could see the livid bruise on his left cheekbone, and the purple stain around his eye.

His hair was dark, soft and glossy, cut short round the sides but flopping forwards over his eyes. It looked rumpled, as if he'd run his fingers through it over and over again, and his jaw was deeply shadowed. He looks awful, she thought, and she wondered briefly what he'd done.

Not that it mattered. It was enough to have brought him home, and that was the only thing that affected her. His injuries were none of her business.

'You wanted to see me,' she said, and waited for the stinging insults to start again.

'I owe you an apology,' he said gruffly, and she felt her jaw drop and yanked it up again. 'I was unforgivably rude to you, and I had no justification for it.'

'I disagree. I'm in your house without your permission,' she said, fairness overcoming her shock. 'I would have been just as rude, I'm sure.'

'I doubt it, somehow. The manners you've drilled into your son would blow that theory out of the water. He's a credit to you.'

She swallowed hard and nodded. 'Thank you. He's a great kid, and he's been through a lot.'

'I'm sure. However, it's not him I want to talk to you about, it's you. You have nowhere to go, is this right?'

Her chin went up. 'We'll find somewhere,' she lied, her pride rescuing her in the nick of time, and she thought she saw a smile flicker on that strong, sculpted mouth before he firmed it.

'Do you or do you not have anywhere else suitable to go with your children for Christmas?' he asked, a thread of steel underlying the softness of his voice, and she swallowed again and shook her head.

'No,' she admitted. 'But that's not your problem.'

He inclined his head, accepting that, but went on, 'Nevertheless, I do have a problem, and one you might be able to fix. As you can see, I've been stupid enough to get mixed up with an avalanche, and I've broken my wrist. Now, I can't cook at the best of times, and I'm not getting my housekeeper back from her well-earned holiday to wait on me, but you, on the other hand, are here, have nowhere else to go and might therefore be interested in a proposition.'

For the first time, she felt a flicker of hope. 'A proposition?' she asked warily, not quite sure she liked the sound of that but prepared to listen because her options were somewhat limited. He nodded.

'I have no intention of paying you—under the circumstances, I don't think that's unreasonable, considering you moved into my house without my knowledge or consent and made yourselves at home, but I am prepared to let you stay until such time as you find somewhere to go after the New Year, in exchange for certain duties. Can you cook?'

She felt the weight of fear lift from her shoulders, and

nodded. 'Yes, I can cook,' she assured him, hoping she could still remember how. It was a while since she'd had anything lavish on her table, but cooking had once been her love and her forte.

'Good. You can cook for me, and keep the housework under control, and help me do anything I can't manage—can you drive?'

She nodded again. 'Yes—but it will have to be my car, unless you've got a big one. I can't go anywhere without the children, so if it's some sexy little sports car it will have to be my hatchback.'

'I've got an Audi A6 estate. It's automatic. Is that a problem?'

'No problem,' she said confidently. 'David had one.' On a finance agreement that, like everything else, had gone belly-up in the last few years. 'Anything else? Any rules?'

'Yes. The children can use the playroom upstairs on the landing, and you can keep the attic bedrooms—I assume you're in the three with the patchwork quilts?'

She felt her jaw sag. 'How did you guess?'

His mouth twisted into a wry smile. 'Let's just say I'm usually a good judge of character, and you're pretty easy to read,' he told her drily. 'So—you can have the top floor, and when you're cooking the children can be down here in the breakfast room with you.'

'Um…there's the dog,' she said, a little unnecessarily as Rufus was now sitting on her foot, and to her surprise Jake's mouth softened into a genuine smile.

'Yes,' he said quietly. 'The dog. My grandmother had one like him. What's his name?'

'Rufus,' she said, and the little dog's tail wagged hope-fully. 'Please don't say he has to be outside in a kennel or anything awful, because he's old and not very well and it's so cold at the moment and he's no trouble—'

'Millie—what does that stand for, by the way?'

'Amelia.'

He studied her for a second, then nodded. 'Amelia,' he said, his voice turning it into something that sounded almost like a caress. 'Of course the dog doesn't have to be outside—not if he's housetrained.'

'Oh, he is. Well, mostly. Sometimes he has the odd accident, but that's only if he's ill.'

'Fine. Just don't let him on the beds. Right, I'm done. If you could find me a glass, the malt whisky and my flight bag, I'd be very grateful. And then I'm going to lie down on my sofa and go to sleep.'

And, getting to his feet with a grunt of pain, he limped slowly towards her.

'You really did mess yourself up, didn't you?' she said softly, and he paused just a foot away from her and stared down into her eyes for the longest moment.

'Yes, Amelia. I really did—and I could do with those painkillers, so if you wouldn't mind—?'

'Right away,' she said, trying to remember how to breathe. Slipping past him into the kitchen, she found a glass, filled it with water, put the kettle on, made a sandwich with the last of the cheese and two precious slices of bread, smeared some chutney she found in the fridge onto the cheese and took it through to him.

'I thought you might be hungry,' she said, 'and there's

nothing much else in the house at the moment, but you shouldn't take painkillers on an empty stomach.'

He sighed and looked up at her from the sofa where he was lying stretched out full length and looking not the slightest bit vulnerable despite the cast, the bruises and the swelling under his eye. 'Is that right?' he said drily. 'Where's the malt whisky?'

'You shouldn't have alcohol—'

'—with painkillers,' he finished for her, and gave a frustrated growl that probably should have frightened her but just gave her the urge to smile. 'Well, give me the damned painkillers, then. They're in my flight bag, in the outside pocket. I'll take them with the water.'

She rummaged, found them and handed them to him. 'When did you take the last lot? It says no more than six in twenty-four hours—'

'Did I ask you for your medical advice?' he snarled, taking the strip of tablets from her and popping two out awkwardly with his good hand.

Definitely not vulnerable. Just crabby as hell. She stood her ground. 'I just don't want your family suing me for killing you with an overdose,' she said, and his mouth tightened.

'No danger of that,' he said flatly. 'I don't have a family. Now, go away and leave me alone. I haven't got the energy to argue with a mouthy, opinionated woman and I can't stand being fussed over. And find me the whisky!'

'I've put the kettle on to make you tea or coffee—'

'Well, don't bother. I've had enough caffeine in the last twenty-four hours to last me a lifetime. I just want the malt—'

'Eat the sandwich and I'll think about it,' she said, and then went out and closed the door, quickly, before he changed his mind and threw them all out anyway...

[text obscured at top of page]

CHAPTER THREE

EDWARD was waiting for her.

He was sitting on the top step, and his eyes were full of trepidation. 'Well?'

'We're staying,' she said with a smile, still not really believing it but so out of options that she had to *make* it work. 'But he'd like us to spend the time up here unless we're down in the breakfast room or kitchen cooking for him, so we don't disturb him, because he had an accident skiing and he's a bit sore. He needs to sleep.'

'So can I unpack my things again?' Kitty asked, appearing on the landing, her little face puzzled and a bulging carrier bag dangling from her fingers.

'Yes, darling. We can all unpack, and then we need to go downstairs very quietly and tidy up the kitchen and see what I can find to cook us for supper.'

Not that there was much, but she'd have to make something proper for Jake, and she had no idea how she'd achieve that with no ingredients and no money to buy any. Maybe there was something in his freezer?

'I'll be very, very quiet,' Kitty whispered, her grey eyes

serious, and tiptoed off to her room with bag in hand and her finger pressed over her lips.

It worked until she bumped into the door frame and the bag fell out of her hand and landed on the floor, the book in the top falling out with a little thud. Her eyes widened like saucers, and for one awful minute Millie thought she was going to cry.

'It's all right, darling, you don't have to be that quiet,' she said with an encouraging smile, and Edward, ever his little sister's protector, picked up his own bag and went back into the bedroom and hugged her, then helped her put her things away while Millie unpacked all the baby's things again.

He was still sleeping. Innocence was such a precious gift, she thought, her eyes filling, and blinking hard, she turned away and went to the window, drawn by the sound of a car. Looking down on the drive as the floodlights came on, she realised it was Kate.

Of course. Dear Kate, rushing to her rescue, coming to smooth things over with Jake.

Who was sleeping.

'Keep an eye on Thomas, I'm going to let Kate in,' she said to Edward and ran lightly down the stairs, arriving in the hall just as Kate turned the heavy handle and opened the door.

'Oh, Millie, I'm so sorry I've been so long, but Megan was in the bath and I had to dry her hair before I brought her out in the cold,' she said in a rush. 'Where are the children?'

'Upstairs. It's all right, we're staying. Megan, do you

want to go up and see them while I make Mummy a coffee?'

'I don't have time for a coffee, I need to see Jake. I've got to try and reason with him—what do you mean, you're staying?' she added, her eyes widening.

'Shh. He's asleep. Go on, Megan, it's all right, but please be quiet because Jake's not well.'

Megan nodded seriously. 'I'll be very quiet,' she whispered and ran upstairs, her little feet soundless on the thick carpet. Kate took Millie by the arm and towed her into the breakfast room and closed the door.

'So what's going on?' she asked in a desperate undertone. 'I thought you'd be packed and leaving?'

Amelia shook her head. 'No. He's broken his wrist and he's battered from end to end, and I think he's probably messed his knee up, too, so he needs someone to cook for him and run round after him.'

Kate's jaw dropped. 'So he's *employing* you?'

Millie felt her mouth twist into a wry smile. 'Not exactly employing,' she admitted, remembering his blunt words with an inward wince. 'But we can stay in exchange for helping him, so long as I keep the children out of his way.'

'And the dog? Does he even *know* about the dog?'

She smiled. 'Ah, well, now. Apparently he likes the dog, doesn't he, Rufus?' she murmured, looking down at him. He was stuck on her leg, sensing the need to behave, his eyes anxious, and she felt him quiver.

When she glanced back up, Kate was staring at her openmouthed. 'He likes the dog?' she hissed.

'His grandmother had one. He doesn't go a bundle on the Christmas decorations, though,' she added ruefully with

a pointed glance at the light fitting. 'Come on, let's make
a drink and take it upstairs to the kids.'

'He was going to put a kitchen up there,' Kate told her
as she boiled the kettle. 'Just a little one, enough to make
drinks and snacks, but he hasn't got round to it yet. Pity. It
would have been handy for you.'

'It would. Still, I only need to bring the children down
if I'm actually cooking. We're quite all right up in the
playroom, and at least it'll give us a little breathing space
before we have to find somewhere to go.'

'And, actually, it's a huge relief,' Kate said, sagging
back against the worktop and folding her arms. 'I was wondering what to do about Jake—I mean, I couldn't leave him
here on his own over Christmas when he's injured, but my
house is going to be heaving and noisy and chaotic, and I
would have had to run backwards and forwards—so you've
done me a massive favour. And, you never know, maybe
you'll all have a good time together! In fact—'

Amelia cut her off with a laugh and a raised hand. 'I
don't think so,' she said firmly, remembering his bitterly
sarcastic opening remarks. 'But if we can just keep out of
his way, maybe we'll all survive.'

She handed Kate her drink, picked up her own mug and
then hesitated. No matter how rude and sarcastic he'd been,
he was still a human being and for that alone he deserved
her consideration, and he was injured and exhausted and
probably not thinking straight. 'I ought to check on him,'
she said, putting her mug back down. 'He was talking
about malt whisky.'

'So? Don't worry, he's not a drinker. He won't have had
much.'

'On top of painkillers?'

'Ah. What were they?'

'Goodness knows—something pretty heavy-duty. Nothing I recognised. Not paracetamol, that's for sure!'

'Oh, hell. Where is he?'

'Just next door in the little sitting room.'

'I'll go—'

'No. Let me. He was pretty cross.'

Kate laughed softly. 'You think I've never seen him cross?'

So they went together, opening the door silently and pushing it in until they could see him sprawled full length on the sofa, one leg dangling off the edge, his cast resting across his chest, his head lolling against the arm.

Kate frowned. 'He doesn't look very comfortable.'

He didn't, but at least there was no sign of the whisky. Amelia went into the room and picked up a soft velvety cushion and tucked it under his bruised cheek to support his head better. He grunted and shifted slightly and she froze, waiting for those piercing slate grey eyes to open and stab her with a hard, angry glare, but then he relaxed, settling his face down against the pillow with a little sigh, and she let herself breathe again.

It was chilly in there, though, and she had refused to let Kate turn the heating up. She could do it now but, in the meantime, he ought to have something over him. She spotted a throw over the back of the other sofa and lowered it carefully over him, tucking it in to keep the draughts off until the heat kicked in.

Then she tiptoed out, glancing back over her shoulder as she reached the door.

Did she imagine it or had his eyelids fluttered? She wasn't sure, but she didn't want to hang around and provoke him if she'd disturbed him, so she pushed Kate out and closed the door softly behind them.

'Can you turn the heating up?' she murmured to Kate, and she nodded and went into his study and fiddled with a keypad on the wall.

'He looks awful,' Kate said, sparing the door of the room another glance as she tapped keys and reprogrammed the heating. 'He's got bruises all over his face and neck. It must have been a hell of an avalanche.'

'He didn't say, but he's very sore and stiff. I expect he's got bruises all over his body,' Millie said, trying not to think about his body in too much detail but failing dismally. She stifled the little whimper that rose in her throat.

Why?

Why, of all the men to bring her body out of the freezer, did it have to be Jake? There was no way he'd be interested in her—even if she hadn't upset and alienated him by taking such a massive liberty with his house, to all intents and purposes moving into his house as a squatter, she'd then compounded her sins by telling him what to do!

And he most particularly wouldn't be interested in her children. In fact it was probably the dog who was responsible for his change of heart.

Oh, well, it was just as well he wouldn't be interested in her, because there was no way her life was even remotely stable or coherent enough at the moment for her to contemplate a relationship. Frankly, she wasn't sure it ever would be again and, if it was, it *certainly* wouldn't be with another empire builder. She'd had it with the entrepreneurial type, big time.

But there was just something about Jake Forrester that called to something deep inside her, something that had lain undisturbed for years, and she was going to have to ignore it and get through these next few days and weeks until they could find somewhere else. And maybe then she'd get her sanity back.

'Come on, let's go back up and leave him to sleep,' she said, crossing her fingers and hoping that he slept for a good long while and woke in a rather better mood...

He was hot.

He'd been cold, but he'd been too tired and sore to bother to get the throw, but someone must have been in and covered him, because it was snuggled round him, and there was a pillow under his face and the lingering scent of a familiar fragrance.

Kate. She must have come over and covered him up. Hell. He hadn't meant her to turn out on such a freezing night with little Megan. He should have rung her back, he realised, after he'd spoken to Amelia, but he'd been high as a kite on the rather nice drugs the French doctor had given him and he hadn't even thought about it.

Damn.

He rolled onto his back and his breath caught. Ouch. That was quite a bruise on his left hip. And his knee desperately needed some ice, and his arm hurt. Even through the painkillers.

He struggled off the sofa, eventually escaping from the confines of the throw with an impatient tug and straightening up with a wince. The gel pack was in the freezer in the kitchen. It wasn't far.

Further than he thought, he realised, swaying slightly and pausing while the world steadied. He took a step, then another, and blinked hard to clear his head.

Amelia was right, he shouldn't have too many of those damn painkillers. They were turning his brain to mush. And it was probably just as well he hadn't taken them with whisky either, he thought with regret. Not that she'd been about to give him any, the bossy witch.

Amelia. Millie.

No, Amelia. Millie didn't suit her. It was a little girl's name and, whatever else she was, she was all woman. And damn her for making him notice the fact.

He limped into the breakfast room and saw that Edward had done a pretty good job of removing the branches and berries from the floor in front of the fire. He felt his brow pleat into a frown, and stifled the pang of guilt. It was his house. If he didn't want decorations in it, it was perfectly reasonable to say so.

But had he had to be so harsh?

No, was the simple answer. Especially to the kids. Oh, rats. He made his way carefully through to the kitchen, took the pack out of the freezer and wrapped it in a tea towel, then went back to the breakfast room and sat down in the chair near the fire and propped the ice pack over his knee. Better.

Or it would be, in about a week. It was only a bruise, not a ligament rupture, thankfully. He'd done that before on the other knee, and he didn't need to do it again, but he realised he'd been lucky not to be smashed to bits on the tree or the rock field.

Very lucky.

He eased back in the chair cautiously and thought with longing of the whisky. It was a particularly smooth old single malt, smoky and peaty, with a lovely complex after-taste. Or was that afterburn?

Whatever, it was in the drinks cupboard in the drawing room, and he wasn't convinced he could summon up the energy to walk all the way to the far end of the house and back again, so he closed his eyes and fantasised that he was on Islay, sitting in an old croft house with a peat fire at his feet, a collie instead of a little spaniel leaning on his leg and a glass of liquid gold in his hand.

He could all but taste it. Pity he couldn't. Pity it was only in his imagination, because then he'd be able to put Amelia and her children out of his mind.

Or he would have been able to, if it hadn't been for the baby crying.

'Oh, Thomas, sweetheart, what's the matter, little one?'

She couldn't believe he was doing this. She'd fed him just before Jake had arrived home, but now he was awake and he wouldn't settle again and he was starting to sob into her chest, letting fly with a scream that she was sure would travel all the way down to Jake.

He couldn't be hungry, not really, but he obviously wanted a bottle of milk, and that meant going back down to the kitchen and heating it, taking the screaming baby with her, and by the time she'd done that, he would cer-

tainly have disturbed her reluctant host. Unless she left him
with Edward?

'Darling, could you please look after him for a moment
while I get him his bottle?' she asked, and Edward, being
Edward, just nodded and held his arms out, and carried
Thomas off towards the bedroom and closed the door.

She ran lightly downstairs to the sound of his escalat-
ing wails. As she hurried into the breakfast room, she came
face to face with Jake sitting by the fire, an ice pack on his
knee and the dog at his side.

She skidded to a halt and his eyes searched her face. 'Is
the baby all right?'

She nodded. 'Yes—I'm sorry. I just need to make him
a bottle. He'll settle then. I'm really sorry—'

'Why didn't you bring him down?'

'I didn't want to wake you.' She chewed her lip, only too
conscious of the fact that he was very much awake. Awake
and up and about and looking rumpled and disturbingly
attractive, with the dark shadow of stubble on his firm jaw
and the subtle drift of a warm, slightly spicy cologne
reaching her nostrils.

'I was awake,' he told her, his voice a little gruff. 'I put
a gel pack on my knee, and I was about to make some tea.
Want to join me?'

'Oh—I can't, I've left the baby with Edward.'

'Bring them all down. Maybe I should meet them—
since they're staying in my house.'

Oh, Lord. 'Let me just make the bottle so it can be
cooling, and then we'll get a little peace and I can intro-
duce you properly.'

He nodded, his mouth twitching into a slight smile, and she felt relief flood through her at this tiny evidence of his humanity. She went into the kitchen and spooned formula into a bottle, then poured hot water from the kettle on it, shook it and plonked it into a bowl of cold water. Thankfully there had been some water in the kettle so it didn't have to cool from boiling, she thought as she ran back upstairs and collected the children, suddenly ludicrously conscious of how scruffy they looked after foraging in the woods, and how apprehensive.

'Hey, it's all right, he wants to meet you,' she murmured reassuringly to Kitty, who was clinging to her, and then pushed the breakfast room door open and ushered them in.

He was putting wood on the fire, and as he closed the door and straightened up, he caught sight of them and turned. The smile was gone, his face oddly taut, and her own smile faltered for a moment.

'Kids, this is Mr Forrester—'

'Jake,' he said, cutting her off and taking a step forward. His mouth twisted into a smile. 'I've already met Edward. And you must be Kitty. And this, I take it, is Thomas?'

'Yes.'

Thomas, sensing the change of atmosphere, had gone obligingly silent, but after a moment he lost interest in Jake and anything except his stomach and, burrowing into her shoulder, he began to wail again.

'I'm sorry. I—'

'Go on, feed him. I gave the bottle a shake to help cool it.'

'Thanks.' She went into the kitchen, wondering how he knew to do that. Nieces and nephews, probably—although he'd said he didn't have any family. How odd, she thought briefly, but then Thomas tried to lunge out of her arms and she fielded him with the ease of practice and tested the bottle on her wrist.

Cool enough. She shook it again, tested it once more to be on the safe side and offered it to her son.

Silence. Utter, blissful silence, broken only by a strained chuckle.

'Oh, for such simple needs,' he said softly, and she turned and met his eyes. They were darker than before, and his mouth was set in a grim line despite the laugh. But then his expression went carefully blank and he limped across to the kettle. 'So—who has tea, and who wants juice or whatever else?'

'We haven't got any juice. The children will have water.'

'Sounds dull.'

'They're fine with it. It's good for them.'

'I don't doubt it. It's good for me, too, but that doesn't mean I drink it. Except in meetings. I get through gallons of it in meetings. So—is that just me, or are you going to join me?'

'Oh.' Join him? That sounded curiously—intimate. 'Yes, please,' she said, and hoped she didn't sound absurdly breathless. It's a cup of tea, she told herself crossly. Just a cup of tea. Nothing else. She didn't want anything else. Ever.

And if she told herself that enough times, maybe she'd start to believe it.

'Have the children eaten?'

'Thomas has. Edward and Kitty haven't. I was going to wait until you woke up and ask you what you wanted.'

'Anything. I'm not really hungry after that sandwich. What is there?'

'I have no idea. I'll give the children eggs on toast—'

'Again?' Kitty said plaintively. 'We had eggs on toast for supper last night.'

'I'm sure we can find something else,' their host was saying, rummaging in a tall cupboard with pull-out racking that was crammed with tins and jars and packets. 'What did you all have for lunch?'

'Jam sandwiches and an apple.'

He turned and studied Kitty thoughtfully, then his gaze flicked up to Amelia's and speared her. 'Jam sandwiches?' he said softly. 'Eggs on toast?'

She felt her chin lift, but he just frowned and turned back to the cupboard, staring into its depths blankly for a moment before shutting it and opening the big door beside it and going systematically through the drawers of the freezer.

'How about fish?'

'What sort? They don't eat smoked fish or fish fingers.'

'Salmon—and mixed shellfish. A lobster,' he added, rummaging. 'Raw king prawns—there's some Thai curry paste somewhere I just saw. Or there's probably a casserole if you don't fancy fish.'

'Whatever. Choose what you want. We'll have eggs.'

He frowned again, shut the freezer and studied her searchingly.

She wished he wouldn't do that. Her arm was aching, Thomas was starting to loll against her shoulder and if she was sitting down, she could probably settle him and get him off to sleep so she could concentrate on feeding the others—most particularly their reluctant host.

After all, she'd told him she could cook—

'Go and sit down. I'll order a takeaway,' he said softly, and she looked back up into his eyes and surprised a gentle, almost puzzled expression in them for a fleeting moment before he turned away and limped out. 'What do they like?' he asked over his shoulder, then turned to the children. 'What's it to be, kids? Pizza? Chinese? Curry? Kebabs? Burgers?'

'What's a kebab?'

'Disgusting. Anyway, you're having eggs, Kitty, we've already decided that.'

Over their heads she met his eyes defiantly, and saw a reluctant grin blossom on his firm, sculpted lips. 'OK, we'll have eggs. Do we have enough?'

We? Her eyes widened. 'For all of us?'

'Am I excluded?'

She ran a mental eye over the meagre contents of the fridge and relaxed. 'Of course not.'

'Good. Then we'll have omelettes and oven-baked potato wedges and peas, if that's OK? Now, for heaven's sake sit down, woman, before you drop the baby, and I'll make you a cup of tea.'

'I thought I was supposed to be looking after you?' she said, but one glare from those rather gorgeous slate grey eyes and she retreated to the comfort of the fireside, settling down in the chair he'd been using with a sigh of relief. She'd have her tea, settle Thomas in his cot and make supper.

For all of them, apparently. So—was he going to sit and eat with them? He'd been so anti his little army of squatters, so what had brought about this sudden change?

* * *

Jake pulled the mugs out of the cupboard and then contemplated the lid of the tea caddy. Tea bags, he decided, with only one useful hand, not leaves and the pot, and putting the caddy back, he dropped tea bags into the mugs and poured water on them. Thank God it was his left arm he'd broken, not his right. At least he could manage most things like this.

The stud on his jeans was a bit of a challenge, he'd discovered, but he'd managed to get them on this morning. Shoelaces were another issue, but he'd kicked his shoes off when he'd got in and he'd been padding around in his socks, and he had shoes without laces he could wear until the blasted cast came off.

But cooking—well, cooking would be a step too far, he thought, but by some minor intervention of fate he seemed to have acquired an answer to that one. A feisty, slightly offbeat and rather delightful answer. Easy on the eye. And with a voice that seemed to dig right down inside him and tug at something long forgotten.

It was the kids he found hardest, of course, but it was the kids he was most concerned about, because their mother was obviously struggling to hold things together. And she wasn't coping very well with it—or maybe, he thought, reconsidering as he poked the tea bags with the spoon, she was coping very well, against atrocious odds. Whatever, a staple diet of bread and eggs wasn't good for anyone and, as he knew from his experience with the cheese sandwich, it wasn't even decent bread. Perfectly nutritious, no doubt, but closely related to cotton wool.

He put the milk down and poured two glasses of filtered water for Edward and Kitty. 'Hey, you guys, come and get your drinks,' he said, and they ran over, Edward more slowly, Kitty skipping, head on one side in a gesture so like her mother's he nearly laughed.

'So—what *are* kebabs, really?' she asked, twizzling a lock of hair with one forefinger, and he did laugh then, the sound dragged out of him almost reluctantly.

'Well—there are different kinds. There's shish kebab, which is pieces of meat on skewers, a bit like you'd put on a barbecue, or there's doner kebab, which is like a great big sausage on a stick, and they turn it in front of a fire to cook it and slice bits off. You have both in a kind of bread pocket, with salad, and your mother's right, the doner kebabs certainly aren't very healthy—well, not the ones in this country. In Turkey they're fantastic.'

'They don't *sound* disgusting,' Kitty said wistfully. 'I like sausages on sticks.'

'Maybe we can get some sausages and put sticks in them,' Edward said, and Jake realised he was the peacemaker in the family, trying to hold it all together, humouring Kitty and helping with Thomas and supporting his mother—and the thought that he should have to do all that left a great hollow in the pit of Jake's stomach.

No child should have to do that. He'd spent years doing that, fighting helplessly against the odds to keep it all together, and for what?

'Good idea,' he said softly. 'We'll get some sausages tomorrow.' He gathered up the mugs in his right hand and limped through to the breakfast room and put them down on the table near Amelia. She looked up with a smile.

'Thanks,' she murmured, and he found his eyes drawn down to the baby, sleeping now, his chubby little face turned against her chest, arm outflung, dead to the world. A great lump in his throat threatened to choke him, and he nodded curtly, took his mug and went back to the other room, shutting the door firmly so he couldn't hear the children's voices.

He couldn't do this. It was killing him, and he couldn't do it.

He'd meant to sit with her, talk to her, but the children had unravelled him and he couldn't sit there and look at them, he discovered. Not today. Not the day before Christmas Eve.

The day his wife and son had died.

CHAPTER FOUR

WELL, what was that about?

He'd come in, taken one look at her and gone.

Because she'd sat in his chair?

No—and he'd been looking at Thomas, not her. And had she dreamed it, or had there been a slight sheen in his eyes?

The glitter of tears?

No. She was being ridiculous. He just wanted to be alone. He always wanted to be alone, according to Kate, and they'd scuppered that for him, so he was making the best of a bad job and keeping out of the way.

So why did he want to eat with them? Or was he simply having the same food?

She had no idea, and no way of working it out, and knowing so little about him, her guesswork was just a total stab in the dark. But there had been *something* in his eyes…

'I'm just going to put Thomas to bed, then I'll cook you supper,' she told the children quietly and, getting up without disturbing the baby, she took him up to the attic and slipped him into his cot. She'd change his nappy later.

She didn't want to risk waking him now—not when he'd finally settled.

And not when Jake had that odd look about him that was flagging up all kinds of warning signals. She was sure he was hurting, but she had no idea why—and it was frankly none of her business. She just needed to feed the children, get them out of the way and then deal with him later.

'Right, kids, let's make supper,' she said, going back in and smiling at them brightly. 'Who wants to break the eggs into the cup?'

Not the bowl, because that was just asking for trouble, and she sensed that crunchy omelettes wouldn't win her any Brownie points with Jake, but one at a time was all right. She could fish for shell in one egg.

She looked out of the window at the herb garden and wondered what was out there. Sage? Rosemary? Thyme? It was a shame she didn't have any cheese, but she could put fresh herbs in his, and she remembered seeing a packet of pancetta in the fridge.

She cooked for herself and the children first, then while she was eating she cooked his spicy potato wedges in a second batch, then sent the children up to wash and change ready for bed.

'I'll come up and read to you when I've given Jake his supper,' she promised, kissing them both, and they went, still looking a little uncertain, and she felt another wave of anger at David for putting them in this position.

And at herself, for allowing him to make them so vulnerable, for relying on him even after he'd proved over and over again that he was unreliable, for giving him the power to do this to them. He'd walked out on them four years ago, and letting him back again two years later had been stupid in the extreme. It hadn't taken her long to realise it, and she'd finally taken the last step and divorced him, but their failed reconciliation had resulted in Thomas. And, though she loved Thomas to bits, having him didn't make life easier and had forced her to rely on David again. Well, no more. Not him, not any man.

Never again, she thought, vigorously beating the last two eggs for Jake's omelette while the little cubes of pancetta crisped in the pan. No way was she putting herself and her family at risk again. Even if Jake was remotely interested in her, which he simply wasn't. He couldn't even bear to be in the same room as her—and she had to stop thinking about him!

She went out and picked the herbs by the light from the kitchen window, letting Rufus out into the garden for a moment while she breathed deeply and felt the cold, clean air fill her lungs and calm her.

They'd survive, she told herself. They'd get through this hitch, and she'd get another job somehow, and they'd be all right.

They had to be.

She went back in with Rufus and the herbs, made Jake's omelette and left it to set on the side of the Aga while she called him to the table.

She tapped on the door of what she was beginning to think of as his cave, and he opened it almost instantly. She stepped back hastily and smiled. 'Hi. I was just coming to call you for supper.'

He smiled back. 'The smell was reeling me in—I was just on my way. Apparently I'm hungrier than I thought.'

Oh, damn. Had she made enough for him?

He followed her through to the breakfast room and stopped. 'Where are the other place settings?'

'Oh—the children were starving, so I ate with them. Anyway, I wasn't sure—'

She broke off, biting her lip, and he sighed softly.

'I'm sorry. I was rude. I just walked out.'

'No—no, why should you want to sit with us? It's your house, we're in your way. I feel so guilty—'

'Don't. Please, don't. I don't know the ins and outs of it, and I don't need to, but it's quite obvious that you're doing your best to cope and life's just gone pear-shaped recently. And, whatever the rights and wrongs of your being here, it's nothing to do with the children. They've got every right to feel safe and secure, and wanted, and if I've given you the impression that they're not welcome here, then I apologise. I don't do kids—I have my reasons, which I don't intend to go into, but—your kids have done nothing wrong and—well, tomorrow I'd like to fix it a bit, if you'll let me.'

'Fix it?' she said, standing with the plate in her hand and her eyes searching his. 'How?' How on earth could he fix it? And why didn't he do kids?

'I'd like to give the children Christmas. I'd like to go shopping and buy food. I've already promised them sausages, but I'd like to get the works—a turkey and all the trimmings, satsumas, mince pies, Christmas cake, a Christmas pudding and cream, and something else if they don't like the heavy fruit—perhaps a chocolate log or something? And a tree. They ought to have a tree, with real decorations on it.'

She felt her eyes fill with tears, and swallowed hard.

'You don't have to do that,' she said, trying to firm her voice. 'We don't need all that.'

'I know—but I'd like to. I don't normally do Christmas, but the kids have done nothing to deserve this hideous uncertainty in their lives, and if I can help to make this time a little better for them, then maybe—'

He broke off and turned away, moving slowly to the table, his leg obviously troubling him.

She set the plate down in front of him with trembling hands. 'I don't know what to say.'

'Then just say yes, and let me do it,' he said gruffly, then tilted his head and gave her a wry look. 'I don't suppose I'm allowed a glass of wine?'

'Of course you are.'

'You wouldn't let me have the whisky.'

She gave a little laugh, swallowing down the tears and shaking her head. 'That was because of the painkillers. I thought you should drink water, especially as you'd been flying. But—sure, you can have a glass of wine.'

'Will you join me?'

'I thought you wanted to be alone?' she said softly, and he smiled again, a little crookedly.

'Amelia, just open the wine. There's a gluggable Aussie Shiraz in the wine rack in the side of the island unit, and the glasses are in the cupboard next to the Aga.'

'Corkscrew?'

'It's a screwtop.'

'Right.' She found the wine, found the glasses, poured his and a small one for herself and perched a little warily opposite him. 'How's the omelette?'

'Good. Just right. What herbs did you use? Are they from the garden?'

'Yes. Thyme and sage. And I found some pancetta—I hope it was OK to use it.'

'Of course. It's really tasty. Thanks.'

He turned his attention back to his food, and then pushed his plate away with a sigh when it was scraped clean. 'I don't suppose there's any pud?'

She chuckled. 'A budget yogurt?'

He wrinkled his nose. 'Maybe not. There might be some ice cream in the freezer—top drawer.'

There was. Luxury Belgian chocolate that made her mouth water. 'This one?' she offered, and he nodded.

'Brilliant. Will you join me?'

She gave in to the temptation because her omelette had only been tiny—elastic eggs, to make sure he had enough so she didn't fall at the first hurdle—and she was still hungry. She dished up and took it through, feeling a pang of guilt because she could feed her children for a day on the cost of that ice cream and in the good old days it had been their favourite—

'Stop it. We'll get some for the children tomorrow,' he chided, reading her mind with uncanny accuracy, and she laughed and sat down.

'How did you know?'

His mouth quirked. 'Your face is like an open book— every flicker of guilt registers on it. Stop beating yourself up, Amelia, and tell me about yourself. What do you do for a living?'

She tried to smile, but it felt pretty pathetic, really. 'Nothing at the moment. I was working freelance as a technical translator for a firm that went into liquidation. They owed me for three months' work.'

'Ouch.'

'Indeed. And David had just run off to Thailand with the receivers in hot pursuit after yet another failed business venture—'

'David?'

'My ex-husband. Self-styled entrepreneur and master of delusion, absent father of my children and what Kate describes as a waste of a good skin. He'd already declined to pay the maintenance when I left him for the second time when I was pregnant with Thomas, so I'd already had to find a way to survive for over a year while I waited for the courts to tell him to pay up. And then I lost my job, David wasn't in a position to help by then even if he'd chosen to, and my landlord wanted out of the property business so the moment I couldn't pay my overdue rent on the date he'd set, he asked me to leave. As in, "I want you out by the morning".'

Jake winced. 'So you went to your sister.'

'Yes. We moved in on the tenth of December—and it lasted less than two weeks.' She laughed softly and wrinkled her nose. 'You know what they say about guests being like fish—they go off after three days. So twelve wasn't bad. And the dog does smell.'

'So why don't you bath him?'

'Because they wouldn't let me. Not in their pristine house. I would have had to take him to the groomer, which I couldn't afford, or do it outside under the hose.'

'In December?' he said with a frown.

She smiled wryly, remembering Andy's blank incomprehension. 'Quite. So he still smells, I'm afraid.'

'That's ridiculous. Heavens, he's only tiny. Shove him in the sink and dry him by the fire.'

'Really?' She put down her ice cream spoon and sat back, staring at him in amazement. 'You're telling me I could bath him in your lovely kitchen?'

'Why not? Or you could use the utility room. Wherever. It doesn't matter, does it? He's only a dog. I can think of worse things. You're all right, aren't you, mate?' he said softly, turning his head and looking at the hearth where Rufus was lying as close to the woodburner as the fireguard would let him. He thumped his tail on the floor, his eyes fixed on Jake as if he was afraid that any minute now he'd be told to move.

But apparently not. Jake liked dogs—and thought it was fine to wash him in the kitchen sink. She stood up and took their bowls through to the kitchen, using the excuse to get away because her eyes were filling again and threatening to overflow and embarrass her. She put all the plates into the dishwasher and straightened up and took a nice steadying breath.

Rufus was at her feet, his tail waving, his eyes hopeful. She had to squash the urge to hug him. 'Do you think I'm going to give you something? You've had supper,' she told him firmly. 'Don't beg.'

His tail drooped and he trotted back to Jake and sat beside him, staring up into his eyes and making him laugh.

'He's not looking convinced.'

'Don't you dare give him anything. He's not allowed to beg, and he's on a special diet.'

'I don't doubt it. I bet he costs more to run than all the rest of you put together.'

She laughed and shook her head. 'You'd better believe it. But he's worth every penny. He's been brilliant.' She bit her lip. 'I don't mean to be rude, but I did promise the children I'd read to them, and I need to change Thomas's nappy and put him into pyjamas.'

He nodded. 'That's fine. Don't worry. I'll see you later. In fact, I might just go to bed.'

'Can I get you anything else?'

He shook his head. 'No. I'm fine, don't worry about me. I'll see you in the morning. If you get a minute before then, you could dream up a shopping list. And thank you for my supper, by the way, it was lovely.'

She felt the cold, dead place around her heart warm a little, and she smiled. 'My pleasure,' she said, and took herself upstairs before she fell any further under his spell, because she'd discovered during the course of a glass of wine and a bowl of ice cream that Jake Forrester, when it suited him, could be very, very charming indeed.

And that scared the living daylights out of her.

His bags were missing.

The cabbie had stacked them by the front door, and they were gone. Kate, he thought. She'd been over while he was sleeping earlier, he knew that, and he realised she must have taken them up to his room. Unless Amelia had done it?

Whatever, he needed to go to bed. Lying on the sofa resting for an hour was all very well, but he needed more than that. And it was already after ten. He'd sat and had another glass of wine in front of the fire in the breakfast room, with Rufus keeping him company and creeping gradually closer until he was lying against his foot, and eventually it dawned on him that he was hanging around in the vain hope that Amelia would come back down and sit with him again.

Ridiculous. And dangerous. They both had far too much baggage, and it would be dicing with disaster, no matter how appealing the physical package. And there was no way he wanted any other kind of relationship. So, although he was loath to disturb the dog, he'd finally eased his toes out from under his side and left the room.

And then had to work out, in his muddled, tired mind, what had happened to his bags.

He detoured into the sitting room and picked up his painkillers, then made his way slowly and carefully up the stairs. He was getting stiffer, he realised. Maybe he needed a bath—a long, hot soak—except that he'd almost inevitably fall asleep in it and wake up cold and wrinkled in the middle of the night. And, anyway, he hated baths.

A shower? No. There was the difficulty of his cast to consider, and sealing it in a bag was beyond him at the moment. He'd really had enough. He'd deal with it tomorrow.

Reluctantly abandoning the tempting thought of hot water sluicing over his body, he eased off his clothes, found his wash things in the bag that had indeed arrived in his room, cleaned his teeth and then crawled into bed.

Bliss.

There was nothing like your own bed, he thought, closing his eyes with a long, unravelling sigh. And then he remembered he hadn't taken the painkillers, and he needed to before he went to sleep or his arm would wake him in the night.

He put the light back on and got out of bed again, filled a glass with water and came back to the bed. He'd thrown the pills on the bedside chest, and he took two and opened the top drawer to put them in.

And there it was.

Lying in the drawer, jumbled up with pens and cufflinks and bits of loose change. Oh, Lord. Slowly, almost reluctantly, he pulled the little frame out and stared down at the faces laughing back up at him—Rachel, full of life as usual, sitting on the grass with Ben in between her knees, his little hands filled with grass mowings and his eyes alight with mischief. He'd been throwing the grass mowings all over her, and they'd all been laughing.

And six months later, five years ago today, they'd been mown down by a drunk driver who'd just left his office Christmas party. They'd been doing some last-minute shopping—collecting a watch she'd bought him, he discovered when he eventually went through the bag of their things he'd been given at the hospital. He'd worn it every day for the last five years—until it had been shattered, smashed to bits against an alpine tree during the avalanche.

An avalanche that had brought him home—to a woman called Amelia, and her three innocent and displaced children.

Was this Rachel's doing? Trying to tell him to move on, to forget them both?

He traced their faces with his finger, swallowing down the grief that had never really left him, the grief that sent him away every Christmas to try and forget the unforgettable, to escape the inescapable.

He put the photo back in the drawer and closed it softly, turned off the light, then lay back down and stared dry-eyed into the night.

She couldn't sleep.

Something had woken her—some strange sound, although how she could know the sounds of the house so well already she had no idea, but somehow she did, and this one was strange.

She got out of bed and checked the children, but all of them were sleeping, Thomas flat out on his back with his arms flung up over his head, Edward on his tummy with one leg stuck out the side, and Kitty curled on her side with her hand under her cheek and her battered old teddy snuggled in the crook of her arm.

So not them, then.

Jake?

She looked over the banisters, but all was quiet and there was no light.

Rufus?

Oh, Lord, Rufus. Did he want to go out? Was that what had woken her, him yipping or scratching at the door?

She pulled on a jumper over her pyjamas—because, of course, in her haste she'd left her dressing gown on the back of the door at her sister's—and tiptoed down the stairs, glancing along to Jake's room as she reached the head of the lower flight.

She'd brought his luggage up earlier while he was sleeping and put it in there, because he couldn't possibly manage to lug it up there himself, and she'd had her first look at his room.

It was over the formal drawing room, with an arched opening to the bathroom at the bay window end, and a great rolltop bath sat in the middle, with what must be the most spectacular view along the endless lawn to the woods in the distance. She couldn't picture him in it at all, there was a huge double shower the size of the average wetroom that seemed much more likely, and a pair of gleaming washbasins, and in a separate little room with its own basin and marble-tiled walls was a loo.

And at the opposite end of the room was the bed. Old, solid, a vast and imposing four-poster, the head end and the top filled in with heavily carved panelling, it was perfect for the room. Perfect for the house. The sort of bed where love was made and children were born and people slipped quietly away at the end of their lives, safe in its arms.

It was a wonderful, wonderful bed. And not in the least monastic. She could picture him in it so easily.

Was he lying in it now? She didn't know. Maybe, maybe not—and she was mad to think about it.

There was no light on, and the house was in silence, but it felt different, she thought. There was something about it which had changed with his arrival, a sort of—rightness, as if the house had relaxed now he was home.

Which didn't explain what had woken her. And the door to his room was open a crack. She'd gone down to let the dog out and tidy up the kitchen after she'd settled the children and finished unpacking their things and he must have come upstairs by then, but she hadn't noticed the door open. Perhaps he'd come out again to get something and hadn't shut it, and that was what had woken her, but there was no sign of him now.

She went down to the breakfast room, guided only by the moonlight, and opened the door, and she heard the gentle thump of the dog's tail on the floor and the clatter of his nails.

'Hello, my lovely man,' she crooned, crouching down and pulling gently on his ears. 'Are you all right?'

'I take it you're talking to the dog.'

She gave a little shriek and pressed her hand to her chest, then started to laugh. 'Good grief, Jake, you scared me to death!' She straightened up and reached for the light, then hesitated, conscious of her tired old pyjamas. 'Are you OK?'

'I couldn't sleep. You?'

'I thought I heard a noise.'

He laughed softly. 'In this house? Of course you heard a noise! It creaks like a ship.'

'I know. It settles. I love it—it sounds as if it's relaxing. No, there was something else. It must have been you.'

'I stumbled over the dog—he came to see me and I hadn't put the light on and I kicked him by accident and he yelped—and, before you ask, he's fine. I nudged him, really, but he seemed a bit upset by it, so I sat with him.'

'Oh, I'm so sorry—he does get underfoot and—well, I think he was kicked as a puppy. Has he forgiven you?'

The soft sound of Jake's laughter curled round her again, warming her. 'I think so. He's been on my lap.'

'Ah. Sounds like it, then.' She hesitated, wondering if she should leave him to it and go back to bed, but sensing that there was something wrong, something more than he was telling her. 'How's the fire?'

'OK. I think it could do with more wood.'

'I'll get some.'

She went out of the back door and brought in an armful of logs, putting on the kitchen light as she went, and she left it on when she came back, enough to see by but hopefully not enough to see just how tired her pyjamas really were, and the spill of yellow light made the room seem cosy and intimate.

Which was absurd, considering its size, but everything was in scale and so it didn't seem big, just—safe.

She put the logs in the basket and opened the fire, throwing some in, and as the flames leapt up she went to shut it but he stopped her.

'Leave it open. It's nice to sit and stare into the flames. It helps—'

Helps? Helps what? she wanted to ask, but she couldn't, somehow, so she knelt there on the hearthrug in the warmth of the flames, with Rufus snuggled against her side, his skinny, feathery tail wafting against her, and waited.

But Jake didn't say any more, just sighed and dropped his head back against the chair and closed his eyes. She could see that his fingers were curled around a glass, and on the table behind him was a bottle. The whisky?

'What?'

She jumped guiltily. 'Nothing.'

He snorted. 'It's never nothing with women. Yes, it's the whisky. No, it doesn't help.'

'Jake—'

'No. Leave it, Amelia. Please. If you want to do something useful, you could make us a cup of tea.'

'How about a hot milky drink?'

'I'm not five.'

'No, but you're tired, you're hurt and you said you'd had enough caffeine today—it might help you sleep.'

'Tea,' he said implacably.

She shrugged and got to her feet, padded back through to the kitchen and put the kettle on, turning in time to see him drain his glass and set it down on the table. He glanced up and met her eyes, and sighed.

'I've only had one. I'm not an alcoholic, Amelia.'

'I never suggested you were!' she said, appalled that he'd think she was criticising when actually she'd simply been concerned for his health and well-being.

'So stop looking at me as if you're the Archangel Gabriel and I'm going off the rails!'

She gave a soft chuckle and took two mugs out of the cupboard. 'I'm the last person to criticise anyone for life choices. I'm homeless, for heavens' sake! And I've got three children, only one of whom was planned, and I'm unemployed and my life's a total mess, so pardon me if I pick you up on that one! I just wondered…'

'Wondered what? Why I'm such a miserable bastard?'

'Are you? Miserable, I mean? Kate thought—' She broke off, not wanting him to think Kate had been discussing him, but it was too late, and one eyebrow climbed autocratically.

'Kate thought—?' he prompted.

'You were just a loner. You are, I mean. A loner.'

'And what do you think, little Miss Fixit?'

She swallowed. 'I think you're sad, and lonely. She said you're very private, but I think that's because it all hurts too much to talk about.'

His face lost all expression, and he turned back to the fire, the only sign of movement from him the flex of the muscle in his jaw. 'Why don't you forget the amateur psychology and concentrate on making the tea?' he said, his voice devoid of emotion, but she could still see that tic in his jaw, the rhythmic bunching of the muscle, and she didn't know whether to persevere or give up, because she sensed it might all be a bit of a Pandora's box and, once opened, she might well regret all the things that came out.

So she made the tea, and took it through and sat beside the fire in what started as a stiff and unyielding silence and became in the end a wary truce.

He was the first to break the silence.

'I don't suppose you've made the shopping list?'

She shook her head. 'Not yet. I could do it now.'

'No, don't worry. We can do it over breakfast. I have no doubt that, no matter how little sleep we may have had, the kids will be up at the crack of dawn raring to go, so there'll be plenty of time.'

She laughed a little unsteadily, feeling the tension drain out of her at his words. 'I'm sure.' She got to her feet and held out her hand for his mug, then was surprised when he reached up his left hand, the one in the cast, and took her fingers in his.

'Ignore me, Amelia. I'll get over it. I'll be fine to-morrow.'

She nodded, not understanding really, because how could she? But she let it go, for now at least, and she squeezed his fingers gently and then let go, and he dropped his arm and held out the mug.

'Thanks for the tea. It was nice.'

The tea? Or having someone to sit and drink it with?

He didn't say, and she wasn't asking, but one thing she knew about this man, whatever Kate might say to the contrary—he wasn't a loner.

'My pleasure,' she murmured and, putting the mugs in the sink, she closed the doors of the fire and shut it down again. With a murmured, 'Good night,' she went upstairs to bed, but she didn't sleep until she heard the soft creak of the stairs and the little click as his bedroom door closed.

Then she let out the breath she'd been holding and slipped into a troubled and uneasy sleep.

CHAPTER FIVE

IT WAS the first time in years he'd been round a supermarket, and Christmas Eve probably wasn't the day to start—not when they even had to queue to get into the car park, and by the time they'd found a space Jake was beginning to wonder why on earth he'd suggested it.

It was going to be a nightmare, he knew it, rammed to the roof with festive goodies and wall-to-wall Christmas jingles and people in silly hats—he was dreading it, and it didn't disappoint.

The infuriatingly jolly little tunes on the in-store speakers were constantly being interrupted with calls for multi-skilled staff to go to the checkouts—a fact that didn't inspire hope for a quick getaway—and the place was rammed with frustrated shoppers who couldn't reach the shelves for the trolleys jamming the aisles.

'I have an idea,' he said as they fought to get down the dairy aisle and he was shunted in the ankle by yet another trolley. 'You know what we need, I don't want to be shoved around and Thomas needs company, so why don't I stand at the end with him and you go backwards and forwards picking up the stuff?'

And it all, suddenly, got much easier because he could concentrate on amusing Thomas—and that actually was probably the hardest part. Not that he was hard to entertain, quite the opposite, but it brought back so many memories—memories he'd buried with his son—and it was threatening to wreck him. Then, just when he thought he'd go mad if he had to look at that cheerful, chubby little smile any longer, he realised their system wasn't working.

The trolley wasn't getting fuller and, watching her, he could see why. She was obviously reluctant to spend too much of his money, which was refreshing but unnecessary, so he gave up and shoved the trolley one-handed into the fray while she was dithering over the fresh turkeys.

'What's the matter?'

'They're so expensive. The frozen ones are much cheaper—'

'But they take ages to defrost so we don't have a choice. Just pick one. Here, they've got nice free-range Bronze turkeys—get one of them,' he suggested, earning himself a searching look.

'What do you know about Bronze turkeys?' she asked incredulously.

He chuckled. 'Very little—but I know they're supposed to have the best flavour, I'm ethically comfortable with free range and, anyway, they're the most expensive and therefore probably the most sought after. That's usually an indicator of quality. So pick one and let's get on.'

'But—they're so expensive, Jake, and I feel so guilty taking your money—'

He gave up, reached over and single-handedly heaved a nice fat turkey into the trolley. 'Right. Next?'

'Um—stuffing,' she said weakly, and he felt a little tug at his sleeve.

'You said we could have sausages and cook them and have them on sticks,' Kitty said hopefully.

'Here—traditional chipolatas,' he said, and threw three packets in the trolley, thought better of it and added another two for good measure. 'Bacon?'

'Um—probably.' She put a packet of sausagemeat stuffing in the trolley and he frowned at it, picked up another with chestnuts and cranberries, which looked more interesting, and put that in, too.

'You're getting into this, aren't you?' she teased, coming back with the bacon.

So was she, he noticed with relief, seeing that at last she was picking up the quality products and not the cheapest, smallest packet she could find of whatever it was. They moved on, and the trolley filled up. Vegetables, fruit, a traditional Christmas pudding that would last them days, probably, but would at least be visible in the middle of the old refectory table in the breakfast room, and a chocolate log for the children. Then, when they'd done the food shopping and filled the trolley almost to the brim, they took it through the checkout, put it all in the car and went back inside for 'the exciting stuff', as Kitty put it.

Christmas decorations for the tree they had yet to buy, little nets of chocolate coins in gold foil, crackers for the table, a wreath for the door—the list was nearly as long as the first and, by the time they got to the end of it, the children were hungry and Thomas, who'd been as good as gold and utterly, heart-wrenchingly enchanting until that point, was starting to grizzle.

'I tell you what—why don't you take the kids and get them something to eat and drink while I deal with this lot?' he suggested, peeling a twenty pound note out of his wallet and giving it to her.

She hesitated, but he just sighed and shoved it at her, and with a silent nod she flashed him a smile and took the children off to the canteen.

Which gave him long enough to go back up the aisles and look for presents for them all. And, because it had thinned out by that point, he went to the customer services and asked if there was anyone who could help him wrap the presents for the children. He brandished his cast pathetically and, between that and the black eye, he charmed them into it shamelessly.

There was nothing outrageous in his choices. There was nothing outrageous in the shop anyway but, even if there had been, he would have avoided it. It wasn't necessary, and he didn't believe in spoiling children, but there was a colouring book with glue and glitter that Kitty had fingered longingly and been made to put back, and he'd noticed Edward looking at an intricate construction toy of the sort he'd loved as a boy, and there was a nice chunky plastic shape sorter which he thought Thomas might like.

And then there was Amelia.

She didn't have any gloves, he'd noticed, and he'd commented on it on the way there when she was rubbing her hands and blowing on them holding the steering wheel.

'Sure, it's freezing, but I can't do things with gloves on,' she'd explained.

But he'd noticed some fingerless mitts, with little flaps that buttoned back out of the way and could be let down to tuck her fingers into to turn them into mittens. And they were in wonderful, ludicrously pink stripes with a matching scarf that would snuggle round her neck and keep her warm while she walked the dog.

He even bought a little coat for Rufus, because he'd noticed him shivering out on their walk first thing.

And then he had to make himself stop, because they weren't his family and he didn't want to make them—or, more specifically, Amelia—feel embarrassed. But he chucked in a jigsaw to put on the low coffee table in the drawing room and work on together, just because it was the sort of thing he'd loved in his childhood, and also a family game they could play together.

And then he really *did* stop, and they were all wrapped and paid for, together with the decorations, and someone even helped him load them into the car and wished him a merry Christmas, and he found himself saying it back with a smile.

Really?

He went into the canteen and found them sitting in a litter of sandwich wrappers and empty cups. 'All set?'

She nodded. 'Yes. We were just coming to find you. Thank you so much—'

'Don't mention it. Right, we'd better get on, because we need to take this lot home and then get a tree before it's too late, and at some point today I need to go to the hospital and have a proper cast put on my arm.'

'Wow! Look at the tree. It's *enormous*!'

It wasn't, not really, but it was quite big enough—and it had been a bit of a struggle to get it in place with one arm out of action in its new cast, but just the look on the children's faces made it all worth it—and, if he wasn't mistaken, there was the sheen of tears in Amelia's eyes.

They'd put it in pride of place in the bay window in the drawing room, and lit the fire—a great roaring log fire in the open hearth, with crackling flames and the sweet smell of apple-wood smoke—and, between the wood smoke and the heady scent of the tree, the air just smelled of Christmas. All they had to do now was decorate the tree, and for Jake it was a step too far.

'I'm going to sit this out,' he said, heading for the door, but Kitty shook her head and grabbed his good hand and tugged him back, shocking him into immobility.

'You *can't*, Jake! You have to help us—we're all too small to reach the top, and you *have* to put the *lights* on and the *fairy* and all the tinsel and *everything*!'

Why was it, he wondered, that children—especially earnest little girls—always talked in italics and exclamation marks? And her eyes were pleading with him, and there was no way he could walk away from her. From any of them.

'OK. I'll just go and put the kettle on—'

'No! Lights first, because otherwise we can't do *anything* until you get back, and you'll be *ages*!'

Italics again. He smiled at her. 'Well, in that case, I'll put the *lights* on *first*, but *just* the lights, and then we'll have a *quick* cup of tea and we'll finish it off. OK?'

She eyed him a little suspiciously, as if she didn't trust his notion of quick and wasn't quite sure about the emphasis on the words, because there was something mildly teasing in them and he could see she was working it out, working out if he *was* only teasing or if he was being mean.

And he couldn't be mean to her, he discovered. Not in the least. In fact, all he wanted to do was gather her up into his arms and tell her it would all be all right, but of course it wasn't his place to do that and he couldn't make it right for her, couldn't make her father step up to the plate and behave like a decent human being.

If he was the man he was thinking of, Jake knew David Jones, had met him in the past, and he hadn't liked him at all. Oh, he'd been charming enough, but he'd talked rubbish, been full of bull and wild ideas with no foundation, and at one point a year or two ago he'd approached him at a conference asking for his investment in some madcap scheme. He'd declined, and he'd heard later, not unexpectedly, that he'd gone down the pan. And it didn't surprise him in the least, if it *was* the same David Jones, that he'd walked out on his family.

So he couldn't make it right for David's little daughter. But he could help her with the tree, and he could make sure they were warm and safely housed until their situation improved. And it was all he needed to do, all his conscience required.

It was only his heart that he was having trouble with, and he shut the door on it firmly and concentrated on getting the lights on the tree without either knocking it over or hurting any more of the innumerable aches and pains that were emerging with every hour that passed.

'Are you OK doing that?'

He turned his head and smiled down at Amelia ruefully. 'I'll live. I'm nearly done.'

'I'll put the kettle on. You look as if you could do with some more painkillers.'

'I'll be fine. It's just stretching that hurts—'

'And bending over, and standing, and—'

'Just put the kettle on,' he said softly, and she opened her mouth again, closed it and went out.

He watched her walk down the hall, watched the gentle sway of her hips, the fluid grace of her movements, the lightness in her step that hadn't been there yesterday, and he felt a sharp stab of what could only be lust. She was a beautiful, sensuous woman, intelligent and brave, and he realised he wanted to gather her up in his arms, too, and to hell with the complications.

But he couldn't, and he wouldn't, so with a quiet sigh he turned back to the tree and finished draping the string of lights around the bottom, then turned them on and stood back.

'How's that?'

'*Really* pretty!' Kitty whispered, awed.

'It's a bit crooked,' he said, wondering if there was any way he could struggle in under the tree and right it, but Edward—typically—rushed in with reassurance.

'It doesn't show,' he said quickly, 'and it looks really nice. Can we put the rest of the things on now?'

'We have to wait for Mummy!' Kitty said, sounding appalled, and so Jake sent them off to the kitchen to find out what she was doing and to tell her to bring biscuits with the tea. He lowered himself carefully on to the sofa and smiled at Thomas, who was sitting on the floor inside a ring of fat cushions with a colourful plastic teething ring in his mouth.

'All right, little man?' he asked, and Thomas gave him a toothy grin and held out the toy. It was covered in spit, but it didn't matter, he was only showing it to Jake, not offering it to him, so he admired it dutifully and tried oh, so hard not to think about Ben.

'That's really nice,' he said gruffly. 'Does it taste good?'

'Mumum,' he said, shoving it back in his mouth with a delicious chuckle, and Jake clenched his teeth and gave a tiny huff of laughter that was more than halfway to a sob.

What was it about kids that they got through your defences like nothing else on earth?

'You're going to be a proper little charmer, aren't you?' he said softly, and was rewarded with another spitty little chuckle. Then he threw down the toy and held out his hands, and it was beyond Jake to refuse.

He held out his hands, hoping his broken wrist was up to it, and Thomas grabbed his fingers and pulled himself up with a delighted gurgle, taking Jake's breath away.

'Are you all right?'

'Not really,' he said a little tightly, massively relieved to see Amelia reappear. 'Um—could you take him? My hand—'

'Oh, Jake! Thomas, come here, darling.'

She gently prised his fingers off Jake's, and the pull on the fracture eased and he sank back with a shaky sigh, because it hadn't only been the fracture, it had been that gummy, dribbly smile and the feel of those strong, chubby little fingers, and he just wanted to get the hell out. 'Thanks. That was probably a stupid thing to do, but—'

'You couldn't refuse him? Tell me about it. Look, I've brought you something lovely!'

'I don't really want a cup of juice,' he said softly, and she laughed, the sound running through him like a tinkling stream, clean and pure and sweet.

'Silly. Your tea's there, with the painkillers.'

He found a smile. Actually, not that hard, with the warmth of her laughter still echoing through him. 'Thanks.'

'And chocolate biscuits, and shortbread!' Edward said, sounding slightly amazed.

'Goodness. Anyone would think it was Christmas,' he said in mock surprise, and Kitty giggled and then, before he could react or do anything to prevent it, she climbed onto his lap and snuggled up against his chest with a smile.

'It *is* Christmas, silly—well, it is tomorrow,' she corrected, and squirmed round to study the tree. 'We need to put everything else on it.'

'Biscuits first,' he said firmly, because he needed his painkillers, especially if Kitty was going to bounce and fidget and squirm on his bruises. And his arm was really aching now after all the silly things he'd done with it that day.

So they ate biscuits, and Kitty snuggled closer, and he caught the anguished look in Amelia's eye and felt so sad for them all that it had all gone wrong, because Kitty's father should have been sitting somewhere else with her on his lap instead of hiding from his responsibilities in Thailand, and he should have been there with Rachel and Ben, and none of them had deserved it—

'Right. Let's do the tree,' he said and, shunting Kitty off his lap, he got stiffly to his feet and put the baubles where he was told.

* * *

He was being amazing.

She couldn't believe just how kind he'd been all day. He'd been so foul to her yesterday, so sarcastic and bitter, but somehow all that was gone and he was being the man Kate had talked about, generous to a fault and the soul of kindness.

He was so gentle with the children, teasing them, humouring them, putting up with their enthusiastic nonsense, and then, when the tree was done and she'd swept underneath it to pick up the needles that had fallen out of it while they'd decorated it, they went into the kitchen and she cooked supper while she danced around the kitchen with tinsel in her hair, singing along with the Christmas songs on the radio and making Thomas giggle.

And then she'd looked up and seen Jake watching her with an odd look on his face, and she'd felt the breath squeeze out of her lungs. No. She was misreading the signals. He couldn't possibly want her—not a destitute woman with three children and a smelly, expensive little dog.

So she pulled the tinsel out of her hair and tied it round the dog's neck, and concentrated on cooking the supper.

Sausages on sticks for Kitty, with roasted vegetable skewers in mini pitta pockets so she could pretend she was having kebabs, followed by the sort of fruit Millie couldn't afford to buy, cut into cubes and dunked into melted chocolate. He'd put little pots on the top of the Aga with squares of chocolate in, and they'd melted and made the most fabulous sauce.

And the children had loved every mouthful of it. Even Thomas had sucked on a bit of sausage and had a few slices of banana and some peeled grapes dipped in choco-late and, apart from the shocking mess, it was a huge success.

'Right, you lot, time for bed,' she said.

'Oh, but it's Christmas!'

'Yes, and it'll come all the earlier if you're in bed asleep,' she reasoned. 'And Father Christmas won't come down the chimney if you're still awake.'

'But he won't come anyway, because of the fire,' Kitty said, looking suddenly worried, but Jake rescued the situation instantly.

'Not a problem,' he said promptly. 'There's another chimney in the dining room, and he'll come down that.'

'But he won't know where to put the presents!' she argued.

'Yes, he will, because he knows everything,' Edward said with an air of patient indulgence that made Millie want to laugh and cry all at once. 'Come on, let's go up to bed and then he'll come.'

'Promise?' Kitty said, staring at her hopefully.

Oh, Lord, there was so little for them. They were going to be horribly disappointed. 'Promise,' she said, near to tears, but then the doorbell rang, jangling the ancient bell over the breakfast room door, and Jake got to his feet.

'I'll get it, it's probably Kate,' he said, and she followed him, meaning to say hello if it *was* Kate or take the children up to bed if not, but as he reached for the door they heard the unmistakable sound of a choir.

'Carol singers,' he said in a hollow voice, rooted to the spot with an appalled expression on his face.

'I'll deal with them,' she said softly, and opened the door, meaning to give them some change for their tin and send them away. But he was still standing there in full view and the vicar, who was standing at the front, beamed at him.

'Mr Forrester! We heard you were back and that you'd been injured, so we thought we'd come and share some carols with you on the way back from evensong—bring you a little Christmas cheer.'

Jake opened his mouth, shut it again and smiled a little tightly. 'Thank you,' he said, and he probably would have stood there with that frozen smile on his face if Amelia hadn't elbowed him gently out of the way, opened the door wide and invited them in, because after all there was no choice, no matter how unhappy it might make him.

'You'll freeze,' she said with a smile. 'Come inside and join us.' And Jake would just have to cope, because anything else would have been too rude for words. And apparently he realised that, because he found another smile and stepped back.

'Yes—of course, come on in by the fire,' he said, and led them to the drawing room, where they gathered round the fire and sang all the old favourites—*Silent Night*, *Away In A Manger* and *O Come All Ye Faithful*, and then the vicar smilingly apologised for not having a chorister to sing *Once In Royal David's City*, and beside her Amelia felt Edward jiggle and she squeezed his shoulder in encouragement.

'Go on,' she murmured, and he took a step forwards.

'I could do it,' he offered, and the vicar looked at him and smiled broadly.

'Well—please do. Do you need the words?'

He shook his head, went over to them and started to sing.

Jake was speechless.

The boy's voice filled the room, pure and sweet, and he felt his throat close. It brought so much back—the pain of his childhood, the respite that music had brought him, the hard work but the immense rewards of being a chorister.

And when Edward got to the end of the first verse and everyone joined in, he found himself singing, too, found the voice he'd grown into as a man, rusty with lack of use and emotion, but warming up, filling him with joy again as he sang the familiar carol. And Edward looked at him in astonishment and then smiled, as if he'd just discovered something wonderful.

And maybe he had.

Maybe Jake had, too, because Edward had a truly beautiful voice and it would be a travesty if he didn't get the opportunity to develop and explore this musical gift. And if there was anything he could do to help with that, he wanted to do it, even if it was just to encourage him to join the school choir.

But in the meantime he sang, and the choir launched into *God Rest Ye Merry Gentlemen*, which was perfect for his baritone, and so for the first time in years he dragged the air deep down into his lungs and let himself go, and the old house was filled with the joyful sound of their voices.

And Edward grinned, and he grinned back, and beside him he could see Amelia staring up at him in astonishment, her eyes like saucers, and Kitty too. When they got to the end they all smiled and laughed, and Amelia ran down to the kitchen and came back with a tray of mince pies she'd made earlier, and he offered them a drink to wash them down but they all refused.

'Sorry, we'd love to, but we have to get home,' was the consensus, and of course they did. It was Christmas Eve, and he'd been fitted in as a favour. A favour by people he didn't know, who'd heard he'd been hurt and had come to bring Christmas to him, and deep down inside, the fissure that was opening around his heart cracked open a little further, letting the warmth seep in.

'Thank you so much for coming,' he said with genuine feeling as he showed them out. 'The children have really enjoyed it. It was extremely kind of you, and I can't thank you enough.'

'Well, there's always the church roof,' the vicar joked, and he laughed, but he made a mental note to send him a cheque. 'And if the boy wants to join us…'

'Ah, they're only visiting,' he said, and the words gave him a curious pang, as if somehow that was wrong and vaguely unsettling. 'But—yes, I agree. He could be a chorister.'

'As you were once, I would imagine. You could always join us yourself. The choir's always got room for a good voice.'

He smiled a little crookedly. 'My choir days are over—but thank you. Have a good Christmas, all of you. Good night.'

They left in a chorus of good-nights and merry Christmases, and he closed the door and turned to see Edward standing there staring at him.

'Did you really sing in a choir?' he asked warily, and Jake nodded.

'Yes, I did. When I was about your age, and a little older. My voice started to break when I was twelve, which rather put a stop to singing for a couple of years, and I never really got back into it after that, but—yeah, I went to choir school. What about you? Do you sing in a choir?'

'We didn't really have a choir at the school, but the music teacher said I ought to have a voice test somewhere. I was supposed to sing in the school carol concert last week, but we had to move to Auntie Laura's and it was too far away, so I couldn't. And I'd been practising for weeks and weeks.'

'I can tell. What a shame. Still, you did it for us, and it was great. You did really well. Here, come with me. I've got something to show you.'

'Is it a picture?'

'No. It's a film of me when I was in the choir. I had to sing *Once In Royal David's City* myself at the start of the carol service when I was twelve, just before my voice broke.'

And it had been televised, but he didn't mention that because it was irrelevant, really. He took Edward into his sitting room, found the DVD he'd had the old video copied onto, and turned it on.

'Wow,' Edward said at the end of his solo, his voice hushed. 'That was amazing. You must have been so scared.'

He laughed. 'I was pretty terrified, I can tell you. But it was worth it, it was fantastic. It was a good time all round. Hard work, but lots of fun, too, and I wouldn't have swapped it for the world.'

He told him more about it, about the fun, about the pranks he'd got up to and the trouble he'd got in, and about the hard work and the gruelling schedule of rehearsals, but also about the amazing thrill and privilege of singing in the cathedral.

'I'd love to do that,' the boy said wistfully.

'Would you? It's a big commitment. I had to go to boarding school, but then I wasn't very happy at home, so actually I enjoyed it,' he found himself admitting.

'Why weren't you happy?' Edward asked.

'Oh—my parents used to row a lot, and I always seemed to be in the way. So it was quite nice when I wasn't, for all of us, really. But you are happy, aren't you?'

He nodded. 'And I couldn't leave Mummy, because she needs me.'

'Of course she does—but, you know, she also needs you to be happy, and if it made you happy—anyway, you don't have to go away to school. Most schools have a choir, and certainly the bigger churches do. I'm sure they'd be delighted to have you. You've got a good voice.'

'But we don't live anywhere properly, so we don't have a church or a school,' he said, and Jake's heart ached for the poor, uprooted child.

'You will soon,' he consoled him, hoping it was true, and he turned off the television and got to his feet. 'Now, you'd better run up to bed or I'm going to be in trouble with your mother. You sleep well, and I'll see you in the morning. Good night, Edward.'

'Good night,' Edward said, and then without warning he ran over to Jake, put his arms round him and hugged him before running out of the door. And Jake stood there, rooted to the spot, unravelled by the simple spontaneous gesture of a child.

Amelia stood in the shadows of the hall, scarcely able to breathe for emotion.

The sound of his voice had been exquisite, the sort of sound that made your hair stand on end and your heart swell, and she'd stood there and listened to it, then to his gentle and revealing conversation with her son, and her eyes had filled with tears. Poor little boy, to have felt so unwanted and unloved. And thank God for a choir school which had helped him through it, given him something beautiful and perfect to compensate in some small way for the disappointments of his young life.

She'd taken Kitty and Thomas upstairs when she'd seen Edward deep in conversation with Jake, knowing he missed the influence of a man in his life, and she'd bathed them quickly, tucked them up and gone back down—and heard the pure, sweet sound of a chorister coming from Jake's sitting room.

She hadn't known it was him until she'd heard him talking to Edward, but she wasn't surprised. It had been obvious when he'd joined in with the carol singers that he'd had some kind of voice training, as well as a beautiful voice, deep and rich and warm. It had shivered through her then, and it had done the same thing now, hearing him as a child.

And he was talking to Edward about it, treating him as an equal, encouraging him, giving him hope—

But too much hope, and it was pointless doing that,

because there was no way she could afford any lessons or anything for him, so it was cruel of Jake to encourage him. It was easy if you had money. Everything was easier, and it wasn't fair to Edward to build him up. She'd have to talk to Jake, to stop him—

She dived into the kitchen and scrubbed the tears away from her eyes while she cleared up the aftermath of their supper, and then she took the presents she'd brought downstairs with her through to the drawing room—the few things she'd bought the children, and the ones from Kate, and of course the beautiful and inevitably expensive ones from her sister—and, by the time she got there, there were some others waiting.

They must be Jake's, she thought. Presents from friends, if not family, and people like Kate, who was bound to have given him a present.

But they weren't. They were for the children, and for her, and, of all things, for Rufus. Her eyes flooded with tears, and she sat back on her heels and sniffed.

Damn him, how could he do this? Squandering money on them all because it was so easy for him, not realising how much worse it made it all, how much harder it would be when it was all over and they came down to earth with a bump. He was even spoiling the wretched dog—

'Amelia?'

'What are these? You shouldn't—' she began, but he just shook his head.

'They're nothing—'

'No. They're not nothing,' she corrected tautly. 'They're nothing to you, but believe me, you have no idea what nothing's like. Nothing is not having anywhere for your children to live, having to take them away from school just before the carol concert your son's been practising for for weeks, having to tell them that Daddy doesn't have any money and he's not even here to see them because he's run away from the law—except of course I can't tell them that, can I, because it wouldn't be fair, so I have to pretend he's just had to go away and lie to them, and I'm sick of lying to them and struggling and the last—absolutely the *last* damn thing I need is you telling Edward he should go to choir school. I'll never be able to afford it and you'll just build his hopes up and then they'll be dashed and it's just another disappointment in his life—'

She couldn't go on, tears streaming down her cheeks, and he gave a ragged sigh and crouched awkwardly down beside her, his hand gentle on her shoulder, his eyes distressed. 'Amelia—Millie—please don't,' he murmured softly. 'It wasn't like that. I didn't build his hopes up, but he's good, and there are places—'

'Didn't you *hear* what I said?' she raged. '*We have no money*!'

'But you don't need money. He could get a scholarship, like I did. My parents didn't pay. If someone's got talent, they don't turn them away—and there are other things. It doesn't have to be choir school. Just because I went there doesn't mean it's right for everyone. It's very hard, and the hours are really long, and you work every Sunday, Christmas Day, Easter—you have to be dedicated, it's a massive commitment, and it's not for everybody—'

'No, it's not, but even if it was for him, it's not for you to decide! He's my son, Jake—*mine*! It's none of your business! You have no right to take him off like that and fill his head with ideas—'

'It wasn't like that! He was asking…I just thought…'

'Well, don't! If you want a son to follow in your footsteps, then get your own, Jake, but leave mine out of it! And we don't need your flashy presents!'

And, without giving him a chance to reply, she scrambled to her feet and ran into the kitchen, tears pouring down her face and furious with herself as well as him because, whatever he'd done, whatever he'd spent or said, they were in his house against his wishes, and he'd busted a gut today to make their Christmas Day tomorrow a good one, and now she'd gone and ruined it for all of them…

CHAPTER SIX

IF YOU want a son…

His legs gave way and he sat down abruptly on the rug in front of the tree, her words ringing in his ears.

It had never occurred to him he was doing any harm by talking to Edward, showing him the recording. He was just sharing an interest, taking an interest—and not because he wanted a son to follow in his footsteps. He'd been there, done that, and lost everything. She thought he didn't know what nothing meant? Well, he had news for her.

Nothing meant waking up every morning alone, with nobody to share your day with, nobody to help you live out your dreams, nobody to love, nobody to love you in return.

Nothing meant standing in a cold and lonely churchyard staring at a headstone bearing the names of the only people in the world you cared about and wondering how on earth it had happened, how one minute they'd been there, and the next they'd been gone for ever.

If you want a son…

Pain seared through him. *Oh, Ben, I want you. I want you every day. What would you have been like? Would you have loved singing, like me, or would you have been tone-deaf like your mother? Tall or short? Quiet or noisy? I would have loved you, whatever. I'll always love you.* He glanced out of the window and saw a pale swirl of snow, and his heart contracted. *Are you cold tonight, my precious son, lying there in the churchyard?*

Oh, God.

A sob ripped through him and he stifled it, battening it down, refusing to allow it to surface. She hadn't meant to hurt him. She hadn't known about Ben, hadn't realised what she was saying. And maybe she was right. Maybe he'd overstepped the mark with Edward.

He needed to talk to her, to go and find her and apologise—but not yet. Not now. Now, he needed to get himself under control, to let the pain recede a little.

And then he became aware of Rufus, standing just a few inches away from him, his tail down, his eyes worried, and when he held out his hand, the dog's tail flickered briefly.

'Oh, Rufus. What's happened to us all?' he murmured unsteadily, and Rufus came and sat down with his side against Jake's thigh, and rested his head in his lap and licked his hand.

'Yeah, I know. I need to talk to Amelia. I need to tell her I'm sorry. But I can't—'

He bit his lip, and Rufus licked him again, and he ruffled his fur and waited a little longer, until his emotions were back under control, because he owed Amelia more than just an apology. He owed her an explanation, and it would mean opening himself to her, to her pity, and he never ever did that. It was just too damned hard.

But eventually he couldn't leave it any longer, so he got

stiffly to his feet, found the whisky and limped down the hall to the breakfast room and pushed open the door.

She was sitting in front of the fire, her legs drawn up and her arms wrapped round her knees, and he could tell she'd been crying. Her face was ravaged with tears, her eyes wide with distress. He went over to her, poured two hefty measures of spirit and held one out to her.

'I'm sorry,' he said. 'I should have thought—should have asked you before showing it to him.'

'No. You were only being kind. I was so rude—'

'Yes, you were, but I'm not surprised, with everything going on in your life. You're just fighting their corner. I can't criticise you for that.'

And then, before his courage failed him and he chickened out, he said, 'I had a son.'

She lifted her head and stared at him.

'Had?' she whispered in horrified disbelief.

'Ben. He died five years ago—five years yesterday, just a month after his second birthday. He'd been Christmas shopping with my wife, Rachel, and they were by the entrance to the car park when someone mounted the kerb and hit them. They were both killed instantly.'

'Oh, Jake—'

Her voice was hardly more than a breath, and then she dragged in a shuddering sob and pressed her hand against her lips. Dear God, what had she said to him? If you want a son…then get your own. And all the time—

'Oh, Jake, I don't know what to say—'

'Don't say anything. There's nothing you can say. Here, have a drink. And please don't worry about the presents, they really are nothing. It was just a gesture, nothing more. They aren't lavish, I promise, so you don't have to worry. I wouldn't do that to you. I just…it's Christmas, and I'd expect to give something small to any child who was staying here. And I promise not to say anything more to any of them that might give you a problem later on. So come on, drink up and let's go and stuff the turkey, otherwise we'll be eating at midnight.'

She hauled in a breath, sniffed and scrubbed her cheeks with her hands. 'You're right. We've got a lot to do.' And just then she couldn't talk to him, couldn't say another word or she really would howl her eyes out, and so she sipped the whisky he pressed into her hand, feeling the slow burn as it slid down her throat, letting the warmth drive out the cold horror of his simple words.

No wonder he didn't do children. No wonder he hadn't been pleased to see them in his house, on the very anniversary…

She took a gulp and felt it scorch down her throat. What had it done to him, to come home and find them all there? His words had been cruel, but not as cruel as their presence must have been to him. And her own words—they'd been far more cruel, so infinitely hurtful, and there was nothing she could do to take them back.

'What I said—'

'Don't. Don't go there, Amelia. You weren't to know. Forget it.'

But she couldn't, and she knew she never would. She couldn't bear the thought that she'd hurt him with her words, that their presence in his house must be tearing him apart, but there was nothing she could do about it now—

the words were said, the children were sleeping upstairs, and all she could do was make sure it all went as well and smoothly as possible, and kept the children away from him so they didn't rub salt in his wound.

'I'm going to get on,' she said, and she set the glass down and stood up, brushed herself off mentally and physically, and headed for the kitchen.

'We still haven't dealt with the decorations in here,' he said from behind her, and she looked up at their makeshift decorations in the light fitting over the breakfast table, still half-finished and looking bedraggled and forlorn.

Damn. 'I'm sorry, I meant to take them down,' she said, tugging out a chair, but he just shook his head.

'No. Leave them. The children made them.'

She stopped, one foot on the chair, the other on the table, and looked down at him.

'But—you said it was tat. And you were right, it is.'

'No. I'm sorry. I was just feeling rough and you took me by surprise,' he said, master of the understatement. 'Please, leave them. In fact, weren't there some more bits?'

She nodded and climbed slowly down off the chair. 'Edward put them out of the back door.'

'Get them and put them in—finish it off. And I'll put the wreath we bought on the front door. And then we ought to do the things you need help with, and then I'm really going to have to turn in, because I'm bushed, frankly. It's been a long day, and I've had enough.'

She felt another great wave of guilt. 'Oh, Jake—sit down, let me get you another drink. I can do everything. Please—just sit there and rest and keep me company, if you really want to help, or otherwise just go to bed. I can manage.'

He smiled wryly. 'I'm sure you can. I get the feeling there's not a lot you can't manage. But I'm OK.'

And he helped her, even though he must be feeling pretty rough, because she got the distinct impression that he didn't give up easily. So she made them both a cup of tea, and finished off the decorations in the light fitting while he put the wreath on the door. Then he sat down in the chair to drink his tea while she stuffed the turkey and wrapped the sausages in bacon, and the next time she looked he'd leant back and closed his eyes, with Rufus curled up on his lap and his legs stretched out in front of the fire. She made another batch of mince pies and peeled potatoes and carrots and trimmed the sprouts while they cooked, and then she woke him up and sent him to bed.

It was almost Christmas Day, she thought as she tiptoed into the children's room and hung their stockings on the end of their beds. Nothing like what they'd had last year or the year before, but they were good kids and they under-stood, in their way, and thanks to Jake they had tiny oranges and chocolates and little bits of this and that to add to her offerings.

And at least they were alive, unlike Jake's little boy.

She stared down at Edward. He was a little older than Ben would have been, she realised with a pang. How painful it must be for Jake, knowing that. How could she have said what she did? How did he cope with the terrible loss? How did anyone?

Edward's face blurred, and she kissed him lightly on the cheek, snuggling the quilt up round him, then tucked Kitty in and went to check on Thomas. He didn't have a stocking, but he was only eight months old, he didn't even know what Christmas was yet. And at least he was in a warm, comfortable house.

They were so lucky. They could have been anywhere, and instead they were here, warm and safe—and, without Jake, it would have been so much worse. He'd done so much for them, and she'd repaid him by throwing his kindness back in his face. And not just his kindness.

If you want a son...

Tears scalded her cheeks, and she scrubbed them away. She could never take those words back, but she owed him more than she could ever repay, and she vowed to do everything in her power to make it right.

Starting with giving him a Christmas to remember...

'Mummy—Mummy, it's snowing!'

She opened her eyes a crack, but it was still dark—except for a strange light that filtered through the gap in the curtains.

'Kitty, whatever's the time?' she whispered.

'It's nearly six—Mummy, get up and come and *see*! It's so pretty!'

She let Kitty drag her out of bed and over to the window, and sure enough, the garden was blanketed with snow, thick and crisp and brilliant white, eerie in the moonlight.

Whatever time was it? The last thing she wanted was for the children to disturb Jake in the middle of the night! She peered at her watch anxiously. 'Kitty, it's only half past five!'

'No, it's not, it's after, 'cos I waited! And we've got stockings! Come and see!'

'Is Edward awake?'

'Of course I'm awake,' her sleepy, rumpled son said as he came in. 'She's been whispering at me for hours! Happy Christmas, Mummy,' he added with a smile and went into her arms, hugging her hard.

She bent her head and pressed a kiss to his hair, knowing the time for such liberties was probably numbered and enjoying it while she could, and then she scooped Kitty up and kissed her, too, and carried her back into their bedroom, closing the door to keep the noise down.

She snuggled into Amelia's side for a moment, but then wriggled down and ran to her bed. 'Can we open our stockings now?' she asked excitedly.

'All right,' she agreed reluctantly. 'But just the stockings. Nothing under the tree until later.' Much later!

'Are there presents under the tree? Did you see them?' Kitty asked, wide-eyed and eager, and Millie could have kicked herself for mentioning it.

'I expect there might be,' she said. *Unless there have been burglars.* 'But you can't go down and look until much, much later, in case you disturb Jake.'

And that wasn't going to happen if she had anything to do with it.

'How much later?' Kitty asked, persistent to the last, and she rolled her eyes and laughed softly.

'Half past eight,' she said, 'and that's only if Jake's awake. And if you wake him by making too much noise, then you'll have to wait till ten,' she added, trying to look stern.

'Ten?' Kitty wailed softly, and scrambled onto the bed. 'I'll be very, very quiet,' she vowed. 'Edward, don't make a noise!'

'I haven't said a thing!' he whispered indignantly, climbing onto his own bed and sliding a hand down inside his stocking. 'You're the one making all the noise—'

'Stop that, or the stockings go.'

There was instant silence, broken only by the tiny squeals of excitement from Kitty and the murmured, 'Oh, brilliant!' from Edward when he found a page-a-day diary. He flashed her a huge smile, and she felt a lump in her throat. It was such a little thing, but since David had left he'd kept a diary every day, and she knew he was using it as a way of working through his feelings.

He was such a good kid—and Jake was right, he deserved every chance. She'd look into getting him that voice test, but she was so afraid of tempting fate, of dangling something under his nose and then having it snatched away yet again.

'A chocolate Father Christmas!' Kitty said in delight, delving deeper. 'And a satsuma! Can I eat them now? Pretty please with a cherry on top?'

She sat down with a chuckle on the end of the bed and watched as her children found innocent pleasure in the simplest things. Then Edward looked up with hopeful eyes and said, 'Can we make a snowman?'

It was on the tip of her tongue to say, Of course, when she remembered it wasn't her garden, and she smiled ruefully.

'We'll have to ask Jake,' she said.

Edward nodded and went back to his orange, peeling it

meticulously and savouring it segment by segment. He was so thorough, so methodical in everything he did. So very unlike his father, who rushed into everything without thought. And out of it again. Like marriage. And fatherhood.

No, she wasn't going to think about that now. She could hear Thomas starting to stir, and she went back and scooped him out of his cot and gave him a hug. 'Hello, my little man!' she crooned softly. 'Happy Christmas. Look, Thomas—it's snowing!'

And, lifting the curtain aside, she looked out into the garden and saw Jake standing out there with Rufus, racing around in the snow and barking his head off as he tried to bite the snowflakes, while Jake laughed at him.

She chuckled and stood there for a moment watching them. Then, as if his eyes had been drawn to hers, Jake turned and looked up and waved.

She waved back and went in to the children. 'Jake's awake,' she said, 'so I'm going to go down and make a cup of tea and get a bottle for Thomas. Why don't you try and get back to sleep?'

'But we have to say Happy Christmas to Jake!' Kitty said, and ran for the stairs before Amelia could stop her. Edward followed, the two of them thundering and whooping down through the house, and she trailed after them with Thomas, hoping that the onslaught of the children wouldn't prove to be too much for him. Especially now that she knew—

She felt the shadow of his grief fall over the day, and paused a moment to think of a little boy she'd never known and would never have the chance to meet, and the woman who should have been greeting her husband and son here in this house this morning.

'I'm so sorry,' she whispered. 'So, so sorry.'

And then she followed the others downstairs to the kitchen.

It was freezing outside, but there was something wonderful about standing in the snow while Rufus raced round like a puppy and chased the snowflakes.

And as he went back in, the children tumbled into the kitchen, eyes sparkling with excitement, and Kitty ran over to him and reached up. He bent and hugged her, feeling the warm, damp kiss land on his cheek. 'Happy Christmas,' she said, her arms tight around his neck for a second, then she let him go and laughed, and he looked up and met her brother's eyes and remembered last night's spontaneous hug and smiled at him.

'Happy Christmas, Kitty. Happy Christmas, Edward,' he said.

His reply was drowned out by Kitty, plucking at his sleeve and giggling. 'You're all snowy!' she said. 'Like a snowman! Can we make a snowman?'

She was jumping up and down, her enthusiasm infectious, and he grinned down at her. 'Sure. It's great snow for that. It'll stick together. We can do it after we've opened the presents and had breakfast. Well, if that's all right with your mother—'

He looked up and met her eyes, and felt warmth uncurl deep inside him at her smile.

'Of course it's all right. It'll be fun. We can do it whenever you like. But maybe we need to get dressed first.'

'Oh, I don't know, it might be fun for the little cats on your pyjamas to play in the snow,' he teased, and a soft wash of colour swept her cheeks.

'Don't be silly,' she said, a trifle breathlessly, and he felt a totally inappropriate surge of longing.

'Can we make a really huge one?' Edward was asking, and Jake nodded, touched at the grin that blossomed on his usually serious young face.

'The biggest.'

'In the *world*?' Kitty said, her eyes like saucers, and he laughed.

'Well—maybe not *quite*.'

'He'll need a hat.'

'I might have a ski hat he can borrow,' Jake suggested. 'And a scarf.'

'And some coal for his eyes and a carrot for his nose—Mummy, have we got a carrot?'

Amelia threw up her hands and laughed. 'Kitty, slow down! Yes, we've got a carrot. You watched me buy them.'

'Awesome,' she said. 'So can we open the presents now? You said we had to wait till Jake was awake, but he's awake already, so can we go and do it now, and then we can get dressed and go and build our snowman?'

Catching the look on her face, Jake intervened rapidly. 'No, it's too early. Let your mother have a cup of tea and feed the baby. I tell you what,' he went on, watching their faces fall, 'why don't you go and see if you can guess what they are? We'll come through in a minute.'

And, as they ran excitedly out of the room, he met Amelia's eyes and they both let out their breath on a soft laugh.

'Kids,' he said, and she nodded, her smile touched with sadness. On his behalf, he realised, and wanted to hug her. Nothing to do with those crazy cat pyjamas under a baggy old jumper that made him want to peel it off over her head and unwrap her as his very own Christmas present.

He cleared his throat. 'Right, how about that tea?'

'Sounds great. What on earth are you doing up this early, by the way?' she added as he went over to the kettle, and she sounded slightly amazed.

'Making tea, letting the dog out.'

'I'm sorry, I didn't hear him.'

'He didn't make a sound, but I was awake and I wanted to see the snow.'

'You surprise me. I wouldn't have thought you were best friends with snow at the moment.'

He chuckled. 'It wasn't the snow's fault. It was the idiot skiing up above me, but we were well off piste and if I hadn't had an avalanche kit with airbags to help me float on the snow cloud, it would have been very different. So, not the snow at fault, just someone who didn't know what they were doing, and anyway, it isn't often we have a white Christmas. Besides, I was already awake.'

She made a soft sound of sympathy. 'Couldn't you sleep?'

'On the contrary,' he told her, pouring their tea. 'I didn't think I'd sleep, but actually I slept better than I have for ages.'

'It must have been the whisky.'

'Maybe,' he agreed, but he knew it wasn't.

It had been the warmth—the human warmth from having a family in a house so obviously built with families in mind. And the fact that it had been a good day, and he'd enjoyed it. Well, most of it. The supermarket had been pretty hellish, but even that had had its high points. 'Here—' he said, handing her some tea, 'and there's a bottle for the baby cooling by the sink.'

'Oh, you star, thank you,' she said softly, sounding stunned. 'You didn't have to do that.'

'I knew he'd be awake soon. I made it according to the directions, so I hope it's all right and not too weak or strong. And it might still be a bit hot.'

'No, it's fine,' she said with a smile that threatened to send him into meltdown. Damn. Last night she was ripping him to shreds, and today he just wanted to undress her and carry her off to bed.

He took a step away and pretended to check the temperature on the Aga. 'What time do you want to put the turkey in?'

'It needs four hours in a moderate oven.'

He frowned at her. 'What does that mean?' he asked, and she laughed, the soft sound running through him like teasing fingertips.

'It means not too hot and not too cold. I'm sure it'll be fine. We've got ages. Why don't we go and see what the children are doing before they "accidentally" tear the paper?'

He chuckled and followed her, the dog trotting between them, not sure if he should be with the woman who fed him and loved him, or this new friend who'd taken him out in the magical white stuff and played with him. It occurred to Jake that he was having a good time—that, although he'd thought this would be his worst nightmare, in fact he was enjoying himself.

And that, in itself, was an amazing Christmas present.

He'd been wrong.

His presents weren't nothing. They were thoughtfully chosen, simple but absolutely perfect. Laura's had been extravagant, as she'd guessed, and just made her feel guilty and inadequate, and Kate's were very simple and sweet, the children's handmade by Megan, and an outrageous pair of frivolous lacy knickers for her to cheer her up, apparently—only she'd opened them in front of Jake and turned bright red with embarrassment and stuffed them in her pocket.

Her presents to the children had been things they needed, because there simply wasn't the money for anything else, but his—they were just fun, and the children were delighted.

'Oh, Mummy, look! It's that book I wanted!' Kitty said, eyes sparkling, and Millie looked up and met Jake's wary eyes and smiled apologetically.

'So it is. You'll have to be careful with the glitter, it goes everywhere. Say—'

But she didn't need to finish, because Kitty had thrown herself at Jake and hugged him hard. Very hard—hard enough to make him wince, but he was smiling, so she didn't think he minded.

'Edward, what's that?' she asked, watching her meticulous son peel away the last bit of wrapping and reveal his present.

'It's a kit to build all sorts of things—it's brilliant. Thank you, Jake!' her son said, and although he didn't hug him, his eyes were shining and she could see Jake was pleased that he'd got it right.

So very, very right. 'Thomas, look at this!' she exclaimed, unwrapping the shape sorter and giving it to him, and he picked it up and shook it and laughed happily.

'Tull!' he said, and Jake's face creased in bewilderment. 'Tull?'

'He thinks it's a rattle,' Edward explained. 'Look, Thomas, it opens, and you can put these bits in. See this one? It's a square. Look!'

And Thomas stared, fascinated, as the little shape went into the hole as if by magic, and Jake stared, just as fascinated, it seemed, and Millie blinked away the tears and looked back under the tree. There were still two presents there, and Kitty dived under and pulled them out.

'This is for Rufus, and this one's for you,' she said, handing Millie a soft, squashy parcel.

'Me?' she said, horribly conscious that she hadn't bought him anything, or made him anything or in fact done anything except make his already difficult life even harder.

She swallowed and met his eyes, and he smiled tentatively. 'Go on, open it. It's only silly.'

'I haven't—'

'Shh. Open it.'

So she did, and when she saw the fingerless mitts that could turn into proper mittens, her eyes filled. He'd listened to what she'd said about not being able to do anything with gloves on, and he'd found her a solution.

A silly, crazy pink solution, with a matching scarf that was soft and cosy and gorgeous, and her eyes flooded with tears that she could no longer hold back.

'You've made Mummy cry,' Kitty said, staring at her, and Edward looked at her worriedly, but she dredged up a smile and scrubbed her cheeks with the heels of her hands and met Jake's eyes.

'I'm fine, really. Thank you, Jake. Thank you for everything.'

'My pleasure,' he said. 'What about the dog's?'

'I hope it's not food.'

'It's not food. Here, open it,' he said, handing it to her, and she knelt up beside him and tore off the paper and her eyes filled again.

'It's a coat!' she said, choked. 'Oh, thank you, he's been miserable in the cold and he hates the rain. Oh, that's lovely.'

And then, because she couldn't hold back any longer, she leant over and hugged him. Not as hard as Kitty, careful of his bruises, but hard enough that he would know she really meant it.

And he hugged her back, his arms warm and hard and strong around her, and it would have been so easy to sink into them and stay there for the rest of the day.

The rest of her life.

No!

She straightened up, blinking away fresh tears and scrambling to her feet. 'Right, let's put all this paper in the bin and tidy up, and then we need to get dressed, and come back down and have breakfast, and then we've got the world's biggest snowman to build!'

CHAPTER SEVEN

It was the most magical day.

They'd all gone upstairs to wash and dress, and Jake had called her back and asked her to help him.

'I could do with a shower, but I don't want to get the new cast wet and I didn't do so well yesterday. Could you tape this bag over my arm?'

'Of course,' she said, putting Thomas on the floor, and he handed her the bag and some tape, and then shucked off his robe so he was standing in front of her in nothing more than snug-fitting jersey boxers that sent her heart rate rocketing. Until she saw his bruises, and they took her breath away.

'Oh, Jake—you're black and blue!'

He smiled wryly. 'Tell me about it. Still, I'm alive. It could have been worse. And it's better today.'

She wasn't convinced, but she stuck the bag on his arm and stood back, trying not to look at him and not really succeeding, because her eyes were relentlessly drawn to his taut, well-muscled chest with its scatter of dark curls, to the strong, straight legs with their spectacular muscles and equally spectacular bruises. 'Can you manage now?' she asked, trying to sound businesslike and obviously failing, because his right eyebrow twitched.

'Why?' he asked, his voice low and his eyes dancing with mischief. 'Are you offering to wash my back?'

'On second thoughts,' she said and, scooping Thomas up, she left him to it and concentrated—barely—on dressing her children and making breakfast for them all before she put Thomas down for a nap and they wrapped up warmly and went out into the snow.

The snowman was huge—probably not the biggest in the world, but huge for all that—and Jake had found his old ski hat and scarf and they'd raided the fridge for a carrot—and two sprouts for his eyes, 'because,' Kitty said, 'they're too disgusting to eat.' Edward found a twig that looked like a pipe to stick in his mouth. Then, when the snowman was finished, standing in pride of place outside the breakfast room window so he could watch them eat, they came back inside, hung their coats in the boiler room to dry, and settled down by the fire in the drawing room to watch a film while they warmed up.

She flitted between the film and the kitchen, making sure everything was set in motion at the right time like a military operation and laying the table in the breakfast room, because, as Jake said, the dining room was too formal for having fun in. Not to mention too beautiful for Thomas to hurl his dinner across the room or for Kitty to 'accidentally' shoot peas off the edge of her plate for the dog to find, and anyway, it was a long way from the kitchen.

So she put out the crackers and the cutlery and the jolly red and green paper napkins with reindeer on, and a big white pillar candle they'd bought in the supermarket standing on a red plate. In between doing that and checking on the meal, she sat with her family and Jake, squeezing up next to Edward, while Thomas sat wedged between him and Jake, and Kitty had found herself a little place on Jake's lap, with his arm round her and her head on his shoulder and her thumb in her mouth. The next time she came in he had Thomas on his lap instead, standing on his leg and trying to climb over the arm of the sofa.

'I think he's bored,' Jake said softly, and Thomas looked up at her and beamed and held up his arms, and she scooped him up and hugged him.

'Hungry too, probably.'

'Is it lunchtime yet?' Kitty asked hopefully. 'I'm *starving*!'

'Nearly.'

'Can I help?'

Could he? Could she cope with him in the kitchen, that strong, hard, battered body so close to hers in the confined space?

She nearly laughed. What was she thinking about? It wasn't confined, it was huge—but it had seemed confined this morning, while he was making her tea and she was in the pyjamas he'd teased her about and he was in a robe with melted snow on the shoulders and dripping off his hair and those curiously sexy bare feet planted squarely on the tiled floor.

And now she knew what had been under that robe, it would be all the harder...

'I don't really know what you can do,' she said, but he followed her anyway, and he managed one-handed to make himself very useful. He helped lift the turkey out of the dish, entertained Thomas while she warmed his lunch, and then blew on it and fed him while she made the gravy and put everything out into the serving dishes he'd found for her.

'Lunch!' she called, sticking her head round the door, and they came pelting down the hall and skidded into the breakfast room.

'Oh, it looks really pretty!' Kitty said. Jake lit the candle and she carried in the turkey and knew how Tiny Tim's mother must have felt when Scrooge gave them the goose.

The food was delicious, and the children piled in, eating themselves to a standstill, and still there was enough there to feed an army.

'I hope you've got a nice line in leftover recipes,' Jake murmured as he carried it out to the kitchen and put it on the side, making her laugh.

'Oh, I have. I can turn anything into a meal. Have you got any brandy to put over the pudding?'

'I have—and holly. I picked it this morning. Here.'

He turned off the lights, and she carried in the flaming pudding by candlelight, making the children ooh and aah. Then, when they couldn't manage another mouthful, they cleared the table and put on their warm, dry coats and went back out in the garden for a walk, with Rufus in his smart new tartan coat and Thomas snuggled on her hip in his all-in-one suit. When the children had run around and worked off their lunch and the adults had strolled all down the long walk from the house towards the woods, they turned back.

And, right in the middle of the lawn outside the bay window, Kitty stopped.

'We have to make snow angels!' she said. 'Come on, everybody!'

'Snow angels?' Jake said, his voice taut, and Millie looked at him worriedly. Was this another memory they were trampling on? Oh, dear lord—

'Yes—all of us! Come on, Jake, you're the biggest, you can be the daddy angel!'

And, oblivious to the shocked reluctance on his face, she dragged him by the arm, made him lie down, and lay down beside him with her arms and legs outstretched and fanned them back and forth until she'd cleared the snow, and then she got up, laughing and pulled him to his feet.

'Look! You're so big!' she said with a giggle. 'Mummy, you lie down there on the other side, and then Edward, and Thomas, too—'

'Not Thomas, darling, he's too small, he doesn't understand.'

'Well, Jake can hold him while you and Edward make your snow angels,' she said, bossy and persistent to the last. She looked into Jake's eyes and saw gentle resignation.

'I'll take him,' he said softly and, reaching out, he scooped him onto his right hip and held him firmly, one-handed, while she and Edward carved out their shapes in the snow, and then she took her baby back and they went inside to look, shedding their wet clothes all over again, only this time their trousers were wet as well, and they had to go up and change.

'Hey, you guys, come and look,' Jake called from his room, and they followed him in and stood in the bay window looking down on the little row of snow angels.

'That's so pretty!' Kitty said. 'Jake, take a picture!'

So he got out his phone and snapped a picture, then went along the landing and took another of the snowman. Afterwards they all went downstairs again and Kitty got out her book, and Edward got out the construction kit, and they set them up at the far end of the breakfast table and busied themselves while she loaded the dishwasher and cleared up the pots and pans.

There was no sign of Jake, but at least Thomas in his cot had stopped grizzling and settled into sleep.

Or so she thought, until Jake appeared in the doorway with her little son on his hip.

'He's a bit sorry for himself,' Jake said with a tender smile, and handed him over. 'Why don't you sit down and I'll make you a cup of tea?'

'Because I'm supposed to be looking after you and all you've done is make me tea!'

'You've been on your feet all day. Go on, shoo. I'll do it. Anyway, I can't sit, I'm too full.'

She laughed at that, and took Thomas through to the breakfast room, put him in his high chair with his shape sorter puzzle and sat down with the children while she waited for her tea.

'Mummy, I can't do this. I can't work it out,' Edward said, staring at the instructions and the zillions of pieces he was trying to put together. It was complicated—more complicated than anything he'd tackled yet, but she was sure he'd be able to do it.

And how clever of Jake to realise that he was very bright, she thought, as she saw the kit was for older children. Bright and brave and hugely talented in all sorts of ways, and yet his father couldn't see it—just saw a quiet child with nothing to say for himself and no apparent personality.

Well, it was his loss, she thought, but of course it wasn't—it was Edward's, too, that he was so undervalued by the man who should have been so proud of him, should have nurtured and encouraged him. It wouldn't have occurred to David to look into choir school. He would have thought it was sissy.

But there was nothing—*nothing*—sissy about Jake. In fact he was a lot like Edward—thorough, meticulous, paying attention to detail, noticing the little things, fixing stuff, making it right.

The nurturer, she realised, and wondered if he'd spent his childhood trying to stick his family back together again when clearly, from what she'd overheard, it had been broken beyond repair. How sad that when he'd found his own, it had been torn away from him.

And then he came out and sat down with them all, on the opposite side of the table, and slid the tea across to her. Edward looked up at him and said, 'Can you give me a hand?'

'Sure. What's the problem?' he asked, and bent his head over the instructions, sorted through the pieces and found the missing bit. 'I think this needs to go in here,' he said, and handed it to Edward. Didn't take over, didn't do it for him, did just enough to help him on his way and then sat back and let him do it.

He did, of course, bit by bit, with the occasional input from Jake to keep him on the straight and narrow, but there was a worrying touch of hero worship in his voice. She only hoped they could all get through this and emerge unscathed without too many broken hopes and dreams, because, although Jake was doing nothing she could fault, Edward was lapping up every moment of his attention, desperate for a father figure in his life, for a man who understood him.

And she was dreading the day they moved out, to wherever they ended up, and she had to take him away from Jake.

She doubted Jake was dreading it. He was putting up with the invasion of his privacy with incredible fortitude, but she had no doubts at all that he'd be glad when they left and he could settle back into his own routine without all the painful reminders.

Sadly, she didn't think it would be any time soon, but all too quickly reality was going to intervene and she'd have to start sending out her CV again and trying to get another job. Maybe Jake would let her use the Internet so she could do that.

But not now. It was Christmas, and she was going to keep smiling and make sure everyone enjoyed it.

Jake included.

He thought the day would never end.

It had been fun—much more fun than he could have imagined—but it was also painful. Physically, because he was still sore from his encounter with the trees and the rocks in France, and emotionally, because the kids were great and it just underlined exactly what he'd lost.

And until that day, he'd avoided thinking about it, had shut his heart and his mind to such thoughts.

But he couldn't shut them out any more; they seeped in, like light round the edges of a blind, and while Millie was putting the children to bed he went into his little sitting room and closed the door. There was a video of them all taken on Ben's second birthday, and he'd never watched it again, but it was there, tormenting him.

So he put it on, and he watched his little son and the wife he'd loved to bits laughing into the camera, and he let the tears fall. Healing tears—tears that washed away the pain and left bittersweet memories of happier days. Full days.

Days like today.

And then he took the DVD out and put it away again, and lay down on the sofa and dozed. He was tired, he realised. He'd slept well last night, but not for long, and today had been a long day. He'd go to bed later, but for now he was comfortable, and if he kept out of the way Amelia wouldn't feel she had to talk to him when she'd rather be doing something—probably anything—else.

She'd done well. Brilliantly. The meal had been fabulous, and he was still full. Maybe he'd have a sandwich later, start on the pile of cold turkey that would be on the menu into the hereafter. Turkey and cold stuffing and cranberry sauce.

But later. Not now. Now, he was sleeping...

'That was the *best* day,' Edward said, snuggling down under the quilt and smiling at her. 'Jake's really cool.'

'He's been very kind,' she said, wondering how she could take Jake gently off this pedestal without shattering Edward's illusions, 'but we are in his way.'

'He doesn't seem to mind.'

'That's because he's a very kind man, very generous.'

'That's what Kate said—that he was generous.' He

rolled onto his back and folded his arms under his head. 'Did you know he went to choir school?'

'Yes—I heard him tell you,' she said. 'I'd just come downstairs.'

'He said it was great. Hard work, but he loved it there. He was a boarder, did you know that? He had to sleep there, but he said his mum and dad used to fight, and he was always in the way, so it was good, really.'

She was just opening her mouth to comment when Edward went on diffidently, 'Were we in the way? Was that why Dad left?'

Her heart aching, she hugged him. 'No, darling. He left because he realised he didn't love me any more, and it wouldn't have been right to stay.'

He hadn't loved the children either, but there was no way she was telling Edward that his father had used them as a lever to get her to agree to things she wouldn't otherwise have countenanced. Things like remortgaging their house so riskily, because otherwise, he said, they'd be homeless.

Well, they were homeless now, and he'd had to flee the country to escape the debt, so a lot of good it had done to prolong it. And why on earth she'd let him back last year so that she'd ended up pregnant again, she couldn't imagine. She must have been insane, and he'd gone again long before she'd realised about the baby.

Not that she'd send Thomas back, not for a moment, but life had become infinitely more complicated with another youngster.

She'd have to work on her CV, she thought, and wondered what Jake was doing and if he'd let her use the

Internet to download a template so she could lay it out better.

'You need to go to sleep,' she said softly, and bent over and kissed Edward's cheek. 'Come on, snuggle down.'

'Can we play in the snow again tomorrow?' he asked sleepily, and she nodded.

'Of course—if it's still there.'

'It will be. Jake said.'

And if Jake had said...

She went out and pulled the door to, leaving the landing light on for them, and after checking on the sleeping baby she went back downstairs, expecting to find Jake in the breakfast room or the drawing room.

But he wasn't, and his study door was open, and his bedroom door had been wide open, too.

Which left his little sitting room. His cave, the place to which he retreated from the world when it all became too much.

She didn't like to disturb him, so she put her laptop in the breakfast room and tidied up the kitchen. The children had had a snack, and she was pretty sure that Jake would want something later, so she made a pile of sandwiches with freshly cut bread, and wrapped them in cling film and put them in the fridge ready for him. Then she put Rufus's new coat on and took him out into the snow for a run around.

He should have been used to it, he'd been outside several times today, but still he raced around and barked and tried to bite it, and she stood there feeling the cold seep into her boots and laughed at him as he played.

And then she turned and saw Jake standing in the

window of his sitting room, watching her with a brooding expression on his face, and she felt her heart miss a beat.

Their eyes locked, and she couldn't breathe, frozen there in time, waiting for—

What? For him to summon her? To call her to him, to ask her to join him?

Then he glanced away, his gaze caught by the dog, and she could breathe again.

'Rufus!' she called, and she took him back inside, dried his paws on an old towel and took off her snowy boots and left them by the Aga to dry off. And as she straightened up, he came into the kitchen.

'Hi. All settled?'

She nodded. 'Yes. Yes, they're all settled. I wasn't sure if you'd be hungry, so I made some sandwiches.'

'Brilliant. Thanks. I was just coming to do that, but I wasn't sure if I could cut the bread with one hand. It's all a bit awkward.'

'Done,' she said, opening the fridge and lifting them out. 'Do you want them now, or later?'

'Now?' he said. 'Are you going to join me? I thought maybe we could have a glass of wine and a little adult conversation.'

His smile was wry, and she laughed softly, her whole body responding to the warmth in his eyes.

'That would be lovely,' she said, and found some plates while he opened the bottle of red they'd started the night before last and poured two glasses, and they carried them through to the breakfast room, but then he hesitated.

'Come and slum it with me on the sofa,' he suggested,

to her surprise, and she followed him through to the other room and sat down at one end while he sprawled into the other corner, his sore leg—well, the sorer of the two, if the bruises were anything to go by—stretched out so that his foot was almost touching her thigh.

And they ate their sandwiches and talked about the day, and then he put his plate down on the table beside him and said, 'Tell me about your work.'

'I don't have any,' she reminded him. 'In fact, I was going to ask you about that. I need to write a CV and get it out to some firms. I don't suppose you've got wireless broadband so I can go online and do some research?'

'Sure. You can do it now, if you like. I'll help you—if you want.'

She flashed him a smile. 'That would be great. Thanks.'

'Any time. Have you got a computer or do you want to use mine?'

'My laptop—it's in the breakfast room. I'll get it.'

He'd sat up by the time she got back in there, so she ended up sitting close to him, his solid, muscled thigh against hers, his arm slung along the back of the sofa behind her. As she brought up her CV, he glanced at it and sat back.

'OK, I can see a few problems with it. It needs more immediacy, it needs to grab the attention. You could do with a photo of yourself, for a start. People like to know who they're dealing with.'

'Really? For freelance? It's not as if I'd have to disgrace their office—'

'Disgrace? Don't be ridiculous,' he said, leaving her feeling curiously warm inside. 'And anyway, it's about how you look at the camera, if you're open and straight-forward and decent.'

'Or if you have tattoos or a ton of shrapnel in your face,' she added, but he laughed and shook his head.

'That's irrelevant unless you're talking front of house and it's the sort of organisation where it matters. In some places it'd be an asset. It's much more about connecting with the photo. Stay there.'

And he limped out stiffly, drawing her attention to the fact that he was still sore, despite all he'd done today for her and her children. He should have been lying down taking it easy, she thought uncomfortably, not making snowmen and snow angels and construction toys. And now her CV.

He came back with another laptop, flipped it open and logged on, and then scrolled through his files and brought up his own CV. 'Here—this is me. I can't show you anyone else's, it wouldn't be fair, but this is the basic stuff—fonts, the photo size and so on.'

She scanned it, much more interested in the personal in-formation than anything else. His date of birth—he was a Cancerian, she noticed, and thirty-five this year, five years older than her—and he'd been born in Norwich, he had three degrees, he was crazily clever and his interests were diverse and, well, interesting.

She scanned through it and sat back.

'Wow. You're pretty well qualified.'

'So are you. How come you can't find a job? Is it that they don't get beyond the CV?'

She laughed. 'What, a single woman with three young children and one of them under a year?'

'But people aren't allowed to ask that sort of thing.'

'No, but they ask about how much time you're able to commit and can you give weekends and evenings if necessary, are you available for business trips—all sorts of sly manoeuvring to get it out of you, and then you can hear the gates slam shut.'

'That's crazy. Lots of my key people are mothers, and they tend to be well-organised, efficient and considerate. And OK, from time to time I have to make concessions, but they don't pull sickies because they've drunk too much the night before, and they don't get bored and go off travelling. There are some significant advantages. I'd take you on.'

She stared at him, not sure if he'd meant that quite how it sounded, because Kate had said in the past that it was a shame he had someone and didn't need her. So it was probably just a casual remark. But it might not have been...

'You would?' she asked tentatively, and he nodded.

'Sure. I could do with a translator. It's not technical stuff, it's more business contract work, but I farm it out at the moment to someone I've used for years and she told me before Christmas that she wants a career break. What languages have you got?'

'French, Italian, Spanish and Russian.'

He nodded slowly. 'OK. Want to try? Have a look at some of the things I need translating and see if you've got enough of the specific vocabulary to do it?'

'Sure,' she said slowly, although she wasn't sure. She wasn't sure at all if it would be a good thing to do, to become even more involved with a man who her son thought had hung the moon and the stars, and on whose lap her daughter had spent a good part of the day cuddled up in front of the fire.

A man whose heart was so badly broken that he had to run away every Christmas and hide from the pain.

A man, she realised, who she could very easily come to love…

He must be crazy.

It was bad enough having them all descend on him without a by-your-leave, taking over his house and his life and his mind. It was only a step from lunacy to suggest a lasting liaison.

Not that it need be anything other than strictly professional, he realised. It could all be done online—in fact, it could be Kate who dealt with all the communications. He didn't have to do anything other than rubber-stamp payment of her invoices. It would solve her financial problems, give her independence from the scumbag of an ex-husband who'd trashed her life so comprehensively with his lousy judgement and wild ideas, and give the children security.

And that, he discovered, mattered more to him than he really wanted to admit. It would give them a chance to find a house, to settle into schools—and that in itself would give Edward a chance to join a choir, church or school, or maybe even apply to choir schools for a scholarship. They could live anywhere they chose, because she wouldn't have to come into the office, and so if he did end up in a choir school he wouldn't necessarily have to board if she was close enough to run around after him.

And she could afford to look after Rufus.

He glanced down at the dog, snuggled up between their feet, utterly devoted to his mistress.

Hell, he'd miss the dog when they moved. Miss all of them. He'd have to think about getting a dog. He'd considered it in the past but dismissed it because of his business visitors who stayed in the house from time to time, but maybe it was time to think about himself, to put himself first, to admit, perhaps, that he, too, had needs.

And feelings.

'Think about it, and we'll go over some stuff tomorrow, maybe,' he said, shutting his laptop and getting to his feet. 'I'm going to turn in.'

'Yes, it's been a long day.' She shut her own laptop and stood up beside him, gathering up their glasses with her free hand. Then, while she put the dog out, he put his computer back in the study and went back to the kitchen, looking broodingly out over the garden at the snowman staring back at him with slightly crooked Brussels sprout eyes, and he wondered if his feelings could extend to a relationship.

Not sex, not just another casual, meaningless affair, a way to scratch an itch, to blank out the emptiness of his life, but a relationship.

With Amelia.

She was calling Rufus, patting her leg and encouraging him away from a particularly fascinating smell, and then the door shut and he heard the key turn and she came through to the breakfast room and stopped.

'Oh! I thought you'd gone upstairs.'

'No. I was waiting for you,' he said, and something

flickered in her eyes, an acknowledgement of what he might have said.

He led her to the landing by his bedroom and turned to her, staring wordlessly down at her for the longest moment. It was crazy. He didn't know her, he wasn't ready, he was only now starting to sift through the raft of feelings left behind by losing his family—but he wanted her, her and her family, and he didn't know how to deal with that.

Sex he could handle. This—this was something else entirely. He lifted his right hand and cradled her cheek. 'Thank you for today,' he said softly, and her eyes widened and she shook her head.

'No—thank *you*, Jake. You've been amazing—so kind I don't know how to start. It could have all been unimaginably awful, and instead—it's been the best Christmas I can remember. And it's all down to you. So thank you, for everything you've done, for me, for the children, even for Rufus. You're a star, Jake Forrester—a good man.'

And, going up on tiptoe, she pressed a soft, tentative kiss to his lips.

The kiss lingered for a second, and then her heels sank back to the floor, taking her away from him, and he took a step back and let her go with reluctance.

There was time, he told himself as he got ready for bed. There was no hurry—and maybe this was better not hurried, but given time to grow and develop over time.

He opened the bedside drawer and took out his painkillers, and the photo caught his eye. He lifted it out and stared at them. They seemed like strangers now, distant memories, part of his past. He'd never forget them, but they were gone, and maybe he was ready to move on.

He opened his suitcase and pulled out the broken remains of the watch, and put it with the photograph in a box full of Rachel's things in the top of his wardrobe.

Time to move on, he told himself.

With Amelia?

CHAPTER EIGHT

'ISN'T it time we bathed the dog? We've been talking about it for days, and we still haven't got round to it.'

She looked up at Jake and bit her lip to stop the smile. 'He is pretty smelly, isn't he?'

'You could say that. And right now he's wet and mucky from the snow, so it seems like a good time. And he's got all night to dry by the fire.'

'I'll get my shampoo and conditioner and run the water in the sink,' she said, getting to her feet from the hearthrug and running up to her bathroom, then coming back to the utility room—because even she drew the line at bathing the dog in the kitchen sink—and a moment later Jake appeared with the dog at his heels and an armful of towels from the cupboard in the boiler room.

'Here—old towels. I tend to use them for swimming, but I'm sure the dog won't object.'

They were better than her best ones, she thought, but she didn't comment, just thanked him, picked Rufus up and stood him in the water and ladled it over him with a plastic jug she'd found in the cupboard under the sink.

'He's very good,' Jake said, leaning against the worktop

and watching her bath him. 'Not that that surprises me. Did you have time to look at any of that stuff I gave you, by the way?'

'Yes. It doesn't look too bad. Do you want me to have a go?'

'Could you?'

'Sure. I'll do it while Rufus dries, if you like.' She lathered him from end to end, drenched him in conditioner to get the tangles out, then rinsed him again even more thoroughly and lifted the plug out and squeezed the water off him and then bundled him up in the towels and carried him back to the fire.

'Have you got a comb?'

'I'll brush him,' she said, and gently teased the tangles out while he stood and shivered.

'Is he cold?'

'No, he just hates it. He's a wuss and he doesn't like being brushed. He'll get over it.'

'Is she being mean to you, sweetheart?' he crooned, and Rufus wafted his skinny little tail, looking pleadingly at his hero for rescue.

'Forget it, big-eyes, you're getting brushed,' she said firmly, but she kissed him to take the sting out of it. It was over in a moment, and then he shook wildly and ran round the room, scrubbing his face on the rug and making them laugh.

'Right, those documents,' she said. 'Shall I do it on my computer?'

'It's probably easier.'

So she sat at the table, and he sat in the chair by the fire, and Rufus settled down on a towel and let Jake brush him gently until he was dry, and she thought how nice it was, how cosy—and she couldn't imagine what she was doing getting herself sucked into La-La Land like this.

So she forced herself to concentrate, and after a while she sat back and blew out her cheeks.

'OK, I've done it.'

'What, the first one?'

'No, all three.'

'Really?'

He sat next to her, produced the translations he'd already apparently had done and scanned the two side by side, and then sat back and met her eyes.

'They're excellent. Better. Better English—cleaner, clearer. So—do you want the job?'

She laughed a little breathlessly. 'Do I—I don't know. That depends on what you pay, and how.' And how much contact I'll have to have with you, and whether it's going to do my head in trying to be sensible—

'Word count, normally. I'm not sure what we pay without looking, but I'm sure it's fair, and if you don't agree with it, I'll match what you've been getting. That's on top of a retainer, of course. I can check for you. I'll have a look through the accounts. We can go over to the office tomorrow—in fact, do you think the kids would like to swim? The pool's there doing nothing, and you'll have it to yourselves unless any of the staff come over to use it, but I would have thought they're unlikely to do so this soon after Christmas. It's up to you.'

'Oh. They'd love to swim,' she said ruefully, contemplating the idea of being on a retainer because her last job had been much more hit and miss than that, 'but they haven't got any costumes. Swimwear wasn't top of my list of priorities when I was packing things up to go into storage. I have no idea where they'd be, either.'

'It doesn't matter. They can swim in pants. So can you. Bra and pants is only what a bikini is, and I promise I won't look.'

She felt her cheeks heat and looked away from his teasing eyes. Since she'd kissed him last night, she'd scarcely been able to think about anything else, and for the whole day it had been simmering between them. It wasn't just her, she was sure of it, but he didn't seem to be about to take it any further, and goodness knows she shouldn't be encouraging him to.

The last thing—well, almost the last thing, anyway—she needed was to get involved in a complicated relationship with the first person to offer her work in months. And she needed a job more than she needed sex.

Except it wasn't that, or it didn't feel like it. It felt like—help, it felt dangerously like love, and that was so scary she couldn't allow herself to think about it. She'd had it with rich, flashy, ruthless men.

Not that he was flashy, not in the least, but he was certainly rich, and however generous he might have been to her, she was sure that Jake could be ruthless when it suited him or the occasion demanded it. Heavens, she knew he could, she'd been on the receiving end of his ruthless tongue on the first night!

But that had been him lashing out, sore and tired and a little desperate, at someone who'd come uninvited into his home, his retreat, his sanctuary. No wonder.

Nevertheless, it was there, that ruthless streak, and

David's ruthlessness had scarred her and her children in a way that she was sure would never completely fade.

'It's not such a hard question, is it?' he murmured, jerking her back to the present, and she met his eyes in confusion.

'What isn't?'

'Swimming,' he reminded her gently. 'What did you think I was talking about?'

She had no idea. She'd been so far away, reliving the horror of David's heartless and uncaring defection, that she'd forgotten all about the swim he'd talked of.

She tried to smile. 'I'm sorry, I was wool-gathering. No, it's not hard. I'm sure the children would both love to swim, but you can't, can you, with the cast on?' And there was no way she was swimming in pants—most especially not the pants Kate had given her!

'No. No, of course not, but it's sitting there. I just thought they might enjoy it. And I'd like to show you the office. Not that you'll be working there necessarily, but you might find it interesting to see the place.'

She would. She found everything about him interesting, and that was deeply worrying. But she accepted, telling herself that it would give her a better insight into his business operation and help her make a more informed decision about whether to take the job or not.

In fact, maybe she should talk to Kate, and she vowed to do that as soon as she had a chance. But, in the meantime, she'd have a look at his offices, let the kids have a swim and think about it.

The following morning, after the children were washed and dressed and she'd taped up Jake's cast so he could shower, and once they'd had breakfast and walked the squeaky-clean Rufus in his smart little coat, they went over to the old country club site and he let them into the offices hidden away behind the walls of the old kitchen garden.

'Sorry, it's a bit chilly. The heating's turned down but we won't be in here long and the pool area's warm,' he said, and pushed open a door into what had to be his office. There was a huge desk, a vast window and the same beautiful view down the long walk that the drawing room and his bedroom enjoyed. A long, low sofa stretched across one wall, and she guessed he sprawled on it often when he was working late, a coffee in his hand, checking emails on his laptop or talking on the phone.

She pictured him pacing, gesturing, holding everything in his head while he negotiated and wrangled until he was satisfied that he'd got the best deal. She'd seen David do it, seen the way he worked, the way he pinned people down and bullied them until he got his way, and a chill ran over her.

Was Jake like that? The iron hand in the velvet glove? She didn't like to think so, but even a pussycat had claws, and Jake was no pussycat. He could be tough and uncompromising, she was sure, and that made her deeply uneasy. But then wasn't everyone who'd survived in business in these difficult times? And she needed that job.

'Come on, kids, more to see and then there's the pool,' he was saying. They scrambled off his sofa and ran back to the door, and she followed them, Thomas in the stroller so she could have her hands free to help the children when they had their swim.

'This is the main office, this is Kate's office, this is reception—I brought you in the back way, but visitors come in via this door from the garden,' he explained, opening it so that the children could go out and run around in the snow, and she looked out over a pretty scene of snow-covered lawn surrounded by what looked like roses climbing up against the mellow brick walls. In the centre was a little fountain. The children were chasing each other round it, giggling and shrieking and throwing snowballs, and she smiled, relieved to see them so happy after such a difficult year.

'It's beautiful. It must be lovely in the summer.'

'It is. The staff sit out there for their coffee and lunch breaks. It's a lovely place to work, and I knew it would be. I saw it just before—' He broke off, then went on, 'I saw it five and a half years ago, and I was committed to it, so I just shifted my plans a little and went ahead anyway, and it's been a good move—and the right one, although I had no choice because the house was sold and we'd started work on this already.'

'That must have been hard,' she said softly, and he shrugged.

'Not really. We'd made the decision. It was the house that was so hard to deal with. We got the builders in and started at the top. We'd planned to live in the rooms up there at first, so that was already commissioned, and then—well, I got an interior designer in to do the rest, but I wouldn't let her interfere with that bit. It went ahead as planned, and I made it the place where people with children stay, because that was always the idea. We were going to put a kitchen up there as a temporary measure but of course that never happened and I lived somewhere else while it was all done and concentrated on the offices at first.'

He was standing staring at the house, visible over the top of the garden wall, his hands in his pockets, a brooding expression on his face, and she turned away, giving him privacy. Why on earth was she imagining he'd be interested in a relationship with her? Of course he wasn't. He was still in love with his wife—the wife with whom he'd planned the rooms she and her family were living in now.

Of all the rooms for them to have chosen—but maybe it was a good thing. It showed that the plans had been right, and Kate, who didn't know about his wife and son, loved the rooms, too, and had stayed there. And he'd designated it the area for families, so maybe she was just being over-sensitive.

What was she thinking? Did she like the set-up, or was she just being polite? Or did she genuinely like it but didn't want to work with him?

Too complicated, too much baggage for both of them?

'We need to talk terms,' he said, hoping that he could coax her into it and that, once coaxed, she would have time to get used to him, to find out the kind of man he was, to learn to trust him. Because she must have trust issues after a bastard like David Jones had messed so comprehensively with her life.

But he couldn't rush her, he knew that. All he could do was make it possible for her to live again, to give her time to draw breath, to get back on her feet. And maybe then—

His phone rang and he pulled it impatiently out of his

pocket and glanced at the screen. Kate. He felt a flicker of guilt but dismissed it and answered the call.

'Well, hello there. Had a good Christmas?'

'Yes…Jake, can we talk?'

'Why? What's wrong?' he asked, suddenly concerned that something might have happened to her.

She just gave a strangled laugh. 'What's wrong?' she exclaimed. 'You told me I hadn't heard the end of it, and I haven't heard a thing from you since, and the last time I spoke to you, you were injured and hopping mad. I didn't know if you were all right, if you'd forgiven me, if I'd even got a job to come back to. So of course I didn't have a good Christmas, you idiot! Oh, I'm sorry, I didn't mean to say that, but—really, Jake, I've been so worried and you didn't return my call, and you always do.'

Damn. He should have rung her. He'd meant to, so many times, but his eye had been so firmly off the ball—

'I'm sorry. I meant to ring. Of course you've got a job. Look, why don't you bring Megan over for a swim and have a chat and a coffee? In fact, swing by a sports shop and pick up some swimming things for Amelia and the kids on the way here. Theirs are in store. See you in—what? An hour?'

'Less—much less. I've got a costume Millie can use, and one of Megan's that Kitty can borrow, so I only need to get something for Edward and I might be able to find something here of his he left behind in the summer. I'll see you soon,' she said, and hung up.

He put the phone back in his pocket and turned to Amelia. 'That was Kate,' he said unnecessarily. 'She's coming over now with swimming things for all of you.'

'I gathered. Did she really think she might not have a job?' Amelia asked, frowning worriedly. 'Sorry, I didn't mean to eavesdrop, but I couldn't help overhearing your remark. I've been meaning to ring. I had a missed call from her on my phone, and I meant to ring her back, but—'

'Ditto. We've been dealing with other things. Don't worry, she's fine. She's far too valuable for me to lose, and she knows that. Or I hope she knows that.'

'I don't know that she does. She certainly doesn't take you for granted. I think she feels you're a bit of a miracle.'

'Me?' He gave a startled laugh and thought about it. 'I'm no miracle. I'm a tough boss. Make no mistake about that, Amelia. I don't pull punches. I expect my staff to work hard, but no harder than I do, and if they give me their best, I'll defend them to the hilt. But I don't suffer fools.'

Fools like her husband. Correction—*ex*-husband. Thank God he was in Thailand, it'd save him the effort of driving him out of the country.

'Jake? Does she know? About your family?'

He shook his head. 'No. Hardly anybody does. A few who've known me for years, but they don't talk about it and neither do I, we all just get on with it.'

'OK. Just so I know not to say anything. I thought she probably didn't because we talked about you and she didn't mention it, but I don't want to put my foot in it and you've obviously got your reasons for not telling everyone.'

He shrugged. 'It's just never come up. Work is work. I don't talk about myself.'

'But you talk about them. Kate said you always ask about Megan, and about other people's families, and you give very generous maternity deals and so on, and you send flowers when people are sick, and when Kate's pipes froze you put them up in the house—so it's only yourself you keep at arm's length,' she pointed out—probably fairly, now he thought about it.

He gave her a smile that felt slightly off-kilter. 'It's just easier that way. I don't want sympathy, Amelia. I don't need it. I just want to be left alone to live my life.'

Except suddenly that wasn't true any more, he acknowledged, feeling himself frown. He didn't want to be left alone. He wanted—

'Can we see the pool now?'

Kitty was under his nose, covered in snow, her cheeks bright and glowing with health, her eyes sparkling, and behind her Edward was stamping snow off his boots and shutting the door and watching him hopefully.

'Sure. Kate rang. She's bringing Megan over and some swimming things for you all. She'll be here in a minute.'

'Yippee, yippee, we're going in the pool!' Kitty sang, and Edward was laughing.

'That's amazing. We've just had a snowball fight and now we're going swimming! That's so weird. Are you coming in?'

He shook his head. 'I can't—my cast,' he explained, lifting up his arm. 'I can't get it wet. But I can't wait. I swim every day at six before everyone gets here, and I really miss it. So you won't mind if I don't watch you, because I'll just get jealous. You guys go ahead and have a really good time, OK?'

And then Kate arrived with Megan, to the children's delight, and he took one look at her and went over and hugged her.

'Hey, smile for me,' he said, holding her by the shoulders and looking down into her eyes. To his surprise, they filled with tears.

'I felt so awful, but I didn't know what to do, and I didn't think you'd mind. You weren't even supposed to be here—'

'Hey, it's fine. And you're right, I wouldn't have minded and you did absolutely the right thing, so stop worrying. I'd probably be more cross if you hadn't done what you did, so forget it. Anyway,' he said, changing the subject, 'the kids are dying to get in the pool, and I'd like a minute to talk to Amelia, so if you wouldn't mind keeping an eye on them. Amelia, is that OK with you?'

'Sure.' Amelia nodded, and Kate shot her a curious look.

'Right—sort yourselves out, and come and find me, Amelia. I'll be in my office.'

And he left them to it, turned up the heating in his office and checked his emails. Grief. There were loads, and he scrolled through them, deleting the majority without a second glance, saving a few, answering a couple.

And then she was there, standing in the doorway looking a little uneasy, and he switched off his machine and stood up.

'Come on in, I was just doing my email. Coffee?'

'Oh—thanks. Will you have any milk or should I go and get some?'

'Creamer. Is that OK?'

'Fine.' She crossed over to the window and stood staring down the long walk. 'How do you get any work done?' she asked softly, and he chuckled.

'It helps. There's nothing going on—well, apart from the odd squirrel. So my mind's free to think. It's good. No distractions, no diversions—it works for me. And it's peaceful. I love it best when there's nobody here, first thing in the morning and last thing at night.'

'And the house?' she asked, turning to face him.

'What about the house?'

'I get the feeling you sleep there.'

'And eat. Sometimes. And entertain. And I do spend time there, in my study or the sitting room. I don't use the rest of it much, it's a bit formal really.'

And lonely, but he didn't add that, because he didn't want to think about it, about how it hadn't been lonely for the last few days, and how empty and desolate it would feel when they were gone.

'I don't suppose you've thought about the job any more overnight?' he asked, handing her a coffee, and she took it and nodded, following him to the sofa and sitting down.

'Yes, but I need to know if it will be enough, if you can offer me enough work to live on. I don't want to be rude, and I'm not trying to push the rate up or anything, but I do need to earn a living and because my time's limited I need to maximise. And I am good, I know that. So I need to do the best I can for my family. I've been thinking about what you said about Edward, too, wondering if I could get him a voice test or singing lessons, but I need financial security before I even consider that. It's a juggling act, work time and quality time, although without the work the quality's pretty compromised so what am I talking about? But I do have to think about this and I know you're shut over

Christmas and New Year, so I don't know when you're thinking of me starting—'

'Whenever,' he said, cutting her off before she talked herself out of it. 'I can find you a pile of stuff. Judith—my translator—has been doing less recently, and there's a bit of a backlog, so if you want to start on that, I'd be very grateful. Some of it's probably getting a bit urgent.'

'So—would I submit an invoice when you're happy?'

'Or I can give you a cheque now,' he said. 'Just an advance, to start you off.' Which would give her enough money to find a rented house and move out, he realised with regret, but he couldn't hold her hostage, even if he wanted to.

'Don't you want references?' she was asking incredulously, and he laughed.

'No. You're a friend of Kate's, I've met your children, I've met your husband—'

'David? When did you meet David?' she asked, her voice shocked.

He shrugged. 'Last year? I believe it was him. He came to me with an idea he wanted to float for a coffee shop chain.'

'Oh, that's him. It was a crazy idea. I had no idea he'd approached you about it. I expect the fact Kate works for you put the idea into his head. Funny she didn't mention he'd been to see you.'

'She didn't know. I met him at a conference.'

'Oh. So what did you say?'

'I turned him down. It was ill-considered, risky and I didn't want to put my money there.' And he'd disliked the man on sight, but he didn't say that, because it was irrelevant and, after all, presumably she'd loved him once, although what came next made him wonder.

'Wise move,' she said, and smiled ruefully. 'Who knows what I saw in him, but by the time I realised what he was like it was too late, we were married and our second child was on the way. And when I tackled him about some things I'd found out, he walked.'

'And Thomas?'

'I let him come back. Don't ask me why, I have no idea. Maybe I felt I owed it to the children to give it another chance. It didn't last, and then when he'd gone—my idea, not his, because I realised he was relying on my income to support him—I discovered I was pregnant again. And that time I did divorce him. But what's David got to do with my job?'

'Just that I know the mess your life's in isn't your fault. I can imagine you trying to hold it all together, and I can imagine him selling it all out from under you without you realising. So I know you aren't in this position because you're incompetent, and you're right, you are good at your job. Quick and accurate. I need that—particularly the accuracy. The exact meaning of a contract is massively important, and although a lot of the stuff is standard, there are some sneaky little clauses. I like those dealt with, and I need to know what they are. So—I'm more than happy to take you on. My HR people will sort out the fine print when they get back, but in the meantime I'll give you the same rate Judith was on plus a twenty per cent enhancement and increase the retainer by forty per cent—I can find out exactly what that translates to in a minute, and you can start as soon as you like.'

She nodded slowly. 'OK. I need to see how the figures stack up. I might need to take on other work from somewhere else—'

'Don't do that,' he said, cutting her off. 'There's plenty of communication with foreign companies on a daily basis that we might need help with, as well as the really important stuff. French and Italian aren't too much of a problem—I speak them well enough for most things and so do a couple of others—but we struggle with Russian and our Spanish is on the weak side, so if you find you aren't earning enough, just shout. I could probably use you getting on for full-time, even maybe phone calls, that sort of thing. We do so much work abroad now and it would be really handy.'

She nodded thoughtfully. 'OK. Let me see the figures, and we'll talk again,' she said with a smile, and he felt the tension go out of his shoulders.

Good. He wasn't going to lose her—not entirely. He'd make sure of that, make sure the money was so tempting she would be mad to turn it down. She might move out once she'd got some financial security, but he could still phone her, ask her to explain something, find excuses to keep in touch personally—and now he was being ridiculous.

'Go and swim with your children. I'll look up the figures, find some material for you to start on and we'll go from there.'

He just hoped he could convince her...

CHAPTER NINE

'So what was that all about?'

She swam over to Kate and propped her arms on the edge of the pool. 'He's offered me a job. Apparently his translator wants to take a career break.'

'Judith? I didn't know that. Wow. Well, you've obviously made a good impression. I'm so sorry you ended up in that difficult situation with him before Christmas, by the way. I've been feeling so guilty, but you've obviously survived it. How did it go?'

How did it go? Between the tears and the heart-searching—

'OK. It was OK. Fun. He was brilliant. We went to the supermarket and bought loads of food, and I cooked Christmas lunch, and he bought the children little presents—he even got the dog a coat.'

'Good grief,' Kate said faintly. 'Still, it shouldn't really surprise me—when he does something, he usually does it well. He's a stickler for detail.'

'Hmm, that's what worries me about taking this job on. What if I'm not good enough?'

'You will be,' Kate said instantly. 'Of course you will

be. He's only got to look at your references to know that. Is he taking them up?'

'He says not.'

Kate's eyes widened, and then she started to laugh. 'Oh, my. Still, it's not the first time, he's a very good judge of character, but…Millie, I have a feeling he really likes you. As in, *likes* you.'

She shook her head. 'No. No way, Kate, it's too complicated. He isn't in the market for that sort of thing and neither am I.'

'How do you know? That he isn't, I mean? Did he say something?'

Damn. 'Well, he wouldn't be, would he?' she said, going for the obvious in the interests of preserving his privacy. 'Three kids and a dog? You'd be insane to want to take that on. And besides, what would I want with another entrepreneur? I've had it with living my life on a knife-edge, waiting for the next roll of the stock market dice to see if I'll be homeless or not. I want security, Kate, and I don't need a man for that. But I will take his job, and as soon as I can I'll find a house and get out of his hair and get our life back on track. Get the kids enrolled in a new school, and start again. And hopefully, this time it'll last longer than a few months.'

'So what's for supper?' he asked, coming up behind her and peering over her shoulder as she stirred the pan on the stove.

'Would you believe a variation on the theme of turkey?' she said with a laugh, and he chuckled.

'Smells good, whatever it is. Sort of Moroccan?'

'Mmm. A tagine. I found all the ingredients in the cupboard—I hope you don't mind?'

'Of course I don't mind. Use what you like. There doesn't look very much there, have you done enough for us all?'

'Oh. I'm feeding the children earlier. This is just for you.'

She caught his frown out of the corner of her eye. 'What about you?'

'I'll eat with the children—'

'Why?'

She turned and looked at him, not knowing what her role was any longer, not sure what he expected of her.

So she said so, and his brow pleated in a frown.

'I thought…I don't know. We seem to have all eaten together since Christmas Day. Breakfast, lunch, variation on a theme of turkey—I rather thought that was the way it was now.'

'But I'm supposed to be looking after you, helping you with the things you can't do, cooking for you—that's all.'

'Does that mean you can't eat with me?'

'Well…no, of course not, but I thought you might want to be alone—'

'No,' he said emphatically. 'Eat with me—please? Or, if there isn't enough, do something else—throw a bit more turkey in, or make a starter, but—no, I don't want to eat alone. And anyway, I thought we could talk about the job.'

The job. Of course. Nothing to do with wanting her company—and she shouldn't want him to, shouldn't be contemplating intimate little dinners *à deux*, or cosy drinks by the fire with the lights off and only the flickering flames to see by.

But that was what they ended up doing that evening, eating alone together after the children were in bed, opening a bottle of wine and then carrying the rest of it through to the drawing room, because they'd been in there during the day with Kate and Megan, doing a jigsaw by the fire while Thomas alternately slept or tried to haul himself up and eat the pieces.

Jake threw another log on, sat down at one end of the sofa at right angles to the fireplace and patted the seat beside him. 'Come and sit with me and talk,' he said. 'I've got some figures for you.'

And so she sat, hitching her feet up under her bottom and turning half towards him, studying him over her wine glass. 'Figures?'

He told her what he was prepared to pay, and she blinked. 'That's generous,' she said, and he shrugged.

'I expect a lot for my money.'

'And if I can't deliver?' she said with a shiver of dread. She hated to miss deadlines, hated letting people down, but— 'What if the children are sick, or Thomas won't sleep—what then?'

He shrugged. 'Then I expect you to let me know, to do the best you can and be upfront with me. Don't tell me you're doing it if you can't. Tell me if you've got a problem and I'll find another way round it. It's not impossible. We do it all the time. I'm not asking for an unbreakable commitment, just a promise to do your best to fulfil your side of the bargain. That's all any of us can ever do.'

'And if you don't think my work's up to scratch?'

'I know it will be. I know Barry Green. I've phoned him. He's gutted he had to let you down, but he's made some investments that have collapsed and it's not his fault. He really didn't have the money to pay you. In fact, he was relieved that I was going to be able to give you a job because he's been feeling really guilty. So—all I need to know is, will you take the job or do I need to look for someone else?'

Still she hesitated. So many reasons to take it—and so many not to.

'You don't have to deal with me, if that's what's troubling you,' he said softly. 'If you're worried about it all getting a bit too cosy, you can deal with Kate or my contracts manager. And it doesn't have to be for ever. If something better comes along, you can go. And Judith only wants a career break, she hasn't said she's stopping for ever—well, not yet. So it's only for the foreseeable future.'

He was making it so easy to say yes, so hard to say no. And the silly thing was, she didn't want to say no, but she was still afraid of getting involved. But she could deal with Kate, he said. That would be all right. Less complicated.

And so she nodded, her heart pounding as she said, 'Yes. OK. I'll take it. Thank you.'

He let out his breath on a soft huff of laughter. 'Good. Welcome to the team,' he said, lifting his glass and clinking it gently against hers, and she felt the smile spread over her face until it felt as if her whole body was glowing with relief.

'Thank you,' she said, and then as she lowered her glass, their eyes met and a breathless silence descended over them, broken only by the sharp crackling of the logs in the grate.

Oh, Lord. She could hardly breathe. Her eyes locked with his, the heat in them searing her to her soul. He reached out and took her glass and set it down beside his, and then his fingers curled around her jaw, his thumb grazing her bottom lip, dragging softly over the moist skin, the gentle tug bringing a whimper to her throat.

His fingertips traced her face, seeking out the fine lines around her eyes, the crease by her nose, the pulse pounding in the hollow of her throat.

'Come to bed with me,' he said softly, his voice gruff but gentle, and she felt her whole body responding to his touch, to his voice, to the need she could feel vibrating through his hand as it lay lightly against her collarbone.

'Is that wise?' she asked, with the last vestige of common sense, and gave a soft huff of laughter and he smiled.

'Probably not,' he said, but he stood up, holding out his hand to her and waiting, and after an endless pause she put her hand in his and let him draw her to her feet.

Her heart was pounding as he led her upstairs, his hand warm and firm around hers, his fingers sure. He closed the door with a soft click and pressed a switch, and the lights came on, soft and low, barely enough to see by.

'I'm not on the Pill,' she said, remembering in time another reason why this was a bad idea and why the last time it had been such a bad idea, too, but he shook his head.

'It's all right, I'll take care of it. Come here.'

And he drew her gently into his arms, folding her against his heart and just holding her for the longest time. Then she felt his warm breath against her neck, the soft touch of his hand easing the hair aside so he could press his lips to the skin, and she arched her neck, giving him access, desperate for the feel of his lips all over her body, the touch of his hand, the feel of his heart beating against hers.

She slid her hands under his cashmere sweater, so soft, and laid them against the heated satin of his skin. Hot skin, smooth, dry, taut over bones and muscles. She ran her palms up his spine, feeling the solid columns tense, the breath jerk in his lungs.

His hand cupped her jaw, tilting her head back, and his lips found hers, firm and yet yielding, his tongue coaxing her lips apart so that she opened for him with a tiny sound of need that brought an answering groan from low in his chest.

She could feel his hands at her waist, but her camisole was tucked into her jeans and his fingers plucked at it, a growl of frustration erupting from his lips. 'Too many clothes,' he muttered. 'I want to touch you, Amelia. I want to feel your skin against mine.'

Her legs buckled slightly and he caught her against him. 'I need you. This is crazy. Come to bed.'

And, moving away from her, he stripped off his clothes—the soft jumper, which was easy, then the jeans, harder, the stud exasperating him so that she took over and helped him, her knuckles brushing the taut, hard plane of his abdomen so that he sucked his breath in with a sharp hiss and seared her with his eyes.

They were like coals now, the slate-grey gone, banished by the inky-black of his flared pupils burning into her. The stud undone, he reached for her, peeling the sweater over her head, then the camisole, wrenching it out from her jeans with a grunt of satisfaction and then slowly sliding it up over her breasts, his eyes darkening still further as he let them linger on her.

And she'd never felt more wanted, had never felt more beautiful. He hadn't said a word, not a single compliment or facile remark, just the look in his eyes, which was turning her blood to rivers of fire.

He reached for her bra, giving her a moment of unease because after three children...but he unclipped it and eased it away, and his lids fluttered briefly before his eyes met hers. 'I need you,' he breathed.

'I need you, too. Jake, make love to me.'

'Oh, I intend to,' he said gruffly, then smiled a little off-kilter. 'Once you've undone the stud on your jeans.'

She laughed, releasing the tension that held her, and then he tugged them down once she'd undone the stud, and she stepped out of them and bent to pick them up, dragging another groan from his throat.

'That was my first view of you,' he said almost conversationally. 'When I walked into the breakfast room and you bent over to pick something off the table.' His hand stroked over her bottom, catching her hip with his fingertips and easing her back against his groin. She straightened up and saw their reflection in a mirror, his hand curled around her hip, his fingertips toying with the hem of her little lace shorts—the ones Kate had given her for Christmas.

Breathlessly she watched as his hand slid round, his fingers inside the edge tangling with the soft, damp curls and bringing a tiny gasp to her lips. He rocked against her, hard and solid and urgent, and she could see the tension in his face, the taut jaw, the parted lips, the dark, burning eyes.

His other arm was round her waist, the cast holding her firmly against him, the fingertips trailing over her skin.

And she couldn't play any more, she couldn't wait, couldn't hold on another moment. She needed him. She'd needed him all her life, and she didn't want to waste another second.

She turned in his arms, sliding her hands down inside his jeans and boxers, pushing them down just far enough, and he lifted her with one arm and carried her to the bed, dropping her on the edge and stripping away the scrap of lace before rummaging in the bedside table.

'Damn, can you help me? I can't do this with one hand,' he growled, and she took over, her fingers shaking as she touched him so intimately for the first time. His breath hissed in sharply, and then he paused, dragging in a ragged breath, his eyes closed, slowing his breathing until finally he opened his eyes and stared down at her body.

'Jake, please,' she breathed, and with a tortured sigh he went into her arms.

'Are you OK?'

She laughed softly. 'I don't know. I'll tell you in a minute,' she said, and he propped himself up on his elbow and stared down at her.

'You've got glitter in your hair,' she murmured, reaching up to touch it and testing the soft, silky strands between her fingers.

'Mmm. That would be your daughter,' he said, laughter in his voice. 'She thought it would be funny to sprinkle it on me—apparently it's fairy dust. It's going to make me rich.'

'Oh, well, that'll be handy,' she said with a chuckle.

He smiled at the irony. 'Do you have any idea how lovely you are?' he murmured, the fingertips of his left hand trailing slowly over her breasts. He brushed the knuckles over her nipple and it peaked for him obligingly, so he bent and took it in his mouth, suckling it hard and making her gasp.

'How is it I've fed three babies and yet that's so erotic?' she asked in wonder.

'I don't know. How about the other one?' he asked, bending over it. 'We ought to be fair and do a proper survey of both, just in case.'

'Idiot,' she said, but then his mouth closed over her and she forgot to speak, forgot her name almost—and forgot the reason why this was such a dangerous idea, such a silly thing to do as she gave herself up once more to the touch of his hands, the warmth of his lips, the solid, masculine body that could drive her to madness…

For the next week, while the office was still closed and the housekeeper was on her annual leave, they fell into a routine.

In the morning they had breakfast together, and then after they'd walked the dog and Thomas was back in his cot for his nap, Jake would go over to the office and she'd work on the laptop in the playroom upstairs while the children were amusing themselves, something they were very good at and which she encouraged.

And then Jake would come back and they'd have lunch,

and Thomas would nap again, and when he woke they'd have a swim while Jake worked again, and then she'd cook supper for all of them and after the children were in bed she'd fit in another couple of hours before he'd come and shut down her laptop, give her a glass of wine and then take her up to bed.

She didn't sleep with him, because of the children, but every night she went upstairs with him and he made love to her, slowly, tenderly, until her nerves were stretched to breaking point and she was pleading with him to end it.

But it couldn't go on like this, and they both knew it.

'I need to find a house,' she said, as they were standing in the attic on New Year's Eve watching the fireworks in the distance at midnight. 'New Year, new start. And now I've got a job, I can contact the agents and see what they've got—'

'You don't have to go,' he said quietly. 'You could stay— you and the children. Move in properly.'

'Live with you?'

'Yes.'

'No.' She shook her head. 'No, Jake, I can't,' she said, feeling the fear close in round her. 'I can't put us in anyone else's hands, ever again. I can't do that to myself, never mind my children. They've been through enough, and I can't ask it of them. I can't—' She broke off and shook her head again. 'I just can't. I'm sorry. Anyway, it's really sweet of you, but you don't mean it—'

'Sweet?' he said, his voice stunned. 'There's nothing sweet about it, Amelia. I want you. I need you. And I thought…hell, we were getting on so well.'

'We are—but that doesn't mean I can give up my independence, Jake—or theirs. I thought you understood that. I swore I'd never let another man have that much power over me.'

'How do I have power over you? You'd be sharing my life. I'd have no more power over you than you'd have over me.'

'But you would, because it's your house, and my only money is from you, and—it's called having all your eggs in one basket. Not a good idea.'

'It's OK if it's the right basket. Most of us do that, emotionally, at least, if not financially. Get another job if that's what's worrying you, although I have to say I'd be extremely reluctant to lose you. Don't walk away just because there's a chance it may not be right, because there's a much bigger chance, from where I'm standing, that it *is* right.'

'And how do I know? How do I know if it's right, Jake?'

He cradled her shoulders in his hands and met her eyes searchingly. 'You have faith,' he said softly. 'You have faith, and you give it your best shot, and if you're lucky, and you work at it, then all's well.'

'And if it's not? If we find out it's no good, that we aren't the people we thought we were?'

He sighed and dropped his hands. 'OK. It's too soon, I'm rushing you. But think about it. Don't dismiss it. Get somewhere else to live, and give us time. We can still see each other, have dinner, take the kids out—'

She shook her head. 'No. I don't want the kids coming to think of you as part of their life. This is different, we're staying here for a short time, you're doing us a favour. But if we move in properly, if it all gets too cosy and then it goes wrong—bang! Another rug out from under their feet. And I can't do it. I'm sorry.'

She felt tears clog her throat, and turned away. 'I'm sorry, Jake. It's been wonderful, but it ends when I leave. Or now. It's your choice.'

'Then come to bed with me,' he said, his voice rough with emotion. 'If I've only got you for a short while longer, I want to savour every moment.'

He thought it would tear him apart. Making love to her, knowing she was going, knowing he was losing her— It nearly broke him, but he needed to hold her, to love her, to show her without words just how infinitely sweet and precious she was to him.

He'd been a fool, imagining he could win her. She'd been so hurt, so damaged by her life with David and all its tortured twists and turns that it was no surprise she found it hard to trust. But he wouldn't give up. Somehow he'd find a way to convince her. He had to.

But then a week later, just before his housekeeper was due to return, she told him she'd found a house.

'Where?'

'About ten miles away—so I can still come in and see you if I need to for work.'

'Where is it?'

'In Reading.'

'Whereabouts?'

She sighed. 'Does it matter?'

He wanted to tear his hair out. 'Yes! Yes, it matters. What's it like? What's the area like?'

She wouldn't look at him, and that worried the hell out of him. 'Fine.'

He didn't believe her for a minute.

'Have you signed?'

'No. I'm going to see him tomorrow. I looked round it today.'

'And?'

She swallowed. 'It'll be perfectly all right.'

Damn it! He paced across the kitchen, then came back to her. 'I have an alternative—'

'I'm not living here, Jake!'

'Not here. Another house. You remember I said I lived somewhere else while this place was being done? It's empty. I was going to sell it, put it on the market in the spring. It's got four bedrooms, it's detached, the furniture's reasonable—it needs a clean, the tenant left yesterday, but it's close to Kate, it's in a good school catchment area, it's got a nice garden… Can you have pets in this house you've found?'

She sighed. 'I had to convince the letting agent he was all right. He's going to talk to the landlord.'

He stopped pacing and leant back against the worktop, his arms folded across his chest. 'And if he says no?'

She stared at him. 'Then I try again—Jake, why do you *care*?'

'Because I do,' he said honestly, and to hell with giving her time and not rushing her and letting her learn to trust him, because if she was going to go and live in some vile little house in a horrible area and send her kids to a grotty school, he was damned if he was going to stand back and let her do it. 'Because I love you, dammit!' And then his voice softened, his throat clogging. 'I love you, Amelia, and I can't make you stay here, but I can still keep you safe, and make you more secure. Take my rental house—I'll put it in your name, and you can have it. And you can work for me, or not. Your choice. But don't take your kids to some horrible area and put them in a ghastly school just—'

'Just what? Just what, Jake? Just because it's the best I can afford to do? Some of us don't have your options—'

'But I'm trying to *give* you options, and you're turning them down!'

'Because they're not options, Jake. They're just a honey trap—and I can't let you do this for us.'

'Then let me do it for the children. Let me put the house in their names, not yours. Let me give you the freedom to choose whether or not you want me, whether or not you can trust me enough to take my love at face value, and marry me. No strings, no ultimatums. The house is yours. The job is yours. And I'm yours—if you want me. Think about it. I'll get my solicitor on it in the morning. Let me have their full names.'

And he walked out of the room before he said anything else that might prejudice her against him, because he felt so close to losing her this time, and he didn't know what he'd do if he couldn't win her back.

CHAPTER TEN

'RIGHT, that's everything. Time to say goodbye. Say thank you to Jake.'

'I don't want to say goodbye,' Kitty wailed, wrapping her arms around his hips and hanging on for dear life.

'Nor do I,' Edward said, his chin wobbling, and Jake could understand that. His own chin was less than firm, and he had to clench his teeth to stop himself from saying something stupid, like, Stay.

'Jake, don't,' she said, and for a moment he thought he'd said it out loud, but she was just pre-empting him, her voice little more than a breath, and he nodded understanding.

No. Compliance. Not understanding. He couldn't understand for the life of him how she could tear herself away from him when it was going to leave him in tatters and he was pretty sure it would do the same for her, and for the children. But it was her choice, her decision, her life.

And she'd chosen to go. He peeled Kitty's arms away from his hips and lifted her up, hugging her gently and posting her into the car. 'Take care, sweetheart. Let me know how your new school is.'

She sniffed and nodded, and he kissed her wet little cheek and felt the lump in his throat grow larger. 'Take care, Tiger,' he said to Thomas, who just grinned at him, and then he ducked out of the car and turned and Edward was standing there. He dredged up a smile.

'Hey, sport. You'll be all right. Let me know about your voice test.'

'I don't want to go.'

'Yes, you do. Nothing might come of it anyway, but you might get a scholarship. You don't know unless you try. And you wouldn't have to be a boarder. Give it a go,' he encouraged, and then, because he could see Edward needed the reassurance, he held out his arms and hugged him.

'I want to stay here,' he mumbled into Jake's chest.

'I know, but you've got your own house now,' he told him, fighting down the emotion, making himself let go of a boy so like him it could have been him at the same age, with all the same emotional turmoil, the need to do the right thing. And that need was still with him, which was the only reason he could do what he did then, to let the boy go, to unwind his arms and push him gently towards the car and turn away.

To find Amelia there, standing awkwardly, twisting the keys in her hands and biting her lip. As he looked at her, her eyes welled with tears. 'Jake…I can't thank you…'

'Don't. Just go, if you have to. I can't do goodbyes.'

She nodded and got into the car, calling Rufus, but he refused to go. He sat down beside Jake and whined, and stupidly, that was the thing that brought tears to his eyes.

He blinked them savagely away, scooped the dog up and put him into the front footwell.

'Can I ring you?' Edward asked.

'Ask your mother. She's got my number. Take care, now—and good luck.'

He shut the door and stepped back, willing the engine to fail, but it started first turn and she drove away. He watched her until they reached the end of the drive and turned onto the road, and then he went back inside and shut the door.

It was so empty.

The house felt as if the very soul had been ripped out of it, and he wandered, lost, from room to room, the silence echoing with their laughter and tears, the squabbles of the children, the baby's gurgling laugh, the dog's sharp, excited bark, Amelia's warm, sexy chuckle, her teasing glances, the tenderness of her loving.

Gone, all of it, wiped out by her stubborn insistence on being independent.

And, hell, he could understand that. He'd grabbed his independence as soon as he could—as a child first at boarding school, then, with valuable life lessons learned, in senior school, and then in life itself, out there in the real world, cutting himself adrift from parents who'd never stopped bickering for long enough to understand him.

But he'd never walked away from love for fear of being hurt. If he had, he might never have married Rachel, never have known the joy of having a child, and for all it had been snatched away from him, he wouldn't have missed a second of it just because it hurt to lose it.

Better to have loved and lost…

But losing Amelia was so unnecessary! He wasn't *like* David. She didn't need to be cautious, because he wouldn't let them down, he wouldn't fail them with his lousy judgement or turn his back or walk away. He'd cut his own heart out before he'd hurt them, any of them. Even the damn dog.

He went into the sitting room, his sanctuary, and saw the recording of him singing. He'd never be able to listen to it again without thinking of Edward standing by the fire with the carol singers and filling the house with that sweet, pure sound.

He looked out of the window at the lump of slush on the lawn that was the remains of the snowman. The sprouts lay haphazard in the scarf, the carrot on the ground, and his hat had slid off sideways and was lying in a soggy heap.

They'd had such fun that day. They'd made snow angels as well, and eaten mountains of delicious food, and they'd played with their toys. Kitty had made him a picture with glitter, and then she'd sprinkled it in his hair.

Fairy dust.

And Amelia had found it that night, in bed, and teased him. The night he'd made love to her for the first time. He'd be finding glitter all over the house for months. Years, probably—

'Jake?'

There was a tap on the door, and it swung in and Kate stood there.

'Are you all right?'

'Why shouldn't I be?'

'I don't know. Why don't you tell me? You look like hell.'

'Thanks. What can I do for you?'

'I've got George Crosbie on the phone. I've been calling

your mobile and you haven't had it switched on. He's been trying to get you since yesterday.'

'Sorry. Switch it through to my study, I'll take it there. On second thoughts, I'll come over.'

Anything—even George—was better than sitting in the house on his own and listening to the echoes of the children.

He might have to stay over there all night.

'I hate it here.'

'It'll be lovely, Kitty, I promise. We'll soon make it nice. I'll get all our things out of store in the next few days, and we'll get settled in and it'll be home then.'

'Rufus isn't happy. He doesn't like it.'

He didn't. He sat by the front door and howled the whole time, as if he was hoping Jake would come. Amelia knew how he felt. She could have sat there and howled herself.

Edward was just quiet, retreating into himself as he'd done when David left. Not even the upcoming voice test in a week's time seemed to mean anything to him, and Millie didn't know what to do to help.

Apart from ring Jake and tell him it had all been a big mistake, but how could she? What if it all went wrong again? What if he got bored with the idea of another man's family? Your own was one thing, somebody else's was quite another. And David hadn't even wanted his own, so she didn't hold out hope for anyone else.

'Come on, it's time for bed.'

'I don't like my bed. It's lumpy.'

Hers wasn't. There wasn't a lump in it. Nothing so supportive. It was just saggy, saggy and uncomfortable and maybe even slightly damp. And there was a definite musty aroma that came off it, even through the sheets.

But she'd taken the house because the landlord hadn't demanded a huge deposit or dozens of references, he hadn't minded about the dog, and it was in budget. Just. She wanted to put by a good chunk of her money every month, just in case—

That was going to be carved on her headstone. 'Here lies Amelia Jones—Just In Case.'

'Come on, school tomorrow,' she said brightly. 'You need to get to bed.'

'I don't like the new school,' Edward said. 'I asked about a choir and they laughed.'

Oh, no. How much worse could it get?

'Heard anything from Amelia?'

'Yes. She says they're fine. She's done lots of work for you.'

'Yes. She's good.' Missing, but good. And how he missed her. Missed them all. 'Any news of Edward's voice test?'

She sighed and sat back on the sofa and met his eyes. 'Why don't you just ring them?'

'Because it's none of my business.'

She propped her elbows on her knees and planted her chin in her hands. 'You're in love with her, aren't you?'

'Do I pay you for this?'

'Yes. I'm your personal assistant—and, just now, I think you need a little personal assistance, so, yes, you do.'

He grunted. 'I could do with another coffee, if you want

to assist me,' he said bluntly, flicking open a file and scanning the contents.

'He doesn't want to go.'

'What?'

'Edward. He doesn't want to go to the voice test.'

Jake shut the file and stared at her searchingly. 'Why not?'

She shrugged. 'He wouldn't say, apparently. Just announced that he wasn't going, it was rubbish and he didn't want to sing any more, and that was it.'

'Well, maybe he doesn't,' he said slowly, although he didn't believe it for a moment. He'd been really fired up, keen to go, keen to find out all he could, and he'd been really excited when the invitation to attend the test had come through so quickly. So why—?

'I'm going to see her on Sunday. Any message?'

He slammed the door on temptation. 'No. She knows where to find me.'

'You give up easily.'

'No, I don't. But I'm not going to hound her. I gave her the choice, and she went. Her decision. I'm not going to beg.'

'I didn't ask you to beg, just not to give up—'

'Oh, for God's sake, Kate, I poured out my heart to her, told her things I've never told another soul! And she walked away. What else do you expect me to do?' he raged, jack-knifing to his feet and slamming his hand so hard against the window frame that the wood bit into the skin.

'Jake?' Kate's voice was tentative, her hand gentle on his shoulder. 'I'm sorry. I didn't mean to pry. But I can see you're unhappy, and…well, she is, too.'

He stared down the long walk, remembering the children running about having fun, throwing snowballs. 'There's nothing I can do about that. I haven't got the right or the power to do anything about that. Did she tell you I offered her the house in the village?'

'No. Could she afford it? I thought her rent budget was lower than that.'

'No—I mean, I offered to give it to her. Said I'd put it in her name. She said no, so I told her to give me the names of the children so I could put it in their names, and she refused. I thought—if she had a house, if she had independence—'

'But it wouldn't be, would it? It would be like being a concubine. Maybe you should have offered to marry her.'

He turned his head and met her eyes. 'I did. She said no.'

Kate's jaw dropped, and he pushed it up with his finger and smiled tiredly. 'Leave it now. I can't do this any more. I've told her I love her, I've asked her to marry me, I've offered her a house, I've given her a job—and the only thing she's taken is the job, which is her escape route from me. So I've taken the hint,' he said, his voice cracking. He cleared his throat. 'Right, I've done enough today, I'm going home. I'll see you on Monday.'

And he walked out of the office without a backward glance, went over to the house, shut the door of his sitting room, dropped into the sofa with a hefty glass of malt whisky and dedicated the next five hours to drowning his sorrows.

It didn't work.

* * *

'Jake looks awful.'

'Does he?'

'Yes—much like you. He told me he asked you to marry him and you said no. And he said you refused the house.'

'He talks too much,' she said tightly, closing the kitchen door so the children couldn't hear, and Kate laughed.

'I don't think so. Are you crazy? If a man like that asked me to marry him, I'd say yes like a shot.'

'What—because he's rich? It's meaningless.'

'No—because he's *nice*, Millie. He's a lovely guy. I can't understand why he's never been married before— although, come to think of it, he's never said that,' she went on thoughtfully. 'I wonder if he's divorced?'

'Don't ask me,' Amelia said, ignoring Kate's searching look, so Kate gave up and leant back against the worktop, her coffee cradled in her hands.

'He seemed shocked that Edward didn't want to do his voice test.'

Oh, *hell*. 'And how did he know that?'

'I told him.'

Millie sighed abruptly and stared at Kate in frustration. 'Do you and Jake do *nothing* at work except talk about me?'

'Oh, we fit in the odd bit—the occasional company takeover, a little asset-stripping, pruning out the dead wood, rolling the stock market dice—'

'Stop it! I don't want to hear it!'

Kate sighed. 'Millie, he's not like David. He doesn't do that. Yes, he buys companies, but he's considered, thoughtful, and he takes risks, sure, but only calculated ones—and here's the difference, he has a better calculator than David. He knows what he's doing, and he doesn't hurt innocent people along the way. If he did, I wouldn't work for him.'

No, she wouldn't, Amelia thought, staring down the bleak, scruffy little garden at the back of the house. Kate was too intrinsically decent to work for someone who wasn't. But that didn't mean that he was a safe bet personally. Maybe he was just lonely and thought they'd do to fill the gap in his life left by Rachel and Ben. Maybe he thought he could turn Edward into the son he'd lost, the son who could never grow up.

And her boy didn't deserve to be anybody's substitute. Even if that person was his hero—

'Give him another chance. At least see him. I'll babysit for you—you can tell the children you have to work, and they can come to me for a sleepover.'

Oh, she was so tempted. To see him again—it had only been a week, and she was missing him with every passing second. The rest of her life seemed like an eternity, stretching out in front of her without him.

A safe, dull, boring eternity.

'He hasn't contacted me. If he wanted to see me, he could ring.'

'You told him you didn't want him. Don't expect him to grovel. He said you know where to find him.'

So the ball was in her court.

Tough.

'I can't talk about this now. Not with the children here,' she said as their raised voices filtered through the door. 'Come on, we need to supervise this, it sounds a bit lively.'

Which made a change, because all week they'd been quiet and sad. Oh, damn.

'So—aren't you going to ask how they are?'

Oh, hell. He'd promised himself he wouldn't, but Kate would have known that, and she'd waited all day, keeping him in suspense, keeping him dangling.

'No,' he said bluntly. 'I'm not.'

'They're miserable. They were thrilled to see Megan, and Millie said it was the first time they'd laughed since they'd moved. And the dog sat by the door all day and whined.'

'Not my problem,' he said, his heart contracting into a tight ball in his chest. 'I've done all I can, Kate. I can't do more.'

But then later that week Kate came into his office looking worried.

'I've had a call from Millie. She can't finish that work you sent her—there's a problem.'

He leant back in his chair and looked up at her. 'What sort of a problem?'

'Rufus is ill. He's collapsed. She's taken him to the vet, but he's got to go to a referral centre. She's got Thomas with her and the children don't know—they need picking up from school. She's asked me if I can have Thomas and keep the children overnight—Jake, what are you doing?'

'Coming with you. She can't face this alone. I'll take my car and follow you.'

'What about your arm?'

'It's fine. She can drive from the vet's. Are you meeting her there?'

'Yes.'

'Right, let's go.'

He stuck his head into Reception on the way past. 'Clear my diary, and Kate's. We're going out,' he said, and followed Kate to the veterinary surgery.

She was standing by the door, pushing Thomas backwards and forwards in the stroller, trying to stop him crying while she watched the car park entrance for Kate's car.

'Come on, come on,' she muttered, and then she saw it turn in and her eyes flooded with tears of relief. 'Look, Thomas, it's Kate! You like Kate! You're going to stay with her—'

'How is he?'

She jerked upright. 'Jake?' she whispered, and then his arms were round her, and he was folding her against his heart and holding her tight.

'He's on a drip. They've sedated him—they think he might have had a stroke. They get them, apparently. I have to take him to a place miles away and I haven't got any petrol in the car—'

'I've got mine. You can drive it, I probably shouldn't with a cast on. Leave yours here, I'm sure they won't mind. Let's go and talk to them.'

'Where's Kate? I saw her car—'

'I'm here, sweetheart. I'll take Thomas. Give me your house keys. I'll pick up his stuff and some things for the others, and you can come and see me when you get back, OK?'

'OK,' she said, fumbling for her keys with nerveless fingers. 'Thank you.'

Her eyes flooded again, and Kate hugged her hard—difficult, because Jake still had one arm round her, holding her up—and then she was gone and Jake was steering her into Reception and talking to the staff.

Rufus was ready to go—the referral centre was expecting him—and she drove with one eye on the rear-view mirror, where she could see Jake sitting with Rufus beside him, still on the drip, the bag suspended above him clipped to the coat hook on the edge of the roof lining, his hand stroking the dog gently and murmuring soothingly to him.

He'd set the sat-nav to direct her, but although it took the stress out of finding the way, it left her nothing to worry about but Rufus. And the journey was interminable.

'Thank you so much for coming with me,' she said, what seemed like hours later as they sat outside waiting for news.

'Don't be silly,' he said, his voice gruff. 'I couldn't let you do this alone.'

'You always did like the stupid dog,' she said, her voice wobbling, and he put his arm round her shoulders and squeezed gently.

Not nearly as much as he liked the stupid owner, he thought, and then the door swung open and the vet who'd admitted Rufus came out to them.

'Mrs Jones?'

She leapt to her feet, but her legs nearly gave out and he held her up, his arm firmly round her waist, holding her tight as they waited for the news.

'We've done an MRI, and he has had a stroke,' the vet

said, and he felt a shudder go through her. 'It's in the back
of his brain, the cerebellum, which controls balance. It's
quite common in Cavaliers. Their skulls are a little on the
small side and the vessels can get restricted, and he's got
a little bleed, but we're going to keep him quiet and watch
him, and hopefully it will heal and he'll recover. He's still
very heavily sedated and we'll keep him like that for a
while. The first few hours are obviously critical, and he's
got through them so far, but until we can get this settled
down and reduce the sedation we won't know if there's any
lasting damage. I expect the unsteadiness he was showing
will be worse, and he might stagger around in circles or
hold his head on one side or just be unable to sort his feet
out—it may be temporary, it may be permanent, or there
may be a degree of permanent deficit, which is what I
would expect. Do you have any questions?'

'Yes—how long will he be in?' she asked, her voice
tight.

'Maybe a week. Possibly more.'

'Oh, no. Um…my insurance cover is only for three
thousand pounds—'

'Don't worry about that,' Jake said firmly. 'Just do what
you have to do and we'll sort it out later.'

She turned her face up to him, pale and shocked, the
hideous, unpalatable decision clouding her lovely eyes.
'Jake, you can't do that—'

'Don't argue, Amelia,' he said firmly. 'Not about this.
Will you keep in touch?' he added to the vet.

'I can't go—'

'There's nothing you can do here, Mrs Jones,' the vet
said gently but firmly. 'Go home. We'll ring you if there's

any change, and we'll ring you at seven in the morning and seven in the evening every day for an update.'

'Can I see him?'

'Of course. And you can come and visit him later in the week if he's progressing well, but we want him kept as quiet as possible for now.'

She nodded, and they were led through to see him. He was in a cage, flat on his side on a sheepskin blanket, with drips and oxygen and a heat lamp, and he looked tiny and vulnerable and very, very sick.

Jake felt his eyes prickle, and beside him Amelia was shaking like a jelly.

'Come on, I'm taking you home,' he said firmly, and led her out to the car park. He drove—he probably shouldn't have, with the cast on, but she certainly wasn't fit to drive, so he buckled her in beside him and set off. He could see her knotted hands working in her lap out of the corner of his eye, and her head was bent; he thought she was probably crying.

She lifted her head as they crunched onto the gravel drive, and looked around. 'Why are we here?'

'Because Kate's got your house keys, and I think you need a little TLC in private for a while,' he said, and cut the engine. 'Come on.'

He led her inside, and as soon as the door closed behind them, she collapsed against his chest, sobbing.

'I can't lose him,' she wept. 'I can't—how can I tell the children? I can't take him away from them as well—'

'Shh. Come and sit down, I'll get you a drink.'

'I don't want a drink, I want Rufus,' she said, abandoning all attempt at courage, and he steered her into his sitting room, pushed her down onto the sofa and dragged her into his arms.

She cried for ages, not only for the dog, he suspected, but for all the things she'd lost, the things that had gone wrong, the agonies and disappointments and bitter regrets of the past several years.

And then finally she hiccupped to a halt, her eyes puffy and red-rimmed, her cheeks streaked with drying tears, her mouth swollen. And he'd never seen anything more beautiful in his entire life.

'Better now?'

She nodded, sniffing again, and he hugged her and stood up. 'Come on, let's get something to eat and tell Kate what's happening,' he said gently, and she let him pull her up and lead her through to the kitchen.

There was a note on the island from his housekeeper.

CASSEROLE IN FRIDGE. TOP OVEN, HALF AN HOUR. VEG IN MICROWAVE. FIVE MINUTES.

'Hungry?' he asked. She shook her head, but he didn't believe her, so he put the casserole in the top oven anyway and put the kettle on, then rang Kate.

'Hi. He's doing all right, but the next few hours are critical, so I've got her at home. I don't want her by herself. Can you keep the kids?'

'Of course. I won't be in tomorrow, then.'

'No, I know. Nor will I. I'll keep in touch. Thanks, Kate. I think Amelia wants to talk to you.'

He handed the phone over and listened as she tried hard to be brave and upbeat—talking to the children, he guessed, because she said the same thing three times—to Kate, then to Kitty, then to Edward—and then she turned to him. 'Edward wants to talk to you.'

Oh, hell. He took the phone out of her hand. 'Hi, Edward. How are things?'

'Horrible. Is Rufus really going to be OK?'

'I hope so,' he said, refusing to lie to the child. 'They're very skilled, and if he can get through this, he'll do it there, but we're all thinking about him, and if thinking can help, then he'll make it for sure.'

'Thinking doesn't help,' he said. 'I keep thinking about living with you, but it hasn't helped at all.'

'We can't always have what we want,' he said gently. 'You have to change the things you can, and find the strength to deal with the things you can't. Like this voice test. Kate said you didn't want to go.'

'But what's the point? We can't afford it—and anyway, if Rufus dies, I can't leave Mummy, can I?'

'OK. One thing at a time. You have to be offered a place first, and see if you'd like to do it. Then you worry about paying. There might be a way—a scholarship, for instance. That was how I got there. My parents didn't have any money, and the choir school paid my fees. And Rufus hasn't died, and there's every chance he'll live and get better, although it may take a while. And you could probably go to the school as a day boy, so you wouldn't have to leave your mother.'

There was a silence at the end of the line.

'Edward?' he prompted.

'Mmm.'

'Don't shut doors until you know what's on the other

side. It might be what you're looking for, it might not. But you owe it yourself to find that out. Do you want to talk to your mum again?'

'No, it's OK. Tell her I love her.'

'OK. We'll be in touch. Don't worry. He's in the best place.'

He turned off the phone and set it down. 'I have to give you a message,' he said, turning towards her. 'I love you.'

She looked up into his eyes, startled. 'What did you say?'

'I love you.'

Something—hope?—flared in her eyes, and then died. 'That's the message?'

'Yes. So does Edward. That's his message.'

He saw the hope dawn again, then saw her fight it, not allowing herself the luxury of his love, because she didn't dare to trust him—and there was nothing more he could do to prove to her that he loved her, that she and her family and her dog had a home with him, a place in his heart for ever.

He stepped back. 'I'll make the tea,' he said gruffly, and turned away, the pain of knowing he would never have her in his life too great to stand there in front of her and make civilised conversation about her son and her dog and—

'Jake?'

He paused and put the kettle down. 'What?'

'I'm sorry. I've been so stupid. I've kept thinking you were like David, that under it all you were the same kind of person, pursuing the same goals, but you're not, are you? You're just in the same line of business. He always wanted to get rich quick, but you've got where you are by doing what you can to the best of your ability, by working hard, paying attention to detail, doing it right. And you've been successful, not lucky, because you're good at what you do and you do what you're good at.

'And you're good at being a father, Jake. You've been more of a father to my children in the last few weeks than their own father ever has, and a better man to me than he could ever be. And, as for Rufus—there's no *way* David would have done everything you've done for him. He would have told the vet to put him down, because he didn't realise how important he was to the children, how much he's given them. Not that he would have cared. He never gave them anything without considering it first, but you—when your heart was breaking, you gave us Christmas, even though it must have hurt you unbearably, because it was the right thing to do. And you do that, don't you? The right thing. Always.

'So, if the offer's still open—if you really meant it, if you really do love me and want to marry me—then nothing would make me prouder than to be your wife—'

She broke off, her voice cracking, and he turned slowly and stared at her. Her eyes were downcast, her lip caught between her teeth, and he reached out gently and lifted her chin.

'Was that a yes?' he asked softly, hardly daring to breathe, and she laughed, her eyes flooding with tears.

'Yes, it was a yes,' she said unsteadily. 'If you'll still have me—'

'Stuff the tea,' he said. 'I've got a better idea.'

And, scooping her up in his arms, he carried her upstairs to bed.

* * *

'What's that smell?'

'The casserole. Damn.'

He got up and walked, still naked, out of the bedroom and down to the kitchen. She pulled on his shirt and followed him, arriving in the kitchen as he set the casserole dish down on the island. 'Oops.'

'Oops, indeed. Never mind. We'll grab something on the way to Kate's.'

'Kate's?'

'Mmm. I think we need to tell the children—and then we've got wedding plans to make. How do you fancy a January wedding?'

She blinked. 'Two weeks, max? That's tight.'

'Why? We've got the venue. We'll get married in the church, and we'll come back here and celebrate. It's not like it's going to be a huge affair. Your family, our friends— twenty or so? The people from work are my family, really—so more than twenty. OK. It's getting bigger,' he admitted with a laugh, and she hugged him.

'And two weeks isn't long enough to be legal. I don't care when I marry you, or where, just so long as I can be with you.'

It was May, in the end.

Her brother-in-law gave her away—Andy, who'd apologised for the way he and Laura had treated her at Christmas. He had finally told her that they were unable to have children, which was why they'd found it so hard to have the children there. Kate was her matron of honour, with Kitty and a slightly wobbly Rufus in a brand-new collar as her attendants.

And Edward, who'd been practising for weeks with the choir master at his new school, sang an anthem which reduced them both to tears, and then after the service they walked back to the walled garden where the fountain was playing, and in a pause in the proceedings Jake turned to her and smiled.

'All right, my darling?'

'Much better than all right. Have I ever told you that I love you?'

He laughed softly. 'Only a few thousand times, but it took you long enough, so I'm quite happy to hear it again.'

'Good,' she said, squeezing his arm, 'because I intend to keep telling you for the rest of my life…'

A PRINCESS
FOR CHRISTMAS

BY
SHIRLEY JUMP

New York Times bestselling author **Shirley Jump** didn't have the willpower to diet, nor the talent to master under-eye concealer, so she bowed out of a career in television and opted instead for a career where she could be paid to eat at her desk—writing. At first, seeking revenge on her children for their grocery-store tantrums, she sold embarrassing essays about them to anthologies. However, it wasn't enough to feed her growing addiction to writing. So she turned to the world of romance novels, where messes are (usually) cleaned up before The End. In the worlds Shirley gets to create and control, the children listen to their parents, the husbands always remember holidays and the housework is magically done by elves. Though she's thrilled to see her books in stores around the world, Shirley mostly writes because it gives her an excuse to avoid cleaning the toilets and helps feed her shoe habit. To learn more, visit her website at www.shirleyjump.com.

First, to my readers—
there is no more special gift than your letters,
support and warm words.
You make writing an extra wonderful joy.
Second, to my family—
every day with you is a treasured present.

CHAPTER ONE

THE woman in the painting whispered to Mariabella. Her deep green eyes, slightly hooded by heavy lashes, seemed to hold a quiet secret. One she kept close to her heart, one perhaps she hadn't even shared with the man who'd held the paintbrush.

Mariabella reached out, traced the air around the painted woman's eyes. Secrets. This woman had one.

And so, too, did Mariabella Romano.

"You like that painting, huh?"

Mariabella started, jerked out of her reverie. She turned at the sound of Carmen's voice. More friend than employee, Carmen Edelman had worked for Mariabella ever since she'd opened the Harborside Art Gallery in the little coastal Massachusetts town almost a year ago. The quirky college graduate had walked in one day, her arms loaded with paintings, each one a gem. Ever since, Carmen had been unearthing wonderful finds, including the artist who'd painted the portrait of the mysterious woman, titled simply, *She Who Knows*.

Mariabella's twenty-five-year-old assistant had an uncanny eye for quality work, and had been instrumental in helping Mariabella choose the paintings for the gallery's upcoming Christmas show. Carmen's bohemian personality gave the gallery—and Mariabella—a little something unexpected every day.

"I do love this piece," Mariabella said, pointing toward the portrait of the brunette. "It has a certain depth and mystery to it. It is my favorite piece in the collection."

"It does seem to have good karma, doesn't it?" Carmen took a step back, propped a fist beneath her chin, sending dozens of silver and gold bracelets on a jingling race down her arm. "Such deep thoughts in each brush stroke. What do you think it's saying?"

"Probably what she knows…and no one else does."

Carmen turned and caught Mariabella's eye. Her black pageboy haircut swung forward with the movement, and her red-rimmed cat's-eye glasses slipped a little on her nose. "Oh, so perceptive! I can see that now. The way the woman has her chin tilted down just a bit, the way her hair is brushed across her eyes, like she wants to hide behind the bangs but can't because they're not quite long enough. Hmm…though that could just be a bad haircut. And then there's the way her hand is coming up to cover her mouth. It's like she has…"

"Secrets," Mariabella finished, then wanted to catch the word and bring it back. But really, Carmen—like everyone else in town—didn't know anything about the true identity of Mariabella "Romano."

Who wasn't a Romano at all.

Money and privilege provided the opportunity to buy anything—including a new identity and a temporary escape from a life that had chafed at Mariabella like a too-tight yoke.

Carmen's scarlet lips spread in a wide smile. "This is why I love working for you. You're, like, totally psychic about art. You have such a gift."

The genuine compliment washed over Mariabella. She'd lived her life surrounded by people who had dropped compliments on her like confetti at a parade—with the words having about as much depth and meaning. She'd found herself feeling as vacant as those words, and needing something…more.

So a little more than a year ago, she'd left that insular, empty world behind, shedding her true name and her heritage to come here, searching for—

Reality. Peace. Independence.

Here, in Carmen's words, her gaze, and also in the friends who filled the shops lining Harborside's boardwalk, Mariabella had exactly that. People who saw her, not for her lineage, but for herself.

"Speaking of gifts, when are you going to share *your* gifts with the world?" Carmen drifted over to the store's Christmas tree and hoisted one of the faux presents that sat below the tabletop display. "And I'm not talking about these empty boxes."

Sometimes—like when they were dealing with a difficult artist—Mariabella considered her employee's persistence a blessing. And other times when she called it more of a curse. Like now.

"A gallery is not meant to be used as the owner's ego trip."

"Mar, you're not even on the baggage carousel."

"Baggage...what?"

Carmen waved a hand. "American translation, you're not taking any risks. At all. And for your information, it's not a big deal to hang a few of your pieces here. People want to get a peek into who you are, and what's going on in your noggin." Carmen tapped her head.

"Carmen, we go through this argument every week—"

"For good reason—"

"And the answer is always the same."

"Doesn't make it the right answer." Carmen arched a thinly penciled brow.

"My paintings are hardly ready." The lie slipped easily from Mariabella's tongue. She'd been to art school, received her master's degree. She knew when a painting had fulfilled its potential on the canvas. Even though she wouldn't call her art ready for the Louvre, by any stretch, the pieces she'd created could hang proudly on these walls.

If she dared to put her soul on display.

There was something inherently intimate about hanging art on a gallery wall, something that allowed, as Carmen had said, the world a peek inside the artist's true self. And Mariabella knew that as long as she was living a lie, she couldn't permit even a single glimpse.

"In addition," Mariabella went on, when she saw Carmen readying another objection, "we have a number of artists scheduled to exhibit, enough to carry us through next year. Our walls are full, Carmen." Mariabella returned to the front desk of the gallery, and started reviewing the proofs of the catalog for next Tuesday's show. The holiday tourist season was in full swing, and as the calendar flipped closer to Christmas, more and more people flocked to the seaside community looking for unique, locally made gifts. Harborside decorated its boardwalk, revved up its restaurants, brewed up special seasonal lattes, and after a post-summer slumber, came back to life in a new and festive way.

It hadn't been that way in years' past. Before Mariabella came to town, Harborside used to lock its shutters and close its doors for the winter, all the residents and business owners hibernating like bears. Mariabella had joined the Community Development Committee, seeing a potential for more in the little town. That enthusiasm had gotten her elected to committee chair, and also spurred the town into action. This year would be the second that Harborside used the holiday season to bring in much-needed winter revenue through a series of events. The boost in tourism dollars—albeit not a large amount yet, but one that was growing—seemed to have everyone humming Christmas carols.

Carmen's hand blocked Mariabella's view. The bangle bracelets reprised their jingle song. "An excuse is still an excuse, even if you wrap it up with a pretty bow. Or in your case, a European accent."

Mariabella laughed. "Are you ever going to give up?"

"Not until I see a Mariabella masterpiece—" Carmen framed her fingers together and squinted through the square at the wall "—right there. That space would be perfectamundo."

"Uh-huh. And getting this catalog to the printer's before the end of the day would also be…" Mariabella paused. "How do you say?"

"Perfectamundo." Carmen grinned.

"*Perfectamunda,* yes?"

"Close enough. Eventually I'll have you talking all slang, all the time."

Mariabella shook her head and got back to work. Slang—coming from her cultured tongue. She could just imagine her father's reaction to *that.* His stony face, rigid posture. But worst of all, the silence. She'd hated the judgment in that quiet.

She'd never measured up, not to his standards, voiced or not. She'd never sat still enough, smiled at enough people, acted as he'd expected.

Acted as a *princess* should.

If he could see her now, her hair loose and flowing, dressed in jeans and spiky heels, paint beneath her fingernails from a frenzied creative streak this morning—

Well, he couldn't see her, and that was the best part about Harborside being located on the other side of the world. That freedom, to be herself, was a large part of what Mariabella loved about being here. And even talking slang. She smiled to herself.

"Hey." Carmen nudged Mariabella. "Did you see that?"

"What?"

"Eye candy, two o'clock."

"Eye…what?"

"Cute guy, walking past the gallery." She nudged Mariabella's shoulder a second time.

"Mmm…okay." Mariabella kept working on the catalog's corrections.

Carmen let out a frustrated gust. "You should go talk to him."

That got Mariabella's attention. "Go talk to him? Why?"

"Because he's alone, and you're alone, and it's about time you took number one, a few hours for yourself, and number two, a step out of that comfort zone you're so determined to stay glued to."

Mariabella wanted to tell Carmen she had already taken a giant step out of her comfort zone, something beyond opening the gallery. A step that had brought her all the way across the world, from a tiny little country outside of Italy to here, an even tinier town in Massachusetts.

To a new life. A life without kings and queens.

Without expectations.

Carmen did have a point about the dating, though. In all the time Mariabella had been in Harborside, she hadn't dated anyone, hadn't gotten close to a man. She'd made friends, yes, but not true relationships, nothing deep. Part of that was because she'd had no time, as Carmen mentioned, but a bigger part was self-preservation.

She thought again of the woman in the painting. Had that woman dared to open her heart?

If so, was the price she'd had to pay as high as Mariabella's?

"Let's focus on catalogs and canapés, instead of my love life," Mariabella said to her assistant. "I think the artist will be upset if I tell him I spent my time pursuing a hot date instead of concentrating on his show."

Carmen turned to Mariabella and opened her mouth, as if she wanted to argue the point, then shut it again. "Okay. I can see when the stars are out of alignment for this topic. I'll zip down to Make it Memorable and check on the appetizers for Tuesday's opening."

Mariabella sent up a wave, while she kept on checking the page proofs. "Thank you. I'll hold down the tent."

Carmen laughed. "Fort, Mariabella. Fort."

Heat filled Mariabella's cheeks. Her accented English was flawless, but she'd yet to master all those odd little idioms. "I meant fort."

"Hey, a horse is still a horse, even if you call it a pony." Carmen toodled a wave, then left the gallery, with the hurried step that marked her every movement.

Soft, jazzy Christmas music flowing from the gallery's sound system provided companion noise for Mariabella as she got back to work. She settled onto a chair behind the counter, content to be alone, surrounded by the art she loved. All her life, she'd craved this kind of shop, this exact kind of cozy gallery. There were many days when she couldn't believe she actually owned this place, and had seen this dream come true. It made up for all those arguments with her father, all the tears she'd shed.

She paused a moment and cast a glance out the bay window behind her, drawing in the view of the ocean that lay down the dock from the gallery. Through the window, the sun-drenched day could have passed for summer, if the calendar didn't read a few days before Christmas. No snow lay on the ground yet, though the temperature outside was all winter. The ocean curled gently in and out, while seagulls dipped down to the beach for a late morning meal. Bright sunshine cast sparkles of light over the water. How different Harborside was from where Mariabella had grown up, yet how similar, too. She'd lived on the coast then, too, but that coast had been full of rocky cliffs, houses nestled among the stone paths and lush landscape. Here, the land was less hilly, more populated and didn't have hundreds of years of history carved into the side of every building. But Harborside offered something else Mariabella couldn't have in her old home. Something precious.

Anonymity.

A sense of peace draped over Mariabella like a cozy blanket. She loved this town, loved the haven she had found here. She thought of the letter in her purse, and wondered what answer she could possibly give. How she could ever explain she had found something in Harborside that she could never imagine leaving.

But soon, duty demanded her return. As always.

The bell over the door jingled and Mariabella jerked to attention. The man she and Carmen had seen earlier stood in the doorway, his tall figure cutting an imposing stance.

"May I help you?" Mariabella said, moving away from the front desk.

"Just looking, thank you." He stepped inside, giving Mariabella a better view of him.

Dark hair, dark eyes. What appeared to be an athletic build beneath the navy pinstriped suit, clearly tailored to fit his frame. She recognized his shoes as designer, his briefcase as fine leather. No ordinary tourist, that was clear. Most people who came to Harborside wore jeans in winter or shorts in the summer—dressed to relax and make the most of the boating, swimming and fishing the coastal town had to offer.

This man looked ready to steer a corporation, not a catamaran.

He stood about six feet tall, maybe six-two, and when he moved about the open space of the gallery, he had the stride of a man who knew his place in the world.

A zing of attraction ran through Mariabella. No wonder Carmen had called him eye candy. He had more to offer than a ten-pound chocolate bar.

"Our main gallery houses the artist in residence," she said, falling into step a few feet away from him, "who has some mixed media pieces in his collection as well as a number of portraits. In the west room, you will find our sculptures and art deco pieces, and the east room, which overlooks the ocean, features our landscapes, if you're looking for a picture of Harborside to take home or back to your office."

"I'm not looking for something for my home. Or office."

He barely glanced at her as he said the words, but more, he hadn't looked at a single painting. His gaze went, not to the landscapes, portraits and fresco panels, but to the—

Walls. The ceiling. The floors.

Then to her.

A chill chased up her spine.

Had they found her? Was her time here over? No, no, it couldn't be. She had two more months. That was the agreement.

It was too soon, she wasn't ready to leave. She loved her home, loved her gallery, and she didn't want to go back. Not yet.

Mariabella hung back, watching the stranger. He paused to look out the window, the one that provided a view of the entire boardwalk. He took a few steps, as if assessing all of Harborside, then returned to his perusal of the main room of Harborside Art Gallery.

Perhaps he hadn't come here after her. Perhaps he was only sizing up the gallery. Maybe he owned a place in a nearby town and he'd come here to check out the competition.

Except…

Doubt nagged at Mariabella. A whisper of more here, a hidden agenda. But what?

He entered the east room of the gallery, Mariabella's favorite space because of its location facing the harbor. Most of her sales, at least to outsiders, happened in that room. Tourists often selected a painting that captured a moment from their vacation, an image of a sunset, a burst of a sunrise over the ocean. Mariabella often commissioned works based solely on tourists' comments, filling the walls with works that held their visions and happy memories of Harborside.

But this man didn't stop to notice the view of the ocean

outside the window facing the Atlantic. He didn't glance at a single oil or watercolor. He merely strode the perimeter of the room, then exited, and headed into the third room. Again, not a flicker of his gaze toward the exquisite sculptures, nor a blink of the eye when he passed the multicolored art deco pieces.

His silence frayed at the edges of Mariabella's nerves. She paced the small area behind the front desk in the main gallery, unable to concentrate on the catalog. On anything but why he was here.

She needed to find a way to ask his intentions, without seeming to be asking. When he reentered the main room, she crossed to him. "May I offer you a cup of coffee? Tea?"

"Coffee. Black."

Again, barely a flicker of attention toward her. His mind seemed on something else. She let out a breath of relief as she crossed to the small table holding a carafe of fresh coffee, filled a cup, then loaded a small plate with raspberry thumb-print cookies. She turned—

And found him right behind her.

"Here is…here is your coffee. And these cookies—" Mariabella forced herself to breathe, not to betray the nervous-ness churning in her gut "—were baked by a local chef."

His attention perked at that. "Chef? Does he have a restau-rant?"

"She, and no, Savannah Dawson is the owner of Make it Memorable, the catering company in town."

He nodded, taking that in, but otherwise not responding to the information. Damn, he made her nervous. Nor did he accept a cookie. Instead, he merely sipped at the coffee, watching her. "And who are you?"

He didn't know her name. That meant he wasn't here for her.

Unless the question had been a ruse. No, she doubted that. He didn't look like a reporter, and didn't have the accent that said he'd been sent by her parents.

She'd worried for nothing. He was simply another tourist, albeit, not the most friendly one.

"Mariabella Romano," she said, putting out her hand, and with it, a smile, "gallery—"

"Thank you. That's all I needed." Then he turned and began to walk toward the door. That was it? No return of his name? No explanation why he had come here?

On any other day, she would have let this go. Not everyone who walked through the doors of Harborside Art Gallery walked back out with a piece of art. But this man—

This man had an agenda; she could feel it in her bones. And somewhere on his list, was her gallery.

A surge of fierce protectiveness rose in Mariabella's chest, overriding decorum and tact. "Who are you?"

He paused at the door, his hand on the brass handle, and turned back to face her. A shadow had dropped over his face, from the awning outside, but more, it seemed, from something inside him that he didn't want to tell her. "I'm...an investor."

"Well, sir, if you are thinking you are going to buy this shop, think again." She took a step closer to him, emphasizing her point. Like a terrier guarding her territory. "The owner loves this place. She will never sell."

A smile took over his face, but it held no trace of friendliness, not a hint of niceness. "Oh, I don't want this shop."

Relief flooded Mariabella. She'd read him wrong, he wanted nothing to do with her precious Harborside Art Gallery. Or her. Thank God. "Good."

That smile widened, and dread sunk in Mariabella's gut. And then she knew—she'd gotten it all wrong. She hadn't read him right at all.

"I want the entire block," he said. "By the end of the week would be convenient."

CHAPTER TWO

JAKE LATTIMORE peered down the boardwalk of Harborside, Massachusetts, and knew he didn't see the same thing the other people did. The brightly waving flags on the masts of the few covered boats wintered in the marina didn't beckon to him. The shop windows hawking T-shirts and sunglasses didn't attract his attention. The cafes and coffee shops, their doors swinging open and shut as people drifted in and out, sending tantalizing scented snippets of their menus into the air didn't call to his appetite.

No, what Jake saw wasn't even there. Yet.

Condos. A hotel. Maybe even an amusement park, and down the beach, Jet Ski rentals, parasailing stations.

By this summer, if at all possible, so profits could start rolling in immediately.

In other words, a vacation mecca, one that would expand his—and that of his financial backers—portfolio, and take this sleepy little town up several notches.

He glanced again at the boardwalk, at the festive holiday decorations. The notes of a Christmas song carried on the air as someone walked out of the stained-glass shop across the street. The melody struck a memory in Jake's heart, followed by a sharp pang.

A long time ago, this kind of place, this kind of setting,

would have had him rushing in to buy a gift. Humming along with the song. Thinking—

Well, he didn't think that anymore.

He got back to business. That was the only place heartache couldn't take root. Jake returned his attention to the facts and figures in his head, dismissing the sentimental images around him.

He'd done his research, ran his numbers, and knew without a doubt, Harborside was the perfect location for the next Lattimore Resort. Located along the Eastern seaboard, beneath Boston and above New York, away from the already congested areas of Cape Cod and Martha's Vineyard, the tiny town had been tucked away all this time, hardly noticed by tourists, just waiting for someone like him to come along and see its potential.

This was his specialty—find hidden treasures and turn them into profit machines.

This town would be no different. He'd find each shop owner's price, and pay it. Everyone, Jake had found, had a price.

He wouldn't let a little thing like dollars and cents get in the way of adding this resort to the Lattimore Properties empire. Not with so much on the line.

If he didn't land this deal, and went back to New York empty-handed, he knew what would happen. The whispers would start again. People saying he'd only been promoted to CEO because he was the Lattimore heir. Not because he had the chops to handle a project of this scope.

His father had handed him a challenge, sent him to prove he could achieve the goal on his own, and Jake had no intentions of doing anything but exactly that. He'd worked side by side with Lawrence Lattimore for five years, learning the business from the ground up. In the last year or two, though, his father had begun to lose his magic touch. Lawrence's decision making had become less sound, and the Lattimore Properties balance sheet showed the signs of his uneven hand.

The board began talking forced retirement, so his father had put Jake in charge and given him one directive:

Pull off a miracle.

When Jake returned to New York triumphant, with the Harborside jewel in his back pocket, no one could say the junior Lattimore wasn't up to the task of helming the multi-million dollar corporation. Lattimore Properties would once again be on the way to being the powerful company it had once been, and the downward slide that had begun under the last two years of Lawrence's tenure would be reversed.

"Who are you?"

He turned around and found the brunette from the art gallery standing behind him, fists propped on her hips, green eyes ablaze. She had a fiery demeanor about her, one that spoke of passion, in everything she did.

And that intrigued Jake. Very much.

"I told you. I'm an investor," he said. "In towns like this one."

Her lips pursed. "Let me save you some trouble. No one here is looking to sell their shops."

He arched a brow. "And you know this because…?"

"Because I live here. And I'm the chair of the Community Development Committee. It is my job to know."

He smirked. "And that makes you an expert on every resident?"

"It certainly gives me more insight than you."

He loved her accent. Lilting, lyrical. Even when she argued with him, it sounded like a song.

"You think so?" he said, taking a step closer to her. When he did, he caught a whiff of the floral notes of her perfume. Sweet, light. Tantalizing. "I've seen hundreds of towns like Harborside. And met dozens of people like you, people who have this romanticized vision of their town."

"How dare—"

"What they don't realize is that underneath all that coziness," he went on, "is a struggling seaport town that depends on one season of the year, maybe two, for all its financial needs. How much money do you think the people here make off the tourists who visit between the three months of summer and few weeks of Christmas? Enough to sustain every business and every resident for the other eight months of the year?"

She didn't answer.

"You and I both know it isn't." He gestured toward the town, from one end of the boardwalk to the other. This town— and this woman—didn't even realize what a boon a Lattimore resort would be. How it could bring *twelve* months of financial return. Every resident could benefit from a hotel like this, if they'd just imagine something different. "This place is quaint. Off the beaten path. And that's half the problem. Without something to draw visitors in, and really keep them here year-round, you might as well hang up the Going Out of Business signs now."

She glared at him. "We are doing fine."

He arched a brow. He'd read the statistics on Harborside. Talked to several of the business owners. He knew the tax base, the annual business revenue of each of the cottage industries lining the boardwalk.

They needed a bigger draw for tourists to sustain them— they knew it, he knew it. The only one not facing reality was Mariabella Romano.

"We do not need you," she insisted. "Or your coldhearted analysis of our town. Go find someplace else to expand your control of the world."

"Sorry. I'm here to stay."

The fist went back to her hip. She drew herself up, facing him down. Frustration colored her face. "Do not bother to unpack because you will not find anyone who will sell to you here. We all love Harborside just the way it is."

This woman didn't have any idea what she was up against.

This was going to be fun. A challenge. Something Jake hadn't had in a long time.

His pulse raced, and he found himself looking forward to the days ahead. To interacting with her especially. "I can be pretty persuasive, Miss Romano. We'll see how you feel about holding onto that little gallery after you hear my arguments for selling."

"And I can be terribly stubborn." She flashed him a smile of her own, one that held a hundred watts of power, but not a trace of neighborly greeting. "And you will never persuade me to sell so much as a coloring page to you."

Mariabella stood in her gallery and seethed. To think she'd found that man attractive!

No longer. He clearly had some kind of plans for Harborside and for that, she wouldn't give him so much as a single line in her social notebook. Christmas was only a few days away, surely the man would have somewhere to go—some fool who wanted to spend time with him over the holiday—and he could leave, taking his "investment" ideas with him.

Her cell phone rang, the vibrations sending the slim device dancing across the countertop. Mariabella grabbed the phone, just before it waltzed itself right off the edge. "Hello?"

"*Mia bella!* How are you?" her mother asked in their native language, one that was close to the Italian spoken in the country bordering their own country of Uccelli. Their small little monarchy, almost forgotten in Europe, had its own flavor, a mix of the heritages surrounding it.

"*Mama!*" Immediately, Mariabella also slipped into her home language, the musical syllables falling from her tongue with ease. Mariabella settled onto the seat behind her and held the phone close, wishing she could do the same with her mother. "I'm fine. And you? Papa?"

"Ah, we are about the same as always. Some of us are getting older and more stubborn."

Mariabella sighed. That meant nothing had changed at home. After all this time, Mariabella had hoped maybe her father had softened. Maybe he might begin to see his daughter's need for independence, for a life away from the castle.

He never had. He'd predestined his firstborn's path from the moment she'd been conceived, and never considered another option.

"But…" Her mother paused. "Your father is…"

The hesitation caused an alarm to ring in Mariabella's heart. Her mother, a strong, tall, confident woman never hesitated. Never paused a moment for anything. She had sat steadfast by her husband's side for forty years as he led Uccelli, weathering the roller coaster of changes that came with a monarchy. She'd done it without complaint. Without a moment of wavering from her commitment.

"Papa is what?"

"Having a little heart trouble. Nothing to worry about. We have the best doctors here, *cara*. You know that."

The letter in her back pocket seemed to weigh ten times more than it had this morning. Her father's demand that she return home immediately and take her rightful place in the family. She'd brushed it off when it had arrived, but maybe he'd sent the missive because his illness was worse than her mother was saying. Mariabella sent up a silent prayer for her father's health. He'd always been so hearty, so indestructible. And now—

"Is he going to be all right?"

"He'll be fine. Allegra has been wonderful about stepping in for him."

Her middle sister. The one who had always enjoyed palace life. Of the three Santaro girls, Allegra was the one who loved the state dinners, the conversations with dignitaries, the museum openings and policy discussions. She had sat by their father's side for more state business than any of the Santaro women—and for naught, because as the second-born, she was not first in line for the throne.

"I'm glad she's there," Mariabella said.

"I am, too. Your father misses you, of course, but he is happy to have Allegra with him. For now." Unspoken words hung in her mother's sentence.

Mariabella's father had made it clear he expected his eldest to return and take her place as the heir to the throne. Allegra was merely a placeholder.

Her father had voiced his displeasure several times about Mariabella's choice to leave the castle and pursue her dream of painting. At first, he'd talked of disowning her, until her mother had intervened. He'd relented, and given her a deadline. She'd been given a little over a year and a half—the time between college graduation and her twenty-fifth birthday, in February—and then she had to return.

Or—

Abdicate the crown and give up her family forever.

That was what her father had written. Choose the throne or be disowned. Mariabella hadn't told her mother, and suspected neither had her father.

"Don't worry," her mother said. "It will all be fine."

Easier said than done. She thought of her mother, and how worried Bianca Santaro must be about her husband. The miles between mother and daughter seemed to multiply. "I should come home. Be there for Christmas."

"I wish you could, *cara*. I would like nothing more than to have my daughter with me for Christmas." Her mother sighed, and Mariabella swore she could hear her mother begin to cry.

Half a world away, Mariabella's heart broke, too. Christmas. Her favorite holiday, and Mama's, too. The castle would already be decorated top to bottom with pine garlands and red bows. Christmas trees in every bedroom, set before every fireplace. None of them would top the giant tree, though, the twenty-five-foot beauty the palace's landscaper searched far and wide to find, then set in the center hall.

Every year, her mother personally oversaw the decorating of that tree, draping it in gold ribbons and white angel ornaments. And every year, it had been Mariabella's job to hang the last ornament on that tree. To be the one to pronounce it finished, and then to turn on the lights, washing the entire hall in a soft golden glow, sending a chorus of appreciation through the audience of onlookers brought in from the city.

But not this year. Or last year.

No, she had been here, instead. Leaving her mother to handle Christmas with her sisters. Who had lit the tree? Who had hung that last decoration?

"We will miss you," her mother said softly, "but if you come back, you know what will happen."

Mariabella let out a sigh. "Yes."

She would be expected to step back into her role. To go back to being groomed and primped for a crown she neither wanted nor asked to be given.

Because her father would not be convinced to let her go a second time. She knew that, as well as she knew her own name.

"Stay where you are," her mother said, as if reading her daughter's mind. "I know what this time, as limited as it is, means to you." Her mother's gentle orders were firm.

"Mama—"

"Don't argue with me, Bella. I sent you there. I know your father isn't happy, but I will deal with him. You deserve a life outside of this…birdcage."

That was, indeed, how Mariabella had come to think of life back home. A cage, a gilded one she could look out of, but not escape. People could stare inside, see her and judge her, but never really know her.

Then she'd come to Harborside and felt free, like a real person for the first time in her life.

"I'll call you if anything changes," her mother said, "but I have to say goodbye now. I'm late for a state dinner." She sighed. "You know how the prime minister gets. He hates to sit next to the visiting dignitaries from other countries and make small talk. The man has no social graces."

Mariabella laughed. She certainly didn't miss that part of palace life at all. The stuffy meals, the endless dinner parties. "Have a good time. If you can."

"Oh, I will. I seated the prime minister beside Carlita." Her mother let out a little giggle.

"Mama!"

"Your little sister will talk his ear off about horses and dressage. The man may just fall asleep before the soup arrives."

Mariabella laughed. Oh, how she missed some of those moments. The little fun they'd have behind the scenes, the laughter with her sisters, her mother. "I love you, Mama."

Her mother paused, and Mariabella could hear the catch in her voice when Bianca Santaro spoke again. "I love you too, *cara.*"

They ended the call, and Mariabella closed her phone, but held tight to the cell for a long time, as if she could hold her parents in the small electronic device. For a moment, she was back there, in her mother's bedroom, sitting on the chaise lounge, watching her mother get ready for a party. She saw Bianca brushing her hair, heard her humming a tune. Then she'd always turn and open her arms, welcoming her eldest daughter into her embrace. With Mama, there had always been time for a hug, a kiss, one more story before bed.

How she missed those days.

Even if she returned to Uccelli, those moments were gone forever. When her father stepped down, Mariabella was expected to fill the king's shoes. Which meant every day of her life in the palace had been spent grooming her for the throne.

If she returned, she'd be stepping right back into the middle of the very expectations she'd run from.

Her role as future queen.

Mariabella sighed. As much as she missed her parents and her homeland, she couldn't go back. Returning came at too steep a price.

Freedom.

Carmen came bursting through the door. Mariabella slipped her phone into her purse and with that movement, brought her mind back into work mode. She would dwell on the events across the world when she was alone.

"You will *never* believe what just happened when I was in Savannah's shop." Carmen slammed her hand on the counter in emphasis.

"An incredibly rude man offered to buy her place, yes?"

Carmen's jaw dropped. "How'd you know?"

"He was here, a few minutes ago. And wanted my gallery, too."

"The gallery, too?"

Mariabella nodded. "He wants the whole block. For some kind of 'investment.'" She put air quotes and a hint of sarcasm around the last word.

"In Harborside." Carmen said it as a statement, not a question. "That same cute guy we saw earlier."

Mariabella nodded again. "He is not so cute close-up, you know. Not when he is trying to turn our town into some kind of circus for tourists."

"Savannah tried to ask him questions, to find out what his plans are, but he didn't tell her more than boo." Carmen moved to the back of the counter and stuffed her purse underneath. "He's a big mystery man. I still think he's kind of cute, even if his plans might be diabolical. Or, maybe perfectly harmless. We'd have to find out more to know for sure."

"Well, cuteness will not win me over. Or convince me to sell."

Carmen shot her a grin. "You'd be surprised, Mariabella. Stronger women than you have been done in by blue eyes and a nice smile."

Mariabella glanced out the window again at the town she had come to love, to think of as her home. "Not me. And if this man thinks I will fall apart that easily, he can think again." She tucked a strand of hair behind her ear, then returned her attention to the catalog. "Because he has no idea who he is dealing with."

Truly, he had no idea. And neither did anyone in this town.

When the door of the limo shut, the sights and sounds of Harborside dropped away, leaving Jake alone with his thoughts.

Never a place he wanted to be.

He pulled out his PDA and started reading e-mails, at the same time powering up his laptop and scrolling through the reports he'd downloaded earlier about the town. The back of his limo had been his mobile office for as long as he could remember. The automobile had a satellite connection, to give him a link to the Web whenever he needed it, and a small desk installed between the seats for his laptop. Some days, it seemed as if he spent more time in this car than he did at home. If one could call his apartment in New York a home at all.

The passenger's side door opened and another man slid in. "Do you ever stop?"

Jake didn't look up. "I thought you went to lunch."

"I did. I'm done. Unlike you, I took a break from my job. I even made some friends."

Jake stopped working to stare at William Mason, his best friend and chauffeur, who had loosened his tie, and looked as relaxed as an out-of-town uncle at Thanksgiving dinner. Today, Will was sporting a red tie featuring reindeer leaping across the front, a glaring contrast to the white dress shirt with green pinstripes.

No one would call Will conventional. More than once, people had asked Jake why he didn't insist his chauffeur wear a more traditional dark suit and muted tie. Jake told them that if he wanted a conventional chauffeur, he would have hired one out of the phone book.

With Will, he'd gotten something no one else would have brought to the job—

Honesty. Loyalty. Friendship.

Three things Jake didn't seem to have in abundance, not in the vicious world of Lattimore Properties.

Will grinned at Jake, waiting for an answer. His sandy brown hair had been mussed by the wind, his cheeks reddened. He looked like he'd had…fun.

"How could you make friends?" Jake asked. "We've been in this town less than an hour."

"It doesn't take days to say, 'Hey, I'm Will, who are you?'"

"You didn't."

"I did." He shrugged. "Well, maybe something close to that. It would do you good to do the same."

Jake snorted. He could just see himself going into the local diner and introducing himself to a perfect stranger. Will had the affable personality to pull that off. He always had. Jake…well, Jake didn't. "Why would I? I'm here to complete a business deal, not win a popularity contest."

Will leaned forward, propping his elbows on his knees. "Have you ever found it odd that your best friend is a chauffeur? That you spend the last few days before Christmas working obsessively, instead of cuddling by a fire with some hot woman? Which is where I would be, I might add, at home, with my wife, if you weren't keeping me on the road, working more than Santa does. My wife, by the way, has learned to curse your name in three different languages because of the hours I work."

"I pay you well enough."

"Sometimes it's about time, not money, Jake." Will put his hands up before Jake could voice another objection. "I'm just saying, you might want to try the whole staying-home-with-a-girlfriend thing sometime."

"One—" Jake put out a finger "—my best friend is my chauffeur because you have been my best friend since we were kids, and I wanted to hire someone I trusted to drive me around. Especially since I'm going to spend half the day with you. Two—" he put out another finger "—I don't need more friends—"

"One friend is just so many you thought you might lose count after that?"

"And three—" Jake went on, putting out a third finger "—I'm not at home in front of a fire with a hot woman because I'm not dating anyone."

"Exactly the problem. You're going to be thirty this year, Jake. Don't you ever wonder what life would be like if you had one?"

"Had one what?"

"A life. Outside of that." Will waved at the PDA and laptop. "Inanimate objects aren't the most affectionate beings on the planet, in case you haven't noticed."

Jake scowled and ignored Will. He'd had what Will was talking about once before—had even expected by this age to be going home to a wife, just as his best friend did at the end of the day.

But fate had another future in mind. And Jake wasn't about to risk that kind of pain again. Once was enough.

"All I'm saying," Will persisted, "is that it's Christmas and it might be nice if you gave yourself a present this year."

"No one buys themselves gifts on Christmas. Or at least they're not supposed to."

"I meant a *present*. A life outside of work. Someone to wake up to." Will leaned forward and waited until Jake's gaze met his. "You had that once. And it sure would be nice to see you that happy again. Real nice." Will got out of the car and shut the door.

"That's where you're wrong," Jake muttered to the closed door. "That kind of happiness doesn't happen twice." And he went back to where he found peace.

In those inanimate objects that didn't leave him. And didn't die.

CHAPTER THREE

"HE'S back," Carmen said, tugging on Mariabella's sleeve.

Mariabella turned away from the customer she was talking to, and saw the stranger from earlier cross by her front windows. Not him again.

She'd hoped she'd made her feelings clear this morning. Between that, and Savannah's refusal to sell, the man should have let by now, realizing his "investments" weren't welcome in Harborside.

Apparently, he was a slow learner.

"Carmen, can you help this lady find a painting for over her sofa?" Mariabella said, gesturing to the middle-aged woman beside her, who had entered the gallery just a few minutes earlier. "She is looking for something with tones of rose and cream."

"Certainly. Right this way," Carmen said, pointing toward the second room of the gallery. "We have some singularly cool sunsets that I think will be perfect for what you want."

"Wonderful!" the customer exclaimed. "I have this huge blank wall in the great room just crying out for something spectacular."

Carmen grinned. "If you want spectacular, you've come to the right place."

The woman followed Carmen into the next room, the two

of them chatting about the exquisite sunsets each had seen in Harborside, while Mariabella headed out of the gallery and in the direction she'd seen the stranger go earlier.

She didn't see him. But she did see a long, black limousine parked across the street, in the public parking lot.

His, she was sure.

The driver sat behind the wheel, sedate and patient. Probably bored out of his mind, waiting on Mr. Investment to finish his fruitless quest for real estate.

"Mariabella!"

She turned at the sound of the familiar voice. "Miss Louisa. How are things with you?"

The older lady hurried over to Mariabella, her portly dachshund tottering at her feet, his four legs struggling to walk underneath the thick red Santa coat Louisa Brant had buckled around the long, short-haired dog. "Have you heard the latest? About that man trying to buy up our property?"

"I have. And I am not selling."

"I was thinking about it. You know how I hate the winters here. It sure would be nice to retire in Florida. Take me and my little George here down to a sunny little place for the rest of our days." She let out a long sigh, and clasped her thick wool coat tighter, as if just the thought had her feeling winter's chill a little more.

"If you do, who would head the women's tea every New Year?"

Louisa patted Mariabella's hand. "Now, dear, you know that's hardly my doing at all. You're the one who takes care of all of us in this town. Why you're practically a one-woman organizing dynamo. I don't know how little Harborside existed before you came along. You've got us holding dances, and teas, and summer regattas and all kinds of things. This place has become a regular hotbed of activity." Louisa laughed. "Or maybe a hot water bottle, considering how tiny we are."

Mariabella smiled. "I am not doing this alone. I have a lot of help."

"Every spear has a point, you know." Louisa's dog gave a tug on the leash, straining toward the park on the other side of the street. "Well, I must be going."

"Miss Louisa—"

The older woman turned back. "Yes, dear?"

"Promise me you'll talk to me before you consider selling to that man. We businesses in Harborside have to stick together. Surely, as a group, we'll be fine."

Louisa smiled, but her smile shook a little. "Of course, dear."

Then she was gone, the dachshund's tail wagging happily. He seemed to be the only one pleased with the way the conversation had ended.

Mariabella redoubled her determination to rid Harborside of this interloper. As long as he was here, people would continue to be upset and worried about their futures. Louisa loved her shop and had never mentioned retiring before today. Once this stranger was gone, everyone would calm down again and business would return to normal. She returned her attention to his limo, and to the license plate.

Okay, so now she knew two things. He was wealthy. And he was from out of town, but not so far that the distance couldn't be driven. She hurried down the sidewalk and peered around a telephone pole at the limo's license plates.

New York. She started memorizing the numbers, intending to call Reynaldo and have him—

"Checking me out?"

Mariabella jumped at the sound of his voice, and pivoted back. The man stood a mere two feet behind her, close enough that she could see the shades of cobalt flecked with gold in his eyes. See the sharp angle of his jaw, catch the woodsy scent of his cologne. Notice him three times more than she had earlier today.

But not be affected one iota. At all.

"Yes." Damn. She hated having to admit that to him. He'd startled her and she couldn't come up with another excuse.

"I'm no criminal, I assure you, and I have only the best intentions."

"Depends on who you ask, and how you interpret your intentions."

A smirk raised one side of his lips. "Touché."

She glanced back over her shoulder at the limo, trying again to memorize the numbers on the license plate. If this man wasn't going to tell her who he was or why he was here, she would find out for herself.

"Planning on playing detective?" he asked, reading her mind.

"No." Mariabella was not much better at lying than she was with idioms, and a flush filled her cheeks.

"I'll save you the trouble of bothering the local police chief. Not that he seems to have much to do in a town this size." The man reached into his suit jacket, withdrew a slim silver case and produced a business card. "Jacob Lattimore, CEO of Lattimore Properties."

She took the embossed white linen card. It was simple and clean, giving only a New York address and an office telephone number. Nothing that told her who he was, or why he had picked her town—and she *had* come to think of Harborside as hers, ever since the little community had welcomed her, without reservation—and what he intended to do here. "What kind of properties?"

"Resorts. Vacation properties. Condos, hotels."

Mariabella's jaw dropped. "Harborside is not that kind of town."

Another smile, the kind she was beginning to hate. "It can be, once the owners of the shops along this boardwalk see how a Lattimore resort can transform this place into a money machine for everyone." He waved a hand down the length of the boardwalk, as if he were a magician, making all of it disappear, and in its place, creating a gargantuan eyesore of a hotel.

Thus turning Harborside into a cartoon version of what it was right now, something he'd stamp on some silly brochure and market to travelers, as a "destination."

Panic gripped Mariabella. He couldn't be serious. If he did this, he would destroy the very refuge she had found. Ruin the small little town that had wrapped around her, safe and secure, like the cottage she'd been renting. Turning Harborside into a resort town would not only change the very fabric of the community, but worse, it would attract the very people she had tried so hard to avoid all these years—

Her peers. Her family. And worst of all, the media.

If any of the above came to Harborside, her biggest nightmare would come to life.

And her secrets would be exposed.

Her world here would be ripped apart, and she would be forced to return to the one she had left. Forced to step up and take her rightful place beside her mother and father. And eventually, *on* the throne.

No. She wasn't ready, not yet. She had more time, not much, but a little, and she needed it desperately to have this…

Normalcy. Peace. Anonymity.

And then, maybe, yes, she could go back to the birdcage. But on her terms, not Jacob Lattimore's.

She had to stop this man. Had to convince the other business owners on the Community Development Committee to hold firm, and refuse to sell. Surely, as a group, they would have the strength necessary to fend off his offers, no matter how tempting he made his financial proposals. Harborside would be preserved, just as it was, and Mariabella could be sure her town would never change.

"I understand you see this town as some kind of—" he waved vaguely "—step back in time. A little bit of nostalgia.

But nostalgia, unfortunately, doesn't always make money. You have to face reality, Miss Romano, you and the other business owners. Travelers want more on their vacations than a pretty view."

She stared at him and fumed. "There are some people who want a quiet place to stay, not a zoo."

"But not enough people. Your town is struggling, and the sooner you face the fact that you need a property like mine to shake things up, the better off everyone will be." He glanced around at the garland draped between the streetlights and the crimson bows hanging on the storefronts. "No amount of Christmas spirit—" the last two words slipped off his tongue with a taste of sarcasm "—will mask the scent of desperation."

"No one here is desperate."

He arched a brow. A silent disagreement.

Mariabella wanted to throw a thousand arguments in his face. Except, there were a few businesses along the boardwalk that had struggled in recent months, a fact she could not overlook, no matter how hard she tried. A few who would jump at the chance to retire, or find a buyer for buildings that housed inventory that hadn't sold in months. Harborside, like many seaside towns, struggled to compete for tourist dollars, and the members of the Community Development Committee had been brainstorming for months ways to increase traffic flow to the tiny town.

Jake Lattimore would not be the answer, no matter what. The town was not that desperate. To get rid of him, however, meant Mariabella needed to do whatever it took to protect what she loved.

Whatever it took.

Jake watched Mariabella Romano hurry down the sidewalk—in the opposite direction of her gallery—and had to admit he was intrigued.

She hated him.

And he liked that.

Clearly, he needed therapy, or a drink.

He opted for the drink. Faster, cheaper and easier. And in the opposite direction of the limo, where William had undoubtedly witnessed the entire exchange, and was waiting to offer his two cents about fireplaces and Christmas "presents."

Jake didn't need to hear that. Didn't need any more advice from well-meaning people who told him to move on with his life. He'd spent five years moving on—by working.

He gave Mariabella one last glance—she was beautiful, a tall woman with curves in all the right places—before ducking into the Clamshell Tavern. Blues music greeted him, along with a nautical décor. White painted pine walls, navy blue vinyl seats and life rings hanging on the walls printed with the restaurant's name.

All kitsch, all the time. Jake tried hard not to roll his eyes.

"Table for...one?" the hostess asked, peering around him, as if she thought he had a friend hiding in his pocket.

"I'll just sit at the bar. Thanks." He pushed through the glass doors and into the lounge area, which featured more of the same décor.

Good thing he rarely got seasick.

"What'll it be?" asked the bartender, a rotund man in a red-and-white striped shirt, something that was probably supposed to be pirate style, but came off looking more like barber shop clown.

"Your best vodka. Dry. Two olives."

The bartender nodded, then turned and mixed the drink. A minute later, he slid the glass in front of Jake and headed down to the opposite side of the bar.

An unappetizing mix of nuts and something resembling pretzels sat in a bowl to Jake's left. He pushed it away. What he wouldn't give for a tray with a good aged gouda, accompanied by a pear and cinnamon relish. Maybe a salad with grilled endive, apples and glazed fennel. Some *real* food, not this stuff that came out of a bag thrown together in a factory.

If he were back in New York, he'd have any gourmet food he wanted at his beck and call. He'd attended dinners, parties, openings, dining on the best the local chefs had to offer.

Lately, though, those platters had been leaving him with a feeling of emptiness, as if he could eat and eat and never have his fill. Or, as if every meal had too much fluff, and not enough substance.

Restlessness had invaded his sleep, his thought patterns—and at the worst possible time. He needed to be focused, aware, in order to execute this deal and prove himself to the company, while also boosting the bottom line.

Once the Harborside project was underway, surely that hole in his gut would fill.

It would.

"Well, you sure know how to rile people up around here, don't you?" A man slid onto the stool beside Jake. He had a shock of white hair, and wore a long flannel shirt over a pair of thick khakis. He looked about sixty-five, maybe seventy, and sat at the bar with the ease of someone who had been there a time or twenty. "The usual, Tony."

The bartender nodded, reached in the cooler and popped the top on a beer. He slid the dark beer down the bar to the older man, with a friendly hello, then went back to washing glasses.

"So, why are you doing it?" he said.

Jake pivoted toward the other man. "Are you talking to me?"

"Do you see someone else in this bar who's got the whole town in a tizzy?" The older man arched a brow, then put out his hand. "Name's Zeke Carson, short for Ezekiel, though no one calls me that and gets an answer. I'm the newspaper editor for this town, except our paper's more like a newsletter." He chuckled. "Small-town living. You gotta love it."

Jake shook with Zeke. Will would have been proud to see Jake making a friend, of sorts. An acquaintance, really, but at least he could go back to the limo and reassure Will he hadn't remained a hermit.

"Jake Lattimore." No sense keeping his name a secret any longer. Mariabella Romano had undoubtedly set Zeke on him, another guard dog to chase him out of town. If she hadn't already nailed up WANTED: DEAD OR ALIVE posters around town with his name and face on them, Jake figured it was only a matter of time.

Instead of annoying him, as something like that might on any other day, with any other project, it had him even more intrigued.

Charged up. Ready to rise to whatever challenge Mariabella threw his way.

He hadn't felt that way in a while. It had to be the Harborside project, not the woman, that had him feeling so challenged—because that was where his energies lay right now, and where they should lay.

Despite what Will had said, Jake had no intentions of entangling himself in another relationship. Especially not at this time of year.

He stared down into his drink, the frosted clear liquid a mirror to his heart. Five years ago this month.

Five years. Some days, it felt like five minutes.

Zeke took a sip of his beer. "I know who you are. Knew before you got here."

Jake arched a brow, pushing the other thoughts aside. "You did?"

"I may edit a small-town paper, Mr. Lattimore, but that doesn't make me stupid. I read the financial pages. I know all about your company, and I knew you were looking for some coastal properties to add to your portfolio." Zeke grinned. "Read it in an issue last month."

Jake nodded. "I'm impressed."

Zeke tipped his beer in Jake's direction. "I am, too. You're one of those wunderkinds. Rocketship to the top and all that."

Jake shrugged. He hated that label. Maybe he should color his hair gray. That might stop people from commenting on his status at the top of the company before he'd celebrated his thirtieth birthday.

"Must make your dad proud."

"Something like that," Jake said. He tugged his PDA out of his jacket pocket and began thumbing through his e-mails, hoping Zeke would get the hint and stop talking.

He didn't.

"'Cept your dad's had some troubles lately, I read. Company's struggling a little."

"It's fine," Jake said.

"And you…wasn't there something that happened a few years back…?" Zeke rubbed at his chin. "Can't remember what it was. Some accident and—"

"I'm not here to discuss my personal life, Mr. Carson." The words clipped off Jake's tongue. Harsher than he'd intended.

"Zeke, please."

"Zeke."

The other man didn't say anything for a minute. Jake hoped he'd given up on the conversation. Zeke drank his beer, watched the game on television. Then he shifted in his seat toward Jake again. "So, why Harborside?"

Jake thought of cutting off the conversation, then reconsidered. Perhaps talking to the local newspaper editor would be a good idea. Could garner some good press for Lattimore Properties. "You read the financial pages. You tell me, Zeke."

Zeke thought a second, clearly pleased to have his own brain picked. "It's undiscovered. Centrally located. Has just enough beach for one of your fancy-shmancy hotels, but not so much sand that the place'll get crowded with big bucks homeowners and their McMansions."

"So far, so good." Jake pushed the PDA aside, and reached for his drink, but didn't sip it.

"Let's see…" Zeke leaned forward, his gaze meeting Jake's. "You like a challenge, and Harborside is one. We're New Englanders. Stubborn, set in our ways. Not much for change of any kind. Hence, the big challenge. Why pick an unpopulated area, with no one to push around and bully when you corporate giants can go after this place and have a little fun while you're at it?"

Was that how people saw him and the company? As a bully? "I offer a fair price for the land. The buildings. There are no strong-arm tactics at work."

"Maybe that's how you see it." Zeke raised his beer, took a sip, then put it down again. "You oughta read the paper more often. Sometimes it gives you the side of the story you're not seeing."

Jake had little use for the media. He found most reporters intrusive, annoying and hardly interested in anything other than a sensationalized headline to splash across their pages. He called them when he needed press for a new launch, tried to stay under their radar the rest of the time. "I'm only concerned about the business section, Mr. Carson," he said.

"Zeke, please. Mr. Carson makes me sound like my father, and he's *old*."

Jake laughed. Despite everything, he found he liked Zeke. "Zeke it is."

Zeke finished his beer, then slid off the stool. He placed a firm hand on Jake's shoulder and met his gaze, with light blue eyes that had seen and experienced a lot of life. "I'm not here to tell you if your plans for this town are good or bad. There are arguments on both sides of the fence for that, and enough people to battle it out to start World War Three. But take some advice from a young-at-heart newspaperman." He glanced around the bar, not to see if anyone was listening, but as if he was trying to include the Clamshell Tavern in his case. "There are people whose whole lives are Harborside, and what you're proposing will turn their lives upside-down. I've seen and read about the kinds of hotels your company builds, and they may not be the right ones for here. Change isn't always a good thing, and you have to think about what's going to happen *after* you build this thing and head back to your big glass office in New York."

"What do you mean?"

Zeke pointed out the window, at a ship cutting through the cold ocean. "See that boat? It's plowing forward, on to its destination. It doesn't think about what happens in its wake. What the propeller is doing to the fish, the seaweed, all the flora and fauna living in the dark water underneath. That's why those channel markers are out there, to keep the boats in line. Keep them from destroying nature."

"And I'm the big bad boat, ripping up the seaweed in my wake, is that it?"

"You can choose to be, or you can choose to be a sailboat, leaving the ocean more or less as you found it." Zeke gave Jake's shoulder one last pat. "Think about it."

The old man left, and Jake turned back to his drink. Well, he'd been given a warning and a philosophy lesson, all at once. Seemed this town didn't want him around. Jake didn't care. He saw a business opportunity here, one he needed, on a professional and a personal level, and he had no intentions of walking away from it.

Outside the window, he saw Mariabella Romano striding up the boardwalk toward the Clamshell Tavern. As he watched her, he realized something he hadn't noticed before.

She had a way about her that didn't seem to fit this town. Heck, this world. It was more than the accent, the exotic beauty. She carried herself straight and tall, spine absolutely in line, as if she were balancing a book on her head and her stride—well, that could almost be called…

Regal. Yeah, that was the word for it.

Maybe she'd gone to one of those finishing schools or grown up in a wealthy home. Either way, she didn't fit his image of a small-town art gallery owner.

She entered the tavern, then the bar, her fiery gaze lighting on him as if he were the devil incarnate. A grin slid across his face. "Miss Romano. Just the person I wanted to talk to. I have an offer for you."

"And I have one for you." She crossed her arms over her chest. "I would like to pay you to leave Harborside, and find another town for your hotel. Name your price, Mr. Lattimore, and I will pay it."

Just when Jake had thought things couldn't get more interesting—

They did.

CHAPTER FOUR

IT WAS an incredible risk, and Mariabella knew it.

But if money was what it would take to rid Harborside of Jake Lattimore, then she would take that chance. She had resources she could dip into—not an endless pool, of course, but probably more than enough to get this man to change his course. "So," she said, "what is your price?"

He chuckled. "You couldn't pay it. Not unless you have a few masterpieces in the back of your gallery that I don't know about."

"I have the resources I need to make this offer," she said, leaving the issue of where the money was coming from out of the discussion.

He leaned an elbow on the bar and studied her, clearly amused. She shifted under his scrutiny. How long had it been since a man stared at her like that, with such clear interest?

Not just the kind that said he found her intriguing as a woman, but that he saw her as a puzzle, something he wanted to study, read, get to know better.

A charge of electricity ran through the air, and Mariabella's stance faltered. She locked her ankles, then her knees, then her spine. Then her resolve.

This man would not affect her.

At all.

"I have to admit, this is an offer I've never heard before."

His grin widened. She didn't respond to the smile. "I'll have to think about it."

Good. Maybe he'd give her a figure and she could settle this. He met her gaze. "I've thought about it."

"For what, three seconds?"

"I'm not a man who takes long to make a decision."

She let out a gust. "That, I figured."

"And I've decided…" He paused. "No amount of money is going to change my mind."

"What?" Mariabella stared at him. Surely, she'd heard him wrong. "Surely, there must be—"

"No. Sorry."

Just like that. Two words. He'd refused her offer without even giving it serious consideration. Mariabella resisted the urge to shout in frustration. Surely there had to be something that would convince this man Harborside wasn't the right town for him.

"Why are you sure this town is the place for your hotel?"

"I've done my research and the numbers add up."

She shook her head. "So that is what Harborside is to you, a bunch of numbers?"

"Of course. I'm a businessman, Miss Romano. Only a fool would build a project using emotion as his barometer."

And in that answer, Mariabella knew the key to ridding the town of one Jake Lattimore. If she could get him to see the heart of Harborside, make him understand that this town mattered to the people who lived here, people like her, then perhaps, just perhaps, she could get Jake Lattimore to build an emotional connection with Harborside.

And then he couldn't possibly go through with his plans to ruin her sanctuary.

Right?

Maybe. She saw only one flaw in her plan. A man like Jake Lattimore probably had no heart, and wouldn't be swayed by an emotional appeal like this. Either way, she intended to try. After all, she'd fallen in love with this town on her first visit.

Maybe he would, too.

"Then I have another offer for you," she said, and her gut tightened as the words slipped out of her throat. This one was even riskier than the first offer she'd made. This one involved opening herself up to another person, making herself vulnerable. Risking—

Her identity.

No, she could be careful. She wouldn't talk about herself, only Harborside.

"And what are you offering this time?" he said with a smirk. "A famous sculpture in addition to cash on the table?"

"No." She took a step forward, ignoring the butterflies raising havoc in her gut. "I am offering me."

Jake had heard her wrong.

He was sure he had. No way Mariabella had just offered herself as a payment to send him packing. Although, stranger things did happen in business, and maybe she was serious. No. She couldn't be. This woman was too...

Uppercrust. Too proper in her demeanor, her language, her movements, to be the kind who'd sleep with a man merely to get him to call off a business deal. Right?

"You're seriously offering yourself?"

She nodded. "As your personal tour guide of Harborside. To show you the reasons why it's perfect the way it is."

He chuckled, half relieved she didn't mean she'd intended to sleep with him and half disappointed. "Why it doesn't need the big, bad hotelier, you mean."

"Exactly."

He considered that, his gaze connecting with hers as he thought over her offer. It was insane. He never got personal on a deal. Hadn't his father taught him that? When they got personal, the company suffered. It was only by staying on the corporate track, thinking with dollars and cents, that profits soared and megacorporations got built.

Lawrence Lattimore had drilled that lesson into his son for years. Had repeated it over and over again as he'd trained and groomed his son to take over the CEO spot. Don't get to know the locals, don't try to think about the people. Concentrate solely on the bottom line. Lawrence had lamented, several times, the mistakes he'd made in letting his heart rule his brain. Don't do it, he'd warned his son. Think like a CEO, not a person.

Get in, get the papers signed, then move on to the next town, the next project.

If Jake agreed to this, he'd be breaking the one sacred rule he'd been taught—never mix business with pleasure. Only an idiot would tell himself that taking the scenic route through Harborside beside a woman as beautiful as Mariabella Romano would be anything other than pleasurable.

He should be smart. He should leave this bar, get back to work on convincing the locals to sell their shops to him, so the plans for the hotel and condos could move forward. He had too much at stake to screw up this deal. Once Harborside was secure, Lattimore Properties could begin to return to the profitability it had enjoyed, and Jake would have earned the respect of the board.

Then he could fly to San Francisco. Fill his days with the next property. And the one after that. He kept hoping that one day, he'd finally find enough—

Enough work. Enough time away from his apartment. Enough time spent with those inanimate objects Will chided him about.

Enough—

To forget. To be able to move on. To have a life again.

Jake opened his mouth to say no to Mariabella, to tell her

he didn't have the time for such a senseless excursion, then his gaze connected with Mariabella's deep green eyes. Heat grew in the space between them, an awareness uncoiling like a rope. For a second, he saw only her. Not his job, not the papers waiting in his briefcase.

Just her eyes. Her smile.

How long had it been since he'd connected with someone? With a woman, at that? How long had it been since he'd anticipated spending time with a woman and thought of something other than work?

Too damned long.

He rose, put out his hand and closed the gap. When she took his hand, a surge of electricity ran through him.

Before his better judgment could say no, he said, "It would be my pleasure."

"Better button on," Mariabella said, "for our first stop."

"Button on?" Jake gave her a curious look.

She cursed her phrasing. It took a second for her brain to make the connections and find the right word choices, a fact she blamed entirely on her richly appointed surroundings. Plush leather interior, heated seats, even a small wine refrigerator at her feet. When Jake Lattimore bought a limo, he apparently did it right. Christmas music flowed softly from the stereo system, the sound of such high quality she could swear Jake had an entire orchestra in the trunk of the limousine.

She had, of course, been in a limo before. Hundreds of times. Not in the past year and a half, but her entire childhood and teen years had been spent living the life everyone expected of her. That meant dressing the way they thought she should. Living where they thought she should. And yes, even riding in what they thought she should. All to give off the proper image, because Lord knew, her life had been all about images.

Whether or not those images matched the woman inside hadn't mattered, not as long as the people were happy.

"I meant button up," Mariabella said, pushing the thoughts to the side. "It's cold outside, and you do not want to get sick."

He chuckled. "I haven't been sick in years, and even if I was, I wouldn't take the day off. I think my father would have a heart attack if I called in sick."

"Really?"

"I mean that rhetorically. He's gotten so used to seeing me at work every day, that if I ever stopped, it would be a shock. He counts on me to be there, because I'm the one taking over the company now that he's retiring and…" Jake sighed. "There are just a lot of expectations that come with being the one in charge. Like no sick days."

"I know what you mean. I used to be in a similar situation." She should have stopped herself before she said that. What was it with this man? Every time she was around him, she said more than she meant to, as if the brakes on her mouth stopped working.

He arched a brow, studying her. "How so?"

The limo pulled to a stop, and Mariabella tugged on the silver handle the instant the locks clicked. "Here we are!" She stepped out of the car so fast, the door nearly slammed into the chauffeur's gut. "Sorry."

"Happens all the time, ma'am." He gave her a grin. "Though most of the time, it's women running *to* Mr. Lattimore, not *from* him. I'm Will Mason, by the way, should you need anything."

Jake came around the car and gave the chauffeur a clap on the shoulder. "Are you filling her head with nonsense about me, Will?"

"Of course not." Will leaned toward Mariabella. "Only the truth."

Jake laughed, an easy sound that she hadn't heard from him before. "As long as you don't mention that time in Tallahassee, you'll stay on the payroll."

Will made a motion of zipping his lip, then winked at Mariabella.

"*William…*"

"I wouldn't dare tell her how you paraglided into that poor woman's hotel room." Will made a surprised *O* and covered his mouth, but his twinkling eyes belied the gesture. The two men clearly had a more friendly relationship than simply employer and employee. Mariabella had never seen any of the palace staff ever talk to her father like that. If they had, they would have been dismissed on the spot.

She envied Will and Jake's camaraderie. If she'd had a friend in the palace like that, even one, maybe all those long, boring days would have been more tolerable.

"He was quite the flyer that night," Will added. "I think he chose the wrong career. Should have been in the air force, instead of business."

Mariabella glanced over at Jake. "That desperate to see your date?"

Jake scowled. "More like I had troubles with the controls. First time in the air."

"Don't let him fool you. Mr. Lattimore has an adventurous streak that he keeps under wraps," Will said.

"Remind me again why I sign your checks," Jake said.

"Because I'm the only one who can keep up with you on a Jet Ski." Will shivered a bit in the cold. "When I can get you to take time to ride one, which better be soon after making me come to this clone of Alaska."

Mariabella watched the exchange, both surprised and amused. Surprised because Will mentioned that Jake had an adventurous side. Somehow, she couldn't quite see that with this business-only CEO. Secondly, amused because the two men had a repartee that spoke of a long-time friendship, something that showed another aspect to Jake Lattimore.

An aspect she could like, under different circumstances.

"And you can beat me at poker, Will," Jake chuckled again, "but we won't talk about that, either."

"Of course not." Will grinned, then disappeared back inside the driver's side of the limousine, leaving Jake and Mariabella alone. Five minutes ago, this tour of Harborside had seemed like a good idea, but now, out of the cocoon of her gallery, and far from the company of friends, Mariabella's awareness of Jake Lattimore doubled. The way he stood at least a head taller than her, how his shoulders filled his coat, defining the strong *V* of his torso. And most of all, how long it had been since she'd been kissed. Held. Loved.

Jake closed his cashmere overcoat, and fastened the buttons, as the winter wind off the ocean began to kick up. "Well, we're here. At the first stop on your guided tour. What exactly are we seeing?"

Get back to the point, Mariabella. Harborside, not him.

"That." She pointed up, at the top of the black-and-white oblong building beside them.

"The Harborside Lighthouse? I've seen lighthouses before, Miss Romano and—"

"You haven't seen this one." She grabbed his hand, intending only to lead him inside and cut off his protests, but when she touched him, a rush of heat ran through her. She jerked back, and hurried over to the door of the lighthouse. Away from him, and away from the temptation touching him seemed to bring. A quick double knock, then she stepped back to wait.

"Why aren't we going inside?"

"We have to wait for Cletus." She didn't turn around, even though she could sense Jake right behind her. Inches away. The heat of his body mingled with hers. And it felt nice.

Too nice.

"Cletus?" he asked.

"The lighthouse keeper."

"There are still people who do that?"

The note of surprise in his voice made her turn around. As soon as she did, she regretted it, because Jake was so close—the stoop was small, after all, only about three feet square, and sharing the space meant close quarters. "Harborside is a traditional town," she said. Concentrate on the tour, not him.

"Old-fashioned. Behind the times."

"Happy just the way it is."

"If you say so." He gave the rocky shoals around the lighthouse a passing glance, clearly not seeing what Mariabella did. The isolation of the area, the sweet quiet. The utter peace. "I thought lighthouses sat on rocks in the middle of the water."

"Some do. And some are on the coast, used to guide the boats into the harbor. To find their way home." The last word escaped her on a breath. Home.

When she had to return to Uccelli in two more months, if she ever had a chance to come back to Harborside, would that lighthouse guide her back? Most of all, would Harborside still feel like home, still wrap around her with the same comfort?

The door opened on creaky hinges, and a small wizened man peeked his head out. "Better be a damned good reason for you to bother me in the middle of the day," he said.

"And hello to you, too, Cletus," Mariabella said. "Glad to see you are in such a happy mood, what with Christmas just around the corner."

The older man scowled. "Where's my muffins?"

Mariabella propped a fist on her hip. "They will be here Christmas morning, and not a day sooner. And only if you promise to be nice, and come to Christmas Eve dinner with the rest of the family."

Cletus grumbled something under his breath, but opened the door and motioned the two of them inside. "Who's this character?"

"Jake Lattimore, this is Cletus Ridgemont, who for some reason I do not understand—" she winked at Cletus "—did not want to serve on the Welcome New Neighbors to Harborside Committee." Mariabella grinned, then waved between the two men. "Jake is here from out of town, and he wanted to see the view from the lighthouse."

Cletus looked Jake up and down, as if assessing his worthiness to enter the lighthouse. "You treating her nice?"

"Uh, yes, sir." Under Cletus's scrutiny, Jake had a moment of being back in high school, and enduring the inquisition by his dates' fathers. Only this wasn't a date and Cletus wasn't Mariabella's father. Was he? She'd mentioned family. Surely this odd character had no relation to her.

"Good. Our Mariabella deserves the best." Cletus wagged a finger at Jake. "You two go on up, but don't let him touch nothin'. He don't look like the lighthouse-keeper type and I don't want him breakin' my light."

Mariabella grinned. "Thank you, Cletus. We will only be a minute."

"Is that all you're wearing?" Cletus asked, motioning toward Mariabella's white wool coat.

"I'll be fine."

"You take my coat," he said, grabbing a thick khaki parka from a hook by the door. "And you wear it, you hear? Don't need you getting sick before Christmas. Who'll make my muffins if you do?"

Mariabella smiled, then shrugged into the second coat over her own. "Thank you."

Cletus only scowled, but Jake could see a softening in the man's features. He turned away, grumble-grumbling beneath his breath some more.

For all his bluster, the man clearly held a lot of affection for Mariabella. A twinge of envy ran through Jake. He'd been stuck in his office too long, that was for sure, if he was getting sentimental about a gruff lighthouse keeper who thrust his coat onto people.

"This way," Mariabella said, waving Jake toward a circular staircase dominating the room and spiraling toward the top of the lighthouse. Cletus's sparse living room surrounded the staircase, laid out in typical bachelor style. A bare-bones kitchen fed into a living room decorated with a single sofa and a plain maple end table. A TV sat atop a crate and a small oak bookshelf overflowed with paperback suspense novels.

Jake paused to look up the stairs—what appeared to be a thousand of them. The lighthouse had to be a hundred feet tall, and every foot would be climbed by them, not an elevator.

"Ready?" Mariabella asked, taking his hand. Every time she touched him, a surge of electricity ran through Jake, jolting long-dead senses back to life. Parts of him he'd thought had been shut off five years ago reawakened. He hadn't thought he could open his heart or feel that kind of hope again.

Not since—

Not since the future he'd planned had been crushed beneath a tractor trailer on the George Washington Bridge.

"Uh…yeah," he said.

Mariabella released him and started climbing the stairs, and Jake went back to being all business. Every ounce of him slipped back into that persona, as if he'd shed the coat of one man and put on the jacket of another.

The one of the more sensible man. The one who didn't get wrapped up in distractions he couldn't afford.

Except no matter how hard he tried, he couldn't forget the feeling of her touch, how her hand had been delicate and small, the skin as soft as rose petals.

As Mariabella walked ahead of him, he couldn't help but notice her curves. The arches of her calves, the hourglass of her waist, the way her hair hung in dark brown waves nearly to the small of her back. He reached up a hand, aching to run his fingers through those tresses.

He jerked his hand back. Business only. Stay on track. He

was here, not to fall for her or her town, but to utilize this time to sway Mariabella Romano over to his side, to make her understand how a Lattimore Resort could revitalize this sleepy little town.

All business—with no extracurricular activities. He had no intentions of returning to New York with anything other than a handful of signed deeds.

The wrought-iron staircase narrowed with each step, and when they reached the top of the stairs, they were standing in an enclosed, slightly musty space, with rough stone walls, probably hand-hewn a hundred years ago. Above their heads, the wooden ceiling had a small opening, with a ladder Jake guessed they were meant to climb to get to the final destination.

"We have to go up that?"

"You have already climbed a hundred feet, how difficult are a few more?" Mariabella tossed him a grin, then started up the ladder.

Giving Jake an exceptionally good view of her backside. For a moment, he couldn't remember exactly why he had objected to this idea in the first place. Why he had thought Mariabella Romano would bring trouble into his life.

Because right now she was bringing something very interesting to his day.

So much for business-only thoughts.

Jake shook his head and started up the ladder after her.

"Are you ready?" she called down to him.

"Ready for what?"

"The view of a lifetime." Mariabella smiled, then reached out a hand to help him over the edge. He should have refused the hand up—he didn't need it after all—but a part of him started to look forward to touching her.

The part that hadn't realized he could look forward to a woman again. The part that had been buried in work for way too many years.

Jake shook his head. If he let his hormones rule his brain, he'd lose focus. He couldn't afford that, not now. Not with his career and the company's future riding on this deal.

Mariabella released his hand, and stood back. They were at the top of the lighthouse, beside a massive red lantern turning in a constant circle, and blinking every other second. "That thing's huge."

"I didn't bring you up here to see the beacon."

"Then what?" He glanced at his watch. He'd agreed to this excursion, but shouldn't have. He needed to get back to town and convince more people to sign over their properties to Lattimore. *That* was his priority. Not a lighthouse. And not a woman.

"This." She handed him a pair of binoculars and pointed out the glass windows.

He sighed. "Miss Romano—"

"Mariabella."

"Mariabella—" her name slid off his tongue like music, and the distraction started anew "—I don't have time—"

"Everyone has time for one look at the ocean, yes?" She gestured to him to peek through the lenses.

He lifted them to his eyes, and at first, saw nothing but blue. Mariabella leaned over and whispered in his ear, sending a rush of heat through his veins. "A little to the right."

When he shifted position, the circles of the binoculars filled with images of the ocean spreading around them in a vast circle of blue-green, rolling back and forth with choppy white-capped waves. Boats chugged through the channel, plowing through the water like a knife through melted butter. Jake shifted more to the right, and then, far off, he spotted a surge of black above the waves. It disappeared, then reappeared a few feet farther down. He glanced at Mariabella. "Is that…?"

A soft smile stole across Mariabella's face. "A whale. Yes, it is. I could stay here for hours and watch them. They're so incredible, are they not? Almost like…children."

"I'm not the poetry-in-motion kind, you know. I have a business to run." He began to lower the binoculars. "I really don't have time—"

"Shhh." Mariabella placed a finger over his lips, then withdrew it just as fast, as if the touch had seared her skin. "Stay a moment. No moving. No talking. Just...be."

Jake didn't know if it was the confined quarters of the beacon room, or the feel of Mariabella's finger on his lips, or the way she stood there, transfixed, but something in him caused him to take a moment, and breathe in the vast blue space around him.

The sky seemed to be kissing the ocean, and pouring its aqua beauty into the eagerly lapping waters below while a benevolent sun watched it all, and blessed the union with a golden dust. As Jake stood there, a weird sensation took over, first his limbs, then his senses. It was as if he couldn't—no, didn't want to—move.

For the longest time, he couldn't name the sensation. And then, finally he recognized the foreign feeling.

Peace.

"Look," Mariabella whispered, even though they were miles away and encased in a glass tower, "there he is again. And this time, he has a friend."

Jake leaned closer, peering through the salt-spattered glass for the flecks of black. "I don't see anything."

Mariabella shifted to the right, which brought her body within inches of his. She raised her arm and pointed. "There. Do you see him now?"

He saw a woman. With long, dark hair, and soft, soft skin. With every breath, he caught the scent of raspberries and almonds. And when Mariabella moved, as she did just then to look up at him, he fought a primal urge to kiss her.

For five years, he'd existed in a vacuum, and now this woman, this stranger, had stepped into the black hole of his life, like sunshine breaking over a horizon. She was making him set aside everything he should be thinking about.

Making him forget his priorities.

And right this second, he didn't care.

"It is incredible, yes?" she asked.

He watched her lips form the words. Felt them whisper across his skin. Heat rose in the space between them. Desire surged in Jake's chest. "Incredible."

Mariabella opened her mouth to say something else, then stopped. She swallowed. Her green eyes widened, her chest rose and fell, and Jake shifted just enough to close the gap between them.

Their torsos met, and a firestorm of attraction exploded in Jake's gut. Fire. He was playing with fire, and he knew where that led. To someone getting burned.

Step back, get back to business.

He shifted again, and their legs met. Her eyes widened even more.

"What…" she said, then let the sentence trail off.

Stop this before it starts. Be smart.

Jake reached up a hand, and caught one of those impossibly long, tempting tresses in his palm. Just as he'd imagined, the dark brown strands were silky smooth, and slid through his fingers with a whisper. "You were right."

She caught his hand, and met his gaze. "Right about what?"

"The view up here is amazing." He leaned closer, about to kiss her.

But instead, she laughed and stepped back. "Does every woman you meet fall for that one? Do they just collapse at your feet? Run *to* you, as Will said?"

He quirked a grin. "Most of them fall into my arms."

"You poor man." She shook her head again. "If you are done, Casanova, I have more of the town to show you."

"I'm done." Clearly, he'd been the only one who'd felt

anything in the air up here. Maybe it had been altitude sickness or maybe he really had been alone too long—and he'd forgotten how to read the subtle physical cues women sent.

As Mariabella turned and disappeared down the ladder, Jake took one last look out at the vast ocean. In the distance, he saw twin black humps crest, then disappear beneath the blue depths.

"Seems you're having better luck than me, Moby."

CHAPTER FIVE

THAT had been a close one.

Mariabella stuck to her side of the limo, as far from Jake Lattimore—and any potential for bodily contact—as possible. In the rearview window, she watched the Harborside Lighthouse grow smaller and smaller as they headed away from the rocky coastline and back toward town.

For a second in that tower, she'd actually made the mistake of thinking Jake was attracted to her. That he'd wanted her for *her*. For the real Mariabella.

Except he didn't know the real Mariabella, did he?

She clearly had let this American way of life soften her wits, because if she had been back in her own country, in her own element, she never would have fallen for such an obvious ploy to—

Well, to use and manipulate her.

This man was here to buy her building. To use her as an ally in his bid to buy the rest of the buildings on the block. His only interest in her came with dollar signs in his eyes.

Even if his intentions had been true, she had no business getting close to a man. Doing so meant being vulnerable. Opening up. Sharing parts of her past.

Like where she came from.

Why she was here.

And who she really was.

If there was a list of the top three things Mariabella never intended to tell anyone, those were them. The story she'd led people to believe was that she'd come to Harborside on vacation over a year ago and loved it so much, she'd decided to stay. From her accent, people assumed she was Italian, and she'd let those assumptions stand.

Better to let others fill in the blanks than to do that herself—whenever she opened her mouth, she left too much room for error. And so, Mariabella maintained as much distance in her personal relationships as she could, to avoid answering impossible questions. And she busied herself repaying people for their friendship with the skills she had—organizing town events that brought Harborside and that drew in more visitors. Not enough, clearly, if Harborside was vulnerable to a man like Jake Lattimore.

So she didn't talk about her past, her family, or her heritage. She kept her friendships on a surface level, never allowing anyone in too close.

Today, she'd made the mistake of forgetting her commitment to distance, and allowed Jake Lattimore to close the gap. For just a second, she'd let herself think that she was just like every other woman in this town.

One who could date, fall in love, live an ordinary future with a husband, children.

Instead of one living a lie. Instead of one who was living on a ticking clock, and who would be leaving soon to take her place on a throne. Until then her priority was this town, and keeping it out of greedy hands like Jake's.

He wasn't a date—he was the enemy.

Remember that, Mariabella.

"That house there," she said to Jake, pointing out the window as they rounded the corner, "is the oldest home in

Harborside. Built right around the time the founding fathers of America were writing the Declaration of Independence."

He arched a brow. "Who are not your founding fathers, I take it, because your accent definitely isn't native to this country."

She ignored the question. "If you notice the architecture, it has a Georgian style, but an addition was added in 1920—"

"Where are you from?" Jake interrupted. "Italy? Spain?"

"The people who added on didn't stay true to the original style of the building. So, in 1979, when the present owner bought the house—"

"Definitely from a region near Italy," he continued, as if she hadn't said a word. "I've been there several times, mostly on business, sadly. But I did have time for one short visit, a couple years ago."

"He decided to take down the addition and rebuild it from..." Her voice trailed off. They had passed the object of her little speech several minutes ago. "Coming up on your right—" Mariabella pointed past him and out the window, hoping to deflect his attention "—is the first church built in Harborside."

"Are you going to continue to avoid getting to know each other on a personal level?" Jake leaned forward, propping his elbows on his knees. The limo suddenly seemed as small as a subcompact.

"I see little point in it," she said, regardless of that little bit she had let slip earlier today. And that moment in the light-house. Both aberrations. She wouldn't make the same mistake twice. "You are here on business, and I am here to show you the wisdom of taking your business elsewhere."

"What if I'm interested in combining a little pleasure with my business?"

"Then I suggest staying at the Harborside Seaside Inn. They offer a spa service on weekends."

He chuckled. "Are you always this difficult?"

"No. Generally, I am quite pleasant." She offered him a smile as proof.

He returned her smile with one of his own. A smile that hit Mariabella squarely in the gut, sending the hormones that she'd managed to reduce to a slow simmer back up to a full boil.

The man had a heck of a nice smile, she'd give him that. The kind that curved up a little higher on one side than the other, giving him a touch of mischief behind his blue eyes. For a second, she wondered if he was, as Will had said, a man given to fun.

The kind who would say, "Hey, let's go scuba diving this weekend," and book them two tickets to Jamaica. The kind who would throw an impromptu picnic on the living room floor. The kind who would—

Who would bring the kind of fun into Mariabella's life that she had missed living in that caged fishbowl.

"Well, pleasant Mariabella Romano, let's see this church of yours." He pressed a button at his side, and the driver slowed, then pulled over. A moment later, they were out of the car and heading toward the tall white spires of the church.

"I thought you were no longer interested in my tour."

"If I'm going to invest in this town, I need to know as much about it as I can. From bagels to Bibles." He caught her gaze. "Wouldn't you agree?"

Somehow, she suspected he had managed to turn this around, back to his advantage. Mariabella was not used to being in this position. A monarch, even one in training, always maintained control. Always had the upper hand.

Those lessons had been bred into her, and drilled into her again and again over the years. As they headed up the granite stairs of the church, Mariabella vowed to put the very knowledge she had hated learning to use—and get this derailed train back on the right track.

Whether there was a nice smile in the way or not.

* * *

But an hour later, after taking Jake Lattimore through the church, down the block past the dozen or so historic homes that made up the center of Harborside, and then driving back to the boardwalk, she had to admit she had yet to regain her familiar footing at the top.

The sun had begun to set, dropping a blanket of deep orange across the Atlantic. A chill fell over the town, and Mariabella drew her coat tighter against winter's bite when she stepped out of the limo. "You enjoyed your tour of Harborside, Mr. Lattimore, did you not?"

"I did." He waved off the chauffeur, before Will could get out of the car. "And I don't want it to end."

Mariabella pivoted, gesturing toward the buildings they'd just seen. "I don't know of other landmarks, except the boardwalk and you have—"

"I didn't mean that."

She turned back toward him. Jake's blue gaze held hers, steady and sure. He had a way of looking at a woman that pierced through the layers she'd put in place. The ones meant as keep-out signs, the ones that had worked so successfully with other men.

Every other man, it seemed, but this one.

"Then what do you mean?" she asked.

"I saw a sign back there for something I haven't done in a really long time. Something I suspect you haven't done either."

"If it's skiing, I assure you, I have—"

"The Christmas Dance at the town hall."

Her jaw dropped. She started to say a word, couldn't think of one, then tried again. Nothing.

He was asking her out? To a dance? On a date?

She had organized the dance with several other business owners in Harborside as a way to celebrate the holiday and bring together the townspeople. She had learned in the palace that celebrations had a way of reducing political tensions and forming new alliances among old foes. Something about the flow of wine and the music of laughter got people building bridges they wouldn't otherwise form.

"I haven't been to a dance myself since…probably high school," he went on. "It's a good way to get to know the townspeople in a more casual setting, and that will work toward my goal, too."

"Your goal?"

"I can change some of those negative impressions that I'm sure are springing up all over town like crocuses in April. And if you go with me," he said, grinning, "you can remind people behind my back how awful I am."

She cocked her head and studied him. "That is *against* your plans, is it not?"

"Ah, but it's part of another plan of mine." The grin widened. "I don't know about you, but I work much too many hours, and I could use a break."

"A break?" The echo escaped her in a whisper. Her concentration seemed to have flown south with the geese. This was bad. Very bad.

She was a princess, a royal—and a royal maintained order, both personal and national, no matter what. If she didn't, disaster would result.

Mariabella had heard this lesson from her father, spoken in his dispassionate, quiet voice, over and over again. Never allow passion to rule over logic. If you did, people got hurt.

People like her.

"I shouldn't—" she began.

"You should. Have some fun tonight, Mariabella."

Fun. He'd spoken the magic word. Wasn't that exactly what she'd been seeking all her life? The one thing she'd been denied? She'd grown up imprisoned by expectations and decorum—as the future queen, her prison was even tighter than that of her sisters'—and she'd always wished for some-one, something to break her out.

She'd come to this town, hoping to find that escape, and instead been imprisoned in a different way. By her own lies. So she'd buried herself in her gallery, in helping the town, and backed away from personal relationships.

Now Jake Lattimore stood before her, offering the very gift she'd always wanted, like her own personal Santa.

Did she dare accept?

"Come on, Mariabella. Everyone deserves a break. That's just smart business." He took a step forward, buffeting her from the cold air, warming the space between them. But most of all, tempting her to use him as a shield from the long, cold days ahead. "That's what this would be. Business only."

"Business only? You have no ulterior motives at all?"

The smile quirked up a little higher on one side than the other. "Well, I may want to perfect my waltz while I'm at it."

Logic over passion. Never let her heart get ahead of her brain. If she could keep that in mind tonight, and use all that she had been taught to her advantage, then she'd be fine. She could do that and still have fun, couldn't she?

"All right, I will go with you," Mariabella said. And made a date with the enemy.

"What the hell are you doing?" Will asked, glancing at the flyer Jake had handed him, before tossing it onto the dash and putting the car in gear.

"Going to a dance. And working at the same time."

Will muttered something under his breath that sounded close to "idiot."

"Excuse me?"

"You should go to the dance, and *dance*. Not work at all." Will swung the limo through Harborside's streets and stopped in front of the town hall where the dance was being held, and

Jake had agreed to meet Mariabella. "There's a beautiful woman in there, and if you think about anything other than her legs tonight, then you need a lobotomy."

He had far too many things on his work plate right now to consider adding in a relationship. Will would tell him he was making an excuse. Again. The same excuse he'd made for the last five years.

Ever since he'd lost Victoria.

For a minute there in the lighthouse, he'd considered something else, but in the time since he'd dropped off Mariabella, he'd come back to his senses. "My mind will be on balance sheets, Will. Not anything *between* the sheets. I'll be back in an hour."

Will muttered something else a lot less flattering than "idiot."

"What?"

"Number one, you're at a dance, Jake. I don't know who taught you Dating 101, but that's the easiest way to get close to a woman without having to pay for dinner first."

Jake chuckled.

"And if you want to dance with her, you might want to change."

Jake looked down at his dark navy suit and blue striped tie. "What's wrong with what I'm wearing?"

"You look like you're heading to a convention for undertakers." Will unknotted his own tie and tossed it over the seat. The silk fabric unfurled in a cacophony of red, green and white. "Here. Wear mine."

"I'm not—"

"*Act* like a fun guy, Jake, and one of these days, you might just turn back into one."

Fun. The very thing he'd proposed to Mariabella earlier. Trouble was, Jake wasn't so sure he was ready for fun in his life again. It was far easier to stay in the familiar world of work. Jake reached for the door handle, then heard a familiar click.

"Wear the tie," Will said. "Surprise her. You might surprise yourself in the process. What's the worst that can happen?"

"For one, she might laugh her head off."

"So fire me, if she does. And if she kisses you instead, I want a raise." Will winked.

Kiss Mariabella Romano? Just the thought sent a roar of anticipation running through Jake. Today, he'd almost...

He pictured her lush lips beneath his, her curvy body in his arms, her thick dark hair tangled in his hands.

He changed his tie.

"Get involved," Will said before Jake got out of the car. "It won't kill you."

"Maybe," Jake said. "Maybe not."

Outside, a gust of winter wind cut down the sidewalk, cold, sharp, vicious. Jake inhaled, and drew his coat closed against the sudden frigid temperature. Mother Nature's fury held nothing over the ice binding his heart, a self-protective shield he'd thought would keep him from ever feeling that pain again.

But as he gripped the door handle to the Harborside Town Hall, he wondered if he was fooling himself. Did avoiding a topic mean it went away—or was he just killing time, filling those empty holes with balance sheets and architectural plans?

He entered the building, and was immediately greeted by a rock band belting out Christmas songs, a crowd of people filling the dance floor and milling about the perimeter of the room, and a burst of red and green decorations, broadcasting Christmas spirit loud and clear.

His gaze skipped over all of it. The logical, left side of Jake's brain told him to move around the room, to start networking, warm up the residents of Harborside, start convincing the more reluctant sellers that this deal was in their best interests. He had a limited window of time, after all, and every minute he wasted cost the company.

Except, he couldn't seem to focus on anything except finding Mariabella Romano. He scanned the room, seeking her familiar face, telling himself he'd start with her. She was the most logical choice, after all. Head of the Community Development Committee, and all that.

Uh-huh.

Then why did his pulse kick up a dozen notches when he spied her across the room? Why did he start weaving through the crowd, mumbling vague hellos to the half dozen or so people he'd already met in Harborside, instead of focusing on the job at hand?

"You look...stunning," he said when he reached Mariabella. The rest of the room dropped away, the space seeming to close in to just him. And her.

She'd accented her curves with an emerald sweater in a V-neck, decorated with rhinestones that peppered the front like snowflakes. A black skirt cut away from her knees in a swirl of ruffles, and drew his eye down to spiky black-and-silver high heels that only made her already amazing legs look even more amazing. She'd curled her hair, and piled it on top of her head in a riot of curls that begged a man to find every pin, and release the tendrils one by one.

"Thank you." A slight blush filled her cheeks. "Is that how you convince everyone to sell you their properties, Mr. Lattimore?"

"Please, call me Jake." He took a step closer, his gaze catching her green eyes, the color as deep and vibrant as a forest on a stormy day.

"Jake."

His name rolled off her tongue in a sweet song he'd never heard another woman sing. Impartiality kept yielding to testosterone, making it impossible to think about anything but kissing her.

Oh, he was in trouble.

She stepped forward and ran a finger down his tie. A smile curved across her face. "What's this?"

Her touch nearly sent him over the edge. He drew in a breath, fought the urge to take her in his arms. "A little Christmas spirit."

"I like it. You surprise me, Jake. I didn't think you were a snowman fan."

He sure as hell was now.

The band segued into a slow song, and couples began making their way onto the dance floor. Jake put out his hand. "Shall we?"

She hesitated, then nodded, took his hand and followed him out to the dance floor. Her palm was delicate, she had long, fine fingers, and when she put one hand on his back, the other still clasped inside his larger one, he thought how like a hummingbird she was. Fragile, yet strong, determined, and impossible to pin down.

"I thought this was business only," she said.

"It's Christmas. Surely we can have a little fun, too." Will would have laughed if he could have heard Jake right now.

They began to waltz in a slow, easy circle, Mariabella's steps surer and better than his. Clearly, she'd done this a time—or a hundred.

"You're not only beautiful, you're a wonderful dancer," he said.

"Is that how you get what you want in business? By sweet-talking the other side?"

He chuckled. "No. I don't usually call the people I'm in the midst of negotiating with 'stunning.'"

Her green eyes met his. "Is that what this is, a negotiation?"

"Isn't that what all dancing is? A negotiation?" Except he'd stopped doing any kind of business the minute he'd stepped on the dance floor. Something else had started between them, something far more serious and with far higher stakes than a real estate transaction.

He knew it. She knew it.

A smile curved across her face, lighting her eyes, and lighting a flame in Jake's gut, one he had thought died a long time ago. He found his hold on her tightening ever so slightly, his head dipping just a little, enough that if he wanted to, he could close the gap between them with a whisper—

And kiss her.

"If this is a negotiation," Mariabella said softly, "then that means one of is going to lose, yes?"

They stepped to the right, her body moving in perfect rhythm with his. Jake moved a half inch closer, and the silky ends of her hair brushed against his cheek. The scent of raspberries and almonds wafted up to tease at his senses. An errant curl had tugged loose from one of the bobby pins holding it in place, and Jake fought the urge to tug the tendril down, to let it slip through his fingers.

"Perhaps," he whispered, his voice nearly a growl, as desire roared in his gut, "we can compromise instead."

"You do not strike me as the type of man who compromises." She took a step forward, bringing her torso in contact with his for an all too brief second. Every sane thought in Jake's head disappeared.

"And what about you?" He slid his palm up her back and twirled her to the right. She didn't miss a step, matching him move for move. "Are you a compromiser, or a winner?"

"Oh, I am very accustomed to always getting exactly what I want," she said. "To people always doing what I tell them to."

"Pity."

"Why do you say that?"

"Because I am exactly the same way."

"Then it looks like we have a problem."

Her perfume intoxicated him. The curve of her neck riveted his attention, and every step she took knocked him off guard. For a man used to being in control, the feeling was new, unexpected. "Or maybe," Jake said, as the band began to sing the last few notes, "we'll find a way to make this work out for both of us."

The song ended, and the band announced they were taking a break. People began to leave the dance floor, and music from a CD player replaced the live instruments.

"Or maybe," Mariabella said, stepping away from him and breaking the spell between them, "one of us *will* win. Thank you for the dance, Mr. Lattimore. I think it will be smart if we stick to business instead of fun. Don't you agree?"

She headed for a table laden with appetizers and a massive bowl of red punch. He took two steps to follow her, then turned away.

And did the smart thing.

Got back to work.

What had she been thinking?

For five minutes, Mariabella had let herself get swept up in a dance, in a romantic moment, fooled into thinking the arms around her held interest in her, not her gallery. She'd forgotten the identity she'd worked so hard to protect, forgotten the life she'd built, and considered—

Considered kissing him.

Again.

Twice in one day.

She'd broken the cardinal rule her father had drilled into her. The one thing he had insisted on over and over, and made clear in the way he lived his life and interacted with his family.

Reason over emotion. Never, ever let your desires do the thinking for you. That was the kind of mistake that started wars, for goodness sake.

"He must be a Leo," Carmen whispered in her ear.

"A what?" Mariabella asked, turning away from the dance

floor, and focusing on the trays of food, even though her appetite had disappeared.

"You know, the astrological sign? He's like a lion on the prowl tonight."

"I have no idea who you are talking about."

Carmen propped a fist on her hip. "Did you just dance with Mr. Invisible? Because I thought I saw you waltzing around the floor with Prince Charming a second ago."

"He is no prince. Trust me, I know. And far from charming."

Carmen leaned against the table and watched Jake cross the room. "Sure looks like every prince I've read about in a fairy tale. Tall, dark, handsome—"

"Incredibly boorish, self-centered and after one thing."

"A beautiful princess?"

The word hit Mariabella with the force of a rogue wave. She swallowed hard and glanced away for a second, hoping that surprise didn't show on her face. "Well, he should look elsewhere." A skittish laugh escaped her.

"Why? I mean, you're *here*."

"What?" Alarm raised the pitch in the word.

Carmen draped an arm around her boss. "In case you haven't noticed, you are a very eligible catch. I've even heard Cletus say he'd marry you and that guy is the biggest hermit to come along since Bigfoot."

Mariabella laughed. "Cletus? He just likes my cooking."

"Come on, Mari. You're gorgeous. You have that accent thing going on, and you're…mysterious."

"Did they spike the punch this year?" Mariabella asked. Change the subject. Get the focus on something other than herself and mysteries to be solved. "I think I'll try a cup and see."

"Men love that stuff," Carmen went on. "They love women who are a puzzle."

Mariabella ladled some punch into cup. Gulped half of it down. "No. No liquor."

"Let me give you one hint about guys. You don't want to play Mystery Woman for too long."

"Did you see these cookies? They are like little Christmas trees. Cute, yes?" Mariabella grabbed one but didn't eat it.

Carmen didn't move off topic. "It's like doing the Sunday crossword. That sucker's hard. Eventually you give up because you get frustrated. Unless you're like a genius, and then maybe you stick it out. Most of us, we just let it go after twenty-nine down, know what I mean?"

"Jake Lattimore is the puzzle, not me," Mariabella said.

Carmen grinned. "A lot of women wouldn't mind figuring out what's making him run across and down."

"Easy. He wants to buy this town." Mariabella wagged a cookie in Carmen's direction. "Do not let his smile fool you."

"So you *did* notice his smile."

"Only because he insists on using it as a lethal weapon."

Carmen laughed. "He's not that bad."

"He wants to take over Harborside, Carmen. What is good about that?"

Carmen leaned in to Mariabella and lowered her voice. "Did you ever think this town could use some extra oomph? That maybe its destiny is to become something more than a sleepy little place for people to work on their tans in the summer?"

"You have no idea how that could ruin a place," Mariabella said. "How a man like him can destroy a perfect world."

"I've been reading his auras, Mariabella, and I think his intentions are all for good. You should—"

"No," Mariabella said, interrupting Carmen before she could add another argument to the pile. Or worse, return to the Prince Charming and princess matchmaking conversation. That could lead to nothing good. "What I should do is gather the Harborside business owners together so we can come up with a plan to stop him. Before it's too late."

CHAPTER SIX

HE WATCHED them leave, one after another, following Mariabella Romano out of the room like chicks behind a mother duck. Every one of the people he had talked to that morning left the dance.

He leaned against the wall and smiled.

Well, hell. She was a step ahead of him, and he admired that. It had been a while since he'd met such a challenge—on a personal and business level.

Not to mention such a mystery. He'd spent an entire day with Mariabella Romano and knew less about her than he knew about the doorman who worked at Lattimore Properties.

And that guy just started working for the company last week.

Jake rubbed his chin, and plotted a new strategy. Looked like he had an uprising in the making. He had to get creative.

And that meant outflanking Miss Romano, before she did the same to him.

Except, this time, a part of him resisted. Somewhere deep inside Jake, a rebellion had started, a whisper telling him to back away. To let this project go. To let Mariabella keep her town just as it was.

Why?

He'd never done that before. Never treated anything he'd

pursued with kid gloves. This was business, pure and simple. Heart didn't figure into the equation.

That was dangerous thinking. *Bad* thinking. He had to nip that in the bud and quick. No way was he going to deviate from the plan, from the proven formula.

His father would never approve of him thinking with anything resembling sentimentality. Once upon a time, Lawrence Lattimore had been a man who'd run his company with his emotions. But as he'd told Jake over and over, he hadn't gotten rich until he'd left his heart on the curb and started thinking with his brains.

And neither would Jake. No. He'd convince Mariabella Romano that a Lattimore Resort was a good thing for this town—and do it in a way she'd never forget.

A half hour later, Mariabella reentered the room, her business owner ducks again following, then dispersing. The band had started up again, launching into a rousing rendition of a popular Christmas carol. Someone in a snowman suit climbed onto the stage and began gyrating along to the song, boogying close enough to the cymbals to provide an extra clash here and there.

Jake crossed to Mariabella, his pulse kicking up as the gap between them closed. Damn. She had a certain mystique about her, like a veil blocking anyone from seeing the real woman. Even as he fought his attraction to her and told himself to stick to business, the rest of his body mutinied.

"I'd like to make you an offer," he said.

Wariness filled her gaze. "An offer?"

"Come with me tomorrow. And let me show you what a Lattimore resort can be like. Find out firsthand what my company can bring to Harborside." She began to protest, but he put up a finger and laid it against her lips. When he touched her mouth, a surge of desire roared through him. He lowered his hand.

"I can't possibly leave. I have an opening in two days and—"

"You have an assistant. Let her assist."

"I—"

"If you want to battle the enemy, what better way to do so than to see exactly what you're up against?"

He would give her a visual image—one she couldn't argue with. Let her see the dollars and sense in his designs. In one of the diamonds of the Lattimore jewelry case. Then surely all her arguments about a megahotel would disappear.

She considered him. "All right, I'll go. But do not think I can be persuaded by a fancy room or a steak dinner. I am not like other women. At all."

Then she walked away, leaving Jake even more mystified than he had been when the evening started.

Who *was* this woman? And where exactly had she come from?

Mariabella loved mornings. But not early mornings.

She stood outside the gallery, shivering in her winter coat, at a few minutes before four, and wondered what insanity had driven her to agree to Jake Lattimore's proposal last night. The dark wrapped around her with an icy chill, the boardwalk eerily quiet, everything still closed up for the night. Behind her, the ocean whooshed back and forth, whispering its constant music.

The limo glided down the street, tires crackling on the half-frozen road. Mariabella didn't wait for Will to open her door. She hopped inside and closed the door, glad to be cocooned in the heated leather interior.

"I would have been happy to pick you up in front of your house," Jake said.

She knew Jake Lattimore had no idea who she really was, but still, she wanted to put as many layers of protection between herself and her true identity as she could. Hence, meeting him at the gallery this morning. "I had some work to do before I left."

"You sound like me. No time for a personal life."

She laughed. "Small business owner. It goes with the territory."

"It's the same for big business owners." He handed her a cup of coffee, and she thanked him. "What do you know? We have something in common."

Mariabella simply sipped her coffee. The blend was hearty but wonderful. The rich, warm aroma helped awaken Mariabella's senses, and draw her into the land of the living, despite the ridiculously early hour. "I can't believe you found coffee this early."

"We brought it with us."

"You brought your own coffee?"

"I like what I like, and I didn't want to bother the B and B owner this early. Will brewed it for us at the inn this morning before we left." He gestured toward a silver carafe sitting on the small table to the right.

The joys of having exactly what you wanted when you wanted it—how Mariabella missed that. She loved living in Harborside, but there were aspects of palace life that she did miss. Being able to call down to the kitchen at two in the morning because she had a sudden craving for pizza. Waking up to breakfast in bed every morning. Having someone there to tend to everything she needed—from new shoes to making the bed.

Of course, that had all come at a price. A lack of privacy. Her entire life dictated from the day she was born. A public face she could never stop wearing. She'd brew her own coffee, thank you very much, and have her life to herself.

"Where are we going?" she asked.

"If I told you, it wouldn't be a surprise." He grinned, then shifted in his seat to face her. "I have only one rule for this trip. We don't talk about Harborside or the argument we're having about its future for the entire trip. Instead, we act like—" he paused, and met her gaze "—friends."

Mariabella nearly spit out her coffee. "Friends? You? And me?"

"Am I that much of an ogre?"

She bit back a smile at his choice of words. If he only knew who she was, he wouldn't reference fairy-tale creatures. "No. Not an ogre."

"Then is it that unbelievable that you and I could be friends under different circumstances?"

Her gaze locked with his blue eyes. A shiver of awareness ran through her, and she thought of the moment in the light-house. How close they had come to kissing. How much she had *wanted* him to kiss her. How lonely she had been over the last year, heck, her whole life. She hadn't been seen as just Mariabella, as an ordinary woman living an ordinary life, by any man.

Until now.

She had a chance, for a few hours, to sit and play the game. To pretend. Would that be so bad?

"Perhaps not so unbelievable," she said.

A smile curved along his face, feeding the desire that had been coiling in her gut with the memory of that near kiss. When he smiled, it lit up his eyes, crinkled along the corners, and made her wonder—

What if?

"So what do non-ogre friends talk about?" she asked.

He laughed. "Well, for starters, where did you grow up?"

Under any other circumstances, with any other person, that question would be ordinary. Something that wouldn't send out the palace guards on a rescue mission. Or the media on a "find the princess" frenzy. There was no way to answer that with the truth, not if she wanted to keep her identity secret. "Along the coast of Italy," she said finally. A small lie. Uccelli was north of Italy's coast.

"From your accent, I assumed that. I've traveled there. Beautiful country."

"And you?" she asked, before he could probe deeper into her past. "Did you always live in New York?"

"I've never known another home, if you can call an apartment a home."

"And you do not."

He shrugged. "It's a place to lay my head at night. When I'm there."

"I know how that feels," she said quietly. Darn. How did that slip out?

"Isn't Harborside a home for you?"

"It is the closest thing to home I've ever known." That was the truth. She could feel the smile filling her face, the joy she'd found in the tiny seaport exploding in the gesture. "I love it there."

"You didn't love your life in Italy?"

"I was not—" she paused, choosing her words carefully "—as happy there. As...comfortable, not like I am in Harborside."

"You're lucky." His gaze went to the window, and she wondered if he was watching Harborside in the distance, or something else. "I haven't found a place like that. And I've been all over the world."

"I think home is where you make it. I think I would have been just as happy in New York or California or London."

"Yet you didn't find home where you grew up."

"There were...other issues involved."

He arched a brow. "Like what?"

She peered at him over the rim of her coffee cup. "We are just friends getting to know each other, are we not? I do not have to tell all on the first trip."

"You are a mysterious woman, Mariabella."

Her name rolled off his tongue like a song. A craving to hear him say it again rose inside her, and she found herself leaning forward, as if moving nearer would make Jake repeat his words. "I thought men liked mystery."

"We do." A smile, a twinkle in his eyes. "Very much."

Flirting. They were flirting.

She should stop.

"And what about you?" she asked. "Do you like a woman with a little mystery?"

Jake paused a moment, then leaned closer. He reached up and caught a tendril of her hair between his fingers. She held her breath, her heart pounding a furious beat. "I didn't think I did." A second passed. He let the tendril of hair slide through his fingers. "Until now."

Desire roared inside her. Her gaze locked on his eyes, then his mouth. Her thoughts drifted to what those lips could do, given half a chance. Oh, my. "Then I suppose I should stay mysterious."

Why had she said that? Why hadn't she backed away?

She needed to stay uninvolved. Unencumbered. It was the only way to protect the freedom she had worked so hard to achieve.

And yet...

His touch drifted along her cheek now, and she forgot to breathe, forgot her name. "It's been a long time since I've had to unravel a puzzle," he said.

"Me, too."

"Am I a puzzle to you?"

She nodded. Her voice seemed to have gone south, too.

"How is that? I thought most men were pretty easy to figure out."

"Your intentions are...not always so clear." Like whether he wanted just the land in Harborside, or whether he wanted her, too. Or whether this whole seduction scene was merely an attempt to talk her into signing on the dotted line.

"It is getting a little muddled, isn't it?"

She nodded again.

"Then let's stick to just the ride." He sat back against his seat, and disappointment filtered into the space between them.

She should have been happy. She should have been thrilled to return to her comfort zone, the one that didn't involve the encumbrance of a relationship.

Except the empty spots in her heart, her life, kept crying out for someone else to bring another dimension to her days and nights. Someone who understood her. Who knew the real Mariabella.

Ha. That would mean starting with telling a man who she really was. And she couldn't do that, not without giving up everything that mattered.

The rest of the ride, she and Jake exchanged small talk, as if both of them had decided to maintain their distance. He took several calls; she pulled a sketch pad out of her purse, and kept herself busy making drawings of the landscape around them, as the sun came up and kissed the winter land with light.

A few hours later, they crossed into New York City. The buildings and noise surrounded them in an instant, a cacophony of noise and color. Mariabella set her sketchbook aside and sat back, taking in the view, enthralled by the massive skyscrapers, the congestion of people, the burst of holiday decorations on every building, every street corner.

"Have you been here before?"

"Twice," she said, not explaining both trips had been state business with her father, never vacations. "But every time, it is like seeing New York all over again."

"Then we'll have to return when we have more time," he said.

She glanced back at Jake, trying to read the meaning in those words. But his gaze was on the view outside, and not on her.

A few minutes later, William stopped the limo in front of an elaborate hotel, seated across from Central Park. The Lattimore Resort and Hotel had the appearance of being trimmed in gold, and featured four-story columns, and a two-story all-glass front door that revealed a marble foyer and massive water fountain inside.

Jake made a long-winded speech, explaining the hotel's virtues, listing its rooms, its five-star spa, its technologically advanced business center. "It's one of the best Lattimore Resorts available, and we'd bring a lot of these features to Harborside, so that many of the upscale clientele could find these same amenities when they go on a small-town vacation."

"It is certainly impressive," Mariabella said.

Jake put up a finger, motioning for William to wait before getting out to open the doors. "But you don't love it."

"Well…I don't mean to be rude, but anyone can build a hotel. Even an impressive one. I've stayed in many like this one."

"And would you stay in this one?"

She shrugged. "Perhaps."

"I hear a 'but' in that sentence." He draped an arm over the back of the seat and studied her. "What is it?"

"Jake, we drove all these hours and miles. I do not want to criticize your hotel before I have seen it. We should go in, and I will give it a fair view."

"You've seen enough to make a judgment, though, haven't you?"

She wanted to lie. Thought about lying. But really, where would that get her? And him? "I…" She sighed. "I simply like something different."

He chewed that over for a minute. "But this is what we have planned for Harborside."

"I know." She placed her palm against the window, as if she could block the hotel, which reminded her so much of the castle. "Don't you have anything…simpler?"

"All of our resorts are like this. Studies show—"

She wheeled toward him. "I do not read studies. I read in here." She laid a hand on her heart. "And there must be something else. Something less…gaudy."

He rubbed at his chin, thinking about her words for so long, Mariabella was sure she had offended him. She shouldn't have said a thing. After all, if someone had come in and criticized her gallery, she would have been upset. Jake probably felt the same way about his hotel. It would have been better just to exclaim over every feature and leave it at that.

Hadn't she learned to be polite? To keep her opinions to herself? A princess didn't voice her opinions, not in front of others. A princess was, above all, polite and sweet. Never disparaging, never disagreeable.

And always, always diplomatic.

She touched Jake's hand. "We can go inside. I am sure this is a lovely hotel with a great deal to offer your guests."

"No." He shook his head. "You made very valid points. And I happen to agree with them, even if the research shows otherwise. I just happen to be a guy who likes a different kind of vacation experience."

She laughed. "Me, too. This—" she waved toward the hotel "—is not my idea of a vacation."

He nodded. "Then let me show you something else." He picked up a phone beside him and told Will to start driving again. The limo pulled away from the curb and glided down the road.

"Well, I had hoped that building would impress you."

She shook her head. "I am sorry. I am a simple person. I like home and what do you call it…? Hearth. If you had something like that, maybe then—"

Jake grabbed the phone again. "Will, do you remember that place in New Jersey?" He paused. "Yeah, that's the one. Let's go there." Another pause. "I know, I know, but I can call in a favor and we can get in there."

"Where are we going?"

"Somewhere that has home and hearth. A lot of it." Jake glanced out the window and watched New York rush by. "This city may be my address, but where I'm taking you, that's the only place I ever felt at home."

Woodsmoke curled from the chimney and scented the air with hickory. Two white rocking chairs on the long wrap-around porch waved lazily in the chilly breeze. Snowdrifts danced in waves across the lawn, swinging up the trunks of the trees, as if trying to catch the white mushroom snowcaps above.

"It is…beautiful." Mariabella's breath escaped her in a cloud. She stood with Jake on the stone walkway of the Firefly Inn, and felt as if she'd stepped into a Christmas song.

"You like it. I can hear it in your voice."

"I…I love it. I had no idea places like this existed outside of books." She looked up at him. "You own this?"

"Not anymore. My father sold it a few years ago. This used to be what a Lattimore property was like."

"And you changed for…" She waved behind her, in the direction they had traveled.

"For dollars and cents. There's not as much money in little inns tucked away in the country as there is in megahotels in major cities."

"Oh." She drew in a breath, letting the crisp winter air revive her after all the hours in the limousine.

"Do you want to go inside?"

"I thought you did not own it anymore."

"I called in a favor. Come on." He put out his hand.

She slid her palm into his, and even though they were both wearing gloves—his leather, hers wool—she could feel the heat in their touch. Feel the solidity of his large, firm grip. She'd thought today could be just business. A day of nothing but looking at properties and convincing Jake Lattimore why none of his offerings would work in Harborside.

Except she kept forgetting that part of it. And she kept forgetting she was part of the royal Santaro bloodline, and should be acting as such. Using the authoritative mannerisms she had learned to take control of this situation.

But more than that, use the common sense she had learned and stop letting the rest of her body overrule her common sense.

A jingle of bells caught her attention. "What is that?"

Jake glanced at the barn that sat on the right side of the inn. He let out a little laugh. "Can't get any more Christmasy than that."

"What?"

"A sleigh ride." He gestured toward the barn, and then Mariabella saw it. Two horses, attached to a sleigh, like something out of a book or a song.

"I have never seen one in real life."

"Then you've never ridden in one, either?"

"No." She let out a long sigh. "I have always wondered what it would be like. You know, you hear the song on the radio? It sounds so…wonderful. So perfect."

A light dusting of snow had begun to fall, as if Mother Nature wanted to cast the perfect spell over the moment. Jake took her hand and led her down a stone path that led toward the sleigh. "Then let's go."

"Now? I thought we had a schedule to keep."

"The world won't fall apart if the two of us take ten minutes to ride across the snow."

A few minutes later, Mariabella found herself bundled beneath a plaid blanket, seated on a crimson velvet padded seat, while Jake sat beside her, a Thermos of hot chocolate between them. The driver snapped the reins, and the horses started, jerking the sleigh onto the snowy path. The move sent

Mariabella and Jake on a collision course, their torsos meeting, their faces coming within inches. "Sorry," he said.

"Not a problem." She brought the blanket closer to her chin. The faster the horses went, the more winter's cold wind whistled beneath the blanket, her coat, her sweater. She shivered.

Jake put his arm around her, and drew her against his body. Warmth infused her, and so did a heat of a different kind.

She didn't pull away from either.

Instead, she drew the blanket over both of them, and snuggled against him. The horses charged lightly forward, pulling the sleigh through the woods, the bells on their harnesses singing a soft song to match the heavy thudding of their hooves in the snow.

Jake poured her a cup of hot chocolate, and made a joke she laughed at but couldn't remember five seconds later. All she knew was that she was laughing, and he was laughing, and a détente had sprung up between them made all that much sweeter by the cocoa and the snow.

It was, as she'd said earlier, beautiful. And perfect. And so amazingly ordinary.

"Are you having fun?" Jake asked. He brushed his lips against the top of her head, and she leaned closer. Seeking more. Just for now.

"Yes."

"Me, too."

Too soon, the sleigh ride drew to a close, the horses circling back to the barn. Jake helped her down, a smile lingering on his face. "We'll have to do that again sometime."

Did he mean a future with that remark, or was he merely making conversation?

Did it matter, really? When next Christmas came, she'd be in Uccelli. Far from sleigh rides, hot cocoa—

And Jake Lattimore.

"Can we go inside?" Mariabella asked, rubbing her hands up and down her arms. "It is very cold."

"Of course."

Inside, they were greeted by a matronly woman with a wide smile, who told Jake to make himself at home. Several guests filled the downstairs rooms, sitting on the dark brown leather sofas in front of the crackling fire, or in the wingback chairs playing checkers. Others read books by the large picture windows. The scent of apples and cinnamon carried on the air from the kitchen, promising a sweet treat later.

"Let's go upstairs," Jake said. "I want to show you my favorite room in the whole place."

She hesitated, then saw the bright excitement in his gaze, and headed upstairs with Jake Lattimore, even as her better judgment told her being alone with him kept tangling her deeper with a man who awakened a side of her she thought she'd had under control. Yet, every time they were together, she forgot herself. Forgot the objections she had to him.

Forgot her priority—preserving this town.

Every wall in the inn held a photograph, a painting, a piece of memorabilia, that spoke of decades of guests and history. An eclectic mix of furniture, from the rose-patterned wingback chairs to the thick burgundy leather sofa, sent out an air of comfort. Unlike the castle in Uccelli, the charm of this inn existed in its quirkiness, in rooms decorated by chance, not by a professional.

Perhaps this was the key to getting Jake to see how important leaving Harborside alone was to her. If she could equate her town to this place, then maybe he'd understand her fierce love for the town—just as it was—and give up this crazy idea of turning it into a tourist circus. Into the nightmare she had seen in New York.

They went up the first flight of stairs, then turned, headed down the hall and stopped before a small door. Once inside,

Jake flicked on a light switch, then started up another, more narrow flight of stairs. Wood creaked beneath Mariabella's feet, and a slight smell of must and age whispered against her nostrils. She blinked, adjusting her eyes to the dimmer light, provided by a single bulb, then saw where they were.

The attic.

Piles of boxes and sheet-covered furniture pieces filled the space. Cobwebs draped from the corners, and every step they took kicked up a flurry of dust.

"*This* is your favorite room?"

"Not yet." He waved her forward, and she followed, picking her way across the room, dodging crates and stacked chairs, nearly sideswiping a pile of paintings draped with a tarp. A second bare lightbulb sent a harsh stream of light into the room, illuminating a door at the far end of the attic. Jake paused a second, then opened the door, revealing a small, plain room with a twin bed and simple maple dresser. Few decorations accented the space, just a blue braided oval rug, and a pair of white lace curtains hanging like limp soldiers on either side of the lone window.

"You stayed here?" she said. "Why? There are so many rooms downstairs."

"I stayed up here because of that." He pointed out the window, a long, rectangular window that lay so low, one could lie in the bed and stare out at the view all night—a view of the woods, and then, past the forest, the small town nestled at the bottom of the hill. From this distance, the houses and cars seemed to be miniatures, almost doll-sized.

If she hadn't known better, she'd swear she was home in Uccelli. Mariabella moved closer, and rested a knee on the bed. She peered outside, and saw the village below the castle, the people and their homes spread out in a tempting circle around her, a world she could see, but never touch.

The world she longed to be a part of, and couldn't, because of her name. Her station. Her destiny.

She thought of the little boy Jake had once been, who had lain in this bed, and looked out over this view. "You told me you grew up in an apartment in New York," she said.

"I did. A world so different from this one." His voice had softened, dipping into the ranges of memory, of opening a window now to his soul. "But I would come here on vacation once a year with my parents. My father thought I was crazy for wanting this room, but…when I saw this view, and it was just so different from what I had at home, I insisted on staying up here. For a little boy, I guess it was one of those imagination things. Stay up here and dream all day, know what I mean?"

Mariabella nodded, then reached out and touched the pane of glass. "I understand you so much more now."

"You do?"

"We are the same, you and me. At least in what we saw when we looked out the window." She traced the outline of the town below. "From my room, I could see the village below, and at night, when the lights were on, it was like stars had been sprinkled on all the houses. I used to lay there and watch the cars moving, the people walking, then later, after they had all gone inside, I could see them living their lives. Reading by the fire, tucking their kids in at night, laughing with their friends. Just being…normal." She drew in a breath, and looked away from the town. Soon, too soon, she would go back to being the woman in the castle, watching everyone else living the life she wanted for herself. A life she'd only been able to taste, like an appetizer. "It all seemed so…magical from where I was."

Jake had moved to sit behind her on the bed, exchanging warmth. Connection. "Exactly."

Her mind wandered, past the houses below, past the inn, to Uccelli, to the little girl she'd once been, the little girl looking out the window at an impossible dream. "And when the sun came up—"

"It was as if it was coming up just for you. When you're up high like this, the sun seems to be yours alone."

"Yes, it does," she whispered. "It is like you're in your own world. Away from everything that happens below you."

Jake Lattimore understood, she realized, because he had been here, up in this tiny room, just as she had been in her room, at the top of the castle. She could have had any of dozens of bedrooms in the castle, but like Jake, she had chosen the smallest one at the highest point, seeking—

Seeking separation? Seeking distance? Or seeking the best view of the world out there?

"You wanted the same thing, did you not?" She turned around and found herself in his arms. She didn't move back, didn't move away. "The room at the top, so that—"

"I could see what I was missing," he finished.

She swallowed, her gaze connecting with his, wishing, oh, wishing, she had found someone who knew what she had gone through, someone who understood. "And what were you missing?"

His hand came up to cup her jaw. "Freedom."

She closed her eyes. "Yes." The word escaped her on a breath.

"A different life than mine."

"Yes."

And then, his lips were whispering across hers, the heat of his breath caressing her skin. She sank into his arms, and forgot why she shouldn't kiss him—

And just did.

But Jake didn't just kiss her, he awoke a season of feelings in her body, one move at a time. First, with his fingers, dancing along the edge of her jaw, then with his lips, teasing at the edge of hers. She had lived for too long in a winter of nothing, and now she felt as if her body was blooming with emotions, desires, a passion that she had denied, put aside for duty.

For her country.

And yet, Mariabella knew, as wonderful as this was, it had to end. Because it couldn't be, even temporarily. Better to deny herself than have this wonderful thing for a little while, then have it ripped away in two months. She drew back, breaking the contact with Jake, and got to her feet. "That… that should not have happened."

"Because we're at odds over a piece of real estate?"

"That, and because we are from two different worlds."

"It didn't sound so different a minute ago."

She headed for the door, a knife running through her as she remembered she had no right to dream of that life at the bottom of the hill. "We are oceans apart. Further than you will ever know."

CHAPTER SEVEN

THE board had sent out a spy.

Carl Winters leaned against the limo, waiting in the cold. His breath escaped him in a cloud, competing with the smoke coming from the cigar in his hands. A scowl scrunched up his face, darkening his small eyes beneath the black bowler-style hat on his bald head.

"I don't need a keeper." Jake reached past Carl for the door handle.

Carl shifted and blocked Jake's hand. "Seems you do. The board wants action on this deal, and so far, we've got nothing."

"It's Christmas, Carl. People don't make major life decisions four days before Christmas."

"It's your job to make sure they do." He took a step forward. "Your father ran this company into the ground with crazy decisions. That's why we were brought in, to show him how a truly successful corporation is run. He hasn't, however, always listened to our advice, and Lattimore has paid for his…idiocy. We're counting on you to be smarter."

To toe the line, was the unspoken sentence.

"I'm working on it." Jake closed the gap between them, his height giving him a good six-inch advantage over Carl. "Like I told you, I don't need a keeper. I can handle this on my own."

Except, he hadn't done so well with that yesterday, had he?

For a moment there, he'd forgotten business. Actually had the crazy idea of considering the inn, of all properties. What insane sentimental notion had pushed him into driving up there, he didn't know, but he should never have shown it to Mariabella. She needed to understand the more commercially viable property was the one in New York, not a loss leader like the inn.

Given a little more time to make his case, surely he'd show her the downside of those quaint B&Bs she loved, and the benefits of a bustling all-in-one hotel.

Without the distractions of kisses. Definitely no more of those.

"We're just making sure you stick to the plan," Carl said.

As if Jake had any intentions of doing otherwise. He resisted the urge to slam a fist into Carl. "You should remember who is CEO," Jake said, advancing a little on Carl, asserting his authority with his words and height. "I make the plans, and the decisions. I'm the one ultimately in charge of this deal, not you."

"Then stop with the field trips." Carl spun away from Jake, and headed for his car, parked a couple spaces away.

How did the board know where Jake had gone today? No one knew, except Mariabella, Will and his father. He'd told no one else. Jake trusted Will implicitly. Mariabella—

He saw no reason for her to involve the board. That would only go against her goals, rather than work with them.

The only one who could have said anything was Lawrence Lattimore. But why? He was the one who wanted his son to take over as CEO. Unless...

Lawrence doubted Jake's capabilities, too. And had sent out Carl as an insurance policy.

Jake shrugged it off. Until the company was back on solid ground, he'd be proving himself to all the naysayers who thought he'd earned his position through birthright, instead of hard work.

Jake got inside the car, rubbing his hands together to warm them. "There's one guy who's off my Christmas list."

Will laughed. "I saw him coming. Had to resist the urge to push on the gas pedal."

Jake leaned against the seat and ran a hand through his hair. "Maybe I shouldn't work in the family company."

Will stared at him. "You didn't just say that."

"I did. I've been thinking it a lot longer." The empty chasm that had nagged at him for years yawned even wider. Lattimore Properties demanded a type of sacrifice, a compromising of his own ideas and dreams that Jake had accepted when he'd donned the mantle of CEO.

Except, Jake had been wondering lately if he could still make that compromise. Yesterday had only renewed those doubts. Crazy thoughts, yet they kept returning, like boomerangs.

He thought back to the sleigh ride with Mariabella, then the room at the top of the inn. To the blissful happiness he'd seen on her face—and felt in his own chest.

That was the kind of experience he wanted to build. The trouble? Those types of properties didn't make millions. His father and the board would never support such an endeavor. Still…

The empty hole in Jake demanded he fill it with something other than another cookie-cutter hotel. Except cookie cutters sold and sold big.

"Wow. I had no idea," Will said. "I mean, you practically grew up in the company offices."

"Yeah, well, thinking about quitting isn't exactly something I'd bring up at family dinners or at a board meeting."

"Or with your best friend?"

Jake shrugged. "I shouldn't even consider it, that's why I never said anything. My dad is depending on me. Has been for years. I'm his retirement plan." If Jake bucked the company plan, and built a hotel that didn't fit the company model, his father's future would suffer, too.

"Jake, the great savior of the company." Will watched him,

as if trying to gauge his reaction to the words. Will knew Jake better than anyone, knew the expectations that had been heaped on the younger Lattimore for years. "And you have different ideas for your future?"

Jake looked out the window, at the long wooden board-walk lined with shops. A full sidewalk of possibilities for the future of Lattimore Properties, if he did what he was expected to do. "No," Jake said, pulling on the handle and exiting the limo. "I don't."

Carmen had left for lunch, and the gallery had quieted down. The new show would debut tomorrow, the day before Christmas Eve, giving last-minute shoppers both an event to attend and a little something different to buy. All the preparations were done, and Mariabella had turned her attention to her Harborside activities.

She had finished buying the groceries for the annual Christmas Eve dinner she threw for a dozen or so townspeople, and begun the list for the New Year's Eve party at the town hall. She flipped to a clean page in her planner and started working on the wish list for the community center she hoped to have built—or at least started— before she left in February.

So many things to accomplish, and so little time to do them. She'd find a way, though. She'd find a way.

The bell over the door jingled, and Mariabella looked up, expecting a customer. Finding instead Jake Lattimore. Her heart skipped a beat, and her pulse began to race.

She clutched her planner tighter, and refused to let the attraction show on her face.

Ever since that moment in the attic, when he'd kissed her and knocked her completely off-kilter, she'd been unable to concentrate whenever Jake came close. Heck, when she went to sleep last night, she'd dreamed of him, of the laughter they'd shared on the sleigh ride, but most of all, of that kiss.

When she woke up this morning, she'd thought of him. She'd found herself sketching a man with blue eyes in the corner of her planner today.

Insane. She had to shake off these thoughts.

Except a very big part of her didn't want to. That part wanted everything—to find a way to combine duty with the ordinary life she craved like air to breathe.

Jake crossed the room, pausing before the portrait of the mysterious woman. He studied it for a long moment before speaking. "How did you know you wanted to open this gallery?"

The question hit her out of left field. "How did I know? I...I have always loved art. That is what I went to college to study. It is all I have ever known."

More or less. If she left off all that information about the real-life lessons in becoming a queen.

"Yes, but, why a gallery? Why not an art supply store? Or a museum?"

She laughed. "Well a museum is a lot more expensive to own, to stock. To maintain. And, I have been in museums. They are beautiful but not..."

"Not what you wanted." He turned toward her. "Because you had a different vision in mind for your future?"

She thought of the future. There would be no gallery in the days ahead.

Truth be told, she *should* sell Harborside Art Gallery to Jake Lattimore. In a couple of months, she would be leaving for Uccelli, and taking her place beside her father, before finally ascending to the throne.

"No, for my present," she said. Because that was all she had in Harborside.

A slight smile curved up the side of his face, then just as quickly disappeared. "For the present. Of course."

She opened her mouth to tell him she'd given up the fight, she'd sell the shop, then stopped. No. She'd keep the gallery.

Let Carmen run it. She didn't care about making a profit. She simply wanted to know that even if she was on the other side of the world, these days she'd enjoyed wouldn't disappear. It would be like one of those dioramas, something she could peek into with a letter or a phone call, and be transported back to the days when she'd been—

Ordinary.

Jake wandered the room, his gaze roaming over the various pieces of art. He paused by the portrait of the mysterious woman, studying her for a long time, as if he saw the same puzzle in that painting as Mariabella had. "Is this gallery what makes you happy?"

"It…" She paused. "Yes."

He glanced at her. "Why the hesitation?"

"My life is complicated."

He crossed to the window, taking in the view of the ocean. "Complicated. Living here."

She laughed. "Life can be complicated living anywhere."

"True." He spun away from the view and back toward her. The gap between them closed so fast, Mariabella didn't have time to steel herself for his presence, to throw up those defenses she'd worked so hard to convince herself she had in abundance.

"And I have complicated it even more for you," he said.

"Yes. You have."

"Then the best thing to do is to get rid of me."

Her pulse raced, her breath hurried in and out of her chest. She inhaled the woodsy scent of his cologne, and with it, the memory of being in his arms. "It would seem so."

He reached into his jacket pocket and pulled out a sheaf of papers. "This, Miss Romano, is the way to do that."

She stared at him. All this time, she'd thought maybe Jake had come in here to talk about yesterday, about their kiss, about what they had shared on that drive. To tell her that in that room in the inn, he had heard her and now understood her need to preserve Harborside just as it was, because he'd once had the same dreams as her.

Instead, he'd wanted only one thing.

Her gallery.

She swatted the papers away. "I will not sign. Stop asking me."

"Your life is complicated, you told me so yourself. This will make it easier."

"What do *you* know about making my life easier?" She crossed to the desk and flipped open her planner. She dipped her head to study the list of things to do before New Year's Eve. How could she have fallen for that act back at the inn? The romantic sleigh ride? The sweet words?

And that kiss most of all?

Clearly it had all been an attempt to soften her up.

She could read this man like a tabloid. Every time she thought he might be trying to build something on a personal level, might actually be getting to know her—really know Mariabella, the person—Jake Lattimore circled back to what he really wanted. Real estate.

Her cell phone rang, and before she could think about checking the caller ID, she flipped it open, using the call as an excuse to avoid Jake. "Hello?"

"When are you going to end this insanity?"

Her father's voice cut across the phone line with the precision of a knife. Even from the other side of the world, she could hear the disapproval in his tone.

She glanced at Jake, wishing he would leave so she could take the call alone. But he didn't take the hint, and remained in the gallery, a few feet away, yet still close enough to overhear anything she said.

"Are you going to answer me?" None of the sweetness her mother had in his tone.

"How are you feeling?" Mariabella asked, instead of answering the question.

"I'm fine. I'd be better if you were back here. It's been ten months, Mariabella. More than enough time for you to get this craziness out of your system."

She put her back to Jake. "I have until February."

"What difference will two months make? Really, Mariabella, this has gone on long enough. Your place is here, preparing for the throne. Not playing…whatever game you're playing."

"Can we talk about this later?"

"I've sent you an airline ticket by overnight mail. It will arrive tonight, if it hasn't already. I expect to see you here for Christmas. And here to stay."

"But—"

"Your obligations have waited long enough, Mariabella. And so have I." Her father hung up. Discussion over.

Edict issued by His Majesty. No arguments allowed.

Mariabella sighed and tucked her cell phone into her pocket. She would deal with her father later. Somehow.

"Trouble?"

She spun toward Jake and put on a smile. "Everything is fine."

"Good." He slid the papers across the front desk. "About my offer…"

She stared at the purchase and sales he'd put before her. In a few pages, she could sign over the gallery, go back to Uccelli and wash her hands of her life in America. Put it all behind her, dismiss it like a dream she'd once had.

Jake had impeccable timing, she'd give him that. He'd presented her with the way out she needed. The path her father expected her to take.

And take it today.

"What was that yesterday? Who was that man? Because he is not the same one I see today."

Jake scowled. "Forget what I said yesterday. Dreams like that don't make for a successful business."

"And this success you keep talking about, it will make you happy?"

"What does that have to do with anything?"

Mariabella glanced around her gallery, at all that she would soon give up, and relegate to a memory of a time when she had been happy. A man like Jake Lattimore, who had never lived a preordained life of expectations like she had, didn't appreciate what he had. "Happiness fulfills you in a way no amount of money, or privilege, ever can."

He folded the papers into thirds and tucked them inside his jacket. Then he crossed again to the portrait of *She Who Knows.* For a long time, Jake said nothing, then, finally, one quiet sentence. "Have dinner with me."

She hadn't expected that response. "Dinner? With you?"

He pivoted back. "I know there are a hundred reasons why we shouldn't go out again. A hundred more why you probably wouldn't want to see me ever again, especially because I still want to buy your gallery."

"Then why go out at all?"

"Because…" His gaze went past her to the window that looked out over the ocean, to the vast horizon beyond them. "Because my life is complicated, too. And yesterday, when I was with you, it felt a little less complicated for the first time in a long time."

She couldn't say no to honesty like that. Yesterday, she had met a different man. And just maybe, at dinner, she could bring that man back, and persuade him to build the right hotel for this town, before she was forced to meet the demands waiting for her just an ocean away.

CHAPTER EIGHT

"IF YOU don't wipe that smirk off your face, I'll fire you."

The grin widened. Will's smile matched that of the elf's on his blue tie. "Hey, the tie worked, didn't it? You just don't want to admit a bunch of snowmen had more charm than you did."

Jake chuckled. "Okay, so you were right. Half right, anyway. She didn't kiss me. Not that night."

Will arched a brow. "So you *have* kissed her?"

Jake just grinned.

"See? The suggestive power of fun. Give it a day or two and you'll be in love, curled up in front of a fire with her, all cozy for the holidays."

Jake snorted. "It'll take more than that. She's stubborn."

Will glanced at the ceiling. "Like someone else I know?"

"What is this world coming to when the chauffeur is telling the boss what to do?"

"Hey. I prefer the term 'travel director,'" Will said.

Jake laughed again. "Fine. I'll have business cards sent to your office at the front of the limo."

Will's grin had a certain gleam to it, a tease in his gaze, reflected in the rearview mirror. "If you don't mind me saying—"

"You're going to say it either way, so go right ahead."

"—that woman is trouble." Will turned and rested his arm on the back of the leather seat. "Exactly what you need."

Jake scowled. "That's where you're wrong. I don't need any trouble. I need to get this deal done, then get out. I have another property south of San Francisco to look at, then one in Saint Kitts, another in—"

Will mocked a yawn. "Aren't you tired yet?"

"It's six o'clock in the evening, Will. Hardly my bedtime."

"Tired of this grind. Tired of conquering buildings. And going home to…nothing. You don't even have a cat."

"I don't like cats."

"Then get a dog. A goldfish. A parakeet. Something that breathes air into that box you call an apartment."

"Technically, it's a condo. In a building that's netting a fifteen percent return on my—"

Will put up a hand. "Right there. That's the problem. Where do I go on the few days I don't drive you some place?"

"Home."

"Exactly. A real, honest-to-God house. It's nothing much, and I've got a Honey-Do list a mile long, landscaping as over-grown as a rain forest and a dog that my wife walks more than I do, but there's a recliner there with my name on it and a woman who knows exactly how I like my coffee. It's a—" he paused and met Jake's gaze "—home."

"My apartment is a—" Jake stopped. Will was right. The place where Jake put his feet up for a few days a month, the place where he stored his clothes and the books he'd been meaning to read, was a box of walls and windows.

He had once thought he could have a home. Then given up on the idea. Some days he wondered if maybe—

But no. He had a company to run.

Will put out his hands, in a see-what-I-mean gesture. "That's why this woman is trouble."

"Because she has a home?" Jake shook his head. "You

are spending too much time sitting in this car, inhaling carbon monoxide."

His friend let out a sigh, the kind that said his boss had yet to get the point. "Listen, I have no idea if Mariabella Romano lives in a house or a shoebox. What I'm saying is that she's the type of woman who inspires a man to stay home. For a nanosecond, you were that kind of man. And then you became Jake Lattimore, CEO. Apartment guy."

"Then what's the trouble?"

"You're already falling for her." Will turned back around and put the car in gear, pulling away from the curb of the Harborside Inn and heading for the art gallery. The subject closed, but still hanging in the air.

Mariabella stood in the gallery, checking the placement of the paintings for tomorrow night's show, and refusing to check her appearance. Again.

She had already done more than enough primping for an evening that wasn't even a date. It was—

One more opportunity to manipulate Jake Lattimore into leaving Harborside. To convince him he would find bluer waters elsewhere. She had come armed, not just with a dress that showed off her figure—thereby assuring his attention wouldn't wander from her—but also a sheaf of papers in her purse, documenting areas up and down the East Coast that lacked vacation venues.

He wasn't the only one with a few resources up his sleeves.

Except, she fretted, pacing the gallery one more time, dimming the lights for the night as she did, making that call to Reynaldo might have been a mistake. Before, only two people had known her exact location. Now, three did. That multiplied her chances of being found.

Being exposed.

Losing her haven, her serenity.

Mariabella headed into her office, and stopped before a watercolor of a castle. The painting was simple, the lines of the building sparse and stark, but the stone building atop the grassy hill was one very similar to the one where she'd grown up. A local artist had painted it—something the artist had imagined, as a fan of all things fairy tale—and Mariabella had bought the piece for her personal collection because the image was so close, it could have passed for home.

A bone-deep ache bloomed in her chest. She closed her eyes, picturing her parents, wishing she could simply teleport herself back there for one more hug, one more kiss.

Have the best of both worlds. Her freedom, and loving arms.

The bell over the door of the gallery rang, and Mariabella drew herself up. Jake had arrived. And that meant she had to get her game face on, and get down to business. With one last glance at the castle that had been both home and captor, Mariabella strode out of her office and into the main room of the gallery.

She refused to let him know how much he affected her. How she had been thinking, nearly nonstop, about that kiss back in that room in New Jersey.

No. She had to think like a woman in charge, one taking back what was hers—

Harborside.

And that meant using whatever tools she had. She'd learned a long time ago, in dozens of lessons on deportment and protocol, how to make an entrance. She took her time making the walk from the doorway to the center of the room, lengthening her strides, ensuring that the strappy red high heels she wore made her legs look longer, sleeker, beneath the knee-length black dress. Head up, shoulders back, gaze connecting with Jake's.

Commanding the room before she'd even reached him.

His eyes widened, then a smile spread across his face, and

she knew, as she'd known in dozens of state visits and endless balls, that she had his attention. And then some.

"You look…amazing," he said. His voice had dropped into a deeper range, the syllables almost a caress. He took two steps forward, closing the gap between them, and handed her not the traditional chocolates or flowers, but a dozen paintbrushes.

"What is this?"

He smiled. "Carmen told me you paint, too, and I thought this might be a better sign of a truce than a white flag." He pulled a postcard from his jacket pocket and gave it to her. A picture of the inn. "This goes with it."

He'd given her a gift that mattered to her. One that spoke to her passions, and made her remember that day at the inn. Because he was interested in her? Or because he was trying to win her over to his side of the real estate argument by making her think he was on her side, when she knew he wasn't? "Thank you," she said.

"You're welcome." He turned and gestured toward the door. "Are you ready to go?"

She left the gift on the counter, grabbed her coat off the rack, then led the way out of the gallery, locking the shop behind her. Will waited outside the limo, holding the door, a grin on his face. "Good evening, ma'am."

"Hello again, Will." She slid inside the limo. The door shut, sealing Mariabella temporarily in the leather cocoon alone. What was Jake up to tonight? Every time she thought she knew, he reversed course. She found herself wavering between falling for him—and wanting to run him out of town.

Which was the real Jake Lattimore? The one who walked into her gallery that first day, or the one at the inn?

Either way, she knew her only key to getting what this town needed was by appealing to that man she'd glimpsed for a second in the inn. That was the man she had to reach tonight, not the one who had built that New York hotel.

Jake got in on the opposite side, and took the seat across from her. A moment later, the limo pulled away from the curb and began its smooth journey toward the restaurant.

"We could have walked, you know," Mariabella said. "It is only two blocks."

"And it's only about three degrees out. This way, I don't have to worry about you catching pneumonia."

"But then you could take advantage of my weakened state."

He smiled. "Ah, a business strategy I haven't thought of yet. Pump the flu virus into the room, and then bring in the contracts."

"I am sure worse tactics have been employed."

"Not by me." The limo slowed to a stop. "I'm an ethical businessman, regardless of what you might think of me."

She smiled. "I think I will reserve my judgment until after dessert."

He chuckled. "And what if I ask you to go dancing after the crème brûleé?"

"Then poor Will will have an awfully late night, because the closest place for that is Boston."

He leaned forward. "I have all night, Miss Romano, to make my case."

The notes of his cologne carried in the heated air between them. She tried to ignore the dark, woodsy scent, to keep it from affecting her. To keep her gaze from connecting with his cobalt-blue eyes, because in their depths, she saw a heat—

An unmistakable heat, as ancient as the shores that lined the Eastern seaboard. As rocky and treacherous to navigate as the rocky shoals that held Harborside like a north and south cocoon. Desire drew her in, made her forget everything—her goals for this town, her duties back in Uccelli, everything but Jake and how wonderful his kiss had been.

The door opened, ushering in a burst of cold air, and burst of sense. Mariabella jerked back, drawing her coat closed.

Like that put any real distance between them. Still, it was enough to give her mental space, and get her back to reality.

She stepped out of the limousine, thanking Will as she did. "Enjoy your evening, ma'am," he said, then turned to Jake. "Shall I wait, sir?"

"No—" Jake began.

"Yes," Mariabella cut in. "I do not expect us to be out late, Mr. Lattimore. We both have work to do tomorrow, do we not?"

Sending him the clear-cut message with both her words and the use of his last name that this was no date. And he shouldn't expect some endless evening of romance with her.

"As the lady wishes," Jake said, then nodded toward Will, who returned to the driver's side of the limo and pulled it into the parking lot. Jake moved to hold the door for Mariabella, but she had already entered the building herself.

A year ago, she would have waited. Would have expected the man—anyone, really—to treat her in accordance with not just her sex, but her station. Except, after a while, that treatment had grated on her nerves. As if people were treating a title, not a person. Every time Mariabella had tried to do something herself in the castle, she'd been stopped—a princess wouldn't do that; a princess wouldn't behave like that. Since moving to Harborside, Mariabella had enjoyed a sense of self-reliance and strength that went far beyond simply opening her own doors.

She'd opened her own shop. Owned her own home. Mowed her own lawn.

Such simple things, but things she never would have been allowed to do in Uccelli.

"Hi, Mariabella. Table for one? In your usual spot?" Paula, the hostess, asked Mariabella.

"I have a reservation. For Lattimore, table for two, please," Jake said, coming up behind Mariabella and placing a hand lightly on her waist. The familiar gesture, something any date would do, sent a thrill through Mariabella. It was so ordinary, something that wouldn't have happened, had he known she was the princess. There would have been all that stumbling "Your Majesty" stuff in the way.

Paula raised an eyebrow. She stood there for a good three seconds gawking before recovering her hostess manners and managing to look at her reservation book. "Oh, yes, it's right here." She picked up two merlot-colored leatherbound menus. "Uh…right this way please."

"Dine here often?" Jake asked as they made their way toward the dining room.

A hot flush invaded Mariabella's cheeks. She might as well hang a sign around her neck that said Blatantly Single.

"I assume you have a date every night of the week?" she said to Jake. "Some young beautiful woman ready at your beck and call, whenever you jet back to New York?"

"Not quite."

He didn't expound on the answer, and she didn't press. Mariabella got the feeling Jake Lattimore had a few table-for-one evenings in his life, too. Interesting. So she wasn't the only one. Curiosity nudged at her, but she ignored the persistent urge to press him for personal details.

A fire crackled in the wide hearth of the gas log fireplace against the far wall, bathing the room in a soft glow. Pine garland festooned with red bows hung in swags across the mantel, accented with thick vanilla candles sandwiched between pinecones. Wreaths had been hung on the mullioned windows, with electric candles on the sills. The effect was homey and simple, done, Mariabella knew, by the owner herself, complete with all the imperfections that came with homespun décor.

"Can I take your drink order?" Sandy, one of the half-dozen college students who worked at the Captain's Galley in the winter, bounced up to their table, her blond hair back in a ponytail. "The wine list is on the back of the menu."

"Thank you, but I brought along something special of my own. It was an important evening, and I wanted to share my favorite wine with this beautiful lady." Jake flashed Mariabella a smile, then flipped out his cell phone. "Will, could you deliver the 1978 Pinot to the bartender? Thank you."

Sandy headed off, grabbing another waitress on the way, undoubtedly to gossip about the unusual customer who came equipped with his own liquor cabinet.

"You know you will be the talk of the kitchen for days," Mariabella said.

He shrugged. "I'm already the center of a gossip storm. Might as well add to the hurricane." Jake draped an arm over the back of his chair and took in the space. At the same time, the towns-people assessed him, whispers carrying through the room like cold germs in a preschool. "Why do you live in this town?"

"Because I like it here. It is quiet, simple, away from the busy-ness of the city."

"Also what makes it a prime destination spot." He waved toward the windows. Outside, the sun had gone down, and the moon shone a bright white circle above the wreaths. "Harborside has a remote feel without being remote. It's quirky, and yet still maintains some of that uppercrust New England feel. With the right hotel and condos, it can become a mecca for tourists. You have to see the logic in my argument, Mariabella. This idea can work and benefit everyone."

The words grated on Mariabella's senses. "Why are you so set on that idea? Especially after we visited the inn. Something like that would work better, would it not? After all, you loved it so much."

"I do. I did."

She fought the urge to scream at him, to shove him into his limo and drive him out of town herself. "Then why show it to me, if you are still planning on building that other hotel here?"

He put out his hands. "The smart thing for the company to

do is choose the property that will bring in the most return on investment. And while the inn was a nice diversion for the day, it's not smart business."

"The hotel may be the smartest thing to do, but is it the most fulfilling?"

Sandy saved Jake from answering with a glass of his wine, placing one glass before him and another before Mariabella, then leaving the marble carafe holding the bottle beside them. "I'll be back for your order in a minute…unless you have something in your car for dinner, too?"

Jake chuckled. "No, we'll order from the menu."

When Sandy was gone, Mariabella tried her wine. She picked up the glass, lifting the goblet first to her nose, giving the wine a swirl before inhaling the sweet scent, a mixture of citrus with a slight hint of almonds. Then she took a sip. The dry, crisp Pinot slid down her throat smoothly, with a familiar taste.

It couldn't be. That was impossible.

Mariabella took a second sip. But yes, the taste was there. The one she knew. Knew so well.

"Do you like it?" Jake asked. "It's not a common wine, which is part of why I enjoy it so much. Very few people in the States have tasted this one."

She was one of the few who had. She had, in fact, walked the very vineyard that had bottled it. "It is…ah, lovely," Mariabella managed. She put her glass back on the table, careful not to tip it, even as her hands shook.

"I travel quite a bit and sometimes stop off in the tiniest, most out-of-the-way places," he went on, "because I love discovering the best vacation spots. The ones no one else has noticed."

"Really?" The word escaped on a high pitch. Mariabella fought the urge to run. He had to know who she was. He'd done this to set her up.

"Two years ago, I went to Italy, and visited all the normal

spots. Venice, Sicily. I got bored pretty quick, so I decided to go off the beaten path."

Mariabella took another sip of her wine, because she didn't know what to say. Tip her hand now? Or wait until Jake said, *And then I popped into Uccelli and discovered they were missing a princess.*

"So I ditched my driver, rented a car on my own and traveled up the coast." He leaned forward, crossing his arms on the table. His gaze met hers across the small square expanse. "And found the most amazing places."

"Really?" She'd become a one-word parrot.

"Little cafes and shops. Tiny restaurants. Small countries, almost…undiscovered. At least by the corporate lions like me." He let out a laugh.

She tried to join in, but her laughter sounded more like the last-ditch breaths of a strangulation victim.

"My favorite place was this tiny country called Uccelli. Maybe you've been there? Especially where you grew up so close to that area."

What should she say? How much did he know? Panic cut off her air, coiled in her gut. She gripped the stem of the wineglass, so tight, her fingertips turned white.

"So, did you decide?"

Sandy. Thank God. Mariabella could have hugged the waitress for her timing. "I will have…ah…the lobster fra Diablo," Mariabella said. "With a Caesar salad and…and… potatoes au gratin."

Sandy scribbled the order on her pad, then turned to Jake. "The same."

He'd never even opened his menu. Mariabella had a bad feeling about this dinner. What had really been Jake Lattimore's intentions? Business or pleasure?

In Jake's eyes, she didn't read recognition. He didn't know who she was. His interest in Uccelli was a coincidence, nothing more. Relief settled over her, chased by the warm contentment offered by the wine. Perhaps this evening would turn out better than she had expected after all.

"What did you mean when you said your life is complicated, too?" she asked.

He slid his fork to the side, aligning it with his knife. "You know that sleigh ride we took yesterday?"

She nodded.

"I haven't done anything like that in five years. Like Will told you, I used to be a different man."

"Why?"

His mouth worked, as if he were searching for words. "I haven't had a serious relationship in a long time, and I guess I forgot what it was like to enjoy an evening like that."

"Me, too," she whispered.

He raised his glass toward hers, and they clinked. "To more of that, for both of us."

She didn't respond. She couldn't. How could she tell him her time here was nearly through? That the sleigh ride would become nothing but a bittersweet memory?

Instead, she sipped her wine, and thought of Uccelli, and the fate that waited for her there.

"Is that really what you want?" she asked. "More of that fun?"

"If I can find a way to make it work, yes."

It was time to make her move, to show him there was another answer, another option for his plans. To appeal to the side of him that had reappeared, that side she'd seen yesterday.

She pulled the papers out of her purse and slid them across the table. "Then here are several other possibilities for your hotel. All of them far more suitable for your purposes than Harborside. The populations are slightly larger, which gives your vacationers a wider variety of local businesses, there are more amenities available in a fifty-mile radius—" she pointed to the first one on the pile "—this one even has an outlet mall with two-hundred stores, a big plus—"

"You've put a great deal of time into this in a short period of time." He sifted through the thick sheaf of papers. "I'm impressed."

"I wanted to provide you with options."

"Besides Harborside."

"Yes."

Jake leaned back in his chair and crossed his arms over his chest. "Why are you so hell-bent on driving me out of town?"

"We like our town the way it is. It has all the elements of that inn you loved so much. Why can you not see that?"

"If that's so then why did Louisa Hampton already agree to sell her kite shop?"

Louisa? She had given in? Mariabella had thought Louisa would stand firm, and not sell. She couldn't imagine the boardwalk without the kindly elderly woman and her little dachshund. Every morning, Louisa stopped in at each of her neighbors' shops before opening her own, and said a friendly hello. She had been a staple in Harborside for as long as anyone could remember.

"And my team is already working on contract terms with Sam Carter."

The bike shop owner. Business had been down for him for over a year. The summer rentals just hadn't brought in enough income to sustain him the other three seasons. She could understand Sam wanting to sell, but maybe if she talked to the others—

Then what?

Mariabella couldn't single-handedly save every business in Harborside. No matter how much she might want to.

A second couple came into the dining room and sat down at the table beside them. At first, Mariabella gave them a passing glance—a tall blond man dressed in business casual and a thin brunette woman in a red suit and black high heels.

"If you just consider some of the other—" Mariabella gestured toward the papers, then stopped.

The woman at the next table was whispering to the man with her. And at the same time, staring at Mariabella.

"I will think about these possibilities," Jake was saying. "After this project is completed. Harborside needs something to take it to the next level as a vacation spot, not just for tourists, but for the finances of this town. You must agree with me at least on that. But…perhaps you and I can reach a compromise."

"Compromise?"

The woman was now openly gawking at Mariabella. The attention unnerved her, and she shifted in her seat, trying to keep her attention on Jake. What was he saying? Did he still want to build that monstrosity? Was everything they'd done and said yesterday for nothing?

The woman beside them reached out and touched Jake, drawing his attention. "Hi, Jake."

Jake turned and looked at her. "Darcy. Tim. I didn't expect to see you so soon."

"We rode up with Carl. He thought it would be a good idea for us to check out the town early on in the planning process," Tim, the blond man, said. "Get a feel for what you're envisioning."

Jake gave them one short nod, one that didn't show a trace of emotion, then turned to Mariabella. "Mariabella Romano, this is my team. Tim Collins, my architect. Darcy Singer, my marketing director."

A setup, this whole dinner had been a setup. The wine. The table for two. And now, the "team." The betrayal stung Mariabella and it was all she could do to put on a polite smile.

The two other people put out their hands, as polite as dignitaries at a dinner party. Except…

Darcy kept studying Mariabella. She tipped her head one way, then the other.

Mariabella straightened her spine, and tilted her chin, giving Darcy the slight air of haughty disregard that came with her upbringing. In Uccelli, that look reminded those who might have dared to talk down to the princess that royalty came with certain privileges.

Like respect.

Like not being stared at as if she were a science exhibit.

"A pleasure to meet you," Mariabella said. The words choked out of her. She shot Jake a glare. He started to say something to her, but Darcy interrupted.

"Are you…like, a movie star?" Darcy said. "I swear, I know you from somewhere."

Dread dropped in Mariabella's stomach. She'd seen that look before. Knew that tone.

In the space of one slow second, Mariabella could feel the world she'd worked so hard to build fall apart. Crumbling one syllable at a time.

"Your face is so familiar," Darcy went on. "I know it. Give me a second."

Darcy was on to her. Maybe not all the way, but she was inching closer every second Mariabella stayed.

If she could have run out of the restaurant, she would have. But the wall was behind her, Darcy was in front of her, and Jake was beside her.

Jake stared at her. Waited for her answer to Darcy's question.

"I am afraid you have me confused with someone else," Mariabella said.

"No, I don't think so." Darcy squinted. "I *know* I know you. I read that *Famous People* magazine all the time. It's a vice, I know, and I should be reading business magazines on planes, sorry, Jake," Darcy said, glancing at her boss, "but sometimes you just have to indulge, especially when you spend as much time on planes as I do. And I can swear, I've seen your picture in there."

"I need to go," Mariabella said, getting to her feet. Her stomach rolled and pitched, and sweat broke out on her forehead.

Darcy reached for her, but Mariabella shifted quickly to the right, away from the touch. "I'm right, aren't I? Are you like in hiding or something?"

"You have got me all wrong," Mariabella said.

"I don't think so." Darcy stared at her, and in that second, Mariabella knew she'd met her worst nightmare. "I never forget a face."

CHAPTER NINE

JAKE had wondered who Mariabella Romano was. He'd wondered why she was living in Harborside, and concocted dozens of scenarios in his head, most centering around logical premises. She'd come to America to study, or with a boyfriend.

But he clearly should have been looking to the newsstand for his answers.

Mariabella grabbed her purse and coat and got to her feet. "I really have to go."

In a blur, she was gone.

Without ever answering the question.

"Well, that was weird," Tim said.

"I agree." Jake tugged the wine bottle out of the carafe and poured himself a second glass of the Pinot. He was about to put the bottle back into the holder when Darcy stopped him.

"Hey, let me see that." She turned the bottle around, studying the design on the front. "I've seen this painting before." She thought a second. "I know. In the same magazine. They did this whole article on this little country north of Italy, how it was like one of the last monarchies in the world, and—"

She stopped talking.

Stared at Jake, then at where Mariabella had gone.

"That's impossible," she whispered.

"What is?"

Darcy cradled the bottle, running her thumb over the image. "I can't believe it."

"What?"

Darcy handed the bottle over to Jake and pointed at the label. The front had, as Darcy had said, a painting. A stone castle, the same one he'd seen on his brief visit to Uccelli, rising above the rocky shore and lush green paths. It was as he'd remembered, with four turrets topped with purple and gold pennants, surrounded by a massive stone wall, that he imagined had once been manned full-time by guards.

He spun the bottle around to read the back. "'Grown and bottled at a vineyard located just down the hill from the royal palace, an impressive stone structure built in the late seventeenth century. A small but thriving country, Uccelli is one of the few remaining monarchies in Europe.'"

"Monarchy? As in kings and queens?" Tim said.

"That's the place." Darcy pointed to the image on the bottle. "That's the castle I saw in the article."

"And what does this have to do with Mariabella?"

"She was…" Darcy leaned forward, her eyes wide with excitement. "The *princess.*"

Jake scoffed and put the bottle back in the carafe. "Come on. There's no way a princess is living in this little town. And no one knows about it."

Darcy shrugged. "Maybe. Or maybe not. It happens."

"With who? Cinderella?"

Tim chuckled.

"I could be wrong." But as Darcy said the words, Jake got the feeling she doubted she had made a mistake, and knowing his efficient marketing director as he did, he doubted it, too. "Either way, I'll be glad to research it."

Jake gave a single nod. As quickly as Mariabella had left, he sent Darcy and Tim off to research and told them he would have their meals delivered to the Seaside Inn.

That pushed his team off on another mission besides watching his every move, which was undoubtedly what Carl had brought them here to do. To ensure Jake fulfilled the board's orders, got the signatures on the real estate transactions and built a shining example of a Lattimore property. None of those silly sentimental buildings his father had once loved.

He waved over the waitress and paid the bill. For now, the real estate transaction would wait. He had a more important mission of his own to accomplish.

"She doesn't exist," Tim said.

"What do you mean, she doesn't exist?" Jake barked into his cell phone, then lowered his voice and apologized. "There has to be an address, a phone number, something for her. No one lives in this country for almost a year without leaving some kind of paper trail."

"Apparently, she does. And as for Uccelli, all official pictures of her have been taken down. I couldn't find a single one on the Internet. It's like she…vanished."

Jake paced outside the limo, his breath escaping in a cloud. A melody, followed by the rise and fall of laughter, caught his attention. People streamed in and out of the Clamshell Tavern, a few humming along with the Christmas carol playing inside. "She may not have left a paper trail, but I bet she left a people trail." Jake told Tim to keep trying to dig up information, then hung up, gave Will a sign to wait and jogged across the street.

As he'd expected, he found Zeke sitting at the same stool, only this time the tavern was far more crowded, with several people playing pool, a few dancing around the jukebox and a group of men cheering on a hockey team on the big screen at the opposite end of the bar. Jake slid in beside Zeke, and ordered the man a beer. "Hey, Zeke."

"Hey, Mr. Lattimore. You still in town?"

"I'm here until the job is done."

Zeke grinned. "Hard-working man. That's something I can respect. 'Course, can't say I can relate, but I can respect it." He tipped the beer bottle Jake's way. "You working at night?"

Jake was about to say yes, then shook his head. "Thought I'd just have a beer right now." He ordered a second bottle for himself, and settled into a relaxed pose. As if he had all night.

"What do you think of them?" Zeke said.

It took a second before Jake realized the man meant the hockey team battling it out on the television screen. "I like them if you do."

Zeke chuckled. "I do, but I don't say that too loud 'round these parts. You gotta root for the home team, know what I mean?"

"I do."

Jake thought of the season tickets to the basketball team that sat on his desk, year after year, used more often by his assistants than by him. Same with the box seats to baseball. For a second he watched the crowd around him, regular working men and women, who roared at each turn in the action.

And he envied them.

They took the time to go to bars and games, to have lives like Will's. Maybe his friend was right. Maybe it was time to put work aside and live, like he had yesterday.

Except yesterday had been spent with a woman who had been lying to him, who had been hiding a secret the entire time she'd been in his arms. Maybe it was better to stick to work. At least a profit and loss was always written in black and white.

The period ended, and a commercial came on, causing the crowd around the television to break into small groups doing a verbal rehash of the last few moments of play, along with resounding criticism of the refs and the coaches.

"Ah, they're losing." Zeke frowned and turned away. "I know how it's going to end. Badly."

"Then why do you watch?"

Zeke's frown turned into a grin. "Because at heart, I'm one

of those sappy guys who believes in happily ever after. Just don't tell the ladies, or they'll be expecting me to go around with flowers and wine." He puffed out his chest. "Gotta protect my image as a tough guy, you know."

Jake chuckled. "Your secret's safe with me." He toyed with the beer bottle. "Speaking of women, I took Mariabella Romano to dinner tonight."

He didn't add how it had turned out, that he had realized she was leading a double life. From the look on Mariabella's face earlier, Jake doubted anyone in town knew the truth about her.

Zeke's jaw dropped. "And she went? On a date?"

"You're surprised?"

"Our Mariabella doesn't date much," Zeke said, then thought a second. "Actually, I've *never* seen her date."

That would make sense for someone protecting their identity. The question was why. And why she was so fiercely protective of a little town on the other side of the world.

"Things ended badly," Jake said. "And I was hoping to make it up to her."

Zeke gave him a little nudge in the ribs. "A secret flowers-and-wine counterattack? Is that it?"

"Exactly." The one-word lie slid off Jake's tongue easily. But it tasted bitter.

He didn't know why it should. After all, she'd been lying to him from day one. He'd opened up to her and where had it gotten him?

Nowhere but distracted from the plans he should be focusing on. From here on out, things between them would be business, pure and simple. He had no intentions of wooing Mariabella Romano for anything other than her location. And that meant using every tool at his disposal.

Including her identity.

"Our Mariabella might not be the wine-and-roses type."

Zeke rubbed at his beard. "You're going to have to work a little harder, my boy."

"You keep calling her 'our Mariabella.' Is there a reason why?"

Zeke shrugged. "This town unofficially adopted her when she moved here. We took care of her, and she's taken care of us."

"Financially."

"Hell, no. Though what she did for us has brought us up in the dollars-and-cents department. She's started committees, arranged events, just got us organized and thinking in new ways. She's been a real leader 'round here." Zeke took a deep drag from the beer, then put it back on the bar. "Anyway, it ain't none of my business to be talking about her behind her back. You want to know about Mariabella, you have to do your own homework."

He had Tim and Darcy doing some of that homework. The type that could be done on computers, with background checks and phone calls. What Jake wanted to do involved a more…personal connection. "I'd like to get to know her better," he said, "but she's a tough nut to crack."

Zeke chuckled. "She is stubborn, I'll give you that."

"I do feel bad about how things ended tonight," he repeated, hoping to work on Zeke's sympathies, "and if I knew where she lived, perhaps I could tell her in person. If I wait until tomorrow, she'll be so busy at the gallery, that I may miss my chance."

Zeke shifted on the bar stool. "I don't think Mariabella would like me to give out her address."

"You're probably right." Jake signaled for another round. The bartender slid two more beers their way. "Waiting until tomorrow to apologize for spilling a drink on her new dress probably won't hurt…."

"Oh, boy, that's a bad one!" Zeke crowed. "I did that once

to my first wife, and I was in the dog house for a week! Cost me not one, but two new dresses."

Jake nodded, and studied his beer. "I suspect I'll be paying. For quite some time. But I suppose I can make it up to her later. Maybe."

"First date you say, huh?"

He nodded again.

"I know a lot of us around here sure would like to see Mariabella with a fellow." Zeke stroked his beard. "And you seem like a nice enough man."

"My fifth grade teacher will vouch for me." He gave Zeke a grin, one he hoped built camaraderie.

Zeke grabbed a pen from the bar, then scribbled something on a cocktail napkin and slid it over to Jake. "You didn't get that from me. But if this works out, I want to be front and center for the wedding."

Jake's smile wobbled on his face. Wedding? That was as far from his plans as Pluto was from Earth. "You've got it, Zeke."

He left the Clamshell Tavern, leaving behind a promise he didn't mean, made to a man he hardly knew. It was business, he told himself.

Then why did something he did every day suddenly feel so wrong?

"He wants me on the next plane home," Mariabella said. The plane ticket sat on the table before her, bright red and white.

Demanding.

She tucked herself into the chair, the plaid wool afghan drawn tight around her legs, but it didn't block the stress whispering at her nerve endings. She'd come home from the restaurant, terrified that Jake would come running up her walk, announcing he'd recognized her. Calling out her real name. Calling her *Princess*.

He hadn't, so in that area, she was still safe.

Maybe Darcy had gotten her confused with some soap opera star or someone else and the whole incident would blow over. The churning worry in Mariabella's gut said otherwise.

She'd come home tonight to an overnight delivery truck in the driveway, a driver waiting with a pen in his hand and an envelope with her name on it. Her father had done as he'd promised, and sent the ticket. For a few hours today, she'd hoped maybe her father had been bluffing.

She knew better. Franco Santaro never bluffed. Never joked. He ordered—and he got what he ordered.

"I know what your father has said." Her mother let out a long breath. "He is insistent this time. But, I will talk to him. Tell him two months will make no difference."

"You know how he gets, Mama. He won't listen."

"He will. He did the first time."

But her mother's voice lacked conviction, and Mariabella knew the chances of her father changing his mind had dropped from zero to a negative number. The king had made up his mind—and he expected to see his daughter at Christmas dinner in three days.

"I'll come home on the next plane," Mariabella said. "It will make him happy and be easier for—"

"No!" The word escaped her mother in a forceful shout. "Stay where you are until your birthday."

"Mama…"

"No. Once you come back, you will be trapped in this life forever. You know it, I know it. Take this gift of freedom while you have it. I will talk to him, and remind him of his agreement." Her mother paused. "Find your heart, my daughter. You may never have another chance."

"I already did find everything I wanted, Mama," Mariabella said, even though the thought giving up all of that made something shatter inside her. "My gallery is a success—"

"Have you found love yet?"

"I didn't come here for love."

Her mother tsk-tsked. "The right man could be anywhere."

Mariabella laughed. "Mama, I'm not ready to get married. I don't want to get married. I'm happy as I am."

"Are you?"

Two words, a simple question, and yet they hit a nerve both women knew ran deep. Mariabella Santaro had led a solitary life, much like the Rapunzel of fairy tales, stuck in the castle, not by an ogre or an evil prince, but by duty. By honor.

For Mariabella, dating had always been a disaster. Men made too nervous by her position, or too ambitious by her last name. She hadn't met a single one who had seen her as just Mariabella.

Her mother, bless her heart, didn't understand. Franco Santaro had married a woman outside the monarchy, a woman who had not grown up in that steel bubble of judgment. Bianca had been a member of the aristocracy, an approved bride, chosen by his parents, so she would be acceptable, both to the crown and to the populace. Despite the odd beginnings of their marriage, Bianca had fallen in love with her husband, and had been happy for decades.

Mariabella hoped some day to find that kind of happiness, but she had yet to find a man who could see past the crown she would someday wear.

She thought she had, but—

Tonight that had all likely been ruined.

"You need to settle down, Mariabella. You're getting older," her mother said. "Promise me, you'll open your heart, too, while you are in America. And give some man a chance."

Mariabella sighed. "I'll…try."

The image of Jake Lattimore sprang to mind. His deep blue eyes, the way they seemed to pierce through the thick armor she'd built around her true heart. So many times, he'd gotten so close to her, close enough that she could have slipped and nearly told him everything.

If she had, would he have looked at her the same way? Held her, kissed her, the same? Or would he have run from the pressures of being with a royal?

Maybe he had put the pieces together tonight and that was why he hadn't come to her house. Maybe he'd decided a princess carried too much baggage for an ordinary man to handle.

This was why she didn't open her heart. Why she didn't give men a chance. Because once she did, and they knew who she really was, they stopped seeing her as a woman and instead saw her as an object, a crown on a pedestal.

How she wanted to be seen for herself, to have someone look past the exterior and look inside.

"You know the one thing that will change your father's mood," her mother was saying, "and bring back the smiling man we all remember?"

Mariabella tried to think of who her mother meant, because as far as she could think back, her father had always been the monarch, stern and judgmental. "What?"

"Grandchildren."

Mariabella scoffed. "Mama, I'm not even dating anyone. Don't talk about children, too."

Her mother laughed. "If you need someone to date, your father is talking about Ricardo Carlotti again."

Mariabella scowled. "Mama, I don't even like him. He's...dull. Predictable as a cloud. Spends more times reading than he does looking at me. He'd be happier marrying a library."

"Your father thinks he'd make a good match. And," she continued before Mariabella could interject, "your father would like to see you married before you ascend to the throne."

"I don't want to get married. Or ascend."

Her mother was silent. The former might be an optional choice, but the latter was a foregone conclusion. She was the firstborn of three daughters.

The plane ticket glared at her. Waiting patiently, but with one clear message.

Go home.

"Bella, I did not grow up a royal," her mother said, as if reading her daughter's mind, "but because of that, I know what it is like to live an ordinary life. I also know what it is like to become queen, and to see your father's life as king. I have lived both sides of the coin, and understand your frustrations, your desires. As a princess, you had more freedoms than you'll have as the monarch, even if it didn't feel like you did."

"I know." She hadn't had the multitude of state duties, the dinners, the meetings that consumed her father's days. She'd had the expectations of decorum and a number of events, but nowhere near the total her father attended.

"I want you to live the life I had, for as long as you can, before you're…laced into the corset of that crown. Don't get on that plane. Your father can wait two months."

"He won't be happy."

"I know," her mother said quietly.

"He's…" Mariabella paused. "He's never been happy with me."

"He loves you, *cara*."

"That's not the same thing, not when I've never felt loved by him."

There. The words were out. They weren't all of them, but they were a large part of what she had been feeling for so many years. For a long time, her mother didn't say anything, and all Mariabella heard was the crashing of the waves outside her cottage, the hum of the phone line.

"He's a difficult man. A stubborn one."

"That does not give him an excuse, Mama."

Her mother let out a long breath. "No, it doesn't. I think…he is too much of a king. He forgets to be a father."

"If that is the kind of queen I will end up being…I don't want to wear the crown."

"I understand. But you won't be like him. You'll be yourself, Mariabella."

Mariabella glanced out the window, at the country, and the town, she had come to love, because it was here that she had finally become herself. Neither her father nor her mother seemed to understand that. They saw only duty, not Mariabella's heart.

"I'll try, Mama," she said, the words escaping on a sob. She tried to call the tears back, but they pushed past her reserves, fell down her cheeks and dropped onto the only course of action Mariabella had.

The plane ticket home.

Mariabella said goodbye to her mother. She had no other options left. She had better face that now, before she got any more attached to this place.

She rose, crossing the living room, her bare feet padding across the hardwood floors, then meeting the cool tile of the kitchen.

A small house, a cottage really, nothing much by most people's standards. But it sat on the edge of beach, and was kissed by the salty air each morning. The cottage held none of the grandeur or servants of the castle, but Mariabella didn't mind. She loved every inch of the wood frame, the wide pine floors and the white wicker furniture she'd bought herself.

The doorbell rang. Probably Carmen, here to plead her case again about getting Mariabella to hang some of her own paintings in the gallery. Mariabella swiped the tears off her face, then opened the door, expecting a friend.

And got instead Jake Lattimore, with a bouquet of flowers, another bottle of wine and a smile. Not the person she wanted to see, not now, not after the conversation she'd just had. And not after what had happened in the restaurant.

Then she thought of the time in that room in the inn, how he'd looked out over that small town, and seen something similar to what she had seen every day of her childhood. Perhaps he could understand what she felt right now, and realize why she had lied. Perhaps leaning on him could ease the ache in her heart brought on by the thought of leaving.

"May I come in?"

She debated saying no, knew she should say no. She didn't need to entangle herself in a personal relationship, especially not now. She was leaving, probably in the morning. Her moments of normalcy were over. No sense dragging this out another minute. But oh, how she needed someone's shoulders to lean on, someone to hold her and tell her everything would be fine.

Someone who would make her forget for just a minute, when he whispered her name. Touched her. Kissed her.

"I promise, I only want to talk to you." Jake extended the flowers forward. "And to say I'm sorry for tonight."

The fresh scent of white Gerbera daisies, accented with red roses, green kermit poms and holly berries, teased at her senses. An unexpected surge of joy rose inside her. She'd received flowers before—by the truckload, from enraptured suitors determined to win her heart. Once, two wealthy men from Uccelli had gone head to head in their battle to convince Mariabella to go to the annual ball with them. They'd played one-upmanship with flowers, sending so many, the florists in the city had finally begged Mariabella to end the war because they couldn't keep up with the demand.

She'd opted to go alone, and given each man equal time on the dance floor. And donated all of the flowers to the hospital and nursing home.

But these—these were chosen just for her. They were beautiful in their simplicity. "Thank you."

"I apologize for my team being at the restaurant tonight. I had no idea they were coming to town."

Get rid of him. He already knew she wasn't who she said she was. A day, maybe two, and he'd figure out who she was. If it took even that long. Then he would bring in the media, and the frenzy would disrupt the peace in Harborside. Her friends, her neighbors, would be upended by the constant barrage of questions and intrusions into their lives. Not only would the fabric of the town be destroyed by the Lattimore resort, but the tranquility would also be erased simply because of her presence.

Don't let the flowers sway you. Or his words. Or his smile.

"Jake, I'm sorry, but this isn't a good time," she said. "And after tonight—"

His gaze lit on the space behind her. "Wow. You surprise me."

"What are you talking about?"

"I thought you'd be more of a portrait artist. Maybe landscapes. But these…" A smile took over his face. "Amazing."

Mariabella followed his gaze. Her pulse skittered to a stop. Oh, no. Her paintings. He'd seen her paintings.

Suddenly, she felt naked, exposed, as if she'd gotten on a stage and started reading from her diary. She wanted to rush over to the artwork and throw a cloth over the paintings, hide them from his inquisitive view.

"May I?" Jake asked, gesturing toward the art stacked against the far wall.

If letting him into her home was like giving him access to her identity, letting him see her art was like giving him access to her soul. She shouldn't. She hadn't let anyone see her art, except for Carmen, who'd merely had a glimpse when she'd stopped by one time.

And yet, even as everything within her said no, she found her mouth saying "yes."

It had to be the flowers. In the palace, there'd been fresh flowers every week, sometimes every day for special occasions. But none of them had been chosen especially for her.

None of them had been hand-delivered by a man with an apology. And a smile like that.

"First, tell me something."

He cocked his head and studied her. "Okay. What?"

"Why did you bring me a bouquet?"

"Uh…because women like flowers." He rubbed his temple. "Is this a trick question?"

"Why one bouquet? You are a wealthy man and…" She searched for the right words, ones that wouldn't offend him, and yet would say what she needed to say.

"A man who could buy an entire flower shop, if I needed to?" She nodded.

"I thought of that," he admitted. "But then I realized you weren't that kind of woman."

"What made you realize that?"

He took a step closer to her, and her heart began to race. She drew in the scent of his cologne, and with it, the sense of danger that came with getting any closer to this man. To getting closer to anyone. "Back at the inn, I saw another side of you."

He had listened after all. Of all the people who had known her, all the people in her life, this man, this near stranger, had paid attention. Even her mother, who loved her, didn't know her heart the same way. Finally, a man who saw her as a woman, a person, not a princess.

Too bad he was too late.

"What did you see?" she asked, knowing she shouldn't wrap herself in him anymore, but unable to resist.

He caught a tendril of her hair, and let the silky tress slide through his grasp. Her breath lodged in her throat, every ounce of her stilled, waiting. "I saw a woman who has watched the world from a tower, and never got to live in it until she moved here."

Mariabella nodded. "And you, did you ever get to live in the world you watched?"

He shifted away from her, and crossed to the artwork. The conversation had ended as quickly as it had started. One door opened, another slammed shut. "What technique is that?" he asked, bending down to study the work closer. "It looks three-dimensional."

She should be happy. After all, didn't she want to keep things on an impersonal level? Maintain that distance from a relationship, especially for the limited time she had left in America?

Curiosity nudged at her, pushing her closer to him, even as her better judgment told her to back away. "You have asked me a lot of questions. And have told me almost nothing about you," she said. "Who are you, Jake Lattimore?"

"There's not much to know. I work." He grinned. "And I work."

"And watch the world go by instead of getting involved with someone?"

He looked away. She waited, refusing to fill the silence. Time ticked by, seconds marked by the crashing of the waves outside the tiny cottage. Jake crossed to the mantel and fiddled with a ceramic Santa. "There was someone. Once," he said finally.

"What happened?"

He swallowed. The firelight danced across his face, casting the depths of his face into shadows. "She died a month before our wedding. Car accident."

"Oh, Jake, I am so sorry." She went to him, her hands lighting on his back, but he didn't turn around. He held the grief inside him, in a deep place she couldn't reach, couldn't ease for him.

"I never thought—" He heaved a breath. "I never thought I'd get over it."

She leaned her head against the soft fabric of his shirt. The fireplace warmed him from the front, she from the back, but Mariabella knew there was still an ice inside of Jake Lattimore that had yet to thaw.

"And so I worked. It was easier to do that than to live."

"You have been in a prison," she said softly, understanding him so much better now, a man who was a kindred spirit to hers, but for different reasons, "for all these years."

He turned around in her arms. "Yeah, I guess I have."

How she wanted to tell him that she would be here, if he ever decided he was ready to have another life. To move forward. But how could she make that promise? How could she give him a gift she didn't even have?

Across the room, the plane ticket waited. And across the world, her father waited.

"Someday, you will find someone—" the words hurt her mouth as she said them "—and I am sure you will be very happy."

Something flickered in his gaze, something that turned the warmth in his blue eyes cold. "Yeah. Someday."

She broke away from him. She wanted to comfort him more, but she couldn't touch Jake for one more second and fool herself into thinking she didn't care about him.

Because she did.

And forgetting him was already going to be a Herculean task.

He seemed to be thinking the same thing, because he returned to the stack of paintings. "How do you make these 3-D?" His voice had gone distant.

He'd already drawn away from her, too.

She should have been relieved by the change in subject, but a part of her felt disappointment. She brushed off the feeling and focused on her art. "It is called relief painting. I use industrial resin on wood fiber board, to shape the figures, and then I paint the details with oil paints." There. Talk about techniques on canvas.

"They look so real. This one..." He paused. "Incredible."

The one he'd chosen had been one of Mariabella's personal favorites. Two pelicans, diving into the ocean, racing to catch a fish both had spied from the air.

"It was a moment I saw one day, back in the summer, and I wanted to capture that competition, that air war."

"You brought them to life," he said. "The three dimensions make them seem vibrant, so real, and the colors you chose…wow. The way you painted the sun breaking on the horizon behind the birds, it's as if I'm there, standing on the beach."

Heat filled her cheeks. She'd had her work critiqued in college, of course, but never had she had such overt praise heaped on one of her paintings. "Thank you."

"You're incredible, Mariabella." He took her hand, then tugged her over to him, into his arms. She fit perfectly, as if she'd always been made for that space against his chest. Oh, this was trouble. Big trouble.

She was falling for Jake Lattimore. And falling hard. No matter how hard she tried not to, to remind herself she was leaving, that she had to put him in the past now, before it got too hard later, she fell even more.

He looked down at her and smiled, and everything about his face softened, drew her in, captivated her even more. "I lied to you."

"Lied?"

He traced the outline of her jaw, and Mariabella nearly came undone with desire. "When I arrived at the gallery, I lied. I said I wasn't looking for anything for my office. But now I realize I am."

His gaze drifted toward the painting of the pelicans, and she connected the dots. "Oh, no, that is not for sale. It is not ready, I cannot…no."

"If you don't want to sell that one, I'm sure I can find another one I like just as well." Jake released her to flip that painting forward, revealing one with a trio of geese in flight, their wings spread broad, the horizon ahead of them—their new destination blurred—and a rocky, barren landscape to the rear. "Like this."

"I cannot sell that one, either. Or any of my work."

"Why not?"

"I…I just cannot."

"Surely you didn't paint all these just to leave them against the wall?"

"I am just not comfortable with having my work out in the public eye."

"What about my eye? Just mine?"

What was he saying? Did he want something more, something just between them?

Oh, how she did.

But she couldn't have that. Jake Lattimore was like the toy in the window a child wanted for Christmas and the mother couldn't afford. He would always be behind the glass of another world. She had a duty to fulfill, and no matter how much she wished otherwise, he wasn't part of that duty. An ache spread through her chest, her veins. "I cannot let it go," she said, meaning everything but her art. "I am…I am sorry."

I cannot let you go.

I cannot leave.

His gaze met hers, and held for a long moment. "Me, too," he said. "I would have loved to have this."

Did he mean the painting? Or her? Better not to know. Easier.

She didn't answer him. He went back to flipping through the paintings. "Why birds?"

"I like birds." There was more to the answer than that. But telling him the rest involved telling him where she came from, about her quest for freedom, about the constant itch to be anywhere but back in Uccelli.

About the fight in her heart between duty and her own life, as if she were a wild bird caught in a manmade cage.

"Me, too." Jake got to his feet and met her gaze with his own. The quiet of her house, which seemed so peaceful when it was just her, seemed to boil up with tension. "Especially yours."

"Thank you." Heat rose in her cheeks, and she dipped her gaze. When he stared at her like that, the intensity took her to places she hadn't visited before. Opened doors she had always kept shut. Asked her questions she'd never answered.

Could she fall in love? Could she have a life with a commoner?

She didn't ask those questions because she knew the answers. A commoner, particularly an American businessman, would never be acceptable to her father. To the kingdom.

"Why aren't these in your gallery?" Jake asked.

"I am hosting another artist right now." Not a lie, entirely.

"You should host you." His gaze swept over her face. "But if you do, there would be publicity and that would let people know you are…?" He arched a brow.

"I better put those flowers into water before they die." Damn. That's what she got for inviting him in. He circled back around to the one subject she wanted to avoid.

Who she was.

Mariabella hurried into the kitchen. She looked for a vase, then realized she didn't have one. She'd never had a need for one before. She pulled a pitcher out of the cabinet, filled it with water and arranged the bouquet in the glass container, using the ribbon from the package to accent the handle.

"Darcy has this crazy idea," Jake said.

At some point, he had followed her into the kitchen and was leaning against the wall. Mariabella froze at the words. Darcy. That woman who had almost recognized her. Did she know? Had she figured it out after Mariabella left the restaurant?

Impossible. Wasn't it?

"Oh…yeah?" She fiddled with the flowers.

"She thinks you might be a princess."

Mariabella swallowed hard. She plucked out a daisy from the center and shoved into a space on the side, then moved a rose from the right to the left. "Huh. Really?"

"Are you?"

The two words hung in her kitchen, heavy, fat with anticipation. Destructive.

Are you her?

Mariabella planted her hands on either side of the counter. What should she do? Lie and hope he didn't uncover the truth? Or tell him yes, and sit back, wait for the media onslaught that would destroy everything she had worked so hard to build?

Jake Lattimore was a man of means. And those means would lead to the answers he sought, one way or another.

It was over. Her life here. Her fantasy that she could be loved by a man like him, as an ordinary woman. Once she told him who she was, he would never look at her the same way again.

Mariabella closed her eyes and in her mind, said goodbye to a relationship that had never really had a chance to begin. She straightened her back and turned to face him. When she did, her body naturally rose into its perfect alignment, the balance-a-book-on-your-head posture she had learned so long ago. She drew in a deep breath, then released it. "I am, indeed, Princess Mariabella Santaro of Uccelli." She paused, then met his gaze. "But if you tell anyone, I will make sure you never build another hotel in this country or any other."

He had been so sure Darcy was wrong.

But no, here he was, standing in the middle of a tiny cottage in Harborside, Massachusetts, with the heir to the throne of Uccelli. A woman who seemed as ordinary as any other, who could have just come home from buying groceries—and maybe had.

The admission explained everything. Her accent, the way she carried herself, her reluctance to tell him anything about herself. And most of all, the nagging sense he'd had that she was *different*.

He'd never expected *this* kind of different, though.

A princess.

A future queen?

"You are staring at me," she said. "I hate that." Mariabella turned away and crossed to the kitchen cabinets and opened one of the wooden doors, exposing a neatly stacked set of white dishes. She stood there, as if she didn't know what she wanted or why she'd opened the door.

"I'm sorry," he said. "I've just never met a princess before."

"I was a princess when you met me."

"I didn't know you were a princess then."

She pivoted back. "So this makes things different? You see me now as someone else? Someone you should bow to or some such ridiculous thing? Or maybe a curiosity? Like a monkey in a zoo?"

"No. I just…" He took a step closer. "I wonder why you lied to me."

She threw up her hands. "Is it not obvious? I am trying to live my life here as a person, not as a princess. I do not want the media glued to my back, taking a photograph of everything I do, being there when I go into the coffee shop and order an espresso, or go to the grocery and pick up basil. I want to be like everyone else."

"You can do that and still be honest with the people around you." No hurt invaded him, simply a need to understand. He could see how the whole princess thing might have been hard to bring up in a conversation, but still wondered why she had chosen this life of anonymity when she held so much more sway as Princess Mariabella.

She let out a gust. "You think it is so easy? You think I can just say, good morning, I am a princess, but treat me like I am just like you, and that easily—" she snapped her fingers "—it will happen?"

He winnowed the gap even more. "How do you know if you don't give people a chance?"

"People…like you?"

He could easily say no. Mention anyone in town. Cletus. Zeke. The caterer, Savannah, or even Mariabella's assistant, Carmen. Those people had known Mariabella the longest, known her as Mariabella Romano, and never had an inkling that all this time they'd had a real-life princess living among them.

But he'd be lying if he did. From the minute he'd met her, and they'd tangled over the property, over this town, Jake had been intrigued. His senses had been awakened, in a way he'd never thought possible again. For so long, he'd thought his life would never again have that spark, that need for another person.

Until now. Until Mariabella.

"Yeah, people like me," he said quietly, and reached up, to cup her jaw. He lowered his head, his mouth hovering over hers.

She inhaled, and her eyes widened, the light crimson color in her cheeks rising. As tempting as the fabled apple.

The tension between them coiled tighter. Jake gripped her waist, and brought her torso to his. Desire thundered in his head, pulsed through his veins. He didn't see a princess. He didn't see a gallery owner. He saw Mariabella, a woman who made him feel alive for the first time in years.

A woman he had begun to care about. A lot.

And that was the woman he kissed.

When his lips met hers, sensations exploded at every place they touched. She was sweet in his arms, then hot, as she curved against him, and her hands ranged up his back to draw him even closer. His hands tangled in her long, thick dark curls.

Outside, the winter storm kicked up, wind battering the little house, shaking the timbers and whistling under the roof, but it was nothing compared to the storm brewing between Jake and Mariabella. This kiss wasn't like their first one. It wasn't short, it wasn't sweet, it was a storm, like the one outside.

The tumult in their kiss reached a feverish pitch, and they each took a step back, until she was pressed against the counter, and his length was pressed against hers, bodies molding into one, their tongues dancing together, mimicking what their bodies could do. Fire roared through his veins, blinding his thoughts to everything but this. His hands snaked up and ranged over her waist, then her breasts, cupping the generous fullness through the soft fabric of her sweater. Mariabella arched against him, and let out a soft moan. Jake nearly fell apart, and the fire in him reached a level that would not be easily quieted.

Suddenly, she broke away, and stepped over to the sink, her back to him. "What…what are you doing?"

His breath came in heaves, his mind a jumble. "I thought I was kissing you." And he'd thought she'd been responding. Had he misread everything? The invitation in her eyes? The answer in her lips to the question posed by his own?

"Kissing *me?*" she asked, still not facing him, her voice quiet. "Or kissing a princess?"

"Is that what you think this was? I find out who you are, rush right over and grab you, so I can run out and tell the tabloids I kissed a princess?"

She wheeled around. "Is it?"

He wrapped an arm around her waist and pulled her back, the roar of desire she'd awakened in him still sounding so loud in his head, still pounding so hard in his veins, that he wondered whether it would be ever be quieted again. She let out a little yelp of surprise. Jake leaned down. "I don't want to kiss a princess," he said, his voice nearly a growl. "I want to kiss *you,* Mariabella. Only you."

Then he did exactly that again, this time taking no quarter with her, pouring the passion that had built up inside him for years into their embrace. Mariabella let out a mew, and grasped his shirt, curling her fists into his back. He hoisted her up onto the counter, his hands roaming her waist, her back, into her hair, unable to touch enough of her at once. He wanted more, he wanted all of her, right here, right now, but instead did the right thing and pulled back with a groan.

Her lips were swollen and red, her chest heaving with rapid breaths. "We…we probably should not…"

"Why not? Because you're a princess? I don't care about that." And as the words left his mouth, he realized he didn't. She was the same woman now, as she had been yesterday. Okay, so they'd have a few more bumps in their relationship to work around, but he could deal with that. He was alive again, for the first time in forever, and Jake refused to let that go, over something as small as royalty. "I told you, I loved Uccelli when I visited the country. Surely we could find a way to make this work."

"It is more than loving the country, Jake." She shook her head. "Someday, I will be *queen*. You would never be acceptable to my father as a king." She hung her head. "I am sorry, but duty must come first."

He let out a gust. "Duty? You sound like me now. I've spent five years putting duty and work ahead of living and now that I've met you, I've finally begun to realize what I'm missing out on. If you end this now, you will be missing out, too."

Outside, the storm had abated, and the wind stopped its assault on the little cottage. Mother Nature had quieted her war with the coast of Harborside, restoring it to its natural equilibrium.

She gripped the countertop. In her eyes, he saw resignation. "As a royal, my world is almost a…cage of expectations. You do not understand. I cannot have the life others can. I just cannot. Please make this easier on both of us, Jake, and—" she paused, tears filling her green eyes like rain puddling in a lake "—leave."

He stood his ground. He couldn't leave, not until he had the answer he'd come for, the one that had driven him out of the bar, and into her arms, the one answer he hadn't found in her artwork or in her kiss. "Why are you hiding here? And I don't mean just hiding from your name. I mean really hiding."

"What are you talking about? I am living my life."

"You talk about your life being a cage in Uccelli, and yet you've made a cage in Harborside, too."

"I live freely here."

"As yourself?"

"Of course not." She threw up her hands. "What, do you think this is all some fairy tale? That I can just be a princess and live happily ever after?"

"Why not?"

"It does not work that way. Not for me."

"Then how free are you, really, if you're afraid to fall in love? Afraid to be yourself?" He plucked a closed daisy out of the bouquet he had given her, and held it out. "You're like this flower. Shut off, tucked among the others. No one knows the power you hold, because you're just…hiding. You could change this town, make *real* changes, as Princess Mariabella, instead of just Mariabella Romano. You could bring it the kind of publicity it needs, the sort of business that would help these owners survive the other months of the year. And yet—"

She wrapped her arms around herself, anger spiking the color in her face. "And yet what?"

"You choose to be selfish and protect yourself instead of helping the people who have helped you."

"I am doing the least selfish thing possible. Putting this town ahead of everything that matters to me."

Jake laid the single flower on the table, beside one of Mariabella's sketches of a bird in flight. "Are you? Or are you doing the easiest thing possible?"

She advanced on him, her green eyes ablaze with frustration. "Who are you to say that to me? When all you have done since you have arrived in this town is take the easy road?

Followed the company line? Take your own risks, Jake Lattimore, and then tell me how to live my life."

He didn't respond. They'd said it all. Jake turned and left. The flower laid on the table, forgotten and wilting.

CHAPTER TEN

JAKE jerked awake, threw back the thick down comforter and got to his feet. Overnight, frost had coated the windows, blocking the view with a lacy spiderweb of white. Didn't matter. He didn't need to see Harborside to sketch out the plan in his head.

He crossed to the small desk in the corner of his room at the Seaside Inn, drew a pad of paper out of the briefcase sitting on the floor and began to write. At first, full sentences, then, as the frenzy to get it all down overtook him, short bullets, single words, just enough to jog his memory later.

A half hour later, Jake sat back and read over the pages he had composed. The board would undoubtedly think he was crazy. But this…

This would work.

He knew it. Deep in his gut, in that core knot that drove his best decisions, he knew, just knew, this was the decision that would make everyone happy. The company. The town. And most of all—

The princess.

A grin took over his face, the feeling of joy spreading through his chest, his veins. The emotion was so foreign, he nearly didn't recognize it. All these years, his heart had been as frozen as the icicles dangling from the peaks outside, and now—

The fiery woman from Uccelli had brought about a spring thaw. For the first time in forever, Jake imagined a different future. One with someone else in it.

One with Mariabella curled up in his arms, in front of the fireplace on Christmas Day. If he could make this idea work, maybe he could make that work, too.

She'd been right about him, damn it. And it felt real good to admit it.

His cell phone rang, and he flipped it out. "Dad! I was just about to call you. I've got an idea you have to hear."

"There was nothing on the fax machine this morning. No overnight delivery waiting for me. Nothing." His father's voice held a mixture of worry and disappointment. "We need this, Jake. Where are the real estate agreements for Harborside?"

"I'm working on it, Dad. Listen—"

His father sighed. "The board is pushing for me to hire an outsider."

While the mouse was away, the cats plotted. Jake shouldn't have been surprised. The board had always considered him, as the heir, nothing more than a nepotism appointment. "Don't worry about it. I have an idea for this town that can be great. Remember what you used to tell me about the old days, back when you started the company?"

"What do you mean?"

"The first resort you built. That one in New Jersey." Jake waited, allowing the memory a moment to travel across the phone line.

"You mean the inn? The one I took you to when you were—"

"Seven. And eight. And nine, because I begged you to."

His father chuckled, and something heavy that had been carried for so long in Lawrence Lattimore's heart seemed to flow out in that sound. "You loved that place."

"Everyone loved it."

"I have a lot of great memories of that place," his father said. "You and I, we used to take the rowboat out, remember? There was that great fishing hole, the one just you and I knew about. We had more than one dinner we caught ourselves from that place."

"I remember, Dad."

"And the hiking. Saw your first deer in those woods. You were six." His father chuckled. "I think you were more scared of it, than it was of you."

Jake laughed. "I remember that, too."

His father sighed. "It was too bad we couldn't have made that property more profitable. I hated selling it."

"Maybe if we'd handled the inn differently, Dad. Looked at the property from different angles. I think now, with some experience under our belts, we could turn a profit. I had some ideas this morning—"

"Jake, the time for inns like that has passed. Now everyone wants those fancy resorts. Cater to your every whim. Live like the rich do."

"Not everyone wants that, Dad. Some people want the simple life. To feel like…" Jake crossed to the window. He rubbed at the frosted pane with his palm, enough to open up a tiny view of the snowy street below. The garland hung between the street poles, the bows waving in the breeze, the neighbors heading to their shops, waving one another. "To feel like they've gone home."

"When they go on vacation? Not anymore. I wish it wasn't so, but that's the reality of this business. The board says—"

Jake let out a gust. "Think outside the box, Dad. You used to do that, remember?" The Lawrence Lattimore who had founded the company had been a man who charged into deals, who thought with his gut, not with a team of accountants. But as the years wore on, and his father had had to report to more and more people, he'd become less like that, and more of a conformist in business.

"I wish I could. Those days, they were great, but…" His father's sigh seemed to weigh a hundred pounds. "They're over. It's time for me to put my feet up and watch from the sidelines."

Jake could hear the sadness in his father's voice. "What if you didn't have to? What if you could have the company you used to?"

"I don't live like that anymore. It's too crazy. Too risky."

Jake grinned. "Yeah, maybe it is. But I'm going to make it work right here. In Harborside."

"Son, you do that, and you'll ruin this company. We need something powerful. Something big, something that will take Lattimore back up to the top. Use the proven formula, Jake. Trust the board, not the ramblings of an old man who should be retired. We just can't take a risk. Not now."

"No, Dad. That's where you're wrong." Jake turned away from the window, and for the first time since he'd arrived in this town, felt as if everything was going to fall into place exactly right. "We need to go back to where we used to be, lead with our gut, not with the bean counters. That's our ticket to the top."

His father let out a sigh. "I don't know what's gotten into you. Tomorrow's Christmas Eve, Jake. Get this deal done, and fax me the deeds so we can break ground before February. That's the only present I want." His father hung up.

Jake would prove his father's theory wrong. One way or another. And in doing so, maybe he'd help Lawrence Lattimore find the business fire that had long ago died away.

The suitcase lay empty on Mariabella's bed.

Every item she put in, she took back out. She couldn't seem to pack anything. Not her jeans, not her sweaters, not her makeup, not her hairbrush. She clutched the plane ticket, sat on the edge of her bed and cried.

She couldn't do it. Simply couldn't do it. Just the thought of wearing that crown for the rest of her life made her want to run and hide. She looked out the window, at the view that had become as much a part of her as her own hand, and let out a sigh.

Then she made the call.

It took ten minutes before she was connected to the king, a flurry of activity, with people whispering on the other end, the rumors flying about the princess being in contact after her long, unexplained absence. "All I want to hear is when your flight is arriving so I can send Reynaldo to pick you up," her father said when he finally answered. No greeting. No "how are you."

Mariabella took in a breath, and steeled herself. "I'm not coming back, Papa."

She could have cut through the long, icy silence with a razor blade. "You will. I command it."

A year ago, a day ago, Mariabella would have backed down and agreed with her father. He was the king, after all, and she had learned from the day she was born never to disagree with the king.

Her gaze strayed to the Gerbera daisies, and her resolve steeled. She had to do the right thing. Not just for her, but for her country. Jake was right. She'd been hiding too long, from her true self. From what she really wanted. She'd played at being an ordinary woman, and never really done it.

How could she, if the entire time she'd lived in Harborside, she'd been living a lie? How could she ever know if she could be the kind of woman she wanted to be, unless she stepped up and did it as herself? As Mariabella Santaro?

"I can't," she said. "I won't make a good queen and you know it, Papa. My heart isn't in it. I don't think it ever was."

He snorted. "You think this position is about heart? It's *duty,* Mariabella. Now stop this silliness and return at once."

"You already have a daughter who wants to be queen, father. Let Allegra step up to the throne. And let me have my life. If you have ever loved me, even a little, then please, please, Papa—" her voice caught "—let me go."

Then she hung up the phone, and let the tears take over.

She was now a woman without a family or a country. But at least she was finally and truly free.

Jake had his argument ready before Mariabella even opened the door. "I know I'm the last person in the world you want to see right now, but I have a gift for you."

"A gift?"

He grinned. "It's Christmas. People give each other gifts."

She hesitated, and for a second, he thought she might close the door before he could talk to her. "Jake, Christmas isn't for two more days."

"So sue me for being early." He handed her a box, wrapped in bright red paper and topped with a white bow. "I just wanted to show you that I thought about what you said yesterday. And that you were right."

Despite everything, Mariabella smiled, and waved him into her house. One hurdle passed. Maybe there was hope for more. "Do you want some coffee?"

"I'd love some." Hell, he'd drink baby formula if it meant seeing her again.

She put down the box, then went into the kitchen and returned with two mugs of coffee and a small plate of raspberry thumbprint cookies. Then she sat down across from him to unwrap the gift. The bow slid easily off the top, fluttering to the floor. The box lid lifted off, then Mariabella tugged out the tissue-wrapped item inside and peeled away the white paper covering it. "This is…a dollhouse?"

"A mock-up. Of what I want to build here."

She glanced down again and saw, not a monster of a hotel,

like the one he had shown her in New York, but something closer to the inn they had visited in New Jersey. "It looks like…a house."

He grinned and nodded. "That's the plan. I want to put on a big front porch and a long, wide back porch. Lots of chairs, for looking out at the view of the ocean, then benches in the front so people can greet the locals when they walk by. Dinners will be served family style so that when you come and stay here, you'll be able to sit and get to know the other people who are staying in Harborside. There will be boating and swimming. No noisy Jet Skis. We'll have rooms designed with families in mind, and lots of family activities planned. It will be like the vacations from the old days, but taken up a few notches."

"You sound excited."

"I am." His smile widened. "It's all I've been able to think about for hours and hours. I had to drive to Boston this morning and pay a shop to create this—don't even ask me how much it cost—because I couldn't wait to show you my vision for Harborside."

She turned the mock-up around, then lifted it up and peeked inside the tiny windows, the itty-bitty door. She ran a finger down the roof line, along the slender poles of the porch. "This is perfect. I can just see it in town. It matches the buildings we already have, and even looks a little like the light-house, the way the posts curve on the porch here, and the colors that you used."

"I know."

She touched his hand, and fire exploded in her gut. "I did not think you noticed anything on the tour we took."

"It wasn't easy. I was a little distracted by my tour guide." His hand came up to cup her jaw, thumb teasing at her bottom lip. "More than a little distracted."

"All I did was show you some whales."

"You showed me far more than that, Mariabella." Her name slid off his tongue in a whisper, just before he closed the gap and kissed her. Then Jake drew back, and took her hand in his. "If you give me a chance, Mariabella, and support this, I promise, it will work out for the town, for you, for all the residents. This will be a resort that will fit Harborside. That world we saw in the room at the top of the stairs, that's the kind of world I want here. One where people come and they feel like they've come…"

"Home," she finished, the world escaping her on a breath. She glanced down again at the tiny building and saw in it the exact kind of vacation place she would have chosen. A retreat, a haven.

It was, as she'd said, home. Here in Harborside. She couldn't imagine it anywhere else.

"Exactly. When people look out the windows of their room, I want them to see the real Harborside. The one that *you* love." He tipped her chin until her gaze met his. "The one that you've taught me to love, too."

"You…love this town?"

"Lighthouse, boardwalk and all. It took me a while, but it grew on me." He grinned. "It helped that it had such a beautiful ambassador."

"Oh, I am not—"

"You are. Don't sell yourself short. From all accounts, from everyone I've talked to, you've done more for this town in the last year than anyone. Your enthusiasm has brought it back to life."

"But it has not been enough." She gestured out the window. "All your numbers said so, and so did you. I could have done more."

"But if you do, you'll give up part of your life," he said. "I had no right to say that yesterday. I didn't think about what the publicity would do to you. To the privacy that is so important to you." He laid a hand on top of the mock-up of the future resort. "This, however, can make the final difference for Harborside. It can fill in the financial gaps, without you having to be Princess Mariabella. You can be just Mariabella, as you've always been."

She rose and crossed to the fireplace. Beneath her, logs crackled and burned, releasing a cozy comfort. "Except…to make this resort work, you have to have real estate. In a good location, yes?"

"Yes."

They both knew what that meant. He was a businessman, one who wouldn't have reached the position of CEO if he hadn't employed winning strategies.

"The best location is on the boardwalk," Mariabella said, praying he'd disagree.

He didn't. "Yes."

She turned away from the fireplace and looked back at the miniature resort. In it, she saw thought. Caring. A man who had looked around the town she loved—and heard, not just her voice, but those of the other people who lived here.

"You can still have your gallery, I promise," Jake said, reaching for her, knowing what she was thinking. "There will be room for local businesses, every one of them who wants to stay, and even new ones who want to come to town. I'll build you the best and biggest gallery you've ever seen, right here. And give you a wonderful place to hang your art, when you're ready. I'm redesigning the entire complex to have a town-within-a-town feel. I want it to be a community, not just a hotel."

She met his gaze, and saw honesty, integrity, in his blue eyes. Jake Lattimore meant what he was saying. Excitement colored his words, and she knew that enthusiasm would spill over into the town, rejuvenating it in a way nothing else ever had. The boardwalk would be preserved, just in a different form. Everyone would win.

She had done all she could for Harborside, with the events,

the Community Development Committee, but there was much more this building could do. With the Lattimore Inn, Harborside could make that jump from nothing to something big. Everyone she cared about would be taken care of financially, while the town's setting would be preserved.

"Do you still have those papers?" she said.

"Mariabella—"

"Give them to me, Jake. I want to do this."

Without a word, he reached into the pocket of his suit jacket. Mariabella took the purchase and sales agreement from Jake, then she swallowed hard and decided for the first time in her life to take a chance and to trust someone other than herself.

She reached for a pen on the coffee table, then, before she could think twice, signed over ownership of her gallery.

Because she had fallen in love with Jake Lattimore. With the man who had found out she was a princess, and acted the same, who had listened to her when she'd talked about this town, and shown her that he could bring the dreams she had into a reality.

And most of all, because he had made her a promise she couldn't refuse. To take care of everything she loved—and make it even better than it already was.

CHAPTER ELEVEN

MARIABELLA rolled over on Christmas Eve morning, and stretched her full length on the double bed. She had plenty of time before she had to go to work, because the gallery was only open half the day, and Carmen had agreed to handle the morning shift, so that Mariabella could get the cooking done for dinner that night. As Mariabella lay in bed, she smiled.

Had she finally found a man to love?

One she could trust?

One who understood her?

Maybe there was a way to make all of this work after all. Maybe she could live an ordinary life. Live in peace and obscurity here in Harborside, with Jake. She could go on, as she was, without ever telling anyone her real identity.

Except…

Was Jake right? Was she hiding from herself?

But he didn't understand how the reporters could force her again into the very prison she had escaped. No, she would keep her identity secret for as long as possible.

Mariabella got to her feet. She drew her robe around her and started to head toward the shower.

That was when she heard the shouts.

Her name.

Rising in volume.

She halted. Pivoted toward the windows.

And saw what she'd dreaded all this time crowding onto the cottage's small driveway.

Dozens of reporters, their lenses trained on her house. Still cameras, video cameras, television trucks, live feeds—every type of media exposure and kind of media hound—were out there, just waiting to feed on her story.

She stumbled back and collapsed on the bed. No. How did they—

And then the realization slammed into her with the force of a hurricane.

The only one who knew her true identity was Jake.

The betrayal stung, hitting her as hard as a blow to the gut. She'd given up everything—and now she'd lost her trust, too.

Overnight, Harborside had quintupled in population. Jake stepped out of the Seaside Inn, and had to navigate past three television trucks and six rental cars before he could get close to the limo. He stopped in the middle of the street, dread sinking in his stomach. "Oh, God, Mariabella."

It took less than two minutes to track down the source of the leak about Mariabella's identity. Jake hadn't had to search any farther than the small café at the end of the boardwalk. He had to work hard to control the fury rising inside him. "How could you, Darcy?"

His marketing director stared at him like he had grown two heads. "You of all people should know, Jake. This is business, pure and simple. I can't believe *you* didn't do this. My God, you have a perfect opportunity to exploit here and bring a huge amount of publicity to the project. Think about it. A real, honest-to-God princess? Associated with our hotel? You couldn't *pay* for that kind of exposure. The company needs that. When I called New York—"

"Called who in New York? Exactly?"

Crimson filled her cheeks. She dropped her hand to the table and toyed with her silverware.

"What am I missing here?"

"I…I can't tell you."

"What do you mean, you can't tell me?"

Darcy bit her lip, then finally lifted her head. "I don't work for you. I never really did."

And then he knew. The board. Carl Winters showing up, checking on his progress. His father, worried and stressed, mentioning how the board had been pressuring him to hire an outsider. A group of ten men, thinking they could rule the world, simply because they were the board of directors of the corporation.

No longer. Jake would make sure of that.

"And now you don't work for me at all. Darcy, you're fired." Jake exploded out of the seat and stalked out of the restaurant. He wanted to hit a wall, to punch out the nearest window, but more, he wanted to drive up to New York and confront every person in the company. Now.

The minute he hit the street, the reporters leapt on him like dogs on a bone.

"Mr. Lattimore! Did you know you were dating a princess?"

"Mr. Lattimore, how does it feel to have a princess as the spokesperson for the newest Lattimore Resort?"

"Mr. Lattimore, are you going to invite the royal family to the opening of the new hotel?"

The microphones came at him, fast, furious weapons. He put up his arms, fending them off, and ignored the questions, barreling forward through the crush of reporters. They kept up their assault.

"Mr. Lattimore, is it true the new architectural design is based on Uccelli Castle?" A reporter stepped in front of him and waved a newspaper in his face. "Do you have a comment on this article about the design?"

Jake grabbed the paper out of the man's hand. "No. Get out of my way."

"Are you exploiting Princess Mariabella?" another reporter shouted.

He shoved past all of them, and opened the door of the gallery. The reporters moved to follow him inside, but Jake turned around and gave them a look that said not to even try it. They must have read the menace in his face, because they backed off, hanging outside the door like a pack of hungry dogs.

Jake vowed to make every member of the board pay for what they had done to Mariabella. If it was this bad here, outside the gallery, he could only imagine the circus outside her house. He'd do what he could to control the damage. If it wasn't too late.

"Boy, are your stars out of alignment." Carmen, Mariabella's assistant, strode forward, one fist on her slim hip, and shook her head.

"Excuse me?"

"You've made a mess of this. It was all going well, and then wham, you made it as wrong as wrong can be."

"I didn't—" He let out a breath. Explaining the internal subterfuge in Lattimore Properties to Carmen wouldn't solve the big problem. He needed to talk to Mariabella. "Is Mariabella here?"

"She won't talk to you. I don't blame her. You're like a meteor crashing into her planet."

"I have to talk to her, Carmen. I…I didn't do this." He waved at the throng of media outside. "She has to understand that."

Carmen considered him for a long, long moment. Then she let out a sigh, and nodded. "She's not coming in today, and I can't say I blame her. But come to dinner at her house. Tonight. A lot of her friends from town will be there. I have to go to my mother's, but don't worry," Carmen said, grinning, "you'll have a fan club for back up."

Mariabella's house, with the rest of the Harborside residents? All of whom probably blamed him for this mess. Sounded more like a lynch mob to Jake. "I don't know—"

"I do know," Carmen said. "I know this town, and I know Mariabella. And I know what Mariabella's horoscope said for today." She leaned forward, as if she were about to whisper a secret to Jake. "It said she should prepare for a surprise visitor at a gathering. You—" she gave Jake a little swat on the shoulder "—are the surprise visitor. And her Christmas Eve dinner is the gathering. See? It's all in the stars."

He didn't know about stars, or anything being foretold by some newspaper column, but reasoned talking to Mariabella with the crush of reporters outside—and the possibility of them crashing the conversation at any time—made little sense. Better to wait until later. With any luck, even the media would go home for Christmas Eve, and he could find some time alone with Mariabella.

And find an explanation for what had happened.

Cletus sat at the head of the table, Zeke at the opposite end. Louisa sat on one side, while Louisa's dog, George, ran between the legs of the kitchen chairs, hoping for a stray crumb or two. The media onslaught had ebbed slightly, but a good half-dozen dogged reporters still sat outside, determined to talk to Mariabella. She'd finally called the Harborside police chief, and asked him to remind them about the rules of trespassing. That had at least pushed the reporters back, but not sent them away.

As for Jake—

She tried not to think about him. If she did, she wouldn't make it through the day. It was Christmas Eve, and she was going to enjoy her holiday with her friends, even as her heart broke a little more with each passing hour.

"You sure know how to treat us right," Cletus said. "You

make me think I might want to settle down with a woman someday."

Louisa snorted. "You'd have to find a woman who'd take you first."

Cletus shot her a grin. "I'm an eligible bachelor, with a unique home. Any woman in her right mind would love to have me."

Louisa shook her head and tossed her dog a piece of bread crust.

Across from them, Zeke shifted in his chair, and fiddled with his napkin. "If no one else is going to talk about the elephant in the room, I'll do it."

"My dog is not fat!" Louisa smacked Zeke's arm. "He's...husky."

Zeke rolled his eyes. "I meant the princess, Louisa, not George."

"Oh. Well, then, fine. It's just that George is sensitive about his weight." Louisa soothed the dachshund with a pat on the back and a tidbit of bread.

Zeke shook his head, then directed his attention toward Mariabella. "I think I speak for everyone when I say I don't care whether you're a princess, or the last Romanov, or the forgotten stepchild of the Kennedys. To us, you're just Mariabella. So, there."

Mariabella glanced around the table, taking in the faces of these people who had become her friends, her extended family, who had welcomed her into their hearts, their homes, their lives, and now were accepting her as she was, without reservations. "I...I do not know what to say."

"Well then, say grace, for Pete's sake," Cletus said. "We want to eat."

Mariabella laughed, then dropped her head and whispered a prayer, that included gratitude for her friends and for this town. Everyone around the table issued an Amen, and then they began to pass the platters of food, chatting as they dished up generous helpings of lasagna and roasted root vegetables. Conversations flowed as naturally today as they had on any other day.

Except for Cletus. He seemed to hang back, a little more reserved than usual. Mariabella handed him a basket of rolls. "Cletus, is something bothering you?"

He squirmed in his seat. "I don't want to talk about it. Not today."

"If it is about me being the princess of Uccelli—"

"It's not." He scowled. Looked at Zeke, who shook his head, as if warning him not to say what he was going to say. Cletus squirmed some more. "Aw, damn. I was going to let it go, but I can't. You have to know, Mariabella."

Cletus reached into his back pocket and pulled out a page from a Boston newspaper. The article was small, probably inserted at the last minute, among all the holiday stories. But the headline—

The headline stopped Mariabella's heart. Froze her blood.

Lattimore Properties to Build Megahotel in Harborside.

No. He'd promised. He wouldn't—

Would he?

But the words were there, in black and white. Showing Jake Lattimore to be a liar.

And Mariabella to be a fool. A fool taken in by a charming smile and a story a mile long. He'd done far worse than just call the media and tell them who she was. He'd betrayed her, on every single level.

She scanned the article, until the words began to swim in her vision. "Fifteen stories…richly appointed…similar to properties in New York and Miami…offering Jet Ski rental… tiki huts and poolside bar service."

Oh, God, how could he? She had believed him, trusted him.

But worse, she had fallen in love with him. How could she have been so stupid?

She knew better, oh, how she knew better.

Mariabella dropped the article to the table, then glanced up at Cletus, and at Zeke. Wishing they would tell her the whole thing was a joke, some kind of ruse planted by the media to get her riled up.

But the two men nodded slowly. "I checked out the article on the newswires," Zeke said, "before I came over today. It's all over the place. They made the announcement late last night. I read the press release, right on the corporate Web site, Mariabella."

Her mouth worked, trying to form the words. "Did…did the press release have a time on it?"

"It was posted just after eleven o'clock."

An hour after Jake had left last night. After he had shown her that mock-up of a home-like setting for the resort he would build in Harborside. After he had made all these promises—and she had believed them.

And after she had signed over her gallery to him.

She'd thought the hurt couldn't get worse. Thought the pain she'd felt this morning, when she'd seen the media camped outside her house, couldn't run any deeper.

She'd been wrong.

"He promised me he would not do this," she whispered.

"I'm sorry," Zeke said quietly. "I thought he was a good man. I really did."

A tear dropped onto the newspaper, blurring the print into a puddle of black letters. "Me, too."

Louisa's dog scrambled to his feet, nails clacking on the wood floors, and started yapping. He ran for the door, tail wagging, a little brown alarm bell ringing before the doorbell did.

A gust of frustration escaped Mariabella at the sound of the chimes. Just what she didn't need right now—an intrusion from the media. "I am going to call the police chief again. And have him throw those people in prison." Throw Jake in there while he was at it, for good measure.

"I'll help you," Cletus grumbled. "Damned idiots keep interrupting my dinner."

Mariabella opened the door, a tirade prepared for the rude reporter on her doorstep. But she found instead the last two people she'd expected to see in Harborside.

Her parents.

"Mama. Papa. What are you doing here?"

Behind Mariabella, Cletus, Zeke and Louisa gasped. Louisa whispered something about the king and queen.

En masse, the reporters swarmed toward the house, questions spewing from their mouths, as rapid fire as machine guns. Mariabella waved her parents inside, then shut and locked the door. The shouting continued for several minutes, then finally died down as the media realized they weren't going to get an answer. Mariabella double-checked the curtains, ensuring there wasn't an opening for a stray photograph. "I'm sorry. They found out who I am."

Her father's lips pursed. It gave Franco Santaro, normally a tall, distinguished man with white hair and a trim frame, a pinched, bitter look. "I know. All the more reason to come home. Now." He spoke in their native language, keeping the conversation between the three of them.

"I'm sorry you came all the way to America to drag me back, instead of to see me for Christmas," Mariabella said. Of course her father wouldn't fly across the world for a holiday visit, but to demand her return. To tell her he didn't accept her refusal of the crown. Disappointment sunk like a stone in her gut. "It doesn't matter, Papa. I'm not leaving."

"Cara," her mother said, reaching for her daughter, and shooting her husband a sharp look, "we miss you."

"I miss you too, Mama," Mariabella said, the sentiment tearing her throat as she drew her mother's generous frame into a short hug, "but I can't go home and be queen. I'll never be happy. Here, I'm happy."

Her father waved a hand in dismissal. "Childish notions. Come to your senses, Mariabella. There is a car waiting. We'll send for your things."

Had he heard nothing she'd said in that phone call? Why was she even surprised? Her father hadn't heard a word she'd said in twenty-five years. Why would he start now? "Why won't you listen to me, Papa? I won't go. I have found a life here. A life that means something."

"Your life as queen will mean more."

She sighed. "Yes, maybe it would. But what kind of queen would I be, if my heart forever lay elsewhere?"

Her father shook his head and muttered under his breath.

"Papa." Mariabella reached for her father's arm, trying for once to reach him as her father, not as the king. Not caring about decorum, about him being the monarch. They were on American soil now, and if she had learned one thing in all the months she had spent here, it was that relationships were built on connections—physical and emotional—and when she held herself back from those connections, she lost out on everything that mattered.

Except, with Jake Lattimore, she had connected, and lost anyway. Maybe she should have taken a page from her father's book and maintained her emotional distance.

But no. That coldness had hurt her too much over the years. Better to love and hurt than to go on living with this empty hole, waiting for love to fill it.

"Papa," she said again.

His gaze met hers, but he didn't say anything.

"Haven't you ever wanted anything other than to be king?"

Surprise lit his light green eyes. "I've…I've never thought about it."

Bianca gave her husband a knowing stare. "Franco."

"That was a long time ago," he said to his wife.

"Tell your daughter the truth."

He shifted his weight, looking so much like an ordinary man in that moment, that Mariabella wanted to reach out and hug him. But one did not do that to the king of Uccelli, so she refrained. Time ticked by, her father delaying and looking like he'd rather be sitting through a ten-hour speech than answering the question. Finally, he cleared his throat and spoke. "Once—for a moment only—I thought I could be a musician."

He could have hit her with a trombone and she would have been less surprised. "A musician? You don't even play an instrument."

"I did. When I was younger. And I had time. Now my days are filled with the monarchy. With more important duties."

Mariabella looked at her mother, who nodded and smiled, then back at her father. "What…what did you play?"

He shifted his weight again. "The drums. I fancied myself in a band some day."

"You. In a band?"

He waved off the thought. "It was a crazy idea I had for maybe five minutes, then I remembered my duty to the crown. Or, rather, my father reminded me of my duty." He gave her a pointed look. "As should you."

Her mother's gaze connected with hers, soft wisdom in her deep green eyes, shaded by long hair the same color as her daughter's. "Show him, *cara.* Show him what you dream."

"Bianca, talk sense into our daughter. Don't encourage her to—"

"Franco, you promised to listen and not to talk so much." Bianca put a hand on her hip. "You are too much a king and too little a father. See her as your daughter for once, and not as the future queen." She gave her husband a little push, and he stumbled a few steps forward into Mariabella's living room.

Mariabella's guests let out a surprised "ooh."

Annoyance filled the king's features. "Bianca, do you forget who I am?"

"No, I do not," she said. "You are Mariabella's father and my husband before you are anything else. Now take off your crown and act like it."

From across the room, a second collective gasp escaped the group. They might not have understood the language, but they definitely caught the translation of the tension. When Mariabella glanced over, all three heads of her guests swiveled away, and they got busy eating.

Bianca nodded toward her husband. "Do it, Franco. Or you will be flying home alone."

"Bianca, this is insanity." He pursed his lips again, then relented. "All right."

Her mother walked away, and crossed to the kitchen table, slipping into the seat vacated by Mariabella. She said hello to Cletus, Zeke and Louisa, then buttered a roll, and started talking to them about their plans for Christmas, as if they had been her neighbors forever. Once the other three got over their initial shock, the conversation flowed as easily as a river.

Mariabella waved her father over to the sofa, the two of them taking seats on opposite ends. The fire crackled happily, the scent of the wood accented by a cinnamon apple candle burning on the end table. "I'm not changing my mind, Papa. I can't be queen. I'm sorry."

Even though it would be easy to run back to Uccelli. To hide from the media onslaught. To flee from what had happened with Jake. To bury herself in the monarchy, and let that take over her broken heart. After all, she had nothing tying her to this town anymore. She'd sold her gallery, given up her livelihood. If she stayed in Harborside, she'd only watch it become a nightmarish version of the town she loved.

Going back to Uccelli, though, would force her back into the same cage she had fled. No matter what heartbreak this town held, it still offered something she would never find wearing the crown.

Freedom.

Her father draped his hands over his knees and let out a sigh. "I am disappointed, but I understand," he said quietly. "My illness made me think about all the years I have spent as the monarch. They were hard years. But years I wouldn't trade, you know that, don't you?"

"You have been a good king, Papa. Everything I learned from you, I used to help this town grow and prosper. Leadership, diplomacy, organization. It's worked here, and been...fun." She smiled. "I just don't want to do the same thing from the confines of a kingdom."

The wood popped and sizzled in the fire. The elf and Santa clock on the mantel ticked the time away. In the background, the stereo played soft, instrumental versions of Christmas songs. "You have to love the job and the monarchy, to do it right." The king gazed at his daughter for a long time. "You do know what you are giving up?"

She nodded.

He raised his gaze to the ceiling, as if looking for answers from the heavens. Then he paused, and rose. "This is yours?"

Her father's attention had lighted on the painting of the two pelicans. After Jake had left the other day, Mariabella had framed and hung the piece. For too long, she had, as Jake had said, held back from displaying her art—her soul. She had left the rest of the pieces at the framer's, intending to have them readied for a show in January. Except now she no longer owned the gallery, and the building would undoubtedly be demolished by then.

No matter. She'd exhibit either way. Mariabella Santaro was tired of hiding. From her name, from her art. "Yes, it is."

"I had no idea." Her father moved closer, reaching up a hand to trace the outline of the three-dimensional birds. "You have a good eye. An even better hand."

In all the years she had been painting, and going to college pursuing her art degree, her father had expressed nothing but disdain for her passion. He'd seen it as a waste of her time, a distraction from her destiny on the throne. Maybe today, with the revelation of his own dreams, he'd begun to understand her better. "Thank you, Papa."

"This…this is what you want to do?"

"That, and continue my work helping this town. I've made a difference here. A small one, but still, a difference." Yet, if Harborside changed as it would under the Lattimore property, would she stay here? Or move to a place like Harborside used to be?

Her father turned and smiled at her. A genuine smile, one that came from his heart. "I have heard about your work. Your committees, your dances and events. All from your mother, who keeps me apprised."

"Mama tells you what I do?"

He nodded. "I am proud, Mariabella. I don't think I have told you." Her father considered her for a long time, his gaze at first harsh and judgmental, all king. Then his eyes softened, and she saw another man take over, one she had glimpsed so rarely over the years she'd wondered if he really existed. A smile inched across his face, as if carving new territory. "So, you have a little of me in you after all?"

She returned his smile, and reached out a hand toward her father. He took hers, and their touch formed a bridge, a tentative one. "Yes, I think I do."

She saw what she thought might be tears in his eyes, but maybe was just a trick of the dancing firelight. "Then stay," he said. "Have the life I never did."

"You can still have that life, Papa."

"Ah, I am an old man, and the kingdom requires a king to be a certain kind of person."

"Says who? If there is one thing I've learned here, it's that life is in the living of your days, not in the dreaming about living them. A king can play the drums if he wants to," Mariabella said. "After all, he's the king. He makes all the rules."

Her father laughed, and in that sound, Mariabella heard the beginnings of a new relationship between the two of them. She caught her mother's eye. Bianca smiled, and gave her daughter a small nod. They weren't kings or queens or princesses at that moment, merely a family that was beginning to work out its kinks.

CHAPTER TWELVE

"GIVE me your tie."

Will put the limo in Park, and turned around in the driver's seat. "My tie?"

"I would have bought my own, but I've been a little busy. I'll give it back, I promise. Better yet, I'll buy you two dozen for Christmas."

Will shook his head, laughing, then undid his tie and tossed it over the seat. "You really want to wear dancing Santas?"

Jake glanced at Mariabella's cottage. The earlier snowstorm had kissed the entire house with a coating of white. Her Christmas lights twinkled like tiny sprites in the drifts piled on the shrubbery. Smoke curled from the chimney, scenting the air with the perfume of home. Of everything he'd ever wanted. "Yeah. I do."

"Good luck," Will said. "I'll pull the car over there to wait."

Jake shook his head. "No. Go home, Will. I'll see you on January fourth."

Will gaped at his boss. "January fourth? That's…that's almost two weeks off."

"With pay. Go to Jamaica or something with your wife, stay in the best Lattimore property we have. Don't call me, don't send a postcard, just enjoy yourself."

"What about you?"

Jake opened the limo door and stepped into the cold. "I've got a Christmas miracle to pull off."

He drew his coat tighter, then took a deep breath and strode up the walkway to Mariabella's door. He rang the bell, she opened the door—and nearly slammed it again in his face. "I do not have anything to say to you."

Jake put a hand on the oak frame. "I just want to talk to you for five minutes, Mariabella."

"Why? So you can tell me why you betrayed me? I saw the article." She started to shut the door, but he stopped it with his foot. "Just leave, Jake."

"Not until you hear me out." His gaze met hers. The fire in her green eyes sparked, then ebbed.

A bit.

Maybe there was still hope. God, he prayed there was.

Mariabella let out a gust. "Fine. Five minutes." She opened the door and let him in. Cletus, Zeke and Louisa sat at the kitchen table like a posse, shooting him death glares. Even George the dachshund let out a little growl from under the table. Two other people Jake didn't recognize sat on the sofa by the fireplace, sipping coffee.

She saw him glance at the strangers, and with clear reluctance, introduced him. "Jake Lattimore, these are my parents, Bianca and Franco Santaro."

The king and queen of Uccelli? Here in Harborside?

The king had the regal appearance of a man who had ruled for a long time. He sat stiffly, his white hair and defined features making him look imposing, strong. The queen, on the other hand, had more of Mariabella's features, and a softness to her green eyes that seemed to welcome Jake.

Jake crossed to them, and put out his hand, then gave a slight bow. "It's an honor to meet you, Your Majesties."

The queen looked from her daughter then to Jake. "Ah, this is the one for you, is it not, Mariabella?"

The king shot Jake a protective father glare.

"No." Mariabella scowled. "He is no one." She tugged Jake away from the living room and into a small bedroom off to the right. Dead silence fell over the living room. Mariabella shut the door, blocking any attempts at eavesdropping.

Mariabella flicked on the light switch, and illuminated a wide picture window that faced the ocean, then an easel in the center of the room, and a stack of empty canvases along the wall. A half-finished painting of an eagle sat on the easel. Her studio. "You have four and a half minutes," she said.

Okay. So she had no intentions of going easy on him. What had he expected, really?

"Put out your hands."

"What?"

"Just put out your hands."

She did as he asked, cupping her hands together. Jake reached into his coat pocket, then released a pile of something white. As the flecks fluttered down, Mariabella first thought he had dropped snowflakes into her hand, then realized the white pieces were shredded bits of paper. "What...what's this?"

"Every one of the purchase and sales agreements signed by the business owners of Harborside. Including you."

She stared at the pile in her hands. Then him. "Why would you do this? I thought you needed these lots to build your hotel."

"I did, until the board double-crossed me. They pressured my father into going in another direction, and used both of us to get what they wanted. You saw the newspaper article, right?"

She nodded.

"I had nothing to do with that. Nor did I tell the media who you were. That was all Darcy, and the board at Lattimore Properties, trying to exploit every angle they could for 'the good of the company.'" The air quotes and sarcasm in his voice made his feelings clear.

She glanced out the window behind her, the one that faced

the side yard. No curtains hung there, and she half expected a flash bulb to go off, broadcasting a private moment to the world.

"They're gone, Mariabella. And those reporters won't get within a hundred yards of you. Ever. I hired a security detail to keep them away. You can go on living your life here."

The media had left. Her life could return to the way it had been. Private, quiet. She owned her gallery again. She should have been happy.

But she wasn't.

An emptiness invaded her, something still missing, a piece of herself she had yet to find.

She dumped the pile of papers onto the small desk in the corner of her studio. "Why would you do that? You will get fired, Jake."

"No, I won't. My father and I together are the ones in charge now. We just had to join forces and eliminate the board. As a team, we own fifty-one percent of the company. It took a little doing to remind my father of who he used to be, and how we could go back to the kind of company we were. But now he's excited, charged up in a way I haven't seen him in years. He hadn't lost his touch, simply his passion for his job." Jake took Mariabella by the shoulders and drew her over to the large picture window. He pointed to the red light skimming across the water, the telltale sign of a boat riding through the channel. "Zeke issued a challenge to me the first day I was here. He told me I could be like a motorboat, churning up everything in my path, or like a sailboat, leaving the world relatively unchanged after I was here."

"And which have you chosen?" She held her breath, sure she knew the answer, but needing to ask the question anyway.

He leaned down, placing his face beside hers, cheeks meeting. "The sailboat, building an inn that fits Harborside, fits the people, fits the vision of those who love this place. We'll show every business owner, and be sure they all want to be on board, before they sign new agreements. Start at square one, and get community input. Make it a true Harborside property."

She turned in his arms, her gaze meeting his blue eyes. "What if it fails, like the last one?"

He shrugged. "We'll cross that bridge when we get to it. But I have a good feeling about this."

Mariabella's gaze drifted to the eagle half-finished on the painting sitting on her easel. Even birds had a nest to come back to, a place where they roosted, a home they built and tended lovingly. It wasn't just about how far they could soar, but about whether they could fly back to where they wanted to be.

And where she wanted to be was right here. As herself, not as Mariabella Romano. Not as a woman lying every day of her life. There was, as Jake had said, no freedom in lies. "Would it help if a princess ran an art gallery at the inn?"

"Mariabella, you don't have to do that. You can go on being Mariabella Romano. Keep your life the way it is."

"It is no life at all," she said. "Not if I am being someone else. I do not have to be queen to make a difference. I can do it as a princess."

He traced the outline of her jaw, and smiled. "And as a wife."

Had she heard him right? "A wife?"

"I've fallen in love with you, Mariabella. With you, not you the princess, or you, the gallery owner, but just *you*. And I don't want to do any of this—" he swept a hand toward the beach, the town "—without you. You are the dream I was looking for outside my window. And now that I've found you, I don't want to let you go."

A tear escaped and slid down her cheek. "I…I do not know what to say." He'd told her everything she'd always wanted to hear, and the words hummed in her heart.

Jake dropped to one knee, pulled a velvet box out of his pocket and held it open. A simple round diamond glittered back at her. Nothing ostentatious, nothing overdone. The perfect ring. "Say you'll marry me."

Had she once thought there were no Prince Charmings left in the world? That fairy tales didn't come true? She had been wrong, and she'd never been so glad to be wrong in her life. "Yes, Jake, yes, I'll marry you."

He rose, and swung her into his arms. They kissed, at the same time a light snow began to fall outside. The clock struck midnight, and Christmas began. But neither of them noticed, because they both already had the present they'd dreamed of—a present, and a future, with each other.

EPILOGUE

THE palace's landscaper had spent a month finding the perfect tree. He'd hemmed and hawed, until the queen herself had gone out to the woods and chosen the one that now stood proudly in the center hall. Dozens of people had come to see the big event.

"Ah, it is beautiful, isn't it?" Mariabella said to her sister. She stepped back and took in the entire twenty-five-foot-high pine, amazed at the perfect symmetry of the branches, the deep emerald color, offset by the white and gold decorations. Surrounded by the black-and-white marble floors, the two-story hand-carved wood walls, featuring reliefs of Uccelli's history, and the massive windows draped with thick red velvet curtains, the tree stood as an elaborate centerpiece to the castle's main gallery.

Allegra smiled. "It is. But it's still missing something." She handed the final ornament to her eldest sister.

"Shouldn't the queen do this job? After all, I live in America now."

Allegra shook her head, causing her crown to move slightly. The multicolored jewels ringing the gold headpiece sparkled under the pendant lights hanging from the massive, two-story ceiling. "As long as you are home, Mariabella, it is your job."

Mariabella drew her sister into a hug. "You will make a

wonderful queen." Allegra's coronation had been only last week, and the ceremony had been wonderful. Mariabella knew the moment she saw her sister accept the crown, that she had made the right decision in abdicating. Allegra had the passion for the job, the love of the monarchy, and the fortitude for the hard years ahead.

Allegra wiped a tear off her face. "Well, as queen, I am ordering you to hurry up. We have a wedding to go to."

Mariabella laughed, then crossed to the tree and hung the delicate crystal filigree angel on the tree. She stepped over to the wall, then flicked the switch. Thousands of tiny white lights sprang to life, bathing the center room of the castle in a golden light. A collective "ahh" went up among the crowd gathered around the tree.

"It is time, Mariabella." The king touched his daughter on the shoulder.

She nodded, then turned toward her father. He looked younger since he had stepped down and handed over the throne to his middle daughter, happier even. He laid a hand on top of his daughter's arm. "You look like your mother did forty years ago. Beautiful."

"Thank you, Papa."

"You will visit? Often?"

She nodded, tears choking her throat. "Of course. Jake not only loves my family, he loves the Uccelli wine. And you can only buy that here."

Her father laughed. "Then we shall keep on bottling it. By the gallon, if it brings you home more often. I miss you, Mariabella."

"I miss you too, Papa." She had returned to Uccelli a half-dozen times in the past year, and her parents had visited Harborside twice, staying at the Harborside Inn both times, and generating a little media storm with each visit. They'd loved the homey setting, even though it was a major departure from castle life, and vowed to return often. Mariabella had a feeling she and Jake would be putting a lot of miles on his private jet in the years to come.

The bridal march began to play, the organ music swelling and filling the main gallery. Mariabella and her father began the long walk down the hall, along a path littered with white daisies and crimson rose petals.

Candles lit the hall, which had been draped in pine garland and massive crimson bows. White silk shantung hung from ceiling to floor, making it feel as if they'd walked into a winter wonderland.

Jake stood in the chapel, waiting for her, flanked by Will, then Zeke and Cletus. On the bride's side, Allegra had taken her place as maid of honor, followed by Carlita and Carmen. A thousand more white candles flickered in the chapel, the only light for the small room. Beautiful, intimate and as close to a winter setting as she could get. The train of her dress swished along the path, with her veil fluttering softly at her back.

Her father placed a soft kiss on her cheek, then led her to Jake. The wedding march came to an end, and the guests began to take their seats. Neither Jake nor Mariabella noticed anything but each other.

Mariabella took her husband-to-be's hand and smiled, first at the snowman tie he wore, then at him. He matched her smile with one of his own. "I am the luckiest man in the world," he whispered.

"Because you are marrying the princess?"

"No." He placed a soft kiss against her lips. "Because in every fairy tale, the ending is always, 'And they lived happily ever after.' And that, my love, is exactly what I intend to do with you."

* * * * *

JINGLE-BELL BABY

BY
LINDA GOODNIGHT

Winner of the RITA® Award for excellence in inspirational fiction, **Linda Goodnight** has also won the Booksellers' Best, ACFW Book of the Year, and a Reviewers' Choice Award from *RT Book Reviews* magazine. Linda has appeared on the Christian bestseller list, and her romance novels have been translated into more than a dozen languages. Active in orphan ministry, this former nurse and teacher enjoys writing fiction that carries a message of hope and light in a sometimes dark world. She and husband Gene live in Oklahoma. Readers can write to her at linda@lindagoodnight.com.

To Denise and Ashley.
Know you're reading this. Love ya, my friends!

CHAPTER ONE

LESSON NUMBER ONE in birthing class: never drive a car cross-country alone. Especially during the ninth month of pregnancy.

But Jenna Garwood had never taken a birthing class.

For the tenth time in as many minutes, she cast an anxious glance in the rearview mirror, relieved to see that no one had followed her when she'd exited the interstate some miles back.

Since her escape from the Carrington Estate, she'd zigged and zagged from the east toward the west, careful to cover her tracks. After three days, she shouldn't be so worried. But the long arm of the Carrington family reached far and wide. And they didn't give up easily.

When she'd heard the plans they had for her unborn child, Jenna had done the only thing that made sense. She'd run.

She had always been weak, but the little girl beneath her breast had given her strength. After the humiliation and sorrow of the last two years, the baby had given her a reason to try again.

A moan slipped past a bottom lip raw from constant gnawing. She bent forward over the steering wheel to stretch the kink in her back wishing she hadn't spritzed the car's interior with eau de parfum this morning. The stench of dirt and oil intermingled with the honeyed notes of orange blossom rose from the floorboard like an unwanted visitor. Saliva pooled in her mouth. As she tried to focus on the road, she swallowed, regretful, too, of the hamburger she'd eaten for breakfast.

Somewhere in this empty Texas landscape, there had to be a quiet little town where she could rest…and hide…until the ache in her back subsided.

"Only a little farther, darling," she murmured to the hard ball around her middle. "Mommy's tired, too."

Tired was an understatement of monumental proportions.

Her back had hurt nonstop throughout the duration of her pregnancybut during the last twelve hours the discomfort had grown steadily worse. If it had been her belly instead of her back, she would have been scared.

In conjunction with long hours behind the wheel, stress was the likely culprit. She hadn't relaxed once since leaving the estate. Even sleep was accomplished with an ear to the door and her eyes half-open.

The stretching, pressing ache deepened. She really needed to find that town.

She reached for her handbag, a pink crocodile spy bag her mother had purchased for Jenna's twenty-second birthday six weeks ago. The purse, stuffed full of the very best cosmetics, a spa coupon, and a five-thousand-dollar shopping card, had been nothing short of a bribe and Jenna knew it. Unfortunately Mother never understood that monetary possessions had ceased to inspire loyalty in her daughter. Only one thing had her complete and utter devotion—the tiny person who, at this very moment, was causing a great deal of discomfort to Jenna's body.

As her fingers flipped open the purse flap, Jenna hissed a frustrated breath between her teeth. She no longer owned the elegant slider phone, complete with GPS and remote Internet access. Still fully charged and activated, she'd donated it to a bewildered but grateful soldier at an airport in Philadelphia. By the time the device had been located, it would be somewhere in the Middle East.

"Who would you call anyway?" Even 9-1-1 was fraught

with difficulties. Though the Carringtons disdained public attention, choosing to deal with their scandals in a more discreet and private manner, Jenna would allow no chance of alerting anyone to her whereabouts.

She forced herself to breathe slow and deep. The tense, tense muscles in her back only grew tighter.

A flutter of panic trembled in her stomach. What if she went into labor out here alone?

She turned on the radio, praying for a distraction, while also pressing the car's accelerator. She needed to get *some-where* fast.

A male voice, rich in Texas twang, came through the speakers to announce a fall festival at Saddleback Elementary School and a garage sale at 220 Pinehurst behind the Saddleback Pizza Place.

Saddleback must be a town. But where was it?

She gave the radio a pleading glance. "Can't you be a bit more specific?"

The pressure inside her body increased. A new and more insistent discomfort had moved around front to a spot low in her belly. Very low. She gasped and shifted sideways onto one hip. The pressure mounted, deeper, harder, stronger.

A guttural groan erupted from Jenna's throat. The sound was foreign, so different from her normal modulated tone.

From the radio pounded a driving beat of electric guitar and bass. The intensity echoed in her body.

The road ahead seemed to waver.

Fingers of iron gripped her abdomen. She was in trouble. Real trouble.

She blinked, panting, fighting the pressure. Sweat stung her eyes. Texas weather was cool, though not nearly as cold as a Pennsylvania November, and yet, Jenna was roasting inside the small blue economy. She reached for the air-conditioning controls and saw, with concern, how pale and shaky she'd become.

Before she could take another breath, a squeezing pain of epic proportions followed hard on the heels of the intense pressure.

"Oh no." She *was* in labor. Either that or her body was rupturing from the inside out.

Mouth open, panting like a puppy, she gripped the steering wheel with both hands and tried to stay on the road.

"Not yet, baby. Not yet. Let me find a hospital first." She squinted into the glare of an overcast sky, hoping for something, anything. A town, a house, another car.

Nothing but the endless brown landscape and an occasional line of naked trees.

The pressure mounted again, little by little, a warning that another power punch was on the way. Dread tensed her shoulders. "Nooo."

Her body poured sweat. So unladylike. Had Mother perspired this much with her?

She had to escape the pain. She had to. Perhaps if she stopped, got out of the car and walked a bit. Walking had helped in the past to ease the back ache. Even if walking didn't help, she could drive no further. She wouldn't take a chance of having an accident.

She tapped the brake and aimed the car toward the grassy roadside. Her belly tightened again. With one hand, she grabbed for the rock-hard mound, moaning with dread. The terrible pain was coming again. She could think of nothing but the battle raging in her body.

Just before the agony took control, Jenna saw a flash of barbed wire and orange fence posts. The fence moved closer and closer.

And there was nothing she could do about it.

As his King Ranch pickup truck roared down County Road 275, Dax Coleman had two things on his mind: a hot shower and a good meal.

At the last thought, his mouth curled, mocking him. He hadn't had a good meal since the latest of a long string of housekeepers quit two weeks ago. Supper would be microwave pizza or scrambled eggs, the extent of his culinary gifts. His own fault, certainly. He wasn't the easiest man in Texas to live with. Just ask his ex-wife—if you could find her.

A snarl escaped him. He reached over to raise the radio volume and drown out thoughts of Reba.

As he rounded the last lazy curve before the turnoff to the Southpaw Cattle Company, a car in the distance caught his attention. Dax leaned forward, squinting into the overcast day.

The guy up ahead was either drunk, lost or having trouble. Dax took his foot off the accelerator. The car, a dirty blue economy model, was taking its share of the road out of the middle. It wove to the left and then back again as the driver began to slow.

With a beleaguered sigh, Dax tapped the brake. He wasn't in the mood for drunks. He wasn't in the mood for any kind of people, come to think of it.

For the last five years, all he'd really wanted out of life was his son and his ranch. The rest of the world could leave him the heck alone.

The car ahead slowed considerably and aimed for the side of the road. Maybe the fella was having car trouble.

After an afternoon of helping Bryce Patterson separate calves, Dax was too tired and dirty to play nice.

Still, he was a Texan, and the unspoken code of the country was rooted into him as deeply as the land itself. Out here, folks helped folks. Even when it was inconvenient.

Another car might not come along for hours and cell phone usage was spotty. He grabbed the plain black device from the seat next to a pair of dirty leather gloves and a pair of fencing pliers. Sure enough. Not a single bar of connection. He tossed the phone aside.

"Don't know what good the blasted thing is if it never works where you need it."

As he glanced back up, still grumbling, the dirty blue car wobbled off the road, onto the grass, and down a slight incline.

"Come on, buddy, stop. Stop!"

The car ahead kept rolling.

Five strands of brand-new barbed wire bowed outward before snapping like strings on a fiddle. Orange fence posts toppled. Dax's fence posts.

"Blast it!" he ground out through gritted teeth and slammed the heel of his hand against the steering wheel. Somewhere in the back of his mind he was proud of holding back the expletives that tempted his foul-tempered tongue like flirty girls. A few years ago, he would have let fly with enough curses to make the grass blush, but with a mimicking boy dogging his boot prints, Dax had cleaned up his act. At least, that part of his act. Nothing much would clean up the rest.

Braking hard, he slid the truck onto the shoulder and bounded out into a comfortable November afternoon. The metallic slam reverberated over the quiet countryside, joining the rattle and wheeze of the car now captured in his barbed wire like a sad little bluebird.

"Hey, buddy," Dax hollered, as he approached the still-settling vehicle. "You okay?"

His question was met with the slow, painful screech of wire against metal, like fingernails on a blackboard. The driver didn't answer and made no effort to get out of the car.

Dax frowned, slowing his steps to assess the situation. Maybe the guy *was* drunk. Or maybe he was a criminal fixing to bushwhack an unsuspecting rancher. Dax considered going for the wolf rifle resting behind the seat of his truck but fought off the temptation. At six foot one and a hundred and eighty pounds, he could hold his own. Besides, he'd watched the car weave and wobble for a couple of miles. His gut told him something was amiss, either with the driver or the car. Maybe the guy was sick or something.

The car had been moving too slowly for any kind of serious injury so the accident was a by-product of another problem, not the cause. There had been no real impact other than the scraping entanglement with wire and the now-toppled fence posts.

"Blast it," he said again. No matter how tired he was, he'd have to get this fence back up in a hurry or risk having heifers all over the road by morning.

Slapping his Stetson down tight, Dax strode down the slight incline and across the narrow expanse of calf-high weeds toward the blue car. Other than a cloud of dust circling the tires and fenders, there was an eerie stillness around the vehicle.

Dax bent down to peer through the driver's side window. His gut lurched. The occupant was either a guy with really long hair or he was a woman. A real curse drifted through his head. He savored the word like chocolate pie. Women were a lot of trouble.

"Hey, lady." He tapped a knuckle on the glass while tugging the door handle with the opposite hand. "Do you need help?"

The woman was slumped forward, her head on the steering wheel. She was breathing, but her shoulders rose and fell rapidly as if in distress. Dax exhaled a gusty breath. Crying women were the second-worst kind.

Suddenly, the object of his concern arched back against the cloth seat. A cry ripped from her throat, scary enough to make him jump.

The sound shot adrenaline through Dax's veins. He yanked at the door. It was stuck. Strong from years of wrangling five-hundred-pound bovines, he yanked again, harder. The door gave way, digging up dead grass and dirt as it opened.

He reached in, touched the slender shoulder. "Miss. Miss, where are you hurt?"

She turned a narrow, haggard face in his direction. Her eyes were wide with fear. Dark blond hair stuck to a sweaty forehead and cheeks.

"My baby," she managed, the sound more groan than words.

"Baby?" Dax glanced quickly into the backseat, but saw no sign of a child.

The woman squirmed, her hands moving downward to her waist.

And that's when Dax knew. The woman with the wide, doe eyes and the teenager's face was in labor.

All the expletives he knew rushed to his tongue. Somehow he held them back, useless as they were to anyone but him.

"Talk to me, miss. How long have you been in labor?"

"The baby's coming."

The implication froze him solid. "Now?"

She managed a nod and then slid sideways in the seat, lying back against the opposite door. Her body rocked forward. She fought against it, battling the wave of pain he could see on her young face. Nature was taking its course.

Oh boy.

"I'm sorry," she said. "I'm sorry."

Sorry for what? Going into labor? Having a baby? The latter set his stomach churning even harder. He knew about that kind of woman.

But he had no time to ponder the past or the woman's cryptic statement. His brain shifted into warp speed. He had a dilemma here. A real dilemma. A strange young woman was having a baby in a car on his property and he was the only human being around to help.

Great. Just great.

"We need to get you to a hospital."

Her eyes glazed over and she made that deep groaning

sound again. His pulse ricocheted off his rib cage. He'd heard this particular moan before from cows and mares. The woman was right. They were out of time.

"All right, miss, take it easy," he said, as much to calm his own nerves as hers. "Everything will be okay."

She nodded again, her huge eyes locked on his face, clinging to his words, trusting him, a total stranger. Dax got the weirdest feeling in his chest.

"How far along are you? I mean, is it time for the baby?"

"Two weeks away."

Close enough to know this was the real deal. Dang. Dang. Dang.

"How long have you been in labor?" he asked again.

Her body answered for her. Dax was smart enough to know that contractions this close could only mean one thing. Birth was imminent.

Think, Dax, think. What did he need? What could he do, other than wait for the inevitable?

"I'll be right back," he said past a tongue gone dry as an August day.

She managed to lever up, almost heaving toward him. "No! Don't leave. Please. Please."

Her pleading voice ebbed away on the wing of pain, but not before the sound hit Dax in the solar plexus. What kind of jerk did she take him for?

Guilt pinched him. Okay, so he'd resented the interruption to his afternoon. He'd wanted to drive right past. The point was he hadn't. He might be a jerk, but he wasn't a complete slimeball. Most of the time.

He touched her foot, hoping to reassure her. She was barefoot. A pair of fancy-looking silver shoes, complete with a perky bow, rested on the floor. He had the silliest thought that her feet were pretty. Slim and elegant like one of those ballet dancers.

What the devil was she doing out here alone?

"I need some things from my truck," he said. "It's right behind us. Not far at all. I'll only be a minute."

He loped to his Ford and dug out any- and everything he could find in the cab that might be of some use. There wasn't much, but he had an old blanket and plenty of water. A rancher could never be certain when he might be ten miles from the house and need water or a blanket. At least he could wash his hands and wrap the baby when it arrived. A bright-red bandanna on the floorboard caught his eye. Gavin had left it behind. Though the cloth was likely none too clean, he grabbed it anyway and drenched the soft cotton with water.

Back at the car, he leaned in to wipe the wet bandanna over the woman's damp forehead.

"It's me again," he said and then felt stupid for saying it. Who else would it be? The Seventh Cavalry?

The little mama made a small humming noise he took for gratitude. She must have been in between a contraction because her eyes were closed and her expression less tense.

As he straightened, he caught a whiff of some sweet-scented flower. Imagine, smelling like flowers at a time like this. She looked like a nightmare, but she smelled good.

He wondered one final time if he could toss her in the truck and get to the hospital in Saddleback in time.

Just as the thought flitted across his mind, her eyes flew open, distressed. "Oh, no. It's coming again."

She grabbed for his hand and squeezed with a grip that would have taken down a sumo wrestler.

"Easy now. Easy," he said, talking to her the way he would a first-time mare. What else could he do? He was no doctor.

All right, Coleman, he said to himself. You've delivered plenty of calves and foals. A baby can't be much different.

If he believed that he would have gone into the delivery room when Gavin was born.

"You're doing great. Long, deep breaths. Work with the pain, not against it." He didn't know where the advice was coming from, but she seemed to do better when he was talking. "Attagirl. You're doing good."

The contraction subsided and she dropped her head back again. Dax shared her relief. This baby-delivering business was hard work. His back ached from bending over the seat and his pulse pounded so hard against his eardrums, he thought he heard tom-toms.

Having long since tossed his hat aside, Dax wiped a sleeve across his forehead. Even with a cool breeze floating through the open door, he was sweating like a pig. But then, so was the little mama.

Drenched in sweat, her hair a wet wad around her face, she reminded Dax of a drowned kitten. Pitiful-looking little thing. Somebody, somewhere was going to be real upset that she was out here alone on the Texas plains having a baby.

He wondered about the baby's father. About her family. She was young. Though her age was hard to discern at the moment, to an over-the-hill thirty-something like him she looked like a kid. She needed her family at a time like this, not some broken-down old cowboy with a bad attitude, who wanted to be anywhere but here.

She was a brave little thing. He'd give her that. Tough as a pine knot. She had to be scared out of her mind, young as she was, but she hadn't screamed or fought or carried on the way Reba had. She hadn't cussed him or the baby, either.

Dax tasted gall as the old humiliating memory thrust itself into his consciousness.

The little mama shifted slightly, emitting a murmur of dread. Another contraction must be on its way.

He gently rubbed her toes. She captured his eyes; a tiny smile lifted the corners of her mouth. Dax felt oddly heartened.

Here they were in about as intimate a situation as he could think of, and he didn't even know her name. What if something went wrong?

No, he wouldn't think of that. Even if his life was ruled by Murphy's Law, he was not going to allow anything bad to happen to this gritty little lady.

"Name's Dax," he said. "You feel like telling me yours?"

Something odd flickered behind pain-clouded eyes. She licked dry lips. Then her gaze slid away.

Before Dax could decide if her silence was fatigue or reluctance, the wave of nature took over again. As her shoulders rolled forward, straining, she whispered, "I wanted to be brave, but I'm so scared. Don't let anything happen to my baby."

The admission touched Dax somewhere in the cold lump he called a heart. "You're doing fine, little mama."

He wanted to say a lot of other encouraging things, to tell her how courageous he thought she was, but with the blood rushing in his temples and his gut twisting with anxiety at the huge responsibility before him, he just patted her pretty foot and muttered nonsense.

He didn't know how long he'd been there. Couldn't have been more than fifteen minutes though it felt like a lifetime when suddenly she gave one last heaving groan and it was over. She fell back against the car seat, her exhausted breathing loud in the quiet.

A baby, the smallest thing Dax could imagine, slipped into his waiting hands. He'd expected her to be pink and squalling the way Gavin had been. Instead, the tiny form was silent, limp and purplish.

His heart, already jumping and pumping to beat Dixie, rose into his throat. He glanced at the little mama and then down at the infant.

Please God, no. Not this.

CHAPTER TWO

THE BROWN-HAIRED BOY barreling across the yard of The Southpaw in cowboy boots and an open jean jacket lifted Dax's flagging spirits. The last few hours had been rough to say the least.

"Daddy!"

A swell of love bigger than his fifteen-hundred-acre ranch expanded in Dax's chest. He stopped in midyard and hunkered down. The sturdy little boy, smelling of pizza and backyard dirt, slammed into him. Small arms encircled his neck and squeezed.

Dax pressed the slender body to him, clinging to the thought that his son was alive and well. He didn't know what he would do if anything should ever happen to Gavin, a fact that had come home to him with a vengeance during these last few hours with the little mama.

Life was fragile. His thoughts flashed to the tiny newborn baby. Real fragile.

"Where you been?" Gavin was saying. "Rowdy had to stay a long time."

Dax looked up at the young ranch hand ambling lazily toward them, his usual crooked smile in place. Dax figured you could punch Rowdy Davis in the nose and he'd still grin. Sometimes the man's smirky cheer was downright irritating.

"Everything all right, boss?" Rowdy asked, clearly curious. "You were kind of short and not-too-sweet on the telephone. Had us worried some."

Short and not-too-sweet. Yep, that was him, all right. He'd simply told Rowdy to be at the house when the school bus delivered Gavin from kindergarten and stay there. Then, he'd hung up, too wrung out to explain that he was at the emergency room fifteen miles away with a strange woman whose baby he'd just delivered.

"Boys, do I have a story to tell. Let's get in the house first. I could use a cold drink." Since playing doctor on the side of the road, his appetite was gone but he still wanted a cold soda pop and that hot shower.

Gavin wiggled back from his embrace. "A story about Wild Bill and the buffaloes?"

"No, son," Dax said. "Not that kind of story."

He rose, lifting the five-year-old up with him. Gavin looped an arm over his dad's shoulder and patted his opposite cheek. Dax felt that quivery feeling in the center of his chest. He didn't know what he'd done to deserve Gavin, but he was grateful. Without the boy, he would have given up on life long ago. As it was, he clung to the edges of hope, fighting off his own dark tendencies in an effort to give the motherless boy a decent upbringing. It wasn't easy. *Gavin* wasn't easy. And at times Dax no more understood the boy than he could understand Chinese.

A frown cut a deep gash between Gavin's black eyebrows. "It won't be scary, will it?"

Times like these. The boy was scared of his own shadow. Since hearing a ghost story at a fall party he'd been especially nervous.

"No, Gavin, it's not scary." He tried, but failed, to keep the annoyance out of his tone. The boy was skittish as a deer. The teacher had had to peel him away from Dax's side the first day of kindergarten. And Gavin had cried, an occurrence that both worried and embarrassed his father. A sissified kid wouldn't survive in today's mean world, but Dax didn't know how to change his child's disposition.

By now, they'd made the house and were inside. Dax tossed his hat at a heavy wooden end table, shrugged out of his jacket, and collapsed with an exaggerated heave onto a chair. The living room was enormous, compliments of his ex-wife who had insisted on a house big enough to entertain. Trouble was she'd done her entertaining while he was out working. He liked the house, though, liked the warm, golden-brown stone and wood fireplace and the wine-colored leather furniture.

He propped his boots on a squat ottoman. "You ever deliver a baby, Rowdy?"

Rowdy, who had ventured off to the kitchen, reappeared with a glass in hand. "What? Are you serious?"

Dax accepted the glass and gulped the icy drink in three long gulps. "Crazy afternoon. A young woman ran her car through my fence between here and Jake's windmill. I stopped to see what the problem was and she was having a baby."

Rowdy slithered into a chair, the grin forming a surprised O. "Man."

"Yeah. Tell me about it."

"Everything go okay? I mean, you delivered the baby and everything." As the reality of what Dax had done sank in, Rowdy leaned forward, elbows braced on his knees. "Holy smoke, Dax. Are they all right? The mama and baby, I mean?"

"The baby was kind of blue and not moving at first. I thought she was gone." Running a finger around the rim of the glass, he didn't mention how scared he'd been. The telling sounded a lot calmer than the actual event. "Then I thought about how calves are born with a lot of mucous sometimes, so I wiped her nose and mouth off with Gavin's bandana…." He patted the boy's knee. Gavin curled up next to him, listening to every word. "Just as I was getting ready to turn her upside down and swat her bottom, she let out a howl." Sweetest sound he'd ever heard.

"Man." Rowdy said again, seemingly devoid of intelligent comment. Dax understood. He'd been speechless himself at the time. As soon as the baby had cried, he'd wrapped her in the old blanket and made sure the mama was all right. Then he'd jumped behind the wheel of the car, forced the little economy onto the road and sped like a NASCAR racer to the emergency room.

"Where is she, Daddy? Why didn't you bring her home? I want to see her."

"She and her mama are in the hospital in Saddleback." He rattled the ice in his glass, shaking out a few more drops of cola.

Beneath a swatch of thick, dark hair a fretful frown puckered Gavin's forehead. "Are they sick?"

"The doc's going to check them over. But I think they'll be okay."

The child stuck his legs straight out from the couch and tapped the toes of his boots in a steady rhythm. "Noah's mama had a baby. They got to bring it home and keep it. Now he gots two brothers. But a sister would be okay, too."

Dax sighed. He and Gavin had this conversation every time one of the boy's schoolmates welcomed a new sibling. How did he explain to a five-year-old that his daddy wasn't the kind of man women wanted to have babies with?

"Is she from around here?" Rowdy's question gave Dax an excuse not to answer the boy. "The woman. Anybody we know?"

"No. Not even a Texan." He knew that for certain. Her buttery voice with its clipped syllables was upper-class Eastern, a Yankee. He'd stake his ranch on it. Even her clothes were different.

"What was she doing out here on a remote county road all by herself? Visiting someone?"

"Can't say." Though he'd been asking himself the same question. "We didn't exactly have a conversation."

"No, I guess not." Rowdy ran a thumb and forefinger along his chiseled jawline. "What did she look like? Is she pretty?"

Dax shot him a frown. His top ranch hand liked the ladies and had a new one on his arm every week. Women seemed to like him right back. Still, the question didn't sit well with Dax.

"She was a scared kid." Scared but tough and courageous. He couldn't get that out of his head or the thought of the tiny, mewling baby that had been born in his hands.

"I'm sad for her, Daddy, if she's scared. Can we go see her?"

"I told you she's all right." The words came out a little harsher than he'd intended. Gavin blanched and sat back against the couch.

Dax patted the boy's knee, letting him know the sharp retort wasn't aimed at him. Gavin was tenderhearted to his old man's hard-hearted, plain and simple. But Dax refused to feel guilty about wanting the strange day to end here and now. He'd done his part to help the woman. He'd played the good Samaritan. She was receiving expert care and the hospital would contact her family. He had a ranch to run and a downed fence to fix. He'd heard the last of the mysterious young mother and her baby. And that's the way he wanted it.

Jenna heard voices. She opened her eyes in a semidarkened room that smelled of antiseptic and oversteamed food. She faced a wall and a wide pair of windows covered by blinds. The morning sun sliced through, shedding strips of pale yellow across a white woven blanket. Memory flooded in with the sunlight.

The pain, the car, a tall, gruff-talking rancher with gentle hands.

"Oh." Her hands shot to her belly. The baby. The man had

delivered her little girl and brought them to the hospital. A mix of embarrassment and wonder filled her. She'd had her baby in a car with only a stranger to help. Mother would be mortified.

She shifted in the narrow hospital bed. Her body was sore and stiff, but not painfully so, a fact that surprised her. After the torture in the car she'd expected to be half-dead today.

She rolled to her side, eager to hold her new daughter.

The baby was gone.

A tremor rippled through her as the possibilities played through her head. The nurses had left the newborn here, at the bedside, in an Isolette. Jenna was positive.

Had the Carrington machine already discovered her whereabouts?

Fighting the stiff sheets, she sat upright, only to tumble sideways onto the pillow, light-headed and weak. Blood roared in her temples. She took deep breaths, waiting until the black dots dissipated.

For a long moment, she remained still, frustration in every breath. Had someone recognized her and called her family? Was her baby girl even now in the smothering bosom of the Carrington clan?

The heavy wooden door opened with a swish. Jenna braced to face her censuring mother, determined to stand strong for her baby.

When a nurse appeared, backside first, Jenna wilted against the pillow in relief.

"Everything looks great with your little princess," the woman said, rolling the Isolette into the room. "Doctor checked her all out, gave her the requisite medications and said she was perfect."

"I didn't know where you'd taken her." Her voice sounded breathless and scared.

The nurse, a young woman with a long, black ponytail, whose tag read Crystal Wolf, RN, gave her a sympathetic pat.

"Sorry, hon, you were sleepin' like a rock, so I didn't want to disturb you. Not after what you went through. You ready for her? Or are you too tired? You look a little pale."

Jenna held out her arms. Color would return now that she knew her mother wasn't on the premises. "Yes, please let me hold her."

"She's a darling. So pretty with all that fine golden hair and her little turned-up nose."

Jenna thought her daughter looked like an alien. A withered old lady alien. "Will her head always be pointed like this?"

With a shake of dangly white earrings, the nurse laughed. She reached over, flipped the soft pink blanket back and gently massaged the baby's head with a cupped hand. "You do that every day and before you know it, the cone head will be gone."

"Thank goodness." Jenna gave a shaky laugh.

She'd read books and searched the Internet on the topic of parenting and felt competent to be a mother, but now that the moment was upon her, the idea of caring for another human being frightened her. She had no home, no job, and no one to help. For a person who'd never been allowed to do anything for herself, she had a great deal to learn—fast.

"Do you have a name for this little princess?"

A gentle smile lifted Jenna's mouth. "Sophie. Sophie Joy because she is the greatest joy I've ever known."

"Oh, hon, that's beautiful."

Sophie stretched, her tiny face screwing up in an adorable expression. Jenna's whole body seized up with an overwhelming love, a love so powerful tears filled her eyes. This was why she'd run away. This precious bit of humanity deserved to love and be loved for the right reasons. She deserved to grow up free from fear and the hovering, controlling influences that had stymied Jenna's life since birth.

Her family, particularly Elaine Von Gustin Carrington, would not control this baby's life the way they'd controlled hers.

People who envied her opulent lifestyle had no idea what it was like to live in an ivory tower surrounded by hired body-guards and nannies and private tutors. They had no idea the sadness of a child never allowed to play outside or with other children who were "not like us." They'd never sat with their faces pressed against the window watching others play in the snow while wondering what it would be like to build a snowman with someone other than a hired nanny and a burly bodyguard.

The world considered her a spoiled rich princess, but they were wrong. Elaine Carrington's elitism and her kidnapping paranoia had made her only daughter a lonely child, a prisoner of her family's enormous wealth.

Which was exactly the reason Jenna wanted Sophie Joy to grow up in a normal home, in a normal town, doing normal things. She'd play with other children and go to a real school and maybe even join a soccer team if she wanted to. When she was a teenager, she'd hang out at the mall and have sleep-overs and attend school dances with friends of her own choosing.

Sophie would have a childhood her mother had only dreamed of, a wish that sounded foolish to most people—even her late husband, though he'd pretended something far differ-ent in the beginning. Early in their secret relationship, Derek had nurtured Jenna's longing to be a regular wife living in the suburbs. But the Carrington money had followed her in marriage, corrupting the boy who'd claimed to love her, and the few weeks of normalcy had disappeared as quickly as his love.

In the end, her mother had been right about her fortune-hunting husband, and Jenna had gone home to the estate, broken. From Derek, she had learned a cruel fact of life—

never trust a man, no matter how pretty his promises. Men were only interested in someone like Jenna for one thing. As Mother had so succinctly put it, "A trust fund makes any woman attractive."

She swallowed back the festering hurt. She might not be beautiful, but she refused to care anymore. All that mattered now was assuring Sophie the happy, uncomplicated life and freedom she had never known.

To do that, she could never go back to the Carrington Estate or even to Pennsylvania.

As she marveled at her baby's velvet skin, at eyelashes so pale and perfect, the pink rosebud mouth, Jenna made a silent promise. No matter what she had to do from here, her daughter would lead a normal life.

The nurse, whom she'd almost forgotten, patted her arm. In a pleasant drawl she said, "I'll be back in a few, Jenna. We'll get your vitals again and then you'll be good to go."

Jenna's head snapped up. "Go?"

Go where? She'd hoped to stay in the hospital a few days, to get her thoughts together and form a plan. To read the newspaper and make sure the world hadn't been alerted to her disappearance. To figure out where to go and what to do with a newborn.

"Sure thing. Unless there are problems, an OB stays twenty-four hours or less these days. Would you like for me to phone your family?" The young woman reached for the chart at the end of the bed, flipped open a few pages. A frown appeared between her black eyebrows. "Seems we didn't get that information when you arrived yesterday evening. Well, it was a hectic time. No problem. Someone from the business office will be in. They always extract their pound of flesh."

Jenna managed a weak smile at the woman's joke. She hadn't thought about the hospital bill or even about the records a hospital would keep on her and Sophie.

She'd given them her name yesterday and no one had

reacted. But she wasn't surprised no one recognized her face. Due to her family's paranoia, their only child had been publicly photographed very little. Jenna found a certain irony in that. The fear that had made her life a prison might be the very thing that assured her freedom. Unless her parents had released her disappearance to the press, there was a chance no one here in this small Texas town would ever guess that she was one of *the* Carringtons, reluctant heiress to a staggering financial empire.

"Would you like for me to call Dax?"

Jenna blinked. "Who?"

"The rancher who brought you in. Dax Coleman. I thought you knew him."

A warm blush crept up the back of Jenna's neck. She hadn't remembered her rescuer's name. "No."

"Oh, well, I just assumed…" The nurse flapped a hand. "Never mind. My mouth is running away, though it's too bad about Dax. He seemed real concerned, and for a reclusive guy like that, well, we just figured the two of you knew each other."

Was the nurse asking if she and Dax knew each other in the Biblical sense? Did she think Dax Coleman was Sophie's father?

Her flush of embarrassment deepened.

"Mr. Coleman," she said in her most dignified voice, "was kind enough to render aid to a damsel in distress. But no, I had never before made his acquaintance."

The nurse, who was darkly pretty and not much older than herself, looked disappointed. "Well, then, that's really too bad. Dax could use a spark in his life after what happened."

Jenna refused to ask the obvious question. "You know him?"

"Sure. In a region this sparsely populated everyone knows everyone else. Dax is an old friend of mine. Or used to be." The nurse fanned her face with her fingertips. "He's still pretty delicious-looking, too, if you know what I mean. Don't tell my husband I said that." She laughed.

Delicious-looking? Jenna remembered a gravelly, rough voice and strong, calloused hands, though he'd been as gentle as could be with her and Sophie. As far as his looks, she could only recall intense green eyes and dark hair that fell in sweaty waves onto his forehead. A cowboy. She remembered that, too.

En route to the hospital, he hadn't said much. But he'd glared at her and Sophie in the rearview mirror every few minutes until Jenna became convinced she'd somehow angered him. At the time, she'd been too tired and shaky to wonder about her roadside rescuer. Now she did.

"You were lucky he came along," Nurse Wolf said. "Out here you can drive forever and not see a soul."

She almost had.

"Yes, I owe him a debt of gratitude," Jenna muttered, absently rubbing the side of her finger over Sophie's delicate cheek. She'd never been indebted to anyone before, ever. People were indebted to the Carringtons, not the other way around, but the cowboy, a total stranger, had been there for her and her baby when they'd had no one else. She wasn't likely to forget that.

"I'll be back in a few," the nurse said and started out the door.

"Nurse?"

The woman did an about-face. "It's Crystal. Please."

"Crystal," Jenna said, oddly pleased at the simple request. "Would you mind bringing me a newspaper or two?"

"Nothing newsworthy ever happens around here except church dinners and baby showers and school sports, but I'll bring you a paper."

The simple activities sounded like heaven to Jenna who'd never experienced a single one of them. "Thank you."

With a hand wave, Crystal sashayed out of the room, only to lean back into the room with a twinkle in her eye.

"Prepare yourself. A certain delicious cowboy is headed your way."

Jenna was sure her mouth fell open. "You're kidding."

But Crystal had already disappeared, leaving the door open.

Dax kicked himself all the way down the hall. He had no idea what he was doing here. He'd done the right thing already. He'd played the good Samaritan. He should be on the south side of the ranch right now fixing a water gap before snow or rain made the work miserable. But here he was at Saddleback Hospital in the maternity ward, feeling as uncomfortable as if he'd stumbled into one of those ladies' lingerie stores.

But he was here. Might as well get this over with.

Stetson in hand, he used the opposite hand to tap on the open door, doing his level best not to look inside until he was invited.

"Come in," a feminine voice said. He remembered that voice. Soft and educated and worried. He'd dreamed about it last night. Imagine that. Dreaming about a woman's voice. And her bare feet. And the way she'd gazed at him with trust.

Blast it. That's why he was here. She'd haunted his dreams and he'd not been able to get a thing done this morning until he was certain she and her baby were in good shape.

According to the desk nurse the baby he'd delivered was doing well. Thank God. That should have been enough. He should have turned tail and headed for his truck.

But no. He had to see for himself that the brave young woman with the fancy voice was okay.

With a final inward kick, he stepped into the room.

His eyes went straight to the bed. Fluffed up in white sheets, the little mama looked small and flushed. But good. Real good.

Her dark blond hair, sweaty and uncombed yesterday, was

clean and neatly brushed and lay across her shoulders in a soft wave. She was prettier than he'd thought. Her thin face was blessed with long doe-shaped eyes the color of pancake syrup and a mouth that tipped up at the corners.

The thing that really drew his attention was the bundle nestled against her breast. A small egg-shaped head covered with a pink stocking cap protruded from a matching pink blanket. He could see the curve of the baby's cheek, the tiny button nose, the rise and fall of her body as she breathed. Thank God she was breathing smooth and even now.

He allowed himself to breathe, as well, aware that he hadn't quite believed the child would be alive.

The little mama saw the direction of his gaze and looked down at her baby with an expression that punched Dax in the gut. Mother love radiated from her. The kind Gavin had never known.

His admiration for the girl-woman, whatever she was, went up another notch. She loved her baby. She'd be a good mama.

He shifted, heard the scratchy sound of his boots against tile. What now? He'd seen what he came for. Could he just turn around and walk out?

"Would you like to see her?"

The words startled him, breaking through his thoughts of escape. Crushing the brim of his hat between tense fingers, he stepped closer to the bed and cleared the lump out of his throat. "She okay?"

"Perfect, thanks to you." The doe eyes looked up at him, again with that expression of trust.

"What about you?"

Roses bloomed on her cheeks. "Very well. Again thanks to you."

He'd embarrassed her, made her recall the liberties he'd taken with her body. He wanted to apologize, but he never seemed to know the right things to say to women.

"Would you like to hold her?" The little mama stretched the bundle in his direction. The blanket fell away from the baby's face and Dax went all mushy inside. He remembered how Gavin had looked those first few days. All squished and out of shape but so innocent Dax had fallen in instant, over-powering love.

Dax stepped away from the bed. "No."

He'd been to the feed store earlier. He couldn't be clean enough to hold a baby.

"Oh." The little mama's face fell. He felt like a jerk, but didn't figure it mattered. Once he was out of here, he'd never see her again.

"Sophie and I are grateful for everything you did."

"Sophie? Pretty."

"I thought so. Sophie Joy."

Feeling oversize, out of place and like a complete idiot, Dax nodded. "I gotta get back to the ranch. Just wanted to check on you."

"I appreciate it." She reached out a slender hand and touched his arm. Even through the long-sleeved jacket, Dax imagined the heat and pressure of her fingers seeping into his bloodstream. His mind went to the softness of the skin on her bare feet. She was probably silky all over.

Something inside him reacted like a wild stallion. He jerked away. What the devil business did he have feeling at-tracted to a new mother, a woman young enough to be his…well, his niece or something. She was a kid. A kid. And he was a dirty old man.

Without another word, he spun away and hurried out the door, down the hall and out into the gray November where the Texas wind could slap some sense into him.

CHAPTER THREE

STUNNED, JENNA STARED as the cowboy retreated, turning his trim, anvil-shaped back toward her before charging out of the room as if a pack of dogs was after him.

"I don't think he likes us, Sophie," she murmured. Though she couldn't imagine why. He'd behaved the same way in the car yesterday, as though she'd angered him. Yet he'd helped her. And he'd come to visit her in the hospital.

"What a strange man."

He'd left so fast, the scent of a very masculine cologne lingered in the room like a contrail. Were all Texas cowboys so…reticent? Well, it didn't matter. She would likely never see the man again, and the truth was, Dax Coleman had saved her, saved Sophie, and she would be forever grateful.

Before she had time to ponder further, a woman entered the room. Dressed in a black pantsuit and white, round ear-bobs of the 1960s, the woman carried a clipboard and a stack of papers.

"I'm Alice Pernisky from the business office." She rolled an over-the-bed table in front of Jenna. "Let's put the baby in the bassinet while we take care of the paperwork."

Her no-nonsense style brooked no argument, so Jenna did as she said. She was worried enough about completing these forms.

"Let's take care of the birth certificate first." The woman

pushed a paper under her nose. "The doctor has filled in the basics, but we'll need your complete information, your name, the father's name, and of course—" she allowed a thin smile "—the name you've chosen for your baby."

Heart thudding crazily, Jenna stared down at the form and wondered if falsifying a birth certificate was illegal. Ink pen hovering over the sheet, she considered long and hard.

After a few seconds, Alice Pernisky said, "My dear, if you don't want to put the father's name, that's fine. Just take care of the rest. We see more of that kind of thing than we used to."

Heat flushed from her toes to her head. They thought she was an unwed mother who had no idea who Sophie's father was.

"My husband died," she said, which was true, though Derek had been out of her life long before the car crash that killed him.

"I'm sorry," Alice said automatically, although Jenna did not think the woman believed her.

Would people always assume the worst if she didn't put Derek's name on the birth certificate?

Of course they would. This document would follow Sophie all the days of her life. And Jenna would not do that to her daughter.

Taking a deep breath, Jenna bent to the form and began to write. After the divorce, her parents had insisted she return to Carrington and she'd gladly done so. Derek had humiliated her enough. But now, his name might be the one thing that could keep her and Sophie from being discovered.

If she was going to start her life anew with Sophie, she would do it correctly. She would lie only if she had to, and pray her family wouldn't be able to trace her through hospital documents bearing only her married name.

As she handed over the form, another form appeared beneath. "Those are your release forms, your instructions on self-care, and of course your hospital bill. Do you have insurance we can file?"

Jenna gulped. Lie number one. "No."

"How do you plan to take of this? We take check or credit card, of course, and if need be, we can set up a payment plan."

"Cash. I'll pay cash."

The woman pulled back, startled. "Cash?"

"Yes." Accessing her bank accounts or using her credit cards would be too easy to trace. Until she and Sophie were established and on their own, she would not even consider such a thing. Maybe never. Cash was the only way.

Jenna reached for her handbag, aware of how out-of-place the designer crocodile looked in the hands of a woman without health insurance. As she withdrew the funds from her wallet, she had the absurd thought that Alice might think she'd stolen the bag, along with the money. What if she called the police?

Jenna's hand trembled as she counted out the correct amount and handed it over. She could feel the woman's curious stare and almost hear the wheels turning in her head.

When the last paper was signed and the woman left the room, Jenna felt light-headed with relief. Before putting her purse aside so she could hold Sophie again, she counted the remaining bills in her wallet. A quiver of worry drew her brows together. Never in her life had she needed to consider money. A Carrington simply grew up knowing there was plenty. Discussing personal finance was considered vulgar.

But she was no longer a Carrington. She was no longer one of Pennsylvania's old money debutantes with an endless supply of cash and credit cards. She was a single mother alone, scared…and nearly broke.

A tangle of nerves and hormones and uncertainty gathered inside Jenna a short time later as she leafed through two newspapers, including a national one, and waited to be dismissed from the hospital.

After careful scrutiny of each page, she sat back against the scratchy chair and let some of her tension ebb away. There was no mention of a missing heiress. At least, not yet.

She flipped to the classifieds of the local paper, the *Saddleback Sentinel,* and scanned the help wanted ads. After a couple of minutes, her lips curved in wry humor. If she could run a drilling rig or drive an eighteen-wheel truck, she'd be in business before nightfall.

"Looking for anything in particular?"

At Crystal's voice, Jenna jumped. The nurse stood in front of her with a wheelchair, smile curious.

The newspaper crinkled as Jenna refolded it and placed it on the nightstand. Part of her longed to confide in the friendly nurse and admit she needed a job. She opened her mouth to do just that but Sophie chose that moment to awake with a startled cry. All thought rushed to her baby.

"Is she all right?"

Crystal chuckled. "Yes, Jenna. She's fine. Baby's cry. Get used to it. Real used to it. I probably startled her with the noise of the wheelchair."

"Oh." Jenna fought down a blush and gingerly scooped her daughter from the Isolette. "Shh, darling, Mommy's here."

To her joy, Sophie stopped crying immediately. Her scrunched-up face relaxed as she blinked up at her mother. A swell of love ballooned in Jenna's chest.

"You two ladies ready for your free ride in a wheelchair?"

"Can't we walk?"

"Hospital regs, I'm afraid." Crystal patted the black seat. "Hop aboard the Wolf Express for the only free thing in this hospital."

With a smile at Crystal's humor, Jenna complied, jittery to think that in a few minutes, she and Sophie would be alone and on their own. She'd known when she left the estate that this would happen, but she hadn't expected it to happen quite so soon. She'd hoped to be settled somewhere before Sophie's birth, to have the trunk full of layette items set up and ready for the baby's homecoming. She'd even had fantasies of a job where she could keep Sophie with her. Instead, she was down to her last few dollars with nowhere to take her newborn daughter.

Crystal guided the wheelchair down the long, pristine hospital corridor and out the exit toward the parking lot.

"So what did Dax have on his mind?"

The question startled Jenna. She'd tried to put the rugged cowboy out of her thoughts. "I'm not sure."

"What did he say?"

"He asked if Sophie and I were all right and then he left." Crystal chuckled. "He's not a big talker."

"I noticed."

"Hunky, though, huh?"

"I suppose." She really didn't want to talk about the cowboy. "I think I scared him off."

"Nah. He's just quiet. I don't think anything scares Dax Coleman except his ex-wife."

"He's divorced?"

"Yep. For years, but as far as I know, he's never dated again. Reba did a number on him, the witch."

Jenna, in spite of herself, tilted her head in question. "Was she?"

Crystal hitched one shoulder. "I never liked her much, though some folks think the divorce was Dax's fault."

He wasn't exactly Mr. Congeniality, but after the way he'd helped her, she felt compelled to take his side. "Outsiders seldom know the full story."

She knew that from personal experience.

"Too true. And Dax has always been one of the good guys. Or he used to be."

Jenna let the subject of the cowboy drop. Something about him unsettled her in the oddest manner.

Wheels clattered over the concrete parking lot as Crystal

pushed her and Sophie into the weak sunshine. The fresh air felt good on Jenna's skin after the stuffiness of the hospital.

Holding her pink-wrapped daughter snuggled close to her body, a few free baby supplies compliments of the hospital stuffed between her side and the arm of the chair, she couldn't help thinking how different this dismissal would have been in Philadelphia. Surrounded by masses of flowers, a private nurse, and at least two burly bodyguards—one for her and one for Sophie—she would have been gently hustled into a waiting car driven by Fredrick, the family chauffeur, and driven home to the nursery suite especially commissioned and furnished by her mother. There, in the stark white nursery, a nanny would have whisked Sophie from her arms and taken over every nuance of the baby's care. If Jenna was lucky and made enough fuss, she might get to hold her child occasionally.

No, she'd made the right decision, even if she had no idea where she would go or what she would do now.

The wheelchair slowed. "Which way is your car?"

"Out to the left, I think. It's a faded blue." She scanned the parking lot, hoping she'd recognize the still-unfamiliar vehicle. Was it only four days ago when, in an effort to conceal her true destination, she'd taken the train as far as Baltimore and purchased the car from a classified ad?

"There." She pointed, gripping Sophie tighter as Crystal picked up speed.

When they reached the car, the nurse held the baby while Jenna dug out her keys and unlocked the door.

"Someone washed my car," she said in wonder, gazing into the backseat. Someone had even cleaned the interior, which now smelled of vinyl cleaner instead of dust and designer perfume.

"Interesting," Crystal commented. "Must have been Dax."

"Why would he do that?"

The nurse shrugged. "Don't know, but it sure is interesting. Visiting you at the hospital and washing your car. Maybe he has a thing for new mothers."

Shocked, Jenna's snapped around to stare at the nurse. Crystal burst into laughter. "Girl, you should see your face. I was only teasing."

"Oh." But Jenna got that fluttery feeling in her stomach again. What was it about the mention of Dax Coleman that stirred her so?

"Where's your car safety seat?"

"My what?"

"Texas has a child safety seat law. You can't leave the hospital with Sophie until you have one installed."

One more thing she hadn't thought of. "Where can I get one?"

Crystal studied her from beneath black eyelashes. "The hospital sells them. If you'd like I'll run back inside and get one for you."

"Do you mind?"

"Not a bit." She named a price and Jenna extracted the required bills from her wallet.

"Cute purse," Crystal said. "Is that real alligator?"

"Crocodile. It was a gift," she hurried to say, downplaying her ability to purchase such a bag. What she really wanted to say was, "Want to buy it?" The cost of the handbag would go a long way toward apartment rent.

"Wish somebody would buy me gifts like that."

"No, you don't," she nearly said to the nurse's retreating back. You don't want someone to try to control you with money and things and fear.

While Crystal was gone, Jenna thought of her dwindling resources, spirits ebbing lower and lower. Even during her short marriage, they'd always had her considerable bank account, a fact that had changed her average Joe husband to Joe Millionaire in a matter of weeks.

She tasted the bitterness of his betrayal on her tongue.

Before her name was dry on the marriage license, Derek, who had sworn he was not at all interested in Jenna's inheritance, had begun flashing her credit cards, living the high life and leaving her at home when she refused to play along.

"Here we go, Jenna." Crystal reappeared to pop open the back door and installed the car seat in short order. She held out her arms. "Give me the princess."

Jenna complied, happiness replacing the gloom. She wasn't alone anymore.

As the nurse settled the baby and strapped her in, Jenna watched, learning. She wasn't stupid. She was just inexperienced.

"All set." Crystal slammed the back door. Sophie's little arms jerked upward but before Jenna could rush to soothe her, she'd resettled.

"Thank you for everything, Crystal." Jenna slid behind the wheel, uncertainty overtaking her again. What now?

"You are as welcome as summer." Crystal, holding the driver's door open, leaned in, her dark eyes soft with concern. "Honey, are you going to be all by yourself with this new baby? Do you have anyone to help you?"

"Oh, certainly, I'll have plenty of—" Jenna lifted a hand to wave off the suggestion that she had no one and then let the hand fall against the warm steering column.

"No," she admitted, suddenly needing to talk to this young woman who was kindness personified. "My husband died. I'm alone, looking for a place to start fresh. I thought Sophie and I would be happier somewhere new, away from the memories." She gave a pathetic little laugh. "So here we are."

That much was absolutely true.

Crystal draped an arm over the top of the car door, all her weight on one hip. "So that explains it. I knew something was not right, but bless your heart, all alone. That's awful."

The woman's compassion was almost Jenna's undoing. She fought back a wave of self-pity, and then, angry at herself, she refused to acknowledge the emotion. She'd chosen this route even if things hadn't gone quite as smoothly as she'd planned. Starting fresh was the best thing for Sophie, no matter how difficult the first few weeks might be. She could do this. She wanted to do this. For her baby girl and even for herself. Alone was better than lonely and utterly dependent, with your life mapped out before you were out of diapers. Now that she had Sophie, she would never be lonely again.

Stiffening her spine, she said, "Can you direct me to a hotel?"

After a moment's consideration, Crystal took a scrap of paper from her uniform pocket and scribbled on it. "There's a little B and B over on Second Street, not fancy but decent and clean. Terri Wallace runs it. We graduated high school together. Nice gal. Tell her I sent you. I put my phone number on there, too. Call me if I can do anything. Or just to talk. I can always use a new friend."

A friend. Crystal couldn't begin to comprehend how much the offer heartened Jenna.

"Could I ask one more favor?"

"Name it."

"I need a job." She swallowed her pride and said the rest. "In a hurry. Do you have any suggestions?"

The darkly pretty face twisted in thought. "Can't think of anything right off."

Jenna's hopes fell. She pressed her lips together in dismay. Maybe Saddleback wasn't the right town. Maybe she should drive on to Austin or even on to Los Angeles, where she and Sophie could get lost in the masses. But she was too tired and shaky from childbirth to drive that far today.

"Listen," Crystal was saying. "The county employment office is located here in Saddleback. It might be worth a try." She rattled off an address. "In a few days, when you're feeling rested, just drive down Main Street. When you see the boot store—you can't miss it, there's an enormous sign out front shaped like a big red cowboy boot—the employment office is right across the street. Shirley McDougal runs the place. Sweet as pie. She knows everyone and everything in Saddleback. Go talk to her. Tell her I sent you."

"I don't know how I'll ever repay your generosity."

Crystal patted her shoulder. "Just take care of Princess Sophie and give me a call when you get settled. We'll have lunch or something."

Still stunned by the kindness of strangers in this Texas town, Jenna could only nod, fighting back the tears that suddenly clogged her throat.

Crystal stepped back from the car, lifting a hand to wave as Jenna slammed the door, cranked the engine and pulled out of the Saddleback Hospital parking lot.

CHAPTER FOUR

TEN DAYS LATER, Jenna knew she'd recuperated as long as her limited finances would allow. Twice during that time, Crystal Wolf had stopped by the B and B, spreading her brand of Texas hospitality, but Jenna had been afraid to tell her new friend just how desperate things were becoming.

After a sleepless night of baby care and worry, Jenna now stared at a pile of unfamiliar forms at the county employment agency while the woman named Shirley cooed and hummed to Sophie. From the moment she'd started the paperwork, Jenna had been stumped. About the only thing she could fill out easily was her name. She'd finally scribbled the address of the Red Rose Bed-and-Breakfast as her residence, but she had nothing to put in the experience and reference forms.

"What kind of work are you looking for, Jenna, sugar?" Shirley asked, never looking up from Sophie's sleeping face.

"I'm not at all particular, but I would like to secure a position where I could keep my baby with me."

"Hmm. Well, that leaves out the fast-food places. I send a lot of folks to them. The junior high is always looking for substitutes, though you'd have to leave this precious one with a sitter." She glanced up, brows drawing together over her black plastic glasses. "Don't suppose you have a degree in education or computers?"

Jenna shook her head, hopes tumbling. "No."

She'd spent one semester at Brown University under the watchful eyes of her grandparents. Unfortunately, neither theynor her ever-present bodyguards were as watchful as her mother would have liked. She'd met Derek there. Heads had rolled but Mother's fury had come too late.

"How about the medical field? There's always a need for that. Nurses, paramedics, lab techs…"

Again Jenna shook her head. An overprotected heiress was a useless human being.

Shirley studied her beneath thick blond bangs. "Do you have any training? Any experience at all?"

Jenna's hopes fell even further as she bowed her head to the application and didn't answer. She could plan a dinner party for fifty, direct servants and organize a charity auction; none of those skills appeared all that useful in Saddleback, Texas.

Even if no one recognized her here, she might have to move on. Yet, Saddleback's friendliness and easy pace drew her. She wanted to remain in this remote place where her daughter had been born and where people treated her as just another person.

Shirley pushed her glasses up with one finger. "You don't seem the type, but would you mind doing domestic work? We get a few calls for that."

Domestics? As in a maid? Or a cook?

An idea popped into her head. She and Mother had taken a gourmet cooking class from a well-known chef. She'd loved it.

"Could I possibly keep Sophie with me?"

"That would be up to your employer, but I think most people would be all right with a little one around as long as you did the work."

"Then," Jenna said, suddenly thrilled at the idea, "I am a fabulous chef and quite amenable to domestics."

Surely, cleaning a house couldn't be that difficult. She'd watched the maids dozens of times.

Shirley grinned. "My dear girl, I think I may have something for you. A family outside of town needs a cook and general housekeeper. Want to check it out?"

A renewed zip of energy had Jenna sitting up straighter. "Absolutely."

The woman returned a still-sleeping Sophie to Jenna's arms and then riffled through a set of files, pulling out a card.

"Here you go," she said, handing the information to Jenna. "I'll call and let him know you're coming for an interview."

Jenna was beyond delighted, though admittedly a bit nervous as she gripped the index card in her fingers. This was her opportunity to start life all over again, to make a life for herself and Sophie, to finally be her own person.

With held breath, she glanced at the name and address of her prospective employer.

The information she read froze the smile on her lips.

Southpaw Cattle Company. Dax Coleman.

Dax slammed the telephone receiver down, then looked around the living room to be sure no one was listening before letting out a curse.

Last night, he'd dreamed of the little mama and her baby. Again. Then he'd lain awake, staring up at the dark ceiling as he listened to a north wind rattle the trees outside and wondered if the fragile pair was all right.

They haunted him. He couldn't get them out of his head, a fact that infuriated him.

Now a phone call to the hospital told him exactly nothing. What had he expected? The day he'd visited her, he hadn't even thought to ask her name. He'd just asked for the mother and baby he'd brought into the emergency room. How stupid was that? All the receptionist would tell him was that mother and baby had been discharged, but unless Dax was next of kin, and she knew danged well he wasn't, no other information could be shared.

A distant relative of Reba's, the hateful old biddy had never liked him anyway. She'd enjoyed putting him in his place.

"Fine," he said to absolutely no one. The little mama and her baby were gone. They were all right. He could forget them. They were not his responsibility. He had enough of that to choke a horse already. End of topic.

No use fretting over a baby girl he'd never see again when he had his own problems to contend with. Shirley down at the employment office was sending him a new recruit this morning.

He laughed, a mocking sound. Good old Shirley had warned him she was sick and tired of finding him housekeepers only to have him run them off with his cranky-butted attitude. Her words. Cranky-butted. He could almost see her shaking her finger in his face.

He'd laughed when she'd said it. Now he wondered. Was he cranky-butted? Was he a bitter man with a bad attitude? Was that why Reba had walked out, leaving behind a new baby, a husband who'd adored her and an easy life?

He kicked a chair leg. Reba and her betrayal was not allowed in this house.

Dax snatched up the two empty glasses and a corn dog wrapper from the coffee table, toting them to the big, silver, step-levered trash can in the kitchen. Silly to feel nervous about interviewing a prospective housekeeper, but he needed to get this woman on board right away. Rushing home to meet Gavin's school bus each evening took a bite out of his productivity.

He trailed back through the living room, wiping a shirtsleeve over the fireplace mantel then grimaced to discover his shirt was now covered in dust. He batted at it and sneezed when the dust flew upward, dancing in the overhead light.

The doorbell chimed.

As he strode across the carpet toward the foyer, he noticed

two of Gavin's miniature cars and a sock sticking out from under the couch—along with a dust bunny the size of a jack rabbit.

He gave up. He was a rancher. This was why he hired housekeepers.

With a final slap at his dusty shirtsleeve Dax yanked the front door open. His mouth also fell open as he looked down into a familiar face. A very young, slender and decidedly pretty face.

Blast it.

What the devil was the little mama doing on his porch? Please, please. Surely not to apply for the housekeeper position.

Hot on the heels of his plea was a thrill that rocked him to his boot tips. Double blast and a dozen other curses. A burned-out old cowboy like him getting palpitations over a teenager.

"Mr. Coleman?"

Given his wayward thought processes and after what they'd shared in her car, hearing her refer to him as Mr. Coleman was creepy. He should call the sheriff on himself.

"Dax," he growled, wondering why he was in such a weird mood. His gaze went to the pink bundle in her arms and stayed there. "How's the little one?"

"Wonderful. Perfect."

"Good."

They seemed destined to repeat the same sentences to each other. Blast it.

Finding his manners, though admittedly a bit rusty, he stepped aside and motioned toward the interior. "Want to come in?"

She came inside, moving past him with a grace and elegance that had him thinking of ballerinas and her pretty feet again. He caught a whiff of that flowery perfume he'd smelled in her car. As if his eyelids ruled his body, they dropped closed and he inhaled. Nice. Really nice.

"Dax?"

His eyelids flew open. Why had he invited her inside?

"Have a seat," he said, feeling about as awkward as a three-legged horse.

He peered out the door, craning his neck to look down the long, long driveway. Nothing but her blue car. Where was the real housekeeper? Please let her pull up soon.

"Are you expecting someone?" the little mama asked, still standing in the middle of his foyer and close enough for him to see the flecks of gold in her eyes.

He backed up a step.

"A housekeeper applicant from the employment office is on her way out."

The little mama turned bright pink. "Oh," she said. "That would be me."

She handed him a card bearing the logo of the county employment office and her name, Jenna Garwood. Dax's heart stopped. Jenna Garwood was the name Shirley had given him. Oh no.

"You?"

Her pink drained away. "Is there a problem? I can cook. I'm an accomplished chef."

Dax was already shaking his head. "I don't think so."

The last thing he wanted was this new mama who haunted his dreams to live here. She was probably a teenage runaway. He'd get arrested just for thinking about the way her eyebrows took wing at the ends and for noticing how full and pouty her lips were. She was trouble with a baby in arms.

"I need a mature woman to look after my boy."

"I can do that."

"This ranch is far from town. It gets lonely out here."

"I'm accustomed to solitude."

Getting desperate now, Dax pointed to the infant. "You have a new baby."

"I promise to keep up with my domestic duties and care for her, as well. Mothers have maintained homes for millennia while rearing children." Her doe-eyes had widened, almost pleading. "I can do it."

Before he did something really stupid, Dax grumbled, "No."

The little mama—Jenna Garwood—drew up to her full height, which wasn't much, come to think of it. "May I inquire as to why?"

Inquire as to why? What kind of question was that? Finally, he blurted, "How old are you?"

The corners of her too-full lips tilted up. "I'm twenty-two. Why? Age has nothing to do with anything."

Oh, yes it did. He was thirty-four years old and she wasn't.

"A young girl like you—" he started.

"I'm not a girl. I'm a woman—with a baby to support."

Like he didn't know that.

"I know this isn't ideal. Not for me, either, but I really need this job, Mr. Coleman."

"Dax," he growled. And what did she mean, this wasn't ideal for her, either? What was wrong with his ranch? "I have a son. He's in kindergarten."

"I have a daughter. You delivered her."

Jenna Garwood did not play fair. Had she intuitively known he felt some kind of warped sense of responsibility for her and the baby?

The baby in her arms squeaked, squirming. Dax felt a momentary reprieve from this miserable conversation. "She's awake."

That motherly Madonna sweetness moved across Jenna Garwood's face. "Will you hold her for a minute while I get the diaper bag from the car? She's probably wet."

Dax swallowed hard and made no move to take the offered baby.

"She won't bite." That precise, clipped voice chided him for being a coward.

Him? A coward? "Get the bag."

As if he was hypnotized, he reached out, awkward at first as he took the tiny bundle in his arms.

Jenna wasted no time heading for her car.

The front door snapped shut. The baby startled in that special way only newborns do. With fingers too big and thick to be handling an infant again, Dax peeled back the blanket and looked down into a face as pink and new as a rosebud.

His heart did a funny jitterbug in his chest. He remembered when Gavin was this small and helpless. He remembered how scared and alone he'd felt knowing he was the only parent with sole responsibility for another human being.

Did Jenna Garwood feel that way, too? There was dignity in her voice but a look of desperation in her eyes that he understood too well.

The baby mewed and made that squeaky, about-to-cry sound. Tiny, gossamer eyelids lifted. A pair of dark blue eyes snagged him as if he were a marlin and she were a giant hook.

With an inner groan, he knew he was in trouble. Big trouble.

He'd been in Jenna Garwood's shoes. He'd been alone with a newborn—alone and desperate.

And, though he was sure he'd live to regret his rash, emotional decision, he was going to hire her.

CHAPTER FIVE

JENNA MOVED IN that afternoon.

She had plenty of reservations about living on the remote ranch with a man she barely knew, but she and Sophie were out of choices. She was troubled that Dax Coleman hadn't wanted to hire her at first and then had suddenly changed his mind. Troubled and curious.

For those few minutes when she'd gone to the car for Sophie's diapers, she'd been certain he would send her away. She'd returned to the house prepared to beg and lie and make up references, only to discover that his attitude had completely reversed.

The perplexing rancher had been sitting in a leather rocking chair with Sophie cradled against his chest. For one moment, Jenna had remained in the foyer watching and aching with the knowledge that Sophie would not have a father to cradle her. She'd listened as Dax murmured softly to the baby in a way that turned Jenna's insides to warm honey. When she'd made her presence known, he'd gone silent.

But she'd heard. And that moment had told her a great deal about Dax Coleman.

By the time she had driven to the B and B for her belongings, then returned to the ranch, Dax was nowhere to be seen. A slim, nice-looking cowboy who appeared amused with the world greeted her at the front door.

"Well, ain't you a pretty little thing?" His grin widened as his gaze slid over her. "Old Dax must be going blind."

Jenna blinked, startled and uncomfortable. What exactly did he mean? That Dax thought she was ugly? Not that it mattered one iota what Dax thought about her appearance. She had no illusions about her looks, but still, a woman didn't like thinking her appearance was the topic of dinner conversation.

A dry leaf swirled from beneath a fat oak tree in the yard and glided around her head. The weather today was colder and she was eager to get Sophie inside.

"I'm Jenna Garwood, the new housekeeper."

The admission sounded strange on her lips. She was someone's housekeeper.

The ranch hand crossed a pair of muscled arms over his chest. "You sure are. I'm Rowdy Davis, Dax's ranch manager. He said you'd be coming back soon."

No wonder the man was behaving in such an insolent manner. His boss—and hers—wasn't here. For very realistic reasons, she trusted the rancher who'd rescued her and had expected him to be here. Rowdy Davis, on the other hand, made her nervous.

Clutching Sophie closer, she glanced around, suddenly feeling alone and vulnerable. All she saw was barns and fences and acres and acres of serenely grazing cattle. In the distance several cowboys rode horses across a field. They were so far away no sound carried on the wind except the occasional bawl of a calf.

Jenna licked dry lips. It wasn't every day a Carrington hired on as a domestic and encountered a leering cowboy. The man must be either out of his head with loneliness or the kind of guy who thought every female was fair game. Jenna suspected the latter. But she was a new mother with a baby in arms that grew heavier with every second. The opposite sex was the last thing on her mind.

"Where is Mr. Coleman?"

The cowboy got that look again as if he was holding back a laugh. "Gavin got a bloody nose on the playground so Dax went to pick him up."

"Gavin?"

"Dax's son."

Gavin. Of course. He'd mentioned a son.

"Come on in. I'm supposed to help you with your things."

The man pushed the door open and stepped to one side. Finally, he was demonstrating some knowledge of etiquette. Miss Manners would have been aghast at his previous behavior.

Holding Sophie's diaper bag against her side with one elbow, she started into the warm foyer. The cowboy's body crowded the narrow space. Jenna slanted slightly to one side, hoping he'd get the message that with her load, and attired in a heavy woolen coat, she needed more room. He didn't budge. He didn't even offer to help. Her backside accidentally brushed against him. She jerked away, face hot, and moved across the stone-tiled entry to the carpeted area beyond.

When she glanced back, Rowdy remained in the doorway, grinning. Her flush deepened.

"I have a number of things in the car if you wouldn't mind getting them please," she said stiffly, hearing the haughty tone her mother reserved for servants. Hopefully, the man would get the message that she did not want to play his game—whatever it was.

Rowdy's dark eyes glittered and continued staring at her several beats longer before he said, "I'll get them in a minute. Let's get you and baby situated first."

Jenna felt flustered. She wasn't sure what to make of Rowdy Davis. He had done nothing wrong, but he looked at her in a way that was disconcerting, as though he knew her secrets, as though he knew something she didn't.

He was young and good-looking and a tad bit cocky. Maybe that was her problem. His confidence was the antithesis of hers.

The sooner he went on his way, the sooner she could relax.

"Would you mind showing me to my quarters?" she asked. "Then I won't trouble you any longer."

The corner of Rowdy's mouth hiked higher. "Sure thing, ma'am. Your *quarters* are this way." He emphasized the word. "And you aren't troubling me one little bit."

"Thank you," she said, mustering her dignity. "I should like to see them."

Still wearing a strange smirk, Rowdy led the way down a hallway to the left of the massive living/dining area. He ambled in front of her with a slow swagger as if wanting her to notice his lean, fit body and tight blue jeans. Purposefully, she focused her attention elsewhere.

The ranch home was lovely in a Western manner. Spacious and well-appointed in colors and textures that glowed with warmth and reflected light from a pair of large patio doors in the dining area. The ranch was so different from the old mansion she'd escaped, and its modern warmth drew her like a magnet. She could really enjoy tending to such a lovely place.

"Dax wants you to have this section of rooms," Rowdy was saying as he pushed open a door down a hall and to the back of the kitchen area. "This larger bedroom has an adjoining bath and opens into a smaller room intended as a nursery."

"Oh, this should do nicely. Thank you."

Rowdy chuckled again as if she'd said something amusing. She didn't understand his behavior. But then her experience with the opposite sex was limited to one cheating husband, her absentee father and a host of older male employees.

"Dax set up the crib already. Said you could arrange things any way you wanted."

Jenna stopped in the doorway and lowered the diaper bag to the floor. Still unaccustomed to the weight of a baby and a bag, her arm ached. "He bought a crib for Sophie?"

"Gavin's old crib was in storage. Dax just dragged it out of the shed and cleaned it up a little."

The kindness created a warm glow in her chest. After purchasing the blue car, she'd used her credit cards for the final time at a baby store. Then she'd stuffed as many items as possible for Jenna's care into the trunk and headed west. The layette included a folding travel bed—the best she could do in a small car—but a real crib was even better.

"I shall have to thank him."

Rowdy grinned. "Indeed, you shall."

A flush of embarrassment rushed up her neck. Enough was enough. "Mr. Davis, are you making fun of me?"

"We call it teasing around these parts."

"May I inquire as to the reason?"

"You talk funny. All citified and stiff. Kinda tickles the ears."

"Oh, I see." Was her speech the only thing he found amusing? Had she been imagining his insolent stares?

She moved deeper into the room, eager to settle Sophie and to explore her new living arrangements. Rowdy remained in the doorway watching her. "Thank you for showing me the rooms. I'm sure I can find my way around from here."

The ranch hand didn't seem to get the message. He slouched against the door facing, picking at the button on his sleeve.

Determined not to let him bother her, Jenna lifted Sophie to her shoulder and turned her attention to the room.

The suite was different than the rest of the wood and stone and leather ranch house. Here was an English garden, a room filled with lush, print fabrics and graceful furnishings in sage and antique white with splashes of rose and blue. The decor bled over into a sitting room and through to the nursery. Jenna loved it.

"This looks new. As though no one has ever used it," she murmured.

"I don't think it was used much."

Sophie made one of her squeaky noises and squirmed. Jenna patted the tiny back as she turned toward Rowdy. "But these rooms are the nursery. Didn't Gavin sleep here?"

"That was before my time, but I doubt it."

"Why ever not? The rooms are beautiful."

He shrugged. "I guess beauty's in the eye of the beholder."

His answer was no answer at all, but Jenna didn't press the topic. If Dax didn't like the look of an English garden, why should she care? Her job was to cook and clean, not question the tastes of her employer.

A little thrill ran through her veins. She had acquired a job and she would be able to care for her daughter. Like a normal person.

Grateful, she left Rowdy Davis standing in the door while she took Sophie into the taupe-walled nursery and laid her in the crib. As she placed a kiss on her daughter's velvet cheek, the soft scent of baby breath and formula filled her senses. She thought the smell was pure heaven.

She slipped out of her coat and draped it over the railing.

Someone, Dax she supposed, had neatly made up the baby bed and placed pretty quilted bumper pads around the inside. A quilt rack complete with a darling patchwork quilt in sage and taupe stood next to the bed.

Jenna adjusted her daughter's blanket and stroked the miniscule hand, lost in a love that brought a lump to her throat. Sophie looked tiny in the big crib.

"I was just wondering something."

Jenna jumped at the sudden intrusion of a man's voice. She hadn't realized Rowdy had followed her through to the nursery.

She turned slightly to find him standing at her elbow. "Yes? What is it?"

"What's a pretty girl like you doing out here?" He edged closer, overpowering her nose with his heavy-handed cologne. "I can't believe any man would let something like you get away. You married?"

The question startled her like an unexpected spray of cold water.

"I'm a widow. Sophie's father died in a car crash."

"My sympathies." The words didn't quite match the expression in his eyes.

"Thank you." She swallowed and slanted away to fuss with the elephant mobile hanging above Sophie. She expected Rowdy to take his leave.

He didn't. Instead, he reached into the crib and drew a fingertip over Sophie's rose-petal cheek. Jenna had to restrain herself to keep from pushing his hand away.

"So you and the little darlin' here are all alone in the world?" He straightened, turning his probing gaze to her.

"We are making our own way quite well, thank you."

"Good for you. But if you should need a man, give a holler." His words were soft, suggesting something more than helping her unload her car. "I'm always glad to help out."

Jenna had no idea how to handle the man. Pretending a fascination with the little lamp atop the armoire, she moved in that direction. She could feel Rowdy's stare on her back. Maybe he was just being friendly, but his sly, unyielding grin made her uncomfortable as if he could see through her clothes.

Surreptitiously, she glanced down to check her buttons. Though her breasts were uncomfortably full and pushed against her smocked top, she was covered and decent.

"Rowdy!" A gravelly voice called from the front of the house.

Jenna turned toward the sound, a sense of relief flooding her. She was probably being silly but Dax's gruff voice was a welcome sound.

"Back here, boss." Rowdy aimed a wink in her direction and stepped to the doorway. "I'm showing the lady her quarters."

"Her what?" Dax appeared behind Rowdy, a scowl on his face.

"She talks prissified. Called her room *quarters,* like this was the Taj Mahal or something. Pretty little thing, though," he said as if she wasn't standing right there.

Dax's scowl deepened. "Where's her stuff? I told you to help her."

Rowdy pushed off the doorway, seemingly undisturbed by Dax's bluster. "I was just about to get it out of the car."

"Go on then. I'll help you in a minute."

"No problem. I can handle it." With a final flicker in her direction, Rowdy strode out of the room.

Dax's gaze followed him for a minute before he turned his attentions to Jenna. "Everything all right? You getting settled?"

Other than not liking his ranch hand, she was delighted.

"I haven't been here long enough to get settled, but your home is lovely." Although it needed a thorough dusting. "The English garden decor in here is wonderful."

"English garden?" Bewildered green eyes blinked around the room. "Is that what you call this stuff?"

His clueless response made her want to laugh. In his black cowboy hat, sheepskin jacket and a pair of scuffed boots, he didn't exactly fit the image of a man who would be comfortable in an English garden or a room filled with soft colors and ruffles and baby things. Perhaps a nanny had occupied this suite.

"Thank you for thinking of the crib."

"Might as well get some use out of it. Baby need anything else?"

Dax stepped to the crib and gazed down. His shoulders relaxed as though looking at Sophie melted the tension from him. When he reached down and placed his wide hand lightly on the baby's chest, something warm and tender moved inside of Jenna.

The notion puzzled her. She hadn't wanted Rowdy to touch her baby, but she felt differently with Dax. Maybe because those rough rancher hands had brought Sophie safely into the world.

"She breathes so softly," she said, moving to his side, intuitively understanding his reason for touching the newborn. Hadn't she done the same thing dozens of times over the past few days?

Dax turned his head, bringing his face close to hers. "Like a whisper."

Jenna stared into those green, green eyes, the funny, unsettled stirring coming back in full force. Dax made her uncomfortable, too, but in a far different way than she felt with Rowdy. He was short-spoken and puzzling, but she would trust him with her life. A tiny smile quivered on her lips. Indeed, she had already done that.

Dax looked at her for another long, curious moment before moving to the window. He pushed aside the taupe draperies and looked out. "Wonder what's keeping Rowdy?"

Footsteps thudded down the hall. "That must be him."

"Slow as Christmas," Dax grumbled, relieving his ranch hand of a giant carton and a suitcase.

"You wouldn't believe all the junk she crowded into that trunk. Women and their stuff."

Dax made a harrumphing noise in the back of his throat. "Typical."

Jenna wasn't sure what he meant, but from his darkened expression she decided not to ask. She did, however, want to ask about the little boy.

As soon as Rowdy disappeared for another load, she did.

"Rowdy said your son had a bloody nose. Where is he? Did you take him to the hospital?"

Dax made a face as though the notion was ridiculous. "He's all right. I sent him to wash his hands."

A small boy poked his head around the corner. Except for a pair of cobalt-blue eyes, he was a miniature version of his father. "I falled off the merry-go-round. My shirt's all bloody."

"I told you to change clothes."

Gavin's face puckered. "I forgot."

The child looked so small and worried, Jenna crouched in front of him. "I'm Jenna. I'm going to be your new chef."

"I'm Gavin Matthew Coleman."

"A handsome name for a handsome boy. From all that blood on your shirt, I'd say you must be a brave boy, too."

"Noah said I was going to die. He's my friend. I was kinda scart."

Dax made an impatient noise. "No one dies of a bloody nose."

Jenna ignored the irritation in Dax's voice as she tilted the child's chin. Dried blood ringed his nostrils. "I think we need to wash your face a bit, too, and perhaps have a nice warm bath and change that shirt."

"We were about to do that," Dax said. "Go on, Gavin. I'll be there directly."

The boy lingered in front of Jenna. "Are you the new cooker?"

Jenna smiled. Obviously, Gavin was unfamiliar with the term chef. "I am indeed."

The child gave an exaggerated sigh. "What a relief."

Behind her Dax snorted. "Tired of pizza, sport?"

Jenna patted the boy's narrow shoulder. "I shall prepare a dinner fit for two kings. Now head for that bath. Kings must be well-groomed."

"You talk funny, but I like you," Gavin said and surprised her with a quick hug before darting out of the room.

"That's a first."

She stood, turning to look at the rancher. He wore a bemused expression. "What is?"

"Gavin is bashful. I've never seen him hug a housekeeper before."

"Then, I shall take that as a great compliment. He's a darling boy."

"And about that meal fit for two kings?"

"Yes?"

"It might have to wait until you go grocery shopping."

When she laughed, Dax Coleman did a strange thing. He slapped his Stetson on his head, turned on his boot heel and stalked out.

CHAPTER SIX

DAX STOMPED HIS BOOTS at the back door and watched clumps of dirt and unmentionable debris fall away. He should have stayed in the house and made sure the new housekeeper did all right with Gavin. Rowdy could have seen to the cow with the bad foot.

Might as well face the truth, Coleman. The new house - keeper with her big innocent eyes and sexy laugh scared you off.

Jenna Garwood stirred feelings in him that he'd killed long ago. And he didn't like it. Especially from her, a slip of a girl far too young for him to be noticing. Now she was going to be in his house and under his nose, smelling like flowers all the time.

What had he been thinking?

What kind of father was he that he'd leave his son alone with a stranger? He hadn't even asked for references this morning, which showed just how stupid he was. He might have hired Jane the Ripper.

Yet, he wasn't worried about his son in Jenna's care. Not in the least. He'd watched from the doorway while she had filled the bathtub and tested the water with her delicate fingers. She'd told the boy he was brave and strong as Gavin related the bloody nose incident in a child's convoluted manner. And she'd promised to read him a bedtime story.

None of those things kept her from being a serial killer, but Dax simply knew his son was safe with the new mother. Now, it was Dax's job to make sure the new mother was safe from her employer.

As he pushed open the back door, the scent of cooking wafted from the kitchen. He had no idea what the new housekeeper had found to cook in those cereal- and macaroni-laden cupboards, but it sure smelled good.

He chuckled. Anything smelled good to a man who'd been eating his own very bad cooking.

As he entered the kitchen, Jenna shot him a tentative smile. She'd found an apron somewhere and pulled her hair back into a hair clip. She looked about sixteen.

That's the way he needed to think about her. She looked sixteen. A kid. He had never lusted after teenagers.

His traitorous brain registered ample womanly breasts and curvy hips. Her new-mother's body looked far older than sixteen.

Blast his eyes for noticing.

"Dinner in five minutes," she said.

He wanted to tell her the food smelled good and he was starving. Instead, he grumbled, "Where's Gavin?"

She pointed an oversize wooden spoon toward the living room. "Diligently practicing the letter *A. A* is for *apple* and *ant* and *aaa-choo,* you know."

Again that smile that gave him belly flips.

"Gavin," he hollered. "Come on. Wash up."

His son appeared, toting a pencil and a piece of wide-lined paper. "I finished my *A.*"

Dax took the page in hand to admire the squiggly effort. "Looks good, sport."

The smell of flowers and bacon assailed him as Jenna peered over his shoulder. "Lovely job, Gavin. Your teacher will be very impressed."

Gavin beamed up at Jenna as if she'd given him a year's

supply of ice cream. Any fool could see the little dude craved a woman's praise. Blast Reba for her abandonment. Leaving her husband was one thing. Abandoning her son was inexcusable.

"Put your work away and wash your hands for supper," he told the boy.

"I took a bath already," Gavin said as he stuffed the paper down into his schoolbag.

"Doesn't matter." Dax led the way to the back of the house with Gavin dragging his feet behind. By the time they returned to the dining room, the long oak table had been transformed.

The new housekeeper, or chef as she liked to say, apparently had discovered the fancy dishes Reba had purchased and never used—dishes he'd never bothered to use, either. Two places were set with matching plates and silverware, along with dark green cloth napkins and gleaming stemware. A candlestick graced each end of the table—who knew where she'd found those?—and in the center was a slender vase poked full of backyard weeds arranged in artsy beauty.

"What's all this? A party?"

Jenna blinked in surprise. "No, sir. Dinner."

"Never seen such a fancy table for a mere meal." For a bachelor and his child who often ate in front of the television or at the bar, this was like dining at the Ritz.

"Shall I serve now?" she asked, hovering as if worried about pleasing him. The notion made him mad. All he expected was a meal, not subservience.

"Just put the food on the table." He scraped out a chair for Gavin and then for himself. "We aren't helpless."

Face flushed, she did as he said, sliding a steaming casserole in front of him. "You were right about the cupboards being bare. I'll have to rectify that tomorrow."

He eyed the dish with suspicion. "What is this?"

"A macaroni-and-cheese quiche."

"I like macaroni," Gavin said. A doubtful Dax scooped a helping onto both of their plates. Wasn't there some kind of rule that men didn't eat quiche? What *was* quiche anyway?

"And," Jenna went on, standing so close he could still smell perfume, "baked potato soup with herbed toast points."

Toast points? He eyed the toasted triangles arranged in a tidy circle on a serving plate. Some kind of green leaf adorned the center.

He had to hand it to the new cook, the food was pretty. Might as well find out if it was edible.

"Dig in, Gavin." He could have saved his breath because the boy had already shoveled macaroni into his mouth until he resembled a chipmunk. "Slow down, boy."

"It's good, Daddy." Though muffled, the words matched the pleasure on Gavin's face.

Dax took a bite. His taste buds shouted for joy. Whatever quiche was, it included bacon and to his way of thinking, anything with bacon was good.

"Could I get anything else for you?" Jenna asked.

She looked tired. Dax wanted to kick himself. She was a new mama, not much more than a week away from having a baby. She shouldn't be slaving over a stove.

"Sit down," he said.

"Is everything all right with the food?" She drew her pouty bottom lip between her teeth.

Dax frowned. He needed no reminders that she had a mouth made for kissing. "Sit down. Eat."

"I'm the chef, not a guest."

"I'm the boss. Sit. Eat."

Gavin's head volleyed back and forth between the adults, expression worried.

Jenna hovered between the kitchen island and the dining table, looking as anxious as Gavin did. The notion that both of them were getting nervous made Dax feel like a jerk.

"Sit," he bellowed.

Jenna dropped an apple-red pot holder and slithered into the farthest chair from him.

"There is no need to shout," she said with a dignity that turned his annoyance to amusement. Posture stiff and nostrils flared, Jenna Garwood had gone from scared chick to mad hen faster than a mosquito bite.

Dax scooted back from the table and rose. "You need a plate."

She started up. "I'll get it."

"Sit," he said again, this time in a gentler voice. "You've done enough."

He retrieved the plate and utensils and put them in front of her. She looked flustered and pink and tired.

He kicked himself again.

"You've overdone it," he said, taking up his fork. "I shouldn't have let you start tonight."

She flashed him a puzzled look.

"I'm perfectly well, thank you." With graceful fingers she filled her plate and began to eat.

"How's the baby?" He shoved a bite of something cheesy into his mouth and chewed.

Jenna delicately patted her lips with a green napkin. "She sleeps most of the time."

"Don't worry. It won't last. How often does she wake in the night?" He couldn't believe he was having this conversation.

"Twice so far. Nights are the hardest." She dipped a spoon into the steaming soup and stirred. "I'm having difficulty forcing myself to think clearly when I'm half-asleep."

"Yes. I remember the feeling."

"You do?" Her gaze flicked to Gavin, who continued stuffing macaroni into his face as if he hadn't eaten in weeks. It occurred to Dax that he'd neglected teaching his son some common manners.

He tapped Gavin's forearm. "Slow down, sport. There's plenty."

Gavin grinned. Soup dripped on his chin. Before Dax could reprimand him, Jenna handed the boy a napkin and silently indicated the drip. When Gavin successfully swiped the spot, she reacted as though he'd conquered Mt. Everest. "Splendid, Gavin." She clapped her hands once beneath her chin. "I can see your handsome face so much better."

Gavin beamed a hundred-watt grin. "You make good soup."

"Thank you. A chef appreciates hearty appetites." She tasted the soup, her gaze observing Dax above the spoon. "Did you get up with Gavin when he was a baby?"

He hadn't intended to go there. "Yeah."

Her unspoken question hovered like a housefly, annoying him. Where was Gavin's mother? Why hadn't she cared for her son? Well, he wasn't going to talk about Reba, especially in front of Gavin. The boy had enough questions without stirring up more.

"I think that's an admirable thing," Jenna said.

Dax scowled. He'd missed something. "What is?"

"For a father to dedicate himself to the care of an infant." She tilted her head toward Gavin. "You must have been a very special baby."

Gavin looked pleased. "Did your daddy take care of you, too?"

Something tightened in her face. He was certain Gavin wouldn't notice but Dax had. That she was bothered by the question gave rise to new concerns about the woman he'd hired to care for his son. Who was Jenna Garwood anyway?

"No, I lived in the city," she said a little too brightly before glancing down at her plate. Dax wondered what living in the city had to do with Gavin's question about her father.

When she looked up again, her smile was as fake as Reba's fingernails. "You are such a lucky boy. You live on a wonderful ranch with your dad and all these animals. Can you ride a horse?"

Gavin dropped his head and fiddled with a piece of toast. "Not yet."

"Horses scare him." The notion perturbed Dax no end, but he was trying to be patient. Everything scared Gavin. Horses, cows, loud noises, hoot owls. The boy jumped at shadows.

The new housekeeper was all sympathy. "How old are you Gavin?"

"Five. I'll be six February 17."

She waved a hand. "You have plenty of time to learn equestrian skills."

Gavin's fork paused over the cheesy casserole. "Huh?"

"Riding a horse," Dax said. Rowdy was right. She did talk funny. She was far too refined to be a housekeeper. "Equestrian refers to horses."

"Oh." The word was too much for the boy so he let it slide. "When I get big I'll ride. Daddy will get me an old broke pony when I'm ready. All I have to do is the say the word. Right, Daddy?"

Dax's mouth twisted. He'd said that very thing to Gavin a dozen times. "Right, sport."

"And you will become a wonderful horseman, I am certain." Jenna favored Gavin with a smile and reached for another toast point. *Toast points.* He was still tickled over that one.

While the heavy dose of over-the-top kindness floated around his kitchen table, Dax's brain was also shooting off all kinds of warning signals. Jenna Garwood had come into his life in a bizarre manner and, like her pretty little toast points, she no more fit on a ranch than he fit at that pink hotel in Hollywood.

Clearing his throat, Dax interrupted the pleasant chit-chat. "Where you from, Jenna? I forgot to ask this morning during our interview."

Some interview. She'd handed him that soft little baby, looked at him with worried eyes, and he'd forgotten to use the good sense his mama had given him.

"I beg your pardon?" she asked, dragging her attention away from his son.

"Your application was a little short on details. I was asking where you're from."

"Oh." She had that deer-in-the-headlights look. Her hands fidgeted with the napkin. "I'm from back East." She hopped up from the table. "Let me clear away the plates and bring dessert."

Gavin whooped for joy. "Dessert! She made dessert, Daddy."

Jenna disappeared around the bar and into the kitchen. Dax shoved back from the table and stalked after her. She was going to talk to him and she was going to do it now. All the dessert in the world wasn't stopping him from finding out more about her.

Her back was turned when he entered the kitchen area. Busy dishing up something onto his fancy saucers, she pretended not to hear his approach. Incensed, he moved closer. When she still didn't turn around, he slammed a hand down on each side of her. She couldn't run now. He'd trapped her.

Leaning next to her ear, he growled, "Are you trying to avoid my questions?"

With a gasp, Jenna whirled around, eyes wide as those saucers. "What do you mean?"

Cripes. She was so near he could feel her body heat. And smell that tantalizing perfume. What had he been thinking to move in this close?

Sweat popped out on the back of his neck. He dug his fingers into the countertop and hung on tight. Regardless of the unwanted physical reaction to his new employee, he deserved answers.

"I need to know more about you than the fact that you cook weird food."

If such a thing was possible, she drew farther back, pressing into the counter behind her.

"Weird?" Her eyes widened some more, this time in dismay. Her pouty mouth turned down. "You didn't like it?"

Blast and be danged. He'd hurt her feelings. He tried again. "I didn't mean weird. Different."

"Different?" She still didn't look happy. And her too-near chest rose and fell as if she might cry.

"Different but good," he said, growing more unraveled by the moment. A smart man would back away from her lush body and her sweet eyes and her tantalizing mouth. A smart man would never have come in here in the first place. "Real good. You're a great cook."

She was beginning to brighten. He wanted her to smile again the way she'd been smiling at Gavin all through supper… Dinner… Whatever she wanted to call it. "I haven't eaten such a meal in weeks."

Actually, he'd never eaten such a meal, but he knew when to cut his losses and keep his mouth shut.

She relented a little and Dax thought he saw a hint of humor lurking in those eyes. Brown eyes. Like the color of honey. Sweet, warm, delectable honey.

Why didn't someone just shoot him now?

"I'm glad," she murmured, the softness of her breath brushing his lips. Temptation tortured him. If he leaned in the slightest bit, they'd be touching from chest to thigh. A little closer and he could feel the softness of her mouth against his. "I want to do a good job for you."

And he wanted to— With rigid self-control he reined his wayward wants and tried to remember why he'd come in here in the first place.

"You will. You are. It's just that—" What? What was it he wanted to know?

He wanted to know a lot more than he would allow himself to think about.

Oh yes. Now he remembered.

Slowly, he loosened his white-knuckle grip on the counter

and pushed away, leaving enough space between himself and his cook so that she could walk away from this encounter at any time. He'd had no business trapping her against the counter that way. What was the matter with him?

"You'll be taking care of my son," he said.

"A delight I'm looking forward to."

There she went with her fancy talk. "Right, but he's my son. It's my job to protect him."

She got that stricken look again as if he'd slapped her. "I would never do anything to hurt Gavin."

He believed her, but common sense said he needed more information about his housekeeper. "Why are you here, Jenna?"

"I required employment. You offered me a job."

"I don't mean here at Southpaw. I mean here in Texas. You have a new baby. Where is your family? Why aren't you with them? Won't they be concerned about you?"

The sadness that overcame her was a punch in his gut. Her bottom lip quivered. She looked down at her clenched hands. "Sophie's father died in rather embarrassing circumstances. Humiliating for me anyway."

A gentleman wouldn't press but Dax had to. "Meaning?"

She hesitated. And then sighed.

"At the time of the accident Derek was…my husband was…" Color drained from her face while she struggled to say the words. She twisted her fingers until the knuckles whitened. Until Dax had the insane urge to take her hands in his and calm her obvious stress.

"Never mind," he said. "I don't need details."

She looked up, her voice a whisper. "Thank you. It's difficult to discuss."

He got the picture. Her husband had cheated on her and died in the process. Either that or he was a criminal killed during the commission of a felony. The last thought gave him pause, but even if it was true he didn't believe for a minute

that Jenna was involved. She might be running from something, but not that.

"How did you end up here?"

"I wanted to escape the memories and raise my daughter
away from the gossip and the painful past. Texas was an accident."

Dax watched as she twisted her hands over and over again
until the whiteness reddened. Whatever she'd left behind had
hurt her badly. He knew that kind of pain and the need to
escape. Jenna Garwood was a kindred spirit, someone who
understood the hurt that came from loving too much.

His voice gentled. "How was Texas an accident, Jenna?"

"I thought I had more time to find a place and get settled
before Sophie's arrival."

"But Sophie had other plans."

Her face went soft, full of love for her child. "Yes. Once
she arrived, I had to find work and a place to live immediately. A baby changes everything."

How well he knew. But at least, he'd had the ranch and a
job and plenty of money to take care of Gavin. He could hire
help. Jenna was alone with a newborn to support and no
place else to go.

But one thought nagged him. "You're not the type to do
this kind of work."

"Not the type?"

"Too educated or refined or... I don't know how to explain
it but it's pretty clear you don't fit."

A determined glint flickered through her eyes. "I will do
whatever is required to care for my daughter. At this point in
time, domestic work allows me to be with her while earning
a living. That's important to me. Regardless of my background, I am more grateful for this job than you can ever
imagine."

His respect for the tough little mama ratcheted higher.
What an amazing woman. He burned with an irrational need

to pull his housekeeper into his arms and promise to care for her and Sophie.

Dumb. Real dumb.

Yet he had plenty of money. He could assure they lacked nothing. He could support and protect and befriend. He could take care of them both while Jenna mothered her child and his son.

Don't be an idiot, Dax. Women are trouble. Remember?

Finally, to quiet the noise in his head, he muttered, "I'm sorry for all you've been through."

Her chin hitched higher. "Don't be. Sophie and I are delighted with our new environment. It is absolutely perfect. That is, if maintaining my employment and residence here will be a satisfactory arrangement for you and Gavin."

Dax's mouth quivered. She was really cute when she talked like that. Cute and sexy.

Blast his brain! He bit down on the inside of his cheek to punish himself. She wasn't sexy. She was a kid. A new mother in need of help.

But somewhere in the back of that blasted brain a voice laughed at his protestations.

Before he could blurt something foolish and regrettable Gavin came around the corner of the cabinets. A hint of cheese rimmed the boy's lips. He took one look at the adults and slapped his hands onto his hips. "Are you two gonna talk all day or eat dessert? A kid could starve around here."

CHAPTER SEVEN

"MISS JENNA, are you gonna read me a story?"

Jenna sat in the padded rocking chair next to the baby crib, soft lamplight glowing golden around her and Sophie. She glanced up at the small, dark-haired boy standing uncertainly in the door of the nursery.

"Come in, Gavin."

Clad in cartoon image pajamas, the child crept closer. "I got a book in my room."

Jenna's arms and back ached as never before but she couldn't refuse Gavin's request. After all, she was his employee. Caring for him was her responsibility. More than that, she felt an empathy with the child that she couldn't articulate. And she *had* promised a story.

"Do you mind if I bring Sophie along? She's having her dinner now." She dipped her chin to indicate the bottle in the baby's mouth.

He edged closer, hands behind his back, watching in fascination as Sophie's mouth tugged greedily at the nipple. "Is that all she eats?"

"For now. When she's older she'll take cereal and baby food."

"Babies don't got no teeth, do they?"

Jenna hid a smile at the atrocious grammar but intentionally emphasized the correction. "No, babies haven't any teeth."

"Can't you buy her some from the dentist? My Grandpa Joe got some there."

The inner smile moved outward. "She'll grow her own in a few months. Just wait and see." Assuming she and Sophie were still here in a few months.

So far her mother hadn't discovered her whereabouts, and on a ranch this remote, perhaps she wouldn't. Someday Jenna hoped to be strong enough to stand up against her parents, but she never had been before. Even now, with hundreds of miles between them, she went weak and shaky at the idea of going head-to-head with the formidable Elaine Carrington.

Sophie's bottle emptied with a sucking sound. Jenna lifted the baby to her shoulder and patted the tiny back.

Gavin remained at her side, one small hand resting on the arm of the chair.

"She burped," he announced. "Can she say 'Scuse me?"

What an adorable little boy. "Not yet, but when the time comes, I hope you'll help her learn your nice manners."

Gavin's chest puffed with importance. "I will. I promise. I know how to say 'scuse me." He turned his head and emitted a pretend belch and then whipped around with a proud grin. "'Scuse me please, ma'am."

Jenna laughed. "You are excused. Thank you very much."

"Gavin!" Dax's voice rang from the living room. "Time for bed."

One hand supporting Sophie's back, Jenna rose. "Your dad's calling. Let's read that story and get you tucked in."

"Okay!" Gavin took off like a Thoroughbred in the Kentucky Derby.

Jenna followed behind more slowly. Her body yearned for a hot bath and a long slumber.

As she passed through the living room, she paused. Her employer was kicked back in a burgundy recliner that had been drawn too close to the television. He had to know she was in the room, but he chose to ignore her.

Dax Coleman was a puzzling man. One minute he was brusque and crabby. The next he was kindness itself.

The encounter in the kitchen after dinner had shaken her in the oddest manner. Dax had been angry and demanding at first, and then some other emotion had flashed from him that had set her heart to thundering and her belly aquiver. The sparks had almost ignited her hair.

After Gavin's timely interruption, Dax had abruptly withdrawn. Yet their conversation had given her hope that she and her employer would get along. He'd even helped clear the table and put dishes in the washer, gruffly chastising her for overdoing.

Yes, *puzzling* was the word. For all his bluster, perhaps he was, as Crystal had indicated, one of the good guys. He just had a hard time letting anyone know.

She cleared her throat.

A commercial danced across the television screen. The furniture in this room was lovely if badly arranged. To see Dax's face, she had to walk around the chair and stand between him and the television.

"Gavin wants a story. Would you care to join us?" He was the boy's father. Most likely, they shared a bedtime ritual.

Dax squinted in her direction. At some point, he'd run a hand through his longish hair and it stuck up in front. His five o'clock shadow had deepened to a real need for a shave. The quivery feeling returned to her belly and this time she recognized it for what it was. Attraction. Crystal Wolf was right about this, too. Dax Coleman looked delicious. Rumpled, relaxed, and delicious.

Oh dear. The last time she'd been attracted to a man had resulted in disaster.

She pressed a hand to her stomach. Dax followed the motion; a muscle in his jaw twitched before he abruptly turned back to the television.

"Tell Gavin I'll be in later to say good-night."

So that was that.

By the time she reached Gavin's room he had crawled beneath a blue dinosaur comforter and sat with his back bolstered by two fat pillows.

"Sit here." He patted the spot next to him. "I can hold Sophie if you want me to."

Jenna smiled. "You are very thoughtful, but I think I can manage." With Sophie in the crook of her elbow, she picked up a book with the opposite hand. Already she was learning that mothers need three arms. "Is this the story you want?"

"Yep." He propped his hands behind his head. "That's the one."

Jenna rested the baby along her thighs before stroking a hand over the book's colorful cover. "*Peter Rabbit.* I remember this from when I was a little girl."

"Did your mommy read it to you?"

Jenna's chest clutched. "No."

"Mine, neither. I don't have a mom." He said the words in a manner-of-fact tone, but Jenna sorrowed for what he'd missed. At least she'd had a mother on the premises, though Elaine Carrington was not one to dirty her hands with the day-to-day details such as story-reading. A Carrington daughter was a collector's doll to be taken out of the box in pristine condition, displayed briefly at meals or recitals, and returned to the care of servants, not to be seen or heard until the next time. Without the kindness of nannies she'd likely never have heard a bedtime story.

She was determined this would not happen to Sophie.

With a lump in her throat she began to read. By page three Gavin had scooted until his body pressed against her side, bringing with him the pleasant smell of soap and toothpaste. She circled his shoulders with one arm, displaying the book so he could see the pictures. He sighed his approval, leaned closer and grasped the book's edge with one hand.

When the story ended, he said, "I'm glad Peter Rabbit escaped, aren't you, Miss Jenna?"

"Indeed."

"But he shouldn't have gone in the garden. His mama told him not to. Right?"

"Exactly right. Children should always obey their parents." She almost choked on the words. She had always obeyed her parents until Derek.

She closed the book and placed it on the stand next to Gavin's bed. When she turned back, the little boy was looking at the baby in her lap. Tentatively, with surprising gentleness, he touched the top of Sophie's hand with one finger.

"Miss Jenna?"

"Yes?"

"Are you and Sophie going to stay here for always?"

"I don't know."

She could see the answer troubled him. "I hope you stay a long time."

"Why is that?"

"So Sophie can be my baby sister. Noah has a baby brother. I want a baby, too, but Daddy says no. He says we'd have to get a mama to have a baby and he's not ever getting us another mama. So if you stay, Sophie can be my sister."

The child's words were a revelation into the father. Whatever had happened between Dax and his ex-wife cut deep. So much so that he feared getting hurt again, a fear Jenna understood completely.

No wonder Dax Coleman appeared kind and angry all in one package.

The dark-haired boy touched her heart, too. He longed for siblings and probably a mother, as well. Rough and tumble, timid and gentle at the same time, Gavin would be an easy child to love. The notion brought an ache to her chest. Where was his mother? What could have been so terrible about her life here at Southpaw that she would leave this precious, handsome son?

Even though Sophie was little more than a week old, Jenna knew she'd miss her more than life if they couldn't be together.

"Are you ready to have the lights out now?"

"I didn't say my prayers yet."

"All right then. Say them."

Squeezing his eyes closed, Gavin clasped his hands together beneath his chin. Jenna listened as he recited the "Now I lay me" prayer and went through a litany of God blesses before proclaiming with a sigh, "Amen." His eyes sprang open. "Can I have a drink?"

To her surprise, Dax stepped into the room. "He'll do this all night if you let him."

Gavin batted thick black eyelashes. "I'm thirsty, Daddy."

Dax relented with a half chuckle, half sigh. "Go on then. Get your drink, but nothing else."

Gavin scampered off the bed and disappeared. Jenna could hear him rattling around in the bathroom next door.

Dax glanced toward the noise, the hint of a smile on his face. "You read good."

The comment came out of nowhere. "What?"

"*Peter Rabbit*. Read in your voice, he took on a whole different personality."

"Well, thank you, I think." She offered a smile. "You were welcome to come in."

How long had he been standing in the hallway?

"Didn't want to disturb you." He shifted and cast another glance toward the bathroom and the sound of running water and clinking glass. "I need to say something."

Jenna tensed. "Have I done anything wrong?"

He made an irritated sound and swatted the air. "No. Not you. Me. I came on too strong in the kitchen. I apologize."

Relief surged like Hawaiian surf. "You have every right to know about the people in charge of your son."

His mouth twisted. "Don't let me off the hook that easy."

"All right, then." She pointed a finger at him. "Consider yourself appropriately castigated."

Dax surprised her with a laugh. "Castigated. That'll teach me to behave."

Jenna found herself sharing a smile with her employer. He was really handsome when he smiled. She took the thought captive and stowed it away.

"Dax, you have my solemn promise. I will care for Gavin as I will Sophie. With everything in me. You must never, ever be concerned that I would give anything less than my best to your son."

He gave a curt nod. "Can't ask for more than that. He's all I have, you know. He's—"

"Everything." Jenna finished the thought for him, intuitively understanding the depth of his feelings—because she felt the same about Sophie. "Your child is everything."

"Yeah," he said, shifting from one boot to the other. "Everything."

That one spark of kinship ignited a glow in Jenna's heart. Dax Coleman loved his son the way she loved Sophie. And that was a beautiful thing to know about a man. He loved deep. He loved strong. And forever.

The revelation shook her. She'd only just arrived and was the man's employee. She had no right to think of him as a…friend. As a man.

But she did.

Stunned by the emotion splashing around inside like a raft on the Colorado rapids, she stroked Sophie's sleeping face with one finger, thinking.

Dax's gravelly voice scraped across the silence, quiet and dangerously attractive. "She's a good baby, isn't she?"

"I think so, but I haven't been around babies much, so I have no one to compare."

He cocked to one side, resting his weight on a hip. The

tension from earlier tonight had inexplicably dissipated. Puzzling man. Fascinating man.

"No nieces or nephews?"

Jenna shook her head and met his gaze. "I was an only child."

"Are your parents still living?"

She could hear the unasked question. If they're still alive, why aren't you with them? Wouldn't they want to know about their grandchild? She focused her attention on Sophie's fingers, lifting the tiny digits up one by one, unable to look her employer in the eye.

"No. They're dead." At least to her, but her pulse rattled at the lie. "Yours?"

"Dad's gone. Mom moved to Austin some years back to be near my sister, Karina. Once in a while they drive up here or I take Gavin to see them. Not as often as I'd like. Life's busy."

"What about Christmas? Won't you see them then?"

"I don't know yet. Haven't given it much thought."

The holiday was only weeks away. "Doesn't Gavin have a list a mile long?"

"Two miles." He smiled again.

"Who's Grandpa Joe?"

Dax chuckled. "Gavin's good buddy and my ninety-two-year-old great-granddaddy. He's in a care facility over in Saddleback, feeble as a kitten but sharp as a tack."

Gavin wandered back into the room. "Grandpa Joe is my best friend." He hopped onto the bed, his little body slithering beneath the comforter. Water glistened on his hair and around his mouth. He'd apparently combed his hair as well as having that final drink. "I'm ready. Tuck me in."

Dax stepped to the bedside and bent low, pulling the boy into a hug before settling him again with the covers tucked snugly beneath the small chin. "'Night, sport. Sleep tight."

"'Night, Daddy. Don't let the bedbugs bite. 'Night, Miss Jenna."

"Good night, Gavin. Sweet dreams."

Dax gave the child one final pat on the chest and straightened, turning for the door. Jenna, baby in arms, moved past him and started down the hall. As the light snapped out, she heard Gavin's voice one last time. "See, Dad? Having a mama in the house isn't so bad after all."

Dax knew he was dreaming, but the knowledge didn't stop the parade of emotions. In his dream, Gavin was still a baby and he was an exhausted, confused single dad, asleep in his half-empty king-size bed, wishing his wife would come home and help with the baby. And Gavin was crying. Demanding a bottle. Screaming for the mother that would never come.

Dax burrowed deeper into the pillow. Sometimes if he let the baby cry for a few minutes, they could both go back to sleep. After all, he was dreaming. The dream would end, along with the deep ache of regret and the incessant crying.

The cries grew louder.

Reba's mocking face flickered through the dream like a ghost. Ignoring her son's tears, she danced before Dax with a flowy scarf over her face, laughing as she looped arms with another man and flitted away with only a parting glance at her devastated husband and crying child.

The sorrow in Dax's gut turned to acid. He hadn't had this dream in years. He needed to wake up.

Thrashing against the tangle of covers, he fought off sleep and sat upright. A film of sweat covered his body, and his chest heaved, but he forced his breathing to calm. He'd long ago stopped loving Reba. Why had he dreamed about her tonight?

A mewling cry from the far back of the house was his answer.

A baby *was* crying. Gavin? He shook his head. No, couldn't be. The baby was Sophie. Jenna's pink baby doll was crying.

Still mired in a kind of half sleep with cobwebs in his

brain, he threw his feet onto the floor and padded down the hall toward the sound.

The house was dark except for the glow of a three-quarter moon splashing pale whiteness across the carpet. Dax needed no other light to maneuver in his own home. Even the nursery, as little as he'd used those rooms, was familiar. The baby's room had two entries, one from inside Jenna's bedroom and the other from the hall. He quietly pushed open the hallway door and stepped to the crib.

Sophie squirmed within the tight confines of a soft, thick blanket, her cries frantic now. Dax bent low, scooped the bundle into his large hands and lifted her against his naked chest. She was a feather, a dandelion puff, so light and fragile.

As he started out of the nursery toward the kitchen and the supply of formula he'd seen in the refrigerator, the tile was cold against his bare feet. The cooled atmosphere of the house sent prickles over his flesh. He came fully awake.

His heart slammed against his rib cage. This baby creating a single spot of warmth on his chest was not Gavin. This was Sophie, not his child. She was not his responsibility.

The infant whimpered, her head turning this way and that in search of food.

Jenna must be dead tired not to have heard the baby cry. But what did he expect? He'd worked her like a field hand from the very first day, expecting her to clean house, care for Gavin, do the shopping, cook his meals, clean the kitchen and still have the energy to get up at two o'clock with a newborn.

He'd even sent her to town for groceries that second day. She'd come back all rosy and chattery, talking about how much fun she'd had—in the grocery store no less. Picking out cantaloupe and watermelon and showing off Sophie to everyone in the place. He remembered how that worked. Carrying a baby into the grocery store in Saddleback was the same as throwing a party with free food. Everyone came running. He smiled at the memory.

Jenna had reacted to the trip with unbridled enthusiasm, as if she'd never shopped for groceries in her life. She was the same way about everything, come to think of it.

The ranch house was starting to respond to her enthusiasm.

But the truth was Jenna had been at the Southpaw for nearly a week now without a break, working hard enough to drive her into exhaustion.

He was an inconsiderate jerk.

Working in the semidark kitchen, he heated the baby bottle with one hand while holding Sophie securely with the other as he'd done dozens of times with Gavin. "Let your mama sleep, Sophie girl. Uncle Dax will fix you right up."

Okay, so he wasn't her uncle, but he felt like one. He'd been with her from the get-go. Not that he dared let himself get too close. No use getting in an emotional tangle about a baby destined to move on. A woman like Jenna wouldn't be here long. Once on her feet, she'd find a better job. She'd move on to a city somewhere with people of her education and breeding. Even a fool like him recognized quality and class when he saw it. Reba had no class at all, and even she hadn't stayed—which told him a lot about his shortcomings.

Sophie squirmed and let out a howl. Dax grunted away the useless, self-despising thoughts. He wouldn't let himself get attached, but right now, only a heartless jerk could ignore the cries of a hungry infant.

The microwave beeped. Dax took the bottle, shook a drop onto his wrist, then slid the warm nipple into the seeking, rosebud mouth. The crying stopped instantly to be replaced by the small, humming sounds an infant makes at feeding time. He'd always liked that sound. Relieved. Contented.

Padding barefoot back to the nursery, he thought about snapping on the lamp but decided against it. No use disturbing Jenna. He moved to close the door between the nursery and the bedroom beyond. As he did, he caught a glimpse of

Jenna in the moonlight, curled on her side, sleeping like a rock. Her hair was down, spread across the pillow in spiky shadows. He could hear the soft hush of her breathing.

She didn't even stir.

He'd looked in this room many times before when Gavin was tiny and always found it empty. There was something renewing, redeeming even, to have a mother there now, steps away from her child. It eased the tight hard knot in his soul the tiniest bit.

He feasted on the feeling for several seconds, experiencing a connection with Jenna Garwood that he couldn't explain or fully comprehend.

Then, quietly, he shut the door.

CHAPTER EIGHT

JENNA AWOKE WITH A JERK and sat straight up in bed. Daylight streamed through the window. From down the hall came the sounds of people moving around and the undecipherable rumble of conversation. She'd overslept.

Leaping from the bed, she rushed into the nursery. Sophie was gone, her covers tossed aside. The changing table was in disarray. Had she been crying? Had Dax, annoyed by the noise, been forced to tend his employee's child?

Heart thudding, she quickly dressed and headed for the kitchen. Heretofore, she'd risen at six to have breakfast on the table before Gavin's school bus rumbled to a stop at seven.

Things had been going so well up until now, but her mother regularly fired employees for tardiness. Would Dax do the same?

She rushed into the kitchen only to be drawn up short. Dax, barefoot and shirt front unbuttoned, stood over the stove turning bacon with a long fork. Gavin sat at the table dressed for school, hair combed, his face washed and shiny. And Sophie lay in her carrier in front of the little boy. Gavin gently tweaked her onesie-clad toes and shook a rattle above her face. Her eyes, still unable to fully focus, crossed from the effort.

"I'm so sorry," she gushed. "Please forgive me."

Dax offered the long fork. "Save me quick before I create a disaster."

She grabbed an apron from inside a cupboard and tied it around her waist. "Aren't you angry?"

"About?" He offered the fork again. She took it, reached around him, turned the burner down and the range vent on.

"I overslept. This is my job." She poked at the bacon. The crispy strips of pork were nearly done. "I'm supposed to have breakfast on the table by now."

He shrugged. "You were tired."

Fatigue was never an excuse. Domestics executed their duties or found other employment.

"I can't apologize enough."

"You'd better not apologize again." His tone was low and dangerous.

Her pulse skittered. She turned her attention from the bacon to her employer. He was impossibly close, his broad chest naked, the stubble of unshaved beard roguish and attractive. This man who'd taken care of her hungry daughter, started breakfast, dressed Gavin for school and wasn't even upset to have done so.

Since that first night when she'd felt the tug of attraction, she tried to maintain a professional if friendly distance, but this morning, after his incredible kindness, she was especially aware of his appeal. He wasn't classically handsome like Derek but he oozed rugged, masculine sex appeal. And he didn't seem to know it.

She hadn't thought about her appearance in a long time but suddenly she wished she were prettier. Though she'd gained little weight with Sophie, she wished her body was toned and tanned and sexy. The thought made her want to cry. She'd never been sexy. If she had been, her husband wouldn't have found another woman before the ink was dry on their marriage license.

Sophie made a fussy sound. Before she could react, Gavin

poked the pacifier into the baby's mouth. Jenna rewarded him with a smile and then went back to the bacon, lifting the strips out of the pan and onto a plate.

Enough thoughts of sex appeal. She was here to do a job, to provide for her child, not moon over her employer's pectorals. And she was already running late.

"Sophie must have slept through the night," she said, scuttling about the kitchen, quickly taking breakfast items from the refrigerator and cupboards. "I'm sure that's why I overslept. After her two o'clock feeding, I'm usually half-awake until the alarm rings at five-thirty."

Dax leaned his jean-covered behind against the counter and crossed his arms over the appealing chest, expression amused. "Not."

She paused, carton of milk in hand. "What?"

"Sophie didn't sleep through the night. Just her mama."

The milk carton plunked onto the table. "You mean?" Dax had gotten up with her in the middle of the night? "Oh Dax, I'm so—"

Before she could apologize again, he lifted a finger in warning. "Uh-uh. Careful there. A tired mama needs rest. I was already awake. No need troubling you. Sophie and I did all right."

The tension in her shoulders relaxed. He really wasn't angry. "I suppose my brilliant daughter recognized a true expert while I, on the other hand, am still a novice, struggling much of the time to get her diaper on frontward."

Dax grinned. Oh my. He was luscious when he smiled. The tiny lines of weathering crinkled white near his eyes and increased his craggy attractiveness.

Aware she was staring, she spun toward the counter where boxed pancake mix awaited. Thank goodness, she'd had the good sense and had spent enough time researching on the Internet to understand the value of prepackaged goods. She wondered if the Carrington cooks had ever been scowl was meant for her. "Rowdy can handle the situation until I get there. That's what I pay him for."

Rowdy. The thought of Dax's top ranch hand soured the sweet taste of pancakes. For more than a week she'd managed to avoid another encounter with the man, a run of good luck she hoped would continue.

"What's wrong? A sick animal?" Beyond the subtleties of preparing a lovely prime rib, Jenna knew nothing about cattle. Dax had told her a little about the ranch, enough that she was interested. For a woman who'd been sheltered from so much, she wanted to know everything about everything.

"We have an A-I crew here today. They're early." He forked a bite of syrupy pancake and stirred it around his plate.

"May I inquire as to what an A-I crew might be?"

His mouth twitched. "You may. Artificial insemination."

Jenna was certain she turned pink. "I never realized such a thing occurred in cattle."

"Just one select group of experimental cows."

"Experimental cows. How fascinating." Not that she had any idea what he was talking about, but she liked the rumble of that scratchy-rough voice. And she felt rather pleased to have drawn him out. Most mornings, he mumbled hello and goodbye and disappeared out the door. Evenings were somewhat better.

Apparently, she'd been asking the wrong questions because once he started talking about his experimental cows, he didn't stop. Some of the conversation about selective breeding of a certain pasture of purebred cattle went completely over her head, but she listened hard. Dax Coleman was passionate about two things: his son and this ranch.

During a pause, Jenna noticed the clock. "Gavin, you need to brush your teeth. The bus will be here in five minutes." When Gavin scooted away from the table, she turned back to Dax. "Now tell me more about Number Thirty-two and what made her special enough to win 'Supreme Overall Breed' at the San Antonio show?"

Dax pointed his fork at her. "Do you really want to hear this or are you just being your perky self?"

Perky? Was that a compliment?

"I'm learning the nuances of ranch life," she said. "Please continue."

Dax shook his head. "The nuances of ranch life, huh? Okay, you asked for it." He launched into a technical explanation that had her mentally galloping to keep up. Dax Coleman might be a rough cattle rancher but he was a very bright man.

By the time Gavin returned, dragging his camo schoolbag, they'd turned the topic to horses and winter wheat pasture.

"I had no idea there was so much involved in raising cattle."

"Most folks think you turn 'em out to pasture and forget about them."

She smiled. "I can tell by the hours you put in that there is more to the work than that."

Gavin sidled up to his father for a goodbye hug.

"See ya tonight, sport. Be good."

Then the little boy headed toward her. She zipped his coat before pulling him in for a hug. Gavin had won her heart the first night with his precocious charm and obvious need for motherly attention. He seemed to crave her hugs and she was quickly growing to crave his, as well. Gavin was a sweet and gentle child.

She inhaled his clean, school-ready scent before turning him loose.

"Miss Jenna," he said, rustling inside his schoolbag. "I forgot to show this to you."

"What is it?"

He pushed a note in front of her, his face a picture of hope. "Can you make cupcakes for my snack? I told Miss Baker you could. You're a real good cooker."

The compliment brought a smile. Gavin was such a dear little boy with such eagerness to please. Sometimes Dax grew impatient with the child's anxieties, but they touched Jenna's heart. She understood, empathized even, with being afraid. She'd been afraid most of her life.

Thankfully, he'd volunteered her cooking skills and nothing else. The kitchen was the only place she felt comfortable, but so far Dax had not complained about her mistakes in other areas. Like the pink socks. She wondered if he'd noticed those yet?

She shot a quick, relieved glance at his bare feet. She wasn't certain what she'd done wrong yesterday with the laundry but she suspected Gavin's bright red T-shirt was the culprit. Next time she'd separate the colors.

"I would be delighted to bake cupcakes, Gavin. When do you need them?"

With a shrug, the boy bent to zip his schoolbag. "It says on the note. I forget."

Jenna perused the note. "Oh dear."

Dax leaned to peer over her shoulder "What?"

Jenna refused to acknowledge the tingle of awareness where he brushed against her. "Today is Gavin's snack day."

Gavin's hope melted down his face like candle wax. Dax took one glance at his son and his own expression hardened. To Jenna he said, "Forget it then. It's too much trouble. If I have time I'll run into town to the bakery."

"But I wanted Noah to see the baby," Gavin protested.

"Son, don't make promises that aren't yours to keep." His tone was unyielding, angry even, though Jenna couldn't comprehend the reason.

The boy's mouth quivered. "Miss Jenna likes me. I thought—"

A nerve twitched in Dax's jaw. "I'll send your teacher a note and let her know you made a mistake."

The dejected child dropped his head.

"Gentlemen, please!" Jenna slapped down her napkin and rose. "May I speak for myself?"

At the startled glances of both males, she proceeded. "Though I lack the tools for anything artistically decorative, I want to provide refreshments for Gavin's class. I was only lamenting the lack of a pastry bag and tips, not refusing the task. Okay?"

Gavin, bewildered and uncertain, blinked from Jenna to Dax and back again. "Does that mean you'll bring cupcakes?"

In spite of themselves, the adults looked at Gavin and then at each other...and burst out laughing.

CHAPTER NINE

HUMMING A HAPPY TUNE, Jenna shoved at the enormous leather sofa parked directly in the path of the dining room and the gorgeous stone-and-wood fireplace. While Gavin's cupcakes cooled and Sophie watched from her musical swing, Jenna had decided to do something about this ill-arranged living room. As lovely as the design was, the furniture was not being utilized effectively and the result was an unattractive and less-than-comfortable space.

She could actually imagine throwing a wonderful party in this house, maybe for Christmas or New Year's Eve. She already had her eye on some fabulous holiday decorations at the local hobby store and later today, she planned to explore Dax's storage building for others. But first, this space needed rearranging to reach its full potential of design and beauty.

With a groan of effort, she managed to scoot the sofa a few inches. Straining with all her strength while murmuring about her skinny arms, she didn't hear the door open.

"What do you think you're doing?"

At the sound of Dax's furious voice, Jenna jumped and spun around.

He stood, stance wide, hair windblown, looking like a thunderhead.

A hand pressed to her thudding heart, Jenna said, "Dax. I didn't hear you come in."

"Apparently." He slapped both fists low on his hips, billowing out the sides of a sheepskin jacket. "Answer me. What are you doing?"

"Rearranging." She bit her bottom lip. This was the first time he'd objected to any of her changes. She'd washed and moved curtains, rearranged pictures, added touches of color and interest with items she'd discovered in boxes in the garage. She'd even added a Christmas wreath to the front door and bowls of apple-scented potpourri to the tables. Last night, he commented on how good everything smelled and she'd been giddy with pleasure.

Now he was angry. And she had no idea why.

"You have no business moving furniture."

"I'm sorry. I thought you wouldn't mind."

"Well, I do."

"All right then." She pushed at the end of the sofa, edging the heavy item slowly back into the former position.

"Stop!"

She did. "Do you or do you not want this divan back where it was?"

"I don't give a rat's…behind where the couch is."

She blinked at her bewildering boss, lost until he continued.

"You'll hurt yourself. Show me where you want it. I'll move it."

"Oh." He was upset for her sake? Her insides turned to mush. Dax had the most unusual way of showing kindness. She touched his sleeve, surprised to feel the rigid muscle through all that cloth. "You're not angry because of the change in furniture, are you?"

"Why would I get mad about that? The place never looked better."

She smiled, her confidence soaring. Since taking this position, Jenna had discovered something about herself. She was actually good at many things her mother would consider below her station. She was good at them and she enjoyed them, too. She was starting to believe in herself in a way she'd never dreamed possible.

She was also learning some things about her employer. He struggled to express his true feelings, hiding his tender side behind bluster. But the evenings when he listened to her read to Gavin or helped his son with his homework, or even during those times she'd caught him in the nursery talking softly to Sophie, she'd learned the truth he tried to hide. He *was* a good guy. And Jenna was starting to like Dax Coleman. A lot.

"The fireplace should be the focal point of this room," she said. "So if we move the sofa there—" she pointed "—and a chair here and here, we'll open up the space and draw the eye to this beautiful stonework."

Dax contemplated momentarily. "I see your point."

"And the Christmas tree will be positively glorious there." She moved to the side of the fireplace, lifting her hands above her head in imitation of a tree. "See?"

"Couldn't ask for a prettier tree." Then as if he hadn't meant to say such a thing, he gave a curt nod. "Let's get it done."

But just the small hint that Dax thought she was pretty soothed an ache in Jenna's mind.

Biceps bulging and with barely any effort, he moved the furniture as she directed. Once she reached to help and he swatted at her with a growl. She hopped back, laughing, more confident now.

"You don't scare me."

Green eyes danced. "Then why'd you jump?"

She tossed a throw pillow at him. He caught it with one hand and growled again. "Careful, lady."

"Or what? The big bad wolf will get me?" She laughed, feeling free and a little excited.

Dax started toward her. "He might."

A delicious shiver raced up her spine. She grabbed another

pillow, holding the square bit of fluff in the small space between them. Dax snatched the pillow away, advancing. With a squeal, Jenna wheeled away. Her heart thudded and her blood zinged. This was one big bad wolf she wouldn't mind being pursued by.

She glanced back. Dax loomed above her, arms raised, hands forming claws like a bear. He roared.

Jenna screamed and jerked to the side. Her calves encountered a table she'd just moved. She lost her balance and tumbled backward. Dax caught her upper arms and yanked. He was amazingly strong. She was propelled forward and slammed into his chest.

"Are you all right?" He glared down at her, green eyes glittering.

"You saved me." Teasing, she pitter-pattered a hand against his heart. "My hero."

She'd meant it as a joke, as part of the silly game they were playing, but as soon as she touched him, all frivolity fled. She was aware of her body pressed against his, aware that she liked the feel of his arms around her.

"Dax?" she said.

A muscle twitched below his eye. His nostrils flared. After a long aching moment in which Jenna thought—hoped—he might kiss her, his whole body tensed, he dropped his hold and took three steps back.

Without looking at her, he grabbed his hat and jammed it down on his head.

"Let me know if you need any more furniture moved."

He wheeled away and left her standing in the living room alone.

She was getting under his skin in the worst way.

Dax tied off the end of a barbed wire strand and shoved his fencing pliers into his back pocket. For the last two hours, he'd been riding this fence line with Rowdy, checking for gaps, fixing spots and thinking about his house-keeper.

Though his body was warm from his labors, his face was cold. The shiny whiteness of the clouds along with a stiff north wind hinted at a weather change.

He hadn't slept fifteen minutes last night. Instead, he'd lain there in the dark thinking of how close he'd come to stepping over the line with Jenna. He'd never wanted to kiss anyone so much in his life. To kiss her. To hold her. Just to be with her.

To make matters worse, at least for him, after taking the cupcakes to Gavin's school, she'd returned bubbling over with chatter and goodwill. If she'd been affected by the near kiss she didn't let on. A man could get a complex. Not that he wanted her to think anything about that moment in his arms. Maybe she hadn't noticed. Maybe she hadn't been affected. Wouldn't that be for the best?

Right. Good. She'd gone to Gavin's school and had a great time. She'd forgotten all about his unfortunate lapse in judgment.

A shaft of wind slid down the back of his neck. He flipped his collar up.

From the way Jenna had behaved at dinner, you'd think she'd never been in a school building in her life. She'd been all giddy and thrilled to eat cafeteria food and have kindergartner's wipe snot on what he was certain was a very expensive skirt.

Something was going on with Gavin, too. Last night, he'd found the little dude playing quietly in the nursery. He claimed to be guarding baby Sophie so she wouldn't get scared. From a kid who'd always been scared of his own shadow, the gesture was a puzzle.

But then so was his housekeeper. A puzzle and a disturbance.

"Been meaning to ask you something, boss." Rowdy shot a cocky grin his way.

"Yeah?" Dax squinted toward the clouds gathering in the west. Maybe the wind would blow in some much-needed moisture. They'd been irrigating the winter wheat for weeks now.

"How's your new housekeeper working out?"

The question, given he couldn't get Jenna out of his head, caught him completely off guard. He gazed at the clouds another second before turning a squint-eyed gaze at Rowdy. "All right. Why?"

"Just wondering about her. She's single. Pretty. Curved in all the right places."

Dax studied his hand for a moment, not liking the direction of this conversation. "She's a new mother."

He stuck a foot in a stirrup and swung up into the saddle. Rowdy looped a roll of wire over the saddle horn and guffawed. "You're getting old, Dax, if that's all you see."

Thirty-four sounded older every day, but Dax didn't much appreciate the reminder. And he sure wasn't going to tell Rowdy the truth.

"She's doing her job, cooks great food I've never heard of and looks after Gavin." The boy adored her, followed her like a pup hungry for her smiles and hugs. The behavior was pitiful if he thought about it, but he was glad to see Gavin happy.

Rowdy swung into the saddle and they urged the horses to a walk, examining fence line as they rode while keeping an eye out for strays. "What about you?"

Dax ruminated a beat. "What about me?"

"You know what I'm talking about. She taking good care of you, too?"

Dax didn't like Rowdy's implication, though he supposed no insult was intended. The young cowboy was comfortable with horses, cattle and women. Lots of women. Naturally, his r oving eye would land on the only female within fifteen miles. What man with any juice in his veins wouldn't notice Jenna?

"She's a good employee."

Rowdy, holding the reins with a light hand, rose in his stirrups and twisted around, squinting toward a pond dam. "That's all?"

No.

"That's all." Dax heard the growl in his voice, felt the prickle of jealousy beneath his skin.

The saddle creaked as Rowdy settled in again. "Then I guess you won't mind if I stop by the house and pay my respects, maybe ask her out sometime."

Dax rubbed a sleeve across his face, more to avoid looking at his employee than to scratch an itch. What could he say without admitting that he was attracted to his too-young housekeeper? "She stays pretty busy."

"You can't work her 24-7, boss. Every woman likes a night out. Considering she had a kid, she's probably hankering to get away once in a while."

Dax bit down on his molars. Why hadn't he considered that?

As soon as the thought crossed his mind, he mentally kicked himself. He hadn't thought of it because he couldn't, no more than he could consider kissing her. Jenna was out of his league in more ways that one. "She's not your type, Rowdy. Leave her alone. There are plenty of girls in Saddleback waiting for you to call."

Rowdy didn't answer and they rode on, but Dax couldn't get the worry out of his head. He had no right to keep Jenna from having a life. She and that pink princess of hers needed a man to look after them, though she'd probably poison his potato frittata if she heard him say such a thing. Women were testy about that independence business nowadays. But R owdy was probably right. She needed to get out, make friends, do things that young people do. Get away from the likes of him.

Maybe he should encourage a relationship between his

housekeeper and his best ranch hand. Maybe if he did, he could stop thinking about her so much. About her fancy voice and her honey-brown eyes and kissable mouth. About the sweet way she catered to her baby—and his son. About her silvery laugh that caused a catch in his chest as though he couldn't quite breathe.

A cord of tension crept across his shoulders and up the back of his neck. He hoped he wasn't getting one of those headaches—blasted, debilitating things. They made him feel like some kind of sissy.

He kicked the horse into a trot and headed across pasture, leaving the other cowboy in the dust. The rush of wind in his face cleared his thinking.

He'd brought Jenna here to the Southpaw. She was his responsibility. Rowdy might be a good worker, but he was fast and loose with the ladies. Jenna deserved better than that.

Yesterday's near kiss was still on Jenna's mind as she bathed Sophie. She'd mulled over the incident off and on all day, finally coming to a conclusion. She had overreacted. Considering his normal behavior at dinner last night, Dax had already forgotten. Either that or he hadn't been about to kiss her at all.

She heard the back door open. A glance at the elephant clock on the armoire had her frowning. Dax hadn't come in for lunch and the time was long past, though he often skipped the noon meal in favor of work. But someone was certainly here now.

A quiver of concern passed over her. Was something wrong? Worse yet, had someone else come into the house?

Lifting Sophie from her tub, she wrapped the slick little body in a soft, hooded terry cloth towel and went to find out.

Dax stood in the kitchen. He looked weary as he rummaged through the cabinets searching for something. Weary and masculine. She fought back the memory of those strong arms holding her.

"May I help you find something?" she asked. He'd tossed his hat on the counter along with his jacket. His hair was mussed, his shoulders tense. Body heat and cold air radiated from him.

"Aspirin." He rubbed the back of one hand over his eyes.

"Headache?"

He nodded, looking at her through bloodshot eyes with an expression of both embarrassment and suffering.

"I rearranged the cabinets," she said. "All medicines are now in the master bath out of Gavin's reach. I'll get the pain reliever."

Pressing Sophie's still damp body against her shoulder, she started in that direction. Dax followed. "I can manage."

She let him pass her in the hallway, noticing his usual cow-boy swagger was more of a stagger. "Dax. You're sick."

She followed him into the master bath, squelching the hint of impropriety. "Go lie down. I'll get this."

He lifted one arm halfway then let it drop in surrender. "Thanks."

He staggered out of the bathroom. Jenna stared after him.

He really *was* sick. And she was worried. Dax was cowboy tough, almost stoic.

With Sophie in arms, balancing the aspirin and water was a trick, but she managed. By the time she entered the bed-room, Dax was sprawled, fully dressed on a massive brown-and-blue comforter. He levered up on one elbow to accept the medication, then eased back down. His eyes were barely focusing now and his forehead glistened with sweat.

Without giving the action much thought, she lay Sophie next to him and touched his forehead. His skin felt both hot and clammy. He shivered.

"Should I call the doctor?" she asked, growing more worried by the minute.

"No," he murmured. "Just close the blinds and keep Gavin quiet. I'll be fine."

"You aren't fine, Dax. You're really sick." Too sick to re-move his dirty boots.

When she tugged them off, he didn't protest. Oh yes, he was definitely sick. She went into the bathroom and returned with a cool, damp cloth. Dax didn't open his eyes but as she placed the cloth over his forehead, he sighed.

"You might feel better undressed." Her face heated to say such a thing, but the man was miserable.

"Later." Voice weak, he lifted a weak hand. "Go."

Gathering Sophie, she did as he commanded, backing out slowly, her gaze on him as long as possible. What was wrong? What if something terrible happened to Dax? He wasn't one to complain and in fact, she'd noticed the way he shrugged off hurts such as Gavin's bloody nose and his own more recent run-in with an angry cow that had left him with a dis-located finger. With gritted teeth, he'd yanked the joint back into place, slapped some ice on it and never mentioned the accident again.

This was something worse than a dislocation.

Fretting, she dried and dressed Sophie and rocked her for a while. The presence of her daughter soothed her nerves. When Sophie fell asleep again, Jenna put her to bed and tip-toed across the long house to Dax's door.

Peeking through the crack she'd left, she saw a white rim around his lips and the frown of misery between his dark eyebrows.

When Gavin arrived home from school, she met him in the foyer with a finger to her lips. "Your daddy is not feeling very well, Gavin. We need to be extra quiet okay?"

Nodding sagely, the boy placed his schoolbag on the table and slid off his coat, taking special care to make no noise.

"Is it one of his headaches?" he whispered.

"Does your dad often suffer from bad headaches?"

"I can't remember what they're called. Grains, I think. Yeah, that's it. Dad calls them his grains. They're bad."

"Migraines?" she asked, amused at the child's misunderstanding.

The little face screwed up in sympathy. "You get 'em, too?"

"No, sweetheart. Thankfully, I have never suffered with the malady but I have encountered it." Her mother had them at convenient times. Somehow she doubted Dax's were the same. "Will you help me keep Sophie quiet in the nursery tonight so your daddy can recuperate?"

"Yep, but I got homework. The letter *E. E* is for *egg.*"

"Very good. Can you think of anything else that starts with the sound of *egg?*"

"Elephant. Like that clock in Sophie's room." He screwed up his face. "*Elephant* and *egg* and *egg-cited.*"

Jenna's lips twitched. *"Excited?"*

"Yep. The way I feel about Christmas. I'm getting a bulldozer and a dump trunk. We're having a party at school, too."

"You are?"

"Yep. Miss Jenna?" He pulled papers from his bag and carried them to the kitchen table. "Are you coming back to my school?"

"I have to ask your father about it, but I hope to." The day at Gavin's elementary school had been one of the most interesting and enjoyable times she could remember. She'd never been in a public school classroom. The sounds and smells and colorful decor had captivated her. She'd read with a group of children, listened to their adorable chatter, and after serving cupcakes had helped put them down on little mats for a rest. When the teacher had asked her about volunteering once a week, calling her a natural with the kids, she'd been flattered and promised to give the offer some thought. But the answer had to come from Dax. He paid her to be here at the ranch.

"Noah said you're pretty. He said Dad probably likes you." Head bent as he carefully traced the letter *E,* his voice innocent as a lamb, he said, "I told him yes. Dad likes you a lot. Maybe Sophie will be my sister now."

With a pang, Jenna patted his back and headed for the kitchen to prepare dinner. This was Gavin's obsession with having a sibling and nothing more.

She took the marinated beef from the refrigerator, pausing with one hand on the oven dial.

Did Dax like her? She hoped so. She liked her job, loved the beauty of this austere country and was falling fast for Gavin. Most of all, she was safe here. In the days since Sophie's birth, she'd traveled into Saddleback, shopped, had lunch with Crystal, all without hearing mention of the runaway heiress from Pennsylvania.

Her life here grew fuller and more fulfilling every day. She could easily think of Texas as home, and as long as she and her daughter were free of the smothering pressures of her former lifestyle, Jenna didn't care if she was a domestic forever.

As she prepared dinner, she helped Gavin with his work, praised as he practiced writing his name in a laborious hand. She couldn't help thinking this was what a normal family life should be.

When the meal was complete, she debated about disturbing Dax. In the end, she prepared a plate of the beef tournedos and covered it. Though he'd teased her this morning about serving him tornadoes for dinner, she'd looked forward to his reaction to the delicious recipe. But that would have to wait. When and if he felt like eating, his meal would be ready.

After dinner, Gavin asked permission to play with his cars and dinosaurs in Sophie's room. Jenna adjusted the nursery monitor to keep an eye on both children as she cleaned the kitchen. When she poured dishwasher detergent into the holder inside the machine, she grimaced. A few days ago, she'd made the mistake of using laundry detergent. The result had flooded the tile with soapsuds. Gavin had been gleeful over the turn of events and Dax had laughed. She pretended to have accidentally picked up the wrong box, but in truth, she hadn't known the difference. She knew now.

Drying her hands on a dish towel, she checked the monitor again and heard Gavin's voice quietly telling the sleeping Sophie about an incident at school. With a smile, Jenna headed toward the master bedroom to peek in on Dax. As she approached the door, she heard him groan.

She pushed the door open. His covers were a rumpled mess. His hair shot in a dozen directions as though he'd yanked at it in agony.

"Dax?" she whispered.

Bloodshot eyes opened, then closed again, but not before she saw the pain. Needing to help, she went to Dax's office and searched the Internet. The World Wide Web had been her salvation during these days of learning to be a domestic engineer. She liked that term. Now, she searched until she found simple techniques for alleviating the pain of a migraine.

Back in Dax's bedroom, she wet another cloth and replaced the warm one, then eased onto the edge of the bed. Without asking permission, she began to gently massage his temples.

His eyes fluttered open to look at her in glazed curiosity, but he was clearly in too much pain to say anything beyond, "That helps."

She continued the gentle, circular strokes, praying he would find relief. When he tugged at the neck of his shirt, Jenna said, "Would you be more comfortable out of these clothes? I would be happy to assist."

Well, perhaps not happy but willing. The idea of seeing Dax unclothed made her belly quiver.

His body tensed and she could see him holding his breath. Then he exhaled but didn't answer.

Bracing herself to do what was best for her employer, Jenna unbuttoned his shirt. He had a magnificent chest and shoulders. Any woman would notice. She had the craziest urge to smooth her palm over the curved pectorals and discover if they were as rock-hard as she suspected.

Her pulse hammered against her throat. Her fingers tingled at the touch of him. Foolish, silly woman. The man was ill.

With steely resolve, she pushed the sleeves over his shoulders and slid them down his arms. He grunted once. She paused, afraid she'd hurt him.

With the shirt discarded, Jenna drew a deep breath and reached for the silver belt buckle. A hand stopped her. Jenna's gaze flew up to meet his.

Nostrils flared, he grumbled, "I'll do this."

She nodded and backed toward the door. "If you need me…"

"In a minute."

Did that mean he wanted her to return? She stepped outside the room, checked the portable monitor in her pocket to be sure the children were safe, and waited.

She heard rustling and footsteps, then the give of the bed. Her heart beat in her throat and she felt flushed. An embarrassing situation, no doubt, but there was more to her discomfort than that.

"Jenna." The word was slurred.

She reentered the room, finding Dax in string-drawn lounge pants and nothing else. He'd replaced the damp cloth, covering his eyes. His chest rose and fell with the effort of his movements.

Jenna stepped to the bed and reclaimed her place on the edge. Determined to help this man who had helped her, she placed the baby monitor within her line of vision and as gently as she knew how, began to massage his temples again.

"Rest," she whispered. "Relax."

He inhaled deeply and exhaled on a sigh.

She massaged until her fingers numbed and her wrists ached but she refused to stop. Dax hadn't abandoned her when the going had been rough with Sophie, and she would not abandon him.

After the longest time, the tension eased from Dax's body.

His breathing grew deep and even. The furrow between his brows smoothed.

With a tenderness that shook her, Jenna let her fingers drift down his temples, over the whisker-roughened jaw where she paused at the corners of his remarkable mouth.

Relaxed in sleep, he looked young and vulnerable. And incredibly male.

Stunned at the tender feelings he aroused in her, Jenna quietly eased off the bed and slipped from the room.

CHAPTER TEN

THE DAWN HAD YET TO BREAK when Dax entered the kitchen, drawn there by the scent of fresh coffee. He felt washed-out but infinitely better, the rampaging pain but a fading nightmare.

As bad as the dream had been, there had been a good part, too. Jenna. Even in the fog of a migraine, he'd been aware of her soft hands touching him, easing the throb in his temples, sliding his shirt from his body. Had he not been so ill—well, he had been. Otherwise, she would not have taken such liberties.

Yet he remembered.

This morning, Jenna was nowhere to be seen, but from the looks of things she was up and busy, probably tending Sophie. From what he'd gathered, she rose with the baby around six and never let up again until bedtime. He'd seen the fatigue around her eyes, felt a twinge of guilt for working her so hard, but she never complained and any suggestion that she ease up seemed to trouble her. He didn't know why. There was no chance of her being fired, though he figured she didn't know that yet.

After last night, when she'd tended him like a baby, her job was safe for as long as she wanted it.

He was embarrassed at his weakness, but she'd responded with such genuine care. This morning would tell the tale, though. He would know when he looked in her eyes if she considered him less of a man. Reba had.

He poured a thick brown mug full of steaming brew, dumped in two spoons of sugar and stirred. His housekeeper was still a mystery. In the back of his mind a nagging voice claimed she hadn't come completely clean about her reasons for being here. Sometimes she seemed to be looking over her shoulder. Other times she embraced the mundane business of life with the exuberance of a child experiencing things for the first time.

But Dax didn't care where she'd come from or why she'd chosen to stay here. He was simply glad she had.

She'd figured out Gavin faster than a flea hops and the little dude responded like a dry sponge. He was grateful, though his growing feelings for his housekeeper went deeper than gratitude. Every day he reminded himself that she was too young, too smart and pretty and refined. She was wise, too, as if she had an old soul.

With a grunt at his fanciful thoughts, he stepped to the sink and deposited the spoon there for later cleanup. The window over the sink looked out on the backyard and beyond to the barns and corrals and separating pens. The first shifting of dawn's white-pink light cast a halo over the peaceful, drowsy ranch.

The beauty had particular significance this morning now that the Coleman curse of migraines had run its course and he'd survived.

He loved gazing out at the land he'd purchased from the rest of his family. No one else loved the ranch the way he did. No one else could tolerate the long days and 24-7 demands of the cowboy life. Most of all no one wanted to live out here far from the rest of civilization.

Which brought him back to his housekeeper. She seemed to relish the place and even if the pleasure was an act, he'd take it. He'd found her in the horse barns one day, Sophie attached to her front like a baby monkey on some kind of sling thing. He'd been surprised to hear that she had equestrian skills as she called them and after watching her with the horses for a while, he'd believed her. He'd offered to let her ride sometime, refraining from actually offering to ride along with her. No use being stupid.

After Rowdy's comments, though, he was having second thoughts. As much as he liked his ranch hand, he didn't want Rowdy messing with Jenna. She was too sweet and tender and innocent. Rowdy was a rounder.

He sipped his coffee, sighed out his pleasure in such a simple thing as good coffee and sunrise, and leaned against the sink to watch. The silent sun shimmered just beneath the horizon, casting up hints of the coral and yellow to come. The morning sun was magical to him, bringing with it the promise of a new, clean day, uncluttered by yesterday's suffering.

He chuckled and shook his head. He was feeling poetic this morning.

From the corner of his eye he saw movement on the long, back porch and turned in that direction. A figure—Jenna— huddled beneath a blanket on the cedar bench he rarely used. Once, he'd planned for the backyard and patio to be a place for family and friends to gather, a place to watch his children play and grow. Those plans, like so many others, had died in their infancy.

After pouring a second cup of coffee complete with cream, the way Jenna liked it, he eased the back door open with his hip and joined her.

"Good mornin'," he said. Standing with legs wide he breathed in the crisp, clean morning. The air was still as death, though he knew the wind would get up later on. Winter encroached on the perfect fall.

"Good morning." Her voice was a soft melody, blending with the hush of daybreak. "Feeling better?"

He nodded. "Much. Thanks to you."

He watched her eyes, held his breath and waited for the disgust or disappointment he expected. When none was forthcoming, Dax accepted the fact that Jenna Garwood was even more special than he'd originally thought.

"I'm glad."

He held out the mug. "Careful. It's hot."

Expression quizzical, she accepted his offering, wrapping both hands around the cup before sipping daintily. "Thank you."

"Enough cream?"

"Perfect." She started to rise. "I'll finish breakfast now."

The blanket slid away. He replaced it and guided her back down, adding a reassuring squeeze to the delicate bones of her shoulder. "Stay. Weekends are lazy. No rush."

Jenna settled readily and sipped again at the cup. Steam curled upward, wrapping her face in a mist, as if she were a genie who'd appeared to grant his fondest wishes. Ah, if only it were so. But Dax Coleman was the worst kind of realist, a man who barely believed in people, certainly not in pregnant genies. Though if he could believe in anyone, after last night he might believe in Jenna.

Fool that he was.

Turned sideways on the bench, Jenna drew her legs up close to her body and arranged the long ends of a robe and the fleece blanket over them. Her feet peeked out, pink and elegant the way he'd remembered. He hadn't thought about her feet, about those pink-tipped toes, in days. Funny how he wished for an excuse to touch the smooth, soft skin again.

She patted the empty end of the bench. "I'll share my space with you."

Dax hesitated, wondering if spending nonworking time with the housekeeper was a good idea. Considering his fanciful thoughts this morning, it wasn't.

Her mouth curved in a soft smile. "It's so beautiful out here. People should take the time to enjoy these moments."

Hadn't he been thinking the same thing? He eased onto the far end of the bench and leaned forward, letting the coffee cup dangle between his knees. The space between him and Jenna was limited, though, and her toes grazed the side of his thigh. He tried not to think about it but the knowledge that only a layer of denim separated his skin from hers lingered.

"I try to find a few minutes to come out here every morning," she said, her voice soft and dreamy.

He hadn't known that. "No wonder you look tired."

She smiled. "Do I? I'm not really. I'm—" She stopped and sipped at the cup again.

He swiveled his head sideways just enough to watch the thoughts and feelings flit through her eyes. Even in the semi-light, her eyes shone with an inner strength and beauty that had him mesmerized. He didn't know when he'd begun thinking of her this way. Maybe he was still asleep with the remnants of the cursed headache impairing his mental function, but the woman was messing with his mind. As hard as he tried to remember she was hardly out of her teens, he failed more often than not.

And last night, she'd offered to undress him.

A white-hot blaze flared in his gut. He tamped it down, glad for the chill morning, though even the fiercest winter wouldn't have cooled the fire Jenna had started inside him.

This morning she was rumpled and uncombed, still in her robe, the likes of which he'd never seen. It was expensive; he knew that much from watching Reba spend like a queen, but even she had never had anything like this. Jenna's urgent need for a job didn't fit with the fancy clothes or the air of upper-crust breeding she wore like a princess. Had her cheating husband left her penniless? Had he taken everything and caused her to run away in shame, destitute?

"You're what?" he asked, picking up the conversation, wanting to know more than he should have, but not willing to ask the questions about her husband. Had she loved him? Did she still?

"Mmm, I don't know how to express it." Her shoulders lifted. "Grateful, I suppose."

He'd wanted her to say happy. How dumb was that? No woman had ever been happy here. Not his mother or his sister or his ex-wife. Too far from the city. Too far from civilization. Too far from friends and shopping malls.

"Different from where you're from, I suspect."

She made a small amused sound. "Oh, yes. Very different."

He couldn't help himself. "Is that a good thing or a bad thing?"

The early-morning quiet, the intimacy of Jenna in her housecoat and blanket, and him remembering the touch of her cool hands against his temples had him talking in ways he wouldn't normally have.

"A very good thing. A person can feel safe here. Free."

He wondered at the assessment, so different from Reba's. She'd felt confined and alone. Jenna felt safe and free. Though he wondered at how such a young woman could know otherwise, another hitch in the terrible knot beneath his heart loosened.

"Wide-open spaces, fresh air, can't beat 'em."

She inhaled deeply. "Just smell that, Dax. So clean and pure." She touched his shirtsleeve. "I smell winter."

Resisting the urge to put his hand over hers, Dax smiled and looked toward the horizon. She had a cute way of putting things.

"You probably smell rain blowing up from the Gulf. Anyway, I hope you do. Lord knows we need it."

"Do we?"

We. He didn't miss the pronoun. "Always need rain out here. That's why we irrigate."

"Ah." She tilted her head in acknowledgment. "What is that sound?"

Dax listened, hearing only the usual noises of a Texas dawn. "Birds, hungry calves bawling for mama."

"No, that other sound. The popping."

His lips curved against the rim of his coffee cup. He'd lived so long with the noises he hardly heard them anymore. "Oil wells somewhere. Could be miles away. Out here sound travels forever."

"We don't have those in—back East."

That tiny pause caught in Dax's thoughts. What was it about her past that she wanted to hide? Why didn't she want him to know her hometown?

He mentally rolled his eyes. *Get a clue, Coleman. Women like an escape route.* Last night meant nothing beyond an employee showing kindness. Get over it.

The back door groaned open. Gavin poked his head out. "Dad?"

Both adults turned toward the sound.

"Out here, son."

Dressed in flannel pajamas, his dark hair sticking up in horns all over his head, Gavin stumbled out onto the porch. "What are you doing?"

"Talking. Watching the sunrise."

Gavin's face screwed up tight. "Is it time to get up?"

"Only if you want to."

"Okay." He scratched at his underarm, clearly bewildered by the adults' behavior. "Dad?"

"What?"

"Is your grain better?"

"My what?"

Jenna chuckled softly and touched Dax's arm. They exchanged glances. "My grains. Your grains. Understand?"

The light dawned in Dax's eyes.

"Yes, son," he said. "My headache is gone, thanks to Jenna."

"And me. I was real quiet."

"Yes, you were," Jenna said. "You helped me with Sophie, too."

"Yeah." The dark-haired child stretched, yawning loudly. "It's cold out here. Dad?"

The adults shared another amused glance. "What, son?"

"Can Jenna come to my school again? She wants to, don't you Miss Jenna?"

"Yes, I do, but that's entirely up to your father."

"Why would I care if you went to Gavin's school?"

"They'd like me to volunteer one day a week."

"You want to?"

"Very much, but my first duty is here."

Duty. For some inexplicable reason, the word chafed like starched pants. "Gavin is part of that duty. But you have a life, too, Jenna. You aren't a slave here."

"I know, but I want to do the right thing."

"Volunteer. It will be good for both of you." Good for him, too, not to be thinking about her in his house every minute of the day.

She smiled. "Yes, I believe so, too."

Her smile touched a sore spot inside him. The chafing evaporated. Hadn't he been thinking she needed to get out more?

"This reminds me of something I've been meaning to discuss with you." Since the conversation with Rowdy, the thoughts hadn't let up. Along with a near kiss over a rearranged couch, thinking about her had probably given him the migraine. A woman had needs, even a woman with a new baby. Maybe especially then. He didn't want her getting dissatisfied and running off. Though anyone with half a brain would tell you that Dax Coleman no more knew how to make a woman happy than he could sprout wings and fly. But he had to try.

She was a good cook. Gavin needed her. Things ran smoother since she'd come. He needed to keep her happy.

That gnat of a voice buzzing inside his head said he liked having her around, too, but he swatted it. No use thinking the impossible.

"You want to discuss something?" Jenna tilted her head, one finely shaped eyebrow upraised. "Is it something I'm not doing correctly?"

There were lots of those but he wasn't going there. Who cared about pink socks or a fork down the garbage disposal when she served beef tournedos and salmon roulade—and he wasn't even a fish eater.

"You're doing great," he managed, though complimentary words came out of his throat like opening a rusted door.

That smile came again, tickling his stomach. Dax fidgeted, turning the warm mug in his hands. He wasn't doing this for her smiles. It was self-preservation, plain and simple. He needed a housekeeper who would stick around.

"No woman likes being stuck on a ranch all the time. You need to get out now and then."

Jenna went silent. He shifted a glance in her direction. What he saw troubled him. Gnawing that pretty lip of hers, she looked worried.

What did she have to be worried about?

The notion that she was running from something—or someone—came back to haunt him. He'd vowed to protect her and the little pink princess. He couldn't do much else but he could do that. If someone was after her, they'd have to come through him.

The vehemence of the sentiment stunned him.

"I just mean—" What did he mean? Rowdy said women needed to go out and have fun. If he wanted to keep her happily employed, he'd have to make that happen. Though not with Rowdy.

"I thought we might go to a movie," he blurted. "Dinner, too, if you want." He couldn't believe he'd said that.

"You want to take me to a movie?" she asked.

Dax swallowed. Could he handle spending more time with a woman who was already messing with his head? And exactly when had he starting thinking of her as a woman?

"I don't want you to feel trapped here. A night out is good for you now and then. I don't want to put any pressure on you, either. I mean, you're my employee so if you don't want to go, that's fine. Just feel free to go out on your own or with someone else any time you feel like it. Don't let the job stop you. That's what I meant." The last statements ground against him like a handful of rocks in his boot. He didn't want her going out with anyone. "Not one of the hands, though. These cowboys. You can't trust them." He was babbling.

Jenna looked at him as if the headache had caused more mental stress than she'd originally thought. Maybe it had.

Gavin, on the other hand, had come to life. With enough glee to start his own clown act, he began hopping up and down on one foot, slapping his arms. "Say yes, Miss Jenna. Dad will even spring for a Friendly Meal. Won't you, Dad?"

"Oh, Gavin, you charmer." Jenna pressed a hand to her lips and laughed.

Dax's shoulders relaxed. He grinned. "Yeah, I'm a big spender."

Jenna's amused gaze captured Dax's. "Then I shall be delighted to accept your kind invitation. A movie and a Friendly Meal it shall be."

No matter how hard he tried to convince himself he was doing this to keep her happy as well as safely away from Rowdy, Dax realized one thing. He was in big trouble.

CHAPTER ELEVEN

A MOVIE. DAX WAS TAKING her to a movie.

Jenna couldn't keep the smile off her face as she dressed that evening. What did one wear to a movie?

She opened the closet and browsed, regretting the decision to leave her dress clothes behind. The only public movie she'd ever attended was a premiere in New York. Derek had insisted on going, and later she'd realized he was enamored of the starlet who had invited them. She had deplored the ostentatious glitz and posturing, preferring the privacy of their home theater.

A regular movie outing would likely be different. Most people—*normal* people—did not wear Versace gowns to a movie.

Which was fine with Jenna. She'd left the gowns behind with the rest of her life. From her knowledge of the people of Saddleback, she was certain a movie was not a black-tie affair.

The hangers scraped over the metal bar as she sorted through the clothes she'd brought with her. Up to now she'd mostly worn her loose-fitting maternity outfits, but with her tummy regaining shape, she took out a pair of jeans, a long-sleeved top and a pink leather jacket. They weren't Western wear by any stretch of the imagination, but they would do.

She slithered into the jeans, a snug fit, and spritzed eau de parfum in all the right places before sliding the blouse over her head. In front of the mirror, she turned this way and that, casting a critical eye on her appearance. She might not be beautiful, but she knew how to put herself together for the best effect. A Carrington always kept up appearances.

Her hair had lost its trendy cut, but a few minutes with a straightener and some shine serum made it presentable. Humming, she slipped on jewelry and heels, then went to dress the baby for their first night out in Saddleback, Texas.

By the time she entered the living room to await the men of the group, her palms were damp with excitement.

Gavin appeared first, strutting through the house with his chest puffed out, his black-brown hair slicked down and dressed in perfectly creased jeans and a red button-down shirt. His boots gleamed with a fresh polish.

"My goodness. You look immaculate."

"Yeah," he said proudly, craning his neck to one side. "Smell me." He pointed to a spot on his neck. "Right there. Daddy put me on some of his smell-good."

With an inward smile, Jenna inhaled loudly. "Wonderful." If Dax smelled this delicious, she might swoon.

The man in question ambled down the hall into sight. Jenna's heart banged once hard against her rib cage. He was definitely swoonworthy.

"Everyone ready?"

"Yearning for that Friendly Meal," she joked.

"Yeah," Gavin sighed. "I love Friendly Meals."

The adults exchanged glances. For a nanosecond their gazes locked and a feeling of pure pleasure danced between them.

"No headache?" she asked.

He touched his temple. "Good as new."

She reached for Sophie's carrier, but Dax nudged her out of the way. "I've got the princess. You grab the diaper bag."

She did as he said, covertly watching her employer tap the

baby's nose and make faces at her. Sophie, her usual drowsy self, let her eyes cross and then closed them as Dax draped a blanket over the entire baby seat.

Feeling happy in a way she had never dreamed possible, Jenna walked alongside Dax and Gavin out the door and to his truck.

She helped Dax position the car seat in the back with Gavin and smiled her thanks when he helped her into the cab, closed the door and grinned at her through the glass before jogging around to the driver's side.

Yes, indeed, being a normal, everyday woman was beginning to feel very, very good.

Dax sat across the orange plastic table from Jenna watching her and Gavin devour French fries with the same zeal. He'd tried to take them someplace nicer, but she'd insisted on the burger joint. He was sure she'd done so for Gavin's sake and he appreciated that, but she deserved a classier establishment.

Part of him wanted to be sorry he'd asked her out, but tonight he just wanted to laugh and have a good time. When was the last time he'd done that? He didn't even know. From the looks of Gavin, hanging upside down inside the indoor playland, he felt the same. His squeals of laughter mingled with those of a dozen other kids out for a good time on Saturday night.

Dax looked around the colorful dining area, raising a hand to acknowledge a person here and there. He knew most people in Saddleback but hadn't seen them all that much during the last few years. It struck him that the world was moving right along without him to the detriment of his son.

Reba had driven him into a shell. Jenna was bringing him out.

"You have ketchup on your face," he said, pointing.

She took a paper napkin and swiped. "Did I get it?"

"Here." He leaned across the table, took the napkin and cleaned away the drop on her upper lip. "Messy."

The smell of her perfume had driven him batty in the truck, and now he smelled those flowers again. He sat back but the scent lingered in his nostrils.

"You look pretty tonight," he said and then wanted to jam a handful of fries down his throat and strangle himself. He'd brought her out as a means of keeping her employed, not to admire how good she looked in those jeans and that pricey-looking jacket.

Right, and all his cows would jump over the moon at midnight.

Her smile took away the urge to hurt himself. "Thank you. I wasn't sure what to wear."

Women. From the curve of golden hair against her slim face to the silver dangling from her wrist and ears, Jenna was a knockout. "You look great. Perfect." Shut up, Dax.

A hint of pink crested her cheekbones. "What time does the movie start?"

Relieved at the change of subjects, he checked his watch. "Soon. We'd better round up the boy and head that way."

Jenna nodded and began piling discarded wrappers and cups onto the plastic tray before following him to the yellow-and-red tube slide.

"Gavin, come on, son. Time to go."

"He's having such fun."

"Yeah. I liked this stuff when I was a kid, too." An odd look crossed her face. "Didn't you?"

She shook her head. "I've never played on one."

As if she'd said something wrong, she turned away to fiddle with Sophie. Dax studied her, baffled. She'd never played on a playground?

"Why not?"

"Oh, it's not important. Look, here's Gavin," she said a little too brightly as if they hadn't just seen the boy moments ago when he was dancing in ecstasy over a Friendly Meal t oy.

Whatever troubled Jenna about the past, she didn't want to talk about it. Dax decided to let the moment slide. He'd suggested this outing for her pleasure and he wasn't about to mess things up if he could help it. But one of these days Miss Jenna was going to talk to him.

One of these days.

The drive to the movie was a matter of blocks. Once inside the small theater, Dax paid for the tickets. The smell of popcorn enticed Gavin, so they stopped at the concession stand, as well. Cheesy-looking Christmas garland looped from the ceiling, and the walls were plastered with colorful posters of upcoming holiday movies. A cheap, fa ke Christmas tree stood in one corner of the lobby, lights blinking in lazy cheer. Dax would swear it was the same tree from six or s even years ago.

Jenna stared around with a half smile as if thrilled with the decor. While he waited for the slowest clerk in Texas to fill his order, Jenna gazed around, watching the good folks of Saddleback mingle and talk.

Teenagers swarmed the lobby, holding hands and talking too loud over the video games. Dax thought of how Jenna belonged more with them than with him. Though he felt a little better to see she had a serene maturity they all lacked.

He watched her soaking it all in, an enchanted expression on her face, as if attending a two-screen theater in a tiny town was the coolest thing ever. That was Jenna. She had a way of making a celebration out of everyday life.

The clerk finally brought their order.

"Ready?" he said to Jenna.

She nodded, the light of excitement in her eyes almost too much to believe.

Balancing popcorn and sodas along with Sophie and her gear, they wandered down the semilit aisle to a row of seats.

Jostling elbows and baby carrier, they settled in and the

movie started. The loud music startled Sophie who began to whimper. Jenna removed her from the carrier and rocked her back and forth until she settled. The baby scent mingled with popcorn and the distinctive smell of a movie theater. Dax kicked back and relaxed with his snacks. Might as well enjoy himself.

The animated Christmas film had Gavin giggling from the get-go. Thirty minutes in, though, he had to go to the bathroom. When they returned, Sophie was fussing again and Jenna grappled in the dark for a bottle from the diaper bag.

Without giving the action much thought, Dax took the baby while Jenna found the bottle. When she reached for Sophie, he shook his head, taking the bottle from her.

"I got her," he whispered.

Jenna looked more grateful than he'd expected. His conscience tweaked. He'd wanted her to relax and have a good time, but here she was wrestling the fussy baby.

He slipped the bottle into Sophie's mouth. She latched on like a baby 'possum.

Maybe he should have gotten a babysitter, but he'd never hired a sitter and didn't know where to start. Besides, the children made for a good buffer, so the night out didn't feel like a date. It was more like a family outing.

The notion stuck in the center of his brain and wouldn't move until he examined it. Family. This was what he'd always wanted, the thing that was missing in his life, and tonight he felt as if he and Jenna and Gavin and Sophie belonged together.

He squirmed in the chair and tried to concentrate on the pink princess staring up at him as if he was some kind of hero.

When at last Sophie slept again, he handed her over to Jenna who in turn placed her in the carrier.

"Thank you," she whispered, leaning toward his ear. Her arm bumped his from shoulder to elbow. In the flickering light of animation, he saw her smile.

His stomach went airborne.

He reached for her hand and she gave it willingly.

He swallowed hard, pretended to watch the dancing elves and ignored the warning bells going off in his head.

It was only a movie, only a hand. Just that sentimental Christmasy feeling. No big deal.

Tomorrow things would return to normal.

The night air was crisp and quiet when the moviegoers returned to the Southpaw. A banana moon tilted overhead as though paying homage to the stunning spray of stars in the indigo sky.

Careful to cover her daughter against the chilled air, Jenna made her way to the door. Dax strode alongside with a sleeping Gavin slung over one shoulder.

She had never dreamed a night at a fast-food restaurant and a run-down movie theater could be such pleasure. She cast a sidelong glance at her companion. Dax was the main cause of her enjoyment. At the restaurant, he'd teased her about the amount of ketchup she'd dumped on her French fries and told her funny stories about his first few months of taking care of a newborn. Between the lines, she'd read the desperation and sorrow he must have felt. Knowing his struggle matched her own had made his humor all the more endearing.

Then they'd laughed at the funny Christmas movie, and he'd held her hand, such a simple thing, but her entire body had hummed in pleasure. She wondered what it would be like to go on a real date with him, a dangerous thought perhaps, given who she was and the things she'd kept from him. But just this once she wanted someone—a male someone—to see her as something besides a trust fund.

Everything with Derek had been a secret until after their elopement. Secret meetings and stolen kisses in the university library had meant nothing to him but money.

Dax shifted Gavin's lax body, holding on to the child with

one strong arm while he maneuvered the house key and opened the door.

"Youth and beauty before age and treachery," he teased, voice quiet.

He stood to the side, holding the door with his back while she passed through with the baby. She recalled that first day when Rowdy had crowded her in the doorway and she'd been repelled. Not so with Dax. He could stand as close as he wanted.

Of course, he didn't. He padded down the hall with the sleeping Gavin while she headed in the opposite direction to change and settle Sophie for the night, chastising herself for trying to make something significant from the evening. Dax was being kind, asking her to join in an outing with his son. That's all there was to it.

Sophie was sound asleep, rousing only slightly as Jenna changed and swaddled her for the night. After snapping on the elephant night-light, Jenna returned to the living room, hoping for an opportunity to let Dax know how much she'd enjoyed the night out.

She wasn't disappointed. Dax came down the hall toward her, rubbing the back of his neck. When he saw her standing there, he offered a crooked grin. "That boy could sleep through a tornado."

She answered with a smile. "He had fun tonight."

"Yeah. We haven't done that much." He plopped down on the couch. "I like this new arrangement."

The comment brought back the memory of that day when she'd thought he might kiss her.

"Why?"

"Because it looks nice," he said.

"No, I mean why haven't you and Gavin gone out much?"

"Oh. Good question. I don't know."

She smiled and settled on the end of the sofa, wanting to sit near again but unsure if he wanted that. "Would you like something to eat or drink?"

He looked horrified. "Are you kidding?"

"Yes. Nothing like a Friendly Meal and popcorn to fill me up."

"Sorry about that. Next time—"

He stopped but Jenna caught on the phrase. Was he thinking about a next time?

"I'm serious. I loved the Friendly Meal."

He looked dubious, but said, "For a skinny girl you can put away the fries."

"I just had a baby. I am not skinny."

His gaze roved lazily over her, not in an insolent way as Rowdy's had done, but with an appreciation that made her knees wobble.

"I had a good time," he said softly, capturing her eyes with his.

"Thank you for asking me. The evening was wonderful."

"Are you happy here, Jenna?"

What a strange question. "Happier than I've ever been in my life."

The admission came as naturally as breathing. She was happy here, living a dream, bringing her daughter up the way she'd wanted to be. Safe and free and normal.

Dax's nostrils flared.

Everything in her longed to travel the short distance down the couch to him. The memory of his almost kiss stayed with her and she saw it now reflected in his eyes.

"Jenna?" The whisker-rough voice sent tingles down her spine.

"Yes?" she whispered.

A beat of silence quivered in the air before Dax dragged a hand over his face and looked away. "I guess we should call it a night."

Jenna wilted with disappointed. When he said nothing else, only stared at the cold fireplace, Jenna rose. "Then I shall bid you good-night."

Stiffly, she left the room, not daring to look back, lest he see the longing in her face and pity her. Or worse yet, dismiss her. She'd misinterpreted his kindness, for that's all this lovely night had been.

CHAPTER TWELVE

AT HIGH NOON the next Thursday, the tables at Lydia's Lunchbox were jammed with diners. Jenna stood in the crowded entry, soaking up the sights and sounds—the clink of plates and forks, the soft laughter and conversation, the drawling accents she found so entertaining. In the back corner, she spotted a hand waving at her.

"Over here, Jenna." Crystal Wolf had become the kind of friend she'd always wanted.

"This place is really crowded today," she said as she settled into a chair.

"Lydia's is the best place in town for a light lunch. Besides, Pam's Diner is closed until after the first of the year." Crystal peeled the blanket off Sophie. "I swear, hon, she gets prettier every time I see her."

Pride swelled inside Jenna. Her little girl *was* beautiful and she looked adorable today in her hot pink mouse cap with matching jumper and shoes. "Her pointed head went away just as you predicted."

Crystal laughed. "Of course. I didn't go to nursing school for nothing. You look great, too. Wow." The other woman looked her over. "What is going on with you? You look… radiant. If having a baby makes a woman look that good, I need to have five or six."

Crystal and her husband had been married for several years but hadn't started a family.

Jenna shook out a napkin and placed it on her lap. "You saw me at my very worst in the hospital. Anything has to be an improvement on that."

"Sure, but you look different today."

"Same old me," she said, although she wondered if that was exactly the truth. Since the night out with Dax, she'd felt buoyant, excited as though something new and wonderful was just around the corner. "Must be the Christmas spirit. I'm having such fun decorating the house."

The waitress arrived and took their orders. Jenna could care less what she ate. She was delighted with the new freedom to make her own friends and go where she wanted.

Crystal patted Sophie before taking up her own napkin. "Any more domestic disasters?"

Jenna laughed. She'd told her friend about the pink socks and flooded kitchen. "Let's just say learning to be a good housekeeper is an even sharper learning curve than caring for a newborn. If Dax weren't so sweet, he would have fired me the second day."

The waitress appeared with their order of chicken salad sandwiches and veggie slices. Crystal's hand paused over the julienne carrots. "Sweet? Did you just refer to Dax as sweet?"

"Well, maybe *sweet* isn't the right word." Jenna was positive her cheeks flamed. She reached for her glass of water. "He's been very supportive and kind."

"Mmm, I see." The woman's gaze was speculative. "Looks good, too, doesn't he?"

"I'd be lying if I said no. But Dax is more than good-looking, Crystal. He's such a man, so protective and helpful." She refrained from adding that she felt safe with Dax in a way she'd seldom experienced in her childhood or her marriage. Crystal didn't know about her past. "Do you know he wouldn't allow me to move the furniture? He was afraid I'd hurt myself."

"This is getting more interesting by the minute."

Jenna reached for another cucumber slice. "You once told me that Dax Coleman was one of the good guys. You were right. Going into labor in this town was the best thing that ever happened to me. I love my job. The ranch is beautiful. Dax's little boy is a treasure. I'm even volunteering at the school every Tuesday and I'm planning a Christmas party. You're invited, of course."

"Dax is having a Christmas party?"

"Let's just say he has tentatively agreed to this whing-ding, as he calls it." She scrunched her shoulders in excitement. "It will be so much fun, and Dax could use a bit of Christmas cheer."

"There's no doubting that." Crystal stirred her cup of herbal tea and laid the spoon carefully aside. "I'm very impressed by the way you've assimilated, Jenna. When I first met you, I wasn't sure how you'd cope."

Necessity was a fast teacher. "I love it here," she said, drawing in a deep, contented breath. "I'm happier than I've ever been in my life."

Jenna hadn't meant to add the last line but her friend already knew she'd suffered heartache. She just didn't know the real reasons.

"You look happy. You sound happy." Crystal studied her over a bite of chicken salad. "That's it. That's the difference I see in you today. You're in love with Dax."

Jenna nearly choked on a drink of water. She clunked the glass onto the tabletop and stared at Crystal. Blood rushed through her head like a hard rain.

"In love?" she croaked.

Crystal tilted her head. White earrings flashed against her dark skin. "Aren't you?"

"I—" Jenna blinked. Once. Twice. She lifted a hand to her mouth. "Oh dear."

"Honey!" A warm hand closed over Jenna's arm and gave it a shake. "That's fantastic. I'm so happy for you."

"No. I don't know." She floundered. "Dax doesn't…"

"Dax doesn't what? Know you've fallen for him? Or return the feelings?"

"Both." She gripped her friend's fingers. "Promise you won't say a word."

"My lips are sealed. But let me tell you, hon, Dax Coleman is carrying a load of hurt. He may take some time and effort, but I know one thing, when that man falls, he falls hard."

Yes, Dax was the kind of man who would keep a commitment. Hadn't she seen that in the way he'd wanted to be certain she and Sophie were safe and well after the unexpected birth? Maybe that's why he'd never recovered from the divorce. "Do you know what happened with his wife?"

Crystal's long hair fell forward as she nodded. "Everyone in Saddleback knows. She left him for another man."

"After Gavin was born."

"Yes, and to make things worse, the man she ran off with was Sam Coleman, Dax's younger brother."

Jenna's stomach dropped to her shoes. "Oh no. Poor Dax."

"Some thought Reba suffered from postpartum depression, but I never believed that. She was always wild and needed constant male attention. Sam wasn't her first lover. She'd been cheating on Dax for a long time. I guess everyone knew but him."

No wonder Dax had become so reclusive. He'd been as humiliated by Reba as Jenna had been by Derek. More so. Both his spouse and his brother had betrayed him.

Jenna's conscience tugged. Wasn't it betrayal of a different kind not to tell him about her trust fund?

She fought off the worry, convinced she and Sophie were safe as long as no one knew who they were. Not even Dax.

She and Crystal went on talking, jumping from subject to subject. Crystal was a wealth of information about babies and housekeeping, Dax and the people of Saddleback, and the best places for Christmas shopping. Gaining this woman as a friend had been nothing short of a pre-Christmas miracle.

Finally, Jenna glanced at her watch. Gavin would be home soon, so the women reluctantly parted ways with the promise to meet again the following week.

All the way back to the Southpaw, Jenna mulled over the personal revelations that had come out over a chicken salad sandwich. She was falling in love with her employer, her rescuer, a man with deep emotional wounds. Gavin, though he'd never known Reba, was wounded, too. He sensed his father's pain and overprotection. The insecurity had given rise to an inner fear and a timid nature. Jenna didn't know how she understood this, but she did.

Maybe love gave a woman insight.

Casting a glance at Sophie in the rearview mirror, she smiled at the thought. What she'd had with Derek could never compare to this. She was almost ashamed to admit that Derek had been an escape route, a means to escape the prison of her life under Elaine Carrington's paranoid eye. What she felt for Dax and Gavin went deeper—all the way to the center of her heart.

The troubling conscience pressed in again. If she loved Dax, didn't he deserve to know the truth about her situation?

She bit down on her bottom lip, gnawing the skin in the same way the question gnawed away at her heart. Maybe she should tell him.

But what if she was being a fool again? What if her emotions clouded her reason? She'd thought she was in love before and look what had happened.

But this was different. Dax was different. She was different.

But Dax was not in love with her. He didn't even find her

attractive enough to kiss, a fact that had been painfully clear the night of the Christmas movie. He was good to her and Sophie, but kindness did not translate into love. Her nanny was kind. Her bodyguards were kind.

She was an employee just as they had been.

By the time she had taken Sophie into the house and had returned for the shopping bags, she was convinced that keeping quiet was the best thing to do. Any decision she made affected her daughter, and Sophie's life would not be a repeat of hers. Until she could win love on her own terms, without the lure of the Carrington fortune, Jenna would keep her secret.

Bending, she reached into the backseat for the bags. The cold wind swept through the car, beneath her jacket and made her shiver. Paper and plastic crinkled as she hurried, eager to get inside the warm house. A masculine arm snaked from behind her and latched onto a bag. Her heart reacted happily. Dax must have seen her struggling in the wind and come to assist.

She spun around, smile ready. "Dax," she started but then the pleasure drained from her.

Rowdy stood, trapping her between the car door and the backseat, a grocery bag in hand.

"Sorry, darlin', if you were expecting the boss. It's just faithful Rowdy coming to your rescue. You don't mind some help with these bags, do you?"

Jenna swallowed back her disappointment and misgivings. "Thank you. I can manage."

She bent for another bag before realizing that Rowdy was probably staring at her backside.

"Old Dax would have my hide if I let a lady handle this alone. It's cold out here." He stood too close, that insufferable grin taunting her.

Jenna sighed and tightened her jaw. She was not going to let this guy get under her skin. "As you wish, then. I'll offer my thanks if you will please be so kind as to get out of my way. My daughter is already in the house and I don't like to leave her alone."

"Yes, ma'am," he said, though his tone mocked her as he backed off. "Lead the way. I'll bring the rest."

Aware of his eyes on her, Jenna hurried inside. Perhaps she was overreacting. Perhaps the cowboy was genuine in his offer of help. But he gave her the creeps.

Rowdy followed her into the house and though she would have preferred he leave immediately, she didn't want to be rude. She began putting the groceries in the cabinets.

"You wouldn't happen to have a cold drink for a hot man, would you?"

Jenna ignored the double entendre. There was no way he had worked up a sweat in this weather.

She took a can of orange soda from the refrigerator, handed it to him and went back to work. Rowdy leaned an elbow against the granite countertop and watched her.

"I've been meaning to ask you something, Jenna."

She slid a carton of eggs onto the refrigerator rack and shut the door. Cool air wafted out. "What is it?"

"A friend of mine is having a party Saturday night. I thought you might want to get out of here, have some fun."

"Thank you for the kind offer but I have a baby."

"So we hire a sitter. I know lots of girls."

She imagined he did. "I really can't."

"Ah, come on. We'll have fun."

"I—I already have plans." It was a lie worth telling.

"Cancel them."

The man wouldn't take no for an answer.

"I'd prefer not to." She started around him.

He grabbed her elbow. His face hardened. "So what's the deal? You and Dax have something going? Is that why you won't go out with me?"

She stiffened. "I beg your pardon?"

He laughed, though the sound didn't delight. "You sure are cute when you talk prissy. Come on, Jenna, throw me a bone. I'll show you a good time."

She tugged her arm, but his fingers bit into the flesh. "Please let me go."

"On one condition."

She sighed. "I really can't go out with you. Please. I have duties here."

"What kind of duties, Jenna?" He yanked at her, pulling her so close she could smell his breath. He'd been drinking. "What exactly does Dax pay you for?"

She went as cold as ice inside. "I do not appreciate the insinuation. Please unhand me."

"Sure thing, darlin'." He pulled her closer. "Just one little kiss and I'll be on my way."

"I don't think so."

"Well, think again, honey." And his face descended.

Dax wiped his boots on the mat, eager to get inside and tell Jenna the news. That mare she liked was going to foal tonight. But first he took extra care not to track unmentionable stuff onto the clean carpet and tile. She never complained, but she'd given him the evil eye a couple of times. He did not want to make his housekeeper unhappy.

Shaking his head, he chuckled to himself. Fancy-talking Jenna with her real fur house shoes and gourmet meals was quickly becoming more than a housekeeper. She was becoming a part of his life and of Gavin's. The Christmas decor that looked like something out of a magazine wasn't the only thing full of cheer in this once-somber ranch house.

As he crossed the foyer and living room, he heard her voice. She was probably on the phone inviting someone else to the Christmas whing-ding. His smile widened. She even had him looking forward to the invasion of his privacy.

Her tone rose higher. Another voice answered. A male voice. Stomach dropping like a brick, Dax stopped to listen. What was a man doing in the kitchen with Jenna?

A flash of memory made him shudder. Reba, half-naked, in the arms of his brother.

He bit down on his back teeth and shook away the image. Jenna was not his cheating, lying wife.

Yet the dread weighing him down wouldn't go away. He started forward then stopped again to listen.

The pair in the kitchen were not murmuring love words. Jenna's voice sounded strained, frightened. Tension hummed in the air.

Adrenaline kicked in. Something was wrong.

He rounded the wall into the kitchen. His first vision was of Rowdy and Jenna, bodies pressed close. Their mouths were mere inches apart.

The memory of Reba in Sam's arms came again. Pain slammed through Dax, stealing his breath.

Stuck between Rowdy and the counter, Jenna twisted her face to one side. "Stop it, Rowdy. Stop it."

One hand came up to press at Rowdy's chest.

Dax shook his head, battling down the past to understand the present.

Jenna was not inviting Rowdy's attentions. On the contrary. She was resisting.

Relief replaced jealousy. Just as quickly a cold fury washed over him.

Fist clenched, he stormed into the kitchen. "You heard the lady, Davis. Back off."

Rowdy's grip loosened. Jenna jerked to one side, face flaming. She rubbed at her arm. Dax's fury turned white-hot. If she was hurt…

"Hey, boss." Rowdy turned slowly and raised both hands like a criminal. "Everything's cool here. No harm done."

"Doesn't look that way to me." Dax opened his fist,

clenched it again. He was half an inch from punching out his best cowboy. He flicked a glance at Jenna. "You okay?"

Still rubbing her arm, face the color of paste, she nodded. The anxiety radiating off her made him even angrier. Rowdy Davis might be a good hand, but he had no business coming into the house to harass Jenna.

Rowdy shifted backward one step, his eyes never leaving Dax's face. "I'll just be heading back to the barn then."

Dax wagged his head. "I don't think so. You're done here. For good."

Rowdy's mouth dropped. "You're not letting me go because of her, are you?"

"Yeah, I am. Get out, Rowdy, before I lose my temper."

The cowboy's mouth curled in a sneer. "Don't be stupid, Coleman. I'm the best manager around."

Dax was afraid his jaw was going to snap. "We don't need your kind here."

"What about her kind? What's the deal, boss? Why are you so jumpy about an unwed housekeeper with a brat in tow?"

Jenna's gasp drew Dax's gaze. If possible, she'd grown whiter. She pressed a shocked hand to her lips.

"She's a widow."

Rowdy laughed, an ugly sound. "Yeah, and I'm Santa Claus. Ho-ho-*ho*." The last syllable was aimed maliciously at Jenna.

Dax's restraint snapped. He drew back a fist. Before he could throw the punch, a soft hand caught his.

"Please, Dax. No."

Dax turned, incredulous. "You're defending him?"

"No. I just want him to leave me alone." Her voice quivered. "Gavin will be here soon. I don't want him to witness fisticuffs."

Jenna's concern was for Gavin, not for herself. The anger toward Rowdy increased until Dax trembled with the need for a physical release.

"Get your gear and get off my property, Davis, before I satisfy a powerful hankering to break your nose."

Rowdy postured for a few seconds, weighing his options. Apparently, he was smart enough to know when he'd lost. With a curse that Dax hadn't allowed past his own lips in years, the fired cowboy slammed out of the house.

He'd no more than cleared the room when Dax turned to Jenna. "How are you really? And don't say okay."

As she opened her mouth to reply, her lips trembled. That was his undoing. He folded her into his arms. She nestled against him, her soft breath puffing warm against his neck. Her body quivered.

So did his.

He stroked her back and murmured as he'd done the day she'd given birth. The reminder of that shared intimacy swirled inside him, provocative in a way that shook him to his boot heels. He recalled her strength and grit, her frantic concern for her infant. He recalled the way she'd looked at him as though he was the greatest hero ever.

With an inner groan, Dax squeezed his eyes shut.

A hero. He wanted to be a hero. Her hero.

He was a fool. A woman his own age had dumped him. What made him think Jenna, a woman years younger and with far more inner beauty and refinement, would think of him as anything but a worn-out old cowboy?

Yet, he went on holding her against his chest, feeling the thud of her heart so close to his that the rhythms seemed to be one.

A tangle of thoughts coursed through his head.

He wasn't falling for her. No way. It was inappropriate. She was his employee, a young mother, a *very* young mother. She thought of him as a protector, a friend, maybe even an uncle.

Yeah, that was it. An uncle.

"Dax?" Jenna murmured.

He smoothed a hand down the back of her head, over the soft hair, and filled his nostrils with her orange blossom fragrance.

He cleared his throat, thick with some troubling emotion. "Yeah?"

Jenna lifted her head from his chest and tilted her face up to look at him. "Thank you."

Her lips curved, drawing his attention.

He couldn't keep his eyes from a glance at her mouth. He'd thought about it, maybe even dreamed about it.

"Ah, Jenna."

She placed a hand against his cheek, the curved smile deepening. "My hero," she whispered. "Again."

With warning bells clanging like fire engines, Dax groaned, aware he should walk away now while he still could. He started to loosen his hold but Jenna held tight.

"Kiss me this time, Dax. Please." She tiptoed up, waiting.

The request was his undoing.

Just once, he told himself. Just this one time.

With his heart pounding in both fear and hope, Dax cupped her face and pressed his lips to hers.

CHAPTER THIRTEEN

JENNA TUCKED A BLANKET around the sleeping Sophie, kissed her velvet cheek and snapped off the overhead light, though she remained in the semidarkness gazing at her daughter while she thought about the eventful day.

The scene with Rowdy had both embarrassed and unnerved her, but Dax's reaction had shaken her to the core. She still couldn't believe he'd fired his ranch manager because of her. More than that, she couldn't believe he'd finally kissed her. Kissed her in a way she'd never been kissed. Tender and ravenous and with such care, as if she were fragile crystal in danger of shattering.

She'd wanted him never to stop, but they'd both heard the front door open and the sound of Gavin's book bag thump onto the coffee table. With a wry twist of that delicious mouth, Dax had pressed his forehead to hers, given her a look that would melt steel, then gone to greet his son.

Jenna touched a finger to her lips, feeling him there even now and foolishly wishing to repeat the pleasure. Dax Coleman, with only the touch of his mouth, had given hope to an impossible dream.

At dinner he'd been unusually quiet and thoughtful and Jenna wondered what he was thinking. Dare she dream that he was as stunned as she? For stunned she was. Stunned by the emotions roaring through her. Stunned to feel so complete in his arms. Stunned to be falling in love.

Could Dax possibly feel the same? Or was he instead filled with regret about a rash behavior?

All through the meal of beef medallions and pasta, he'd said little and afterward had left the house, using the excuse of a mare about to give birth. She'd wanted to go out to the barn with him to watch the miracle, but he hadn't asked and she didn't quite have the courage to impose.

Perhaps they both needed time to process what had happened. Her optimistic side believed he felt something special for her. He was certainly a better, braver, stronger man than Derek, but it was Derek's betrayal that kept her afraid.

Sensitive Gavin must have felt the tension between the adults because he'd been clingy and whiny all evening. She'd made a special effort to focus on him, finally bringing out the ingredients for baked dough ornaments. Working the dough with his hands and cutting the shapes seemed to ease his stress and by storytime Gavin seemed happier.

Still, when she'd put him to bed, he'd hugged her a long, heart-tugging time. After she flipped off the light and stepped into the hall, he'd called out, "Jenna."

Expecting a request for a drink, she'd said, "Yes, Gavin."

"I love you."

A perfect peace settled in her soul.

She loved him, too. She'd loved him since the first time she'd found him standing guard over Sophie's crib. With every day that passed, she loved him more.

With an ache for the little boy's hungry heart, she'd gone back into the darkened room for another hug. "I love you, too, Gavin." She'd kissed his forehead. "You're a very special boy."

Now, restless and too keyed-up to sleep, she padded down the hall toward the living room. The house still smelled warm and delicious from the cinnamon in the dough ornaments.

Tomorrow they would be cool enough to paint and string with red ribbon for hanging on the tree.

The prelit, flocked spruce Dax had brought from a storage room filled a corner of the dark living room. She plugged in the lights, basking in the beauty she and the Coleman males had created. A lighted wreath sprigged with holly, along with s wags of plush, snow-doused garland hung over the fire-place. More garland, flocked and sprinkled with tiny white lights, draped around fat red candles and down the sides of the mantel. Soon the stockings she'd been personalizing would be ready to hang.

At her parents' estate, she'd never been allowed to partici-pate in Christmas preparations other than shopping. A de-signer had always been retained for the occasion. But Jenna had watched and longed for the day she could create a Christmas of the heart with her own special touches.

Touching a shiny red ball with one fingertip, she smiled softly. That day had finally come in a most unexpected man-ner and in an even more unexpected place.

She heard Gavin stir and tiptoed down the long hall to his room. He tossed restlessly and murmured, then settled again. She waited a moment longer before returning to the living room, where she went to the window and gazed out. A heavy frost lay over the brown grass and glistened beneath the moon. A Texas night could be so still, and yet she knew life teemed all around her.

The quiet snick of the door latch turned her around. Dax, shoulders hunched against the cold, came inside, filling up the room and her heart. Her stomach fluttered, foolishly happy. One kiss shouldn't mean so much, but to her, it did.

"Hey," he said softly.

"Hey." She'd never said *hey* to anyone in her life, but it sounded right in this place and time. Voice as quiet as his, she went on, "How's the mare?"

"Getting close. I thought you might like to be there."

The foolish happiness expanded. "I was hoping you'd ask."

He tilted his head, serious green eyes reflecting the spare light from the Christmas tree. "Were you?"

She nodded, staying still, not wanting to move away from the way he was looking at her. "Yes."

He breathed in through his nose and exhaled. "Smells good in here."

"Gavin and I made ornament cookies. With cinnamon."

"Bet he liked that."

"I think so."

"You've been good for him."

Jenna's mind stumbled on the past tense. Was he going to let her go? Or had the turn of phrase been unintentional?

The balloon of happiness deflated but filled again when Dax motioned toward her end of the house. "Get your coat. It's cold out."

"Don't you want something hot to drink first?"

"Later. The barn is warm enough, and as you know, babies don't wait." His face lightened at the reminder of Sophie's untimely birth.

She laughed softly. "No, they don't."

Feeling both unsettled and excited, Jenna hurried to her closet for coat and gloves, glanced in on Sophie, then slid the baby monitor into her pocket before returning to Dax.

He was in the kitchen, eyeing the pans of cookie ornaments with an unreadable expression. When he felt her approach, he said, "Ready?"

She nodded and they headed outside and across the glistening yard. The air was every bit as crisp and cold as the frost implied.

Dax took her elbow and guided them through the darkness toward a long, lighted horse barn. Neither spoke, and the only sounds were their soft footsteps and the pounding of her pulse against her eardrums. His touch, his nearness set her entire body a-hum.

She shivered once but otherwise ignored the cold. She felt invigorated, alive, her blood pumping through her veins with new strength and clarity. She was in love with Dax Coleman. In love.

She glanced his way. His face was in shadow but the shape was strong and masculine. She felt comforted and safe in this foreign world of rural Texas with Dax at her side.

Did he know what he had done to her? Did he have any idea how much he'd helped her grow and mature? She'd run away from Pennsylvania a scared girl. Today she was a woman.

He felt something for her, she was certain. But what? Gratitude? Responsibility? Did she dare to believe a man as handsome and honorable as Dax could really find her attractive?

"She's in the third stall," Dax said as he released her elbow to slide back the enormous metal door.

Jenna blinked against the bright, overhead light. The barn, surprisingly warm, smelled clean and grassy with the overtone of warm animals. She liked this barn just as she liked the big, soft-eyed horses who resided here. When time permitted, she brought Gavin inside to pet the horses, hoping that exposure would lessen his fears.

She followed Dax inside stall number three, standing just inside while he approached the mother-to-be. Blanca, as white as her name implied, lay on clean straw with her back legs folded beneath her. Her massive chest rose and fell with the effort of labor. Jenna empathized.

"How ya doin', Blanca girl?" Dax asked as he knelt beside the mare and ran a hand over her glossy hip. He tossed a glance toward Jenna. "Ease on over here. She won't mind."

Jenna did as he instructed, crouching next to him.

"Look right there," he murmured.

Jenna's stomach leaped. She grasped the thick quilting of Dax's sleeve. "Is that the baby?"

"Yep. In good position, too, nose and knees first. We should have touchdown any minute now." There was excitement in his voice that matched the rising tide of energy inside her.

"I've never seen an animal born."

His mouth curved. "First time for everything. I'd never seen a baby born before Sophie."

Their gazes collided and held, the memory of that first day a bond between them.

"I'd never had one before, either."

"We did a great job, though, didn't we? Pretty special watching a life come into the world."

The mare rose slightly on her back legs and heaved. Both humans turned their attention to her as the foal's nose and knees inched forward.

"Amazing. So amazing," she muttered. "Do we need to do anything?"

"Not yet. Let nature take its course." He hitched his chin toward a box residing along the edge of the stall. "Unless she goes too long or has trouble, all we have to do is take care of the foal when he arrives. The kit is ready and waiting if we need it."

Jenna had no idea what was in the kit but was not surprised that Dax was ready for any eventuality. Any man who could help birth a baby by the side of the road could handle anything.

The mare rose slightly and strained.

Jenna gasped. "There's his head. Oh, Dax. Look, there he comes."

Dax, who'd been watching the birth, turned to watch Jenna. Instead of feeling self-conscious, Jenna laughed, happy, excited and filled with wonder as the tiny foal slipped onto the clean straw.

"Oh, oh, oh." Tears filled her eyes. In a voice of wonder, she whispered, "Is he okay?"

It occurred to her then that Dax may have felt this way the day Sophie was born. Anxious and awed and overwhelmed by the beauty of new life.

Dax's voice was soft, too. "Watch his mama work. She knows what to do."

Sure enough, the mare pushed to a stand and turned to her newborn, instinctively stimulating and warming him with her tongue. As she did so, Dax examined the foal, applied antiseptic to the umbilical cord and stepped away, motioning Jenna to join him.

Together they watched the mother care for her baby. When the foal struggled to stand, Jenna's whole body tensed with the effort. "Come on, baby. You can do it."

The spotted foal wobbled up. Jenna turned to Dax, realizing for the first time that she held his hand in a death grip. He smiled into her eyes. She smiled back. He took a step closer. She stood her ground. When his calloused rancher's hand slid beneath her hair and caressed her neck, she shivered. He looked pleased by her reaction. Slowly, he titled her face up and brought his down. Jenna's fingers roamed up the front of his open jacket, over the muscular chest and shoulders to twine in the hair at his nape. She breathed in and let her eyes fall closed as Dax's warm, supple mouth caressed hers.

Sensation washed through her. Desire and hope and love and the belief that this was right and good. He kissed her until her heart hammered in her throat and her knees quivered. When at last the glorious torture ended, he went on holding her in his arms. His breath came in soft rasps against her hair. He took one of her hands and pressed it to his heart. The powerful beat hammered against her palm.

Holding his beautiful green eyes with her gaze, she returned the favor, pressing his big hand to her chest. His nostrils flared and he smiled softly.

Without words, they communicated the flood of emotions

rushing in and around them. The feelings were too new and raw to express aloud. At least for Jenna. She wanted to believe she wasn't being a fool and that Dax felt the same.

Behind her, the mare and foal rustled and moved about as the newborn searched for his first meal.

Jenna longed to stay in Dax's warm embrace but a sound from the baby monitor in her pocket ended the moment.

"I should go," she murmured, hearing the tremor in the words.

As he stepped away, Dax dragged a hand over his face and nodded. "Yes. You should. Go."

Jenna tilted her head, trying to gauge his meaning. Gone was the loving look of moments before. An anxious moth fluttered in her chest. What was he not saying?

Maybe he kissed women in the barn all the time. Maybe this meant nothing to him. Maybe she was still the gullible girl that had fallen for Derek.

"Dax?"

He heaved a great sigh. "I apologize. That shouldn't have happened."

He'd kissed her twice in the space of a few hours and it shouldn't have happened? She couldn't believe this.

What was going on inside that complicated head of his?

She stared, waiting with a fragile hope that he would explain.

He clenched his fist and averted his eyes.

Jutting her chin, she said, "No need to apologize. I'm a grown woman and, in case you didn't notice, I was not resisting."

Then with head held high, she rushed outside, the chill in her heart far colder than the December night.

Dax called himself ten kinds of fool and uttered every curse word stored in his memory banks. It was a good thing horses didn't speak English or the mare would have chased him out of the stall.

What had he been thinking to kiss Jenna, not once but twice? The first time he'd convinced himself was to comfort her after the ugly scene with Rowdy. He had no excuse for this second time. He should never have asked her into the barn. He should have left well enough alone. She was his housekeeper, not a girlfriend. His indecently *young* housekeeper.

At least Rowdy was close to her age. Dax had no excuse at all. No excuse except for the fact that he was falling for her. One minute they'd been admiring the new foal, then he'd gazed into those warm brown eyes so filled with the same wonder he always felt at a birthing, and he'd seen a woman after his own heart. A woman who'd returned his kiss with a hungry innocence that turned his insides to jelly. His brain had shorted out. That's all there was to it. He had better self-discipline than to do such a thing.

Anyway, he used to.

No fool like an old fool, Coleman.

He kicked the side of the stall. Pain shot up his leg and he accepted it with a perverse pleasure. The mare turned her head to give him a censorious stare.

"Sorry, old girl." Sorrier than he could ever say.

He cleaned up the stall and after one last examination of mother and baby, he returned to the house.

The tree lights were the only light shining inside the house, and he stood in the entry for several seconds, thinking and admiring the beautiful display. He had erected the tree each year for Gavin's sake but the efforts had been halfhearted. A few ornaments. A few gifts. Gavin's stocking. Jenna had transformed the house into a Christmas wonderland and claimed she wasn't finished yet.

Shucking his boots, he headed for bed, stopping to peek in at Gavin. The night-light—a necessity for his anxious son—illuminated the room enough that he could see the twin bed. The covers were tossed and rumpled but Gavin wasn't there.

His heart leaped. "Gavin?"

He entered the room, flipping on the overhead light as he moved toward the pile of camouflage-patterned covers. Sure enough Gavin was gone.

Sometimes his son had nightmares and climbed into bed with old dad. Dax stepped to his own room and flipped on the light. Gavin wasn't there, either.

There was only one other place he could be.

With a quick stride, Dax crossed the long ranch house to Jenna's room. He dreaded opening the door and seeing her in the bed, but he needed to know that his son was all right. Just the thought of Jenna in a nightgown with nothing underneath drove his imagination wild. He had enough problems with seeing her in the full-length robe, her pretty toes peeking from beneath.

Like an embattled prizefighter, he shook off the fantasy. Jenna was off-limits. If he was any kind of man, she had to be.

As quietly as possible, he turned the knob and entered the nursery first. Sophie lay on her back, little arms flung up and out. His heart squeezed. Once upon a time he'd dreamed of having a baby girl to call him Daddy. And Sophie had no father to love and protect her.

He watched a moment longer, confident that the pink princess was breathing, and then moved to the connecting doorway. At the sight before him, he squeezed his eyelids tight and let the wave of sweetness take him, if only for a moment.

Forever, he would cherish the mental image of his little boy snuggled safely in Jenna's bed. Her body was spooned around his and her arms held him close, one hand on his chest and the other against his cheek as though reassuring him that she was there and all was well.

The noise on the monitor that had sent her scurrying away from the barn hadn't been her child, as he'd thought. It had been his. And yet Jenna had responded to Gavin's call as though she was his mother.

Dax dragged a weary hand over his face and heard the scratchy beard. Jenna disarmed him. Took away his resistance. Touched him to the very soul.

Ah, God, he loved her. He *loved* her.

He loved her enough to do what was right.

The problem was, he hadn't figured out exactly what that was.

CHAPTER FOURTEEN

"BLAST THIS RAIN. Blast this wasted day." Dax stomped into the mudroom and bent to remove his boots. Water sluiced from his hat and rain slicker onto the tile. He shucked the hat and jacket, too, and took a towel from the overhead cabinet, breathing in the fragrance of fabric softener. That was another of Jenna's touches.

Frustrated, he ground his back teeth. He'd risen before sunrise, having slept little, and hurried out to check the mare and foal. Mostly, he'd hurried out to avoid Jenna and the whirlpool of confused emotions she incited. Now a cold December rain had forced him back inside.

Maybe he should have stayed in the barn all day.

But if he was honest, he missed having breakfast with her, missed seeing Gavin off to school, missed the few minutes of playtime with Sophie.

Jenna rounded the corner, carrying a laundry basket. Upon spotting him, she stopped dead still. Her eyes widened. One aristocratic eyebrow twitched.

It was a moment he'd both dreaded and longed for.

"Blasted rain," he grumbled, more to avoid the real issues than for conversation.

"You're soaked." She dropped the basket and dug more towels from the cupboard, handing him one and patting his drips with the other. "You're going to be sick."

Her ministrations felt too good, too…wifely.

He took the towel from her. "I got it."

She stood her ground, watching him. "You need to get warm and dry. I have fresh coffee."

"In a minute. I have to change."

"Clean clothes in the dryer," she said and left the room.

Dax stared after her for a few seconds, contemplating the psychology of women. If he lived to a hundred, he would never understand. She didn't seem angry. She didn't seem upset. She didn't seem anything. After his weird behavior last night, she should have tossed him back out in the freezing rain.

He made a self-mocking noise, glanced down at the pool of water forming around his bare feet and quickly undressed, letting his clothes drop to the floor.

He was standing buck naked in the mudroom while his housekeeper, the woman who was driving him crazy, was in the next room with only a wall between them.

He was chilled to the bone, but his traitorous male body reacted inappropriately anyway. Being a man was an annoyance at times. Jaw clenched, he scavenged in the dryer and sighed with appreciation as he dressed in warm, fragrant clothing.

Once Jenna had gotten the hang of doing laundry, the result was far more pleasant than his pitiful attempts. To his way of thinking, chuck all the clothes in at once and let 'em spin. Jenna's way was magic—and smelled good, too.

Out of long habit, he gathered up the mess in the floor, but the washer was already running, so he dropped them in an empty basket and went in search of that hot coffee.

Jenna wasn't in the kitchen. He wanted to be glad, but instead he poured a steaming mug and went in search of her. Might as well have a little talk, let her know she didn't have to worry about him coming on to her the way Rowdy had. Clear the air.

He found her in the living room, kneeling in front of the fireplace.

"What are you doing?"

She glanced over one shoulder, her hair catching on her mouth. His gaze went straight there as the thought of her kisses came slamming down on him. That puffy bottom lip tasted like sugar and cinnamon and pure delight.

"I thought a fire would be lovely," that mouth said. "And you need to warm up quickly. This is flu season."

His mouth twitched. "Afraid I'll get sick and you'll be stuck taking care of me?"

She studied him solemnly. "Actually, no. I don't want you to miss the Christmas party."

"Ah, yes, the party." He rounded the sectional and set his cup on the table to kneel beside her. Their shoulders brushed and enough electricity arced from his body to start the fire without matches. "Let me help."

She shifted to one side, breaking contact with him, and shoved a handful of crumpled newspaper into the fireplace. "I'm quite capable."

Ah, so she *was* upset with him but too dignified to say so.

Before his brain could engage, he grasped her hands and turned her toward him. "I apologized last night."

"How rude of you!" Color flared on her cheekbones.

Her abrupt words took him aback. He wasn't sure what response he'd expected but certainly not that one.

"Rude?" Since when was apologizing considered rude?

"A gentleman kisses a woman and then apologizes? What does that say to the woman?"

He blinked, baffled. This was a side of Jenna he hadn't seen.

"It says," she went on in that prissy, citified tone, "that he regrets kissing her. That somehow her kisses were unpleasant."

He blinked like a man staring too long at the sun. "It does?"

She nodded. "Isn't that why you apologized?"

"No. You kiss great. I could have stayed out there all night kissing you. You're amazing."

Her face softened. She pressed her fingertips to her chest. With wonder and hope, she whispered, "I am?"

Dax frowned, swallowing hard. She was confusing him. If he didn't shut up, he'd say something he shouldn't. But he couldn't let her go on thinking she'd done something wrong, either.

"I'm the offender here, Jenna. Not you. You—you're very special." He said the last on a rush of air, wishing the words back but thrilled with the joy that leaped into her expression.

"Oh, Dax." She took his chin in her small, soft fingers and held him captive. "What are you afraid of?"

All his resistance seeped out, as though her touch had the power to disarm every carefully erected defense.

"You," he said simply, quietly. "I'm afraid of you."

Her hand fell away. And oh, he wished it back. He wanted her to go on touching him, making him feel alive and real again in a way he hadn't felt in so long.

Bewildered eyes beseeched him. "I don't understand."

"I know you don't. I know." His throat tightened, full of emotion he shouldn't express. Yet he had to find a way to explain. She'd done nothing but make his life better. She deserved everything good.

Helpless to say anything yet, he pulled her head against his chest. The steady rhythm of his life force beat for her, and he didn't know what to do about it. She felt right in his arms and he wanted her there forever.

Her slender arms snaked around his neck. A wild flurry of hope rose inside him.

He tried to beat it back, tried to deny it existed, and still it fluttered there, as fragile as a new butterfly.

"Talk to me, Dax. Tell me what's going on." Her breath tickled his ear. He heard the hurt and confusion, but he also heard something else—determination and strength.

He realized that this woman-child who'd invaded his life was far stronger than he'd given her credit for. With grit and determination, she'd forged a new life for herself and her baby, taking on the role of his housekeeper when he knew very well that she'd never done this kind of work before. Yet, she'd persevered, and learning fast, had turned the Southpaw Cattle Company into a home filled with love.

He closed his eyes and inhaled her scent. Orange blossoms, she'd told him one day when he'd asked. He loved it. He loved her. She was more woman than his ex had ever been.

"Dax?" she murmured again. Only this time, she brushed a soft kiss across his cheek as she leaned back on her heels. "Will you please talk to me? Tell me what's going on in that head of yours."

Talk. He wasn't much good at that. How did a man express his feelings and concerns without opening himself up to heartache? How did he do what was best for her and still keep his sanity?

He licked lips gone dry and turned toward the half-laid fire. "Let's get this fire going."

Jenna said nothing but remained there resting on her heels, hands in her lap. She was thinking, though he had no idea where her thoughts were taking her.

Horses and cows he understood, but he'd never quite figured out women.

Intensely aware of her beside him watching, he arranged kindling on the grate, scraped a long fireplace match along the stone hearth and lit the wadded paper. The flame started small but quickly grew to catch the dry pine.

He'd never been much into analogy, but building the fire reminded him of the woman by his side. He'd been as dry as this kindling. Then Jenna had come along, reminded him of his blessings and the joys of everyday living and started a small spark of hope and light inside him. Now that spark had grown into a flame that burned only for her.

He pivoted to reach for a hickory log. Jenna anticipated his needs, as she'd done for weeks now, and handed him the stick of wood.

His hand trembled the slightest bit as he finished laying the fire and sat back to watch the flames climb higher. Heat began to warm his face.

Jenna shifted away and then stood. Dax looked up. "Where are you going?"

Her mouth curved. "I'll be back."

"Promise?" Ah, man, he was a mess.

Her eyes twinkled. "Are you going to talk to me?"

As worried as he was about screwing up everything and causing her to leave, he still found a certain humor in the situation. "Are you going to nag me if I don't?"

This time she laughed. "What do you think?" And then she hurried out of the living room.

Dax set the fire screen in place, dusted his hands down the sides of his clean jeans and looked around the living room. The place was magazine beautiful since Jenna had rearranged furniture and accessories, added pictures and doodads to the walls and gone all out for Christmas. She'd added a pair of enormous floor pillows for Gavin to flop on when he watched TV. Dax took those now and fluffed them onto the rug in front of the fire, refusing to examine the reasons behind the action.

"Here we go, sir," Jenna said. He scowled at her. The term *sir* didn't sit too well, considering the battle raging inside him. He didn't need any reminders that she was his employee and that he was twelve years older.

Furry slippers snip-snapping against her heels, she came toward him carrying a tray which she deposited on the coffee table. The scent of cinnamon wafted up from a plate piled high with ornament cookies. The tray was jammed with paintbrushes, tiny bowls of colored frosting and red ribbon.

"Are you putting me to work?"

"This is on my to-do list today. I thought you might like to decorate some while you bask by the fireside. It's fun."

Bask by the fireside? Her words tickled him. "What about Gavin?"

"I saved a plate for him. He gets tired after five or six."

Well, decorating cookies wasn't the kind of thing he'd had in mind, but he had to admit her idea was better than his. Cozying up with Jenna in front of a fire could be a dangerous proposition.

"Sophie asleep?" he asked, taking up a paint brush.

"Midmorning nap. Crystal said some babies don't adjust to a schedule right away, but Sophie has. She's the most amazing baby." The light of mother-love warmed her face. Dax's insides squeezed with gladness for Sophie. His baby had never had that kind of female devotion.

A voice in his head said, "Until now," and the vision of Jenna curved protectively, lovingly around his boy rose in his mind.

Taking up a Santa-shaped ornament, he dipped his brush in red frosting. "You gonna tell me about Gavin's nightmare?"

Brush and cookie in hand, she looked at him in surprise. "How did you know?"

"When I came in from the barn, I checked on him." He shrugged. "Always do. He was gone. You heard him on the monitor, didn't you? That's why you came inside last night."

Jenna tilted her head.

Yes, she'd come in for that reason, but also because he'd kissed her and then pushed her away. She was still pondering that turn of events.

"I'm not sure what he dreamed," she said. "But he was shivering and scared."

"Thank you for looking after him."

"No gratitude is required, Dax." Jenna dropped her gaze to the gingerbread boy. "I love him."

There, she'd admitted her love for one of the Coleman men. One down and one to go.

Dax didn't respond to the declaration, just went on painting Santa's hat with red frosting.

After a bit, he said, "You know I'm divorced."

The topic surprised her a little, but she was ready to hear the story from him. "Yes."

"Gavin never really knew his mother. She left when he was a few days old." He laid aside the paintbrush and drew in a deep breath. "She never wanted him."

"How horrible. He doesn't know, does he?"

"No. No. I'd never tell him such a thing, but he has to feel it. Other boys have mothers and he has never even seen his. When he was three years old, he began to notice that baby horses have mamas. Baby calves have mamas. Even his dad has a mama. Now that he's started school, he talks about it more. He's more clingy and the nightmares come more often." He rubbed the side of his neck as though the worry gave him a pain. "I don't know what to do."

"His lack of a mother is not your fault."

"I feel as if it is. I wasn't the best husband in the world. Always working, constantly out in the barn or the fields or off to stock sales and shows."

He looked so sad Jenna couldn't stop herself. She put aside her decorations, reached across the table and touched the back of his hand. "You were making a living for your family. That's as it should be."

"Reba didn't think so. She wanted parties and travel and fun."

"Nothing wrong with those things."

"That's why I blame myself."

"You didn't understand my meaning. There is nothing wrong with those things in small increments, but they aren't a lifestyle. Or they shouldn't be." No one knew that better than her. "My husband was the same way. Life was a party." As long as she was paying the bills and didn't stand in the way.

"Did you love him?"

She lifted a shoulder. "I thought I did. Did you love Reba?"

He nodded. "Yeah. Too much, I guess."

The admission poked at Jenna like a pinprick.

"I need you to know something," he went on. "She started divorce proceedings long before Gavin was born." His Adam's apple rose and fell. "After I caught her in bed with my brother."

The stark pain on his face drove the breath from her lungs. She knew that kind of betrayal, too, although she'd never caught Derek in the act. The newspaper speculation had been humiliating enough.

"You must have been…shattered."

"Yeah. We had just found out she was pregnant. I was overjoyed—and too stupid to see what was going on under my nose. I thought she was finally ready to settle down."

"I'm sorry."

"You know the last words she said to me?" His jaw worked, his fist tightened beneath her fingers, and Jenna could feel the rage and hurt coming off him in waves. "She asked me if I'd always wonder for certain if the kid she'd given me was really mine."

Jenna had never been a violent person, but she wanted to slap a certain female named Reba. The woman was too cruel for words. "Do you?"

He shook his head. "No. Oh, I thought about it when she first left, but after a while I no longer cared. I believe he's mine by biology, but even if he isn't, he's mine in here." He tapped a finger to his breastbone. "I rocked him, walked the floor with him, diapered his bottom and spooned baby food into his bird mouth. With every new thing I did for and with my son, I loved him deeper. He's a trooper, a hearty little soul who survived a stumbling, bumbling daddy. I just wish I could have been a mama to him, too. How could she do that to him? How could she not love a son like Gavin?"

"I don't understand, either, Dax."

He turned his hand over and clasped her palm in his. "I know you don't. That's one of the things I—admire about you."

Jenna heard the hesitation in his speech. Had he almost said love? Her pulse quivered in her chest, a hopeful bird fluttering for release.

Dax had been badly wounded and now she understood that those wounds made him cautious. She wanted to reassure him that she would never hurt him that way. She wanted him to know that the longing to mother Gavin grew stronger every day.

But she didn't tell him. She couldn't. Yet.

Dax took up the paintbrush and cookie again. "This is supposed to be a fun rainy-day project. Didn't mean to get serious on you."

"I asked you to talk to me." The man needed a partner to share his heavy load. And she needed to be needed. For most of her life, she'd been nothing but an ornament like the ones on the massive Christmas tree. Having Sophie and being a part of Dax's life had given her a sense of worth.

He turned the cinnamon cookie in her direction. "What do ya think of Santa?"

So he didn't want to discuss his ex-wife anymore. She understood. Derek wasn't her favorite topic, either. But she did want Dax to have some fun for a change.

She wrinkled her nose. "I thought Santa's boots were black."

Dax made a silly face. "Oops. I'll fix it."

When he leaned in to dip the brush in black frosting, Jenna dabbed paint on the tip of his nose.

"Oh, my goodness," she said with mock seriousness. "You have frosting on your nose."

"I do?" he asked in the same silly tone she'd used. All the while he swirled his paintbrush round and round in the frosting bowl. "Ever heard of face painting?"

Jenna dotted a gingerbread boy with white icing eyes. "Don't they do that at fairs and carnivals?"

Such events were below the status of a Carrington, but she'd seen the activity on television and had envied those lucky children their flowers and cartoon characters.

"And in living rooms on rainy days," he said.

Her gaze flew up to meet his. "Truly?"

He laughed and pointed the brush at her. "First time for everything. What do ya say, Jenna, want to launch my art career?"

She held up a warning finger. "Don't even think about it."

"Too late." Mischief filled his face.

"Dax," she warned, though the rise of energy inside her and the giggle she couldn't stop gave the lie to her warning.

"Ah, come on, Jenna. Play nice. Let me decorate your face. A few dots here, a blue stripe there. Gonna be fantastic." On his knees, he walked toward her, frosting near the drip stage.

"Don't you dare." She crab-crawled backward, but Dax kept coming, brush loaded with bright blue paint.

Like the villain in an old-time movie, he pumped his eyebrows. If he'd had a mustache, he would probably have twirled the ends, too.

Giggling, Jenna scooted back some more, though she couldn't escape—even if she'd wanted to.

Dax pounced. Jenna flung an arm upward to ward off the blue-drenched brush. Bits of cookie paint flicked loose. A laughing, halfhearted wrestling match ensued, but Jenna was no match for the big man's superior strength. In two seconds flat she was pinned to the floor, her wrists manacled above her head by one of his powerful hands while the other advanced toward her face with a glob of shiny blue frosting.

Jenna switched her head from side to side, laughing so hard now that she could barely breathe.

When Dax saw that he couldn't paint a face in motion, he resorted to threats. "Take your punishment or prepare to wash sugar out of your hair."

She stilled but couldn't stop giggling as Dax moved closer with the brush. She'd never seen him playful. He was still a young man but the past and his load of responsibility weighed him down. He needed to laugh and feel young and happy again. And she was thrilled to be a part of the moment—even if it meant having her cheek painted.

But instead of dabbing her cheek, Dax stroked the brush over her mouth. The motion tickled, but Jenna stopped giggling. A tingle of awareness moved from her mouth into her chest and lower.

She became acutely cognizant of Dax's body pressing into hers in all the right places.

"You have the most gorgeous mouth," he murmured.

She tried to joke. "And you think it should be painted blue?"

A tiny smile played at the corners of his mouth as he slowly outlined her top lip with the fine-tipped brush. She shivered. He raised his eyes to hers and then went back to his beguiling work. With painstaking care, while she throbbed at his nearness, he outlined her bottom lip, then dipped his brush again and filled in every millimeter of her mouth.

By now her heart thundered in her ears. Though she tried to control her breathing, her chest rose and fell more quickly. Her tongue snaked out to moisten lips gone dry from nerves and drying sugar. As if she'd issued a command, Dax tossed the brush aside and leaned in to nibble at the corner of her mouth.

"Yum," he said, his breath stirring the sensitive tissues, making her yearn.

She tried to move, to turn her lips into his, but he backed away a fraction of an inch. His eyelids were hooded and sexy.

"Be still." The gravelly command raised goose bumps on her arms. Dax noticed and laughed softly. "I made this mess. I'll clean it up."

While Jenna thought she'd die if he didn't kiss her right then, she played his sensual game. His hot, enticing tongue followed the path of the paintbrush around her lips.

"Sweet as sugar," he murmured, the words flowing into her mouth from his. She smiled a little at the joke.

He nibbled her bottom lip. She let her mouth drop open slightly hoping he'd take the hint.

But Dax was not finished with his delicious torture. He went right on nipping and tasting, making soft moaning sounds that sent her blood racing and alerted every nerve ending in her body.

The taste of sugar mingled with the coffee they'd drunk and a taste that only belonged to Dax—manly, hot and yet cautious as though he was holding himself in check. She didn't want caution. She wanted him.

"Dax," she whispered in a shaky voice.

He raised his head and their eyes locked. The desire she saw there didn't surprise her, but the tenderness did. For all his gruffness, Dax had a way of making her feel cherished.

"I—I—" She longed to admit her love but there were other things she had to tell him first. And yet if she discussed her past, this beautiful spell would be broken. She couldn't bear if he was angry with her for keeping the secret. Not today when she felt more beautiful and special than she'd ever felt in her life. So in the end, she closed her eyes and said nothing. Dax didn't move and she could feel his gaze boring into her. His breath soughed gently and after a moment he shifted slightly, though he never released her hands. He held her captive with his fingers, his body and his lips. She wondered if he knew that he also held her captive with his heart.

Her lips dropped open and this time Dax took full advantage to devour the remaining sugar, caressing her mouth until she thought she might melt into the carpet.

He worked his way over her chin and jaw and to her ear where he puffed softly until she shivered, and then he kissed his way down her throat. It was then he loosened his hold on her wrists. With deep pleasure humming through her body, she laced her fingers in his thick hair and drew him closer.

Just when Jenna thought she would combust with desire, Sophie let out a howl.

Both adults froze. The only sounds in the room were the crackle of the fireplace and the pounding of their hearts.

Sophie cried out again.

Dax growled deep in his throat, and then he chuckled. The sound vibrated inside Jenna's chest. With a wry grin, he rolled to one side and helped her sit up. "Saved by the baby."

She hadn't wanted to be saved from Dax, but common sense would say to take things slowly. She pushed to a stand, using Dax's broad shoulder for leverage. Her knees trembled. "It's time for her bottle."

"Bring her in here." He shoved a hand through his hair, forking it up in all directions. "I missed playtime this morning."

Jenna studied him. He wasn't angry. A little frustrated perhaps, but not angry. Instead he wanted to spend time with her and Sophie.

How could she not love a man like that?

bonnie tenila fingers no steady two ni thun she stroamed
her breathe thing. Dax'd all eleey the wire his small shelf
it than she has that too made he esme Daly to visit at the
sup echo. Brushing over siqued ... Serving her touch tali
... He spread the arm.smn nm hn am he and theowru
onte overriddon, chas.amnu Summed irvned st herlat
one. The absent in her. Its the olen wond butta had ised
tery. Aleliut is so bl em bornio wai ts for the litbbuil on
Rea Ta st festing lesode s nuu wini Shoseminc lardn
the has tishe r tery isr que su cami re Iolae.. the clsee-
lnehes sessio's feces thim. 'rein.mltuyd ldi d duu,

CHAPTER FIFTEEN

DAX LIFTED THE LID on the stew pot and sniffed. Steam and
the aroma of chicken broth warmed his face. Jenna had gone
into town for lunch with Crystal and a couple of other girl-
friends, leaving the stew pot for his lunch. According to
Jenna, they were revising a guest list for the Christmas party
that seemed to grow larger each day. Not that he minded. If
having a party made her happy, she could have one every day.

Taking a thick stoneware bowl from the shelf, he dipped
it full of the Brunswick Stew, sliced a chunk of corn bread
and settled in at the bar for lunch.

The rainy day had changed everything. He could no more
explain it than he could explain why a woman like Jenna
Garwood would choose to remain on the Southpaw with him
and Gavin, but he felt more positive about life than he had in
years. Hope was a magical emotion and he was filled with it.

As much as he'd wanted to make love to Jenna that day,
he now knew the timing had been wrong. They were still
learning and growing together and each day was a discovery.
Jenna in his kitchen. Jenna in his living room. Jenna dancing
in circles to Christmas music with Sophie in her arms.

He loved sneaking up behind her when she was busy. He'd
plant a kiss on her neck or her hair and she'd spin around,
face flushed, to fall against him for a real kiss.

Sometimes at night when he crawled into the king-size

bed, he let himself imagine what it would be like if Jenna was lying beside him. They'd talk about the day's events, laugh at things the kids had done, and then make love sweeter than any cookie frosting ever created.

He spooned the thick soup into his mouth and moaned with appreciation. His Jenna was a fine chef. *His* Jenna. Was she? Did she want to be? He thought she did but he had to be sure. *She* had to be sure.

She was in his house and in his heart. He wanted her in his bed, too.

Making love didn't scare him. Falling in love did.

They'd never spoken of age, but that rainy day in her arms had convinced him that Jenna was far more woman than girl. Part of him still worried that he was too old, too broken and too bitter to give a young, vibrant woman what she needed.

But hope had come to the Southpaw and Dax clung to it like a drowning man to a bit of flotsam. For indeed, he'd been dead inside when Jenna Garwood and her baby had opened the door to his empty heart and made themselves welcome.

Though still convinced that she had secrets, he was afraid to ask. What if he didn't like the answers? What if he drove her away? For now, he couldn't take the chance. Maybe by spring, he'd be more confident—if he could keep his libido in check that long. Jenna deserved more than an employer who took advantage.

He slathered butter on his corn bread and bit down. Jenna had never before baked corn bread but when he'd mentioned a fondness for the Southern dish, it had appeared at the next meal, just the way he liked it with a touch of sugar. He took another bite and realized he was smiling.

She'd left the Christmas tree lights on and last night, she and Gavin had hung the elaborately quilted and personalized stockings on the gleaming wood mantel. The house was alive with her special touches.

Outside he heard the sound of a car and his heart leaped.

Jenna must be back early. Forgetting all about his half-eaten meal, he shoved off the bar stool and hurried to the door. Though she'd only been gone a couple of hours, he missed her.

He yanked the front door open and paused. A long, sleek, black car pulled into his drive. No one he knew drove a car of that caliber, at least not out here in the country. This looked like something a government official would drive.

A sense of foreboding crawled up the back of his neck. He shook it off.

A uniformed driver complete with a flat cap like something out of a movie, exited the car and opened the back door. With a stiff bow, the chauffeur extended a hand to assist the occupant. Out stepped a dark-haired, middle-aged woman in a crisp tan suit. Nose high, she gazed around, taking in the brown landscape and finally coming to rest on him. She looked him over and then squared her shoulders and said something to the chauffeur. From the other side of the car, a burly man exited and came around to stand beside the elegantly clad woman. To Dax's way of thinking, the man looked like a cop—or a gangster.

Normally, Dax went out to greet his company, but something about this group bothered him. He didn't know them, but something didn't feel right.

The dark-haired woman and the burly man came toward the house. Dax stepped out onto the porch.

"You folks lost?"

"I think not." The woman's voice was high-brow and disdaining. "This is the Southpaw Cattle Company, isn't it?"

"It is."

"And may I inquire as to who you are?"

Both the phrasing and the accent sounded eerily familiar. "Dax Coleman. This is my place. And you are?"

"Elaine Carrington. May I come inside please? We have some business to discuss."

He couldn't imagine what business he could possibly have

with a woman he'd never heard of but he motioned toward the house. "Come on in."

He led the way, taking note that the burly fellow followed but hadn't been introduced. The man cast a suspicious eye in all directions as they entered the foyer and passed into the living room.

"Have a seat," Dax said. He waited as politely as possible while the woman settled on the divan and then he perched on the edge of a nearby chair. The burly man didn't sit, rather took up residence at the end of the couch, his arms crossed over his chest.

What was this guy anyway? Some kind of bodyguard?

"I'll get straight to the point," the woman said. "I'm looking for my daughter, Genevieve Carrington."

Dax relaxed the slightest bit. For a minute there, he was scared she was going to mention Jenna. "Sorry, ma'am. I don't know her."

The woman's lips thinned. "That's not what my sources tell me."

Dax was stricken with an overpowering need to get these strangers off his land. "Well, your sources are wrong. So if you'll excuse me, I have a ranch to run."

"Just a moment, Mr. Coleman. I've spent thousands of dollars tracking my daughter. I know she's been here. I know she gave birth to a daughter—my grandchild—in the local hospital. I also know she took a position with your ranch—" her nostrils flared in distaste "—as a domestic."

Oh no. No.

Dax wanted to put a hand over her mouth and stop the flow of words but instead he sat frozen like a plastic snowman.

Mrs. Carrington opened her black leather bag and withdrew a paper which she handed to Dax. "This photo was taken shortly before her husband died."

Before he even looked down, Dax knew who would be smiling out at him, but his heart dropped anyway.

"Jenna," he said. "My housekeeper's name is Jenna Garwood, not Carrington."

"So she is here. Thank God." A world of tension left the woman's body. "Garwood was her married name. Where is she? Where is my granddaughter? We need to get them back to Pennsylvania under medical care right away."

Dax's pulse jumped. "Is Jenna sick?"

"Of course she is. What person in her right mind would run away from her family estate in the ninth month of pregnancy and leave behind a multimillion dollar trust fund?"

His ears buzzed. He could have sworn she said Jenna was rich. "If that's true, why did she come to work here?"

"My point exactly. Jenna is the sole heiress to a vast fortune. Since her husband's death, she has not been well. I blame myself for not getting her the help she needed sooner. Haven't you ever heard of postpartum depression? Hormonal psychosis? Our physician believes this is likely the culprit, and now that she has delivered the baby, the danger increases. So please, Mr. Coleman, tell me where my daughter is so we can take her home where she belongs."

Dax ran a shaky hand over his face. He couldn't believe this. He was living in a nightmare. Jenna, his love, the woman he wanted to keep forever, obviously didn't feel the same. She'd had plenty of chances to tell him who she was, and she hadn't.

He felt as if his heart would burst right out of his chest. What an idiot he was to think a woman like Jenna could care for him. He'd known from the beginning she didn't fit in his world. She was too young, too classy. The warning signs were all around him, and yet he'd shut them out.

The rumble of a car engine sounded, growing closer. His gut knotted to the point of nausea. He had to get out of here before he did something he'd regret forever. Call him a coward, but he couldn't look into Jenna's eyes without losing his cool. It wasn't so much that she hadn't told him, it was that she hadn't trusted him. And more than that, her mother was right. Jenna was a blue blood. She shouldn't be scrubbing floors for a Texas rancher.

"That's Jenna's car," he said, somehow managing to force the words past the knot in his throat. "If you'll excuse me, I'll leave you to your reunion."

With a curt nod, he took his hat and coat and exited out the back way.

They had found her.

The moment she turned down the graveled drive into the Southpaw, Jenna went weak all over. Though she didn't recognize the black luxury sedan parked next to the house, she recognized the Carrington style.

She tapped the brake, blood roaring in her head as she contemplated the best mode of action. If the visitor was, indeed, Mother, she'd already spoken to Dax. By now, he'd be wondering what kind of crazy person would run away from a fortune. Worse yet, he'd be wondering why Jenna had kept such a secret from him even after their relationship had begun to flower.

Now she wondered the same thing. She should have told him. She should have explained about the years of living an overprotected life with a neurotic mother whose fears controlled her every movement.

The memory of her miserable childhood stiffened her spine. She was an adult. Her mother could not force her to return home.

She pulled into the garage, gathered Sophie into her arms and let herself in through the back door. She could hear the clip of her mother's voice speaking to someone.

Holding her baby close, knees trembling, she moved quietly down the hall and through the house until she stood in the entry between the dining and living rooms.

"Hello, Mother." Jenna's voice sounded cool, but her insides wobbled.

"Jenna, darling." Elaine rose and reached toward her. Jenna remained aloof and on guard, but an unexpected surge of emotion struck her. Tears pressed at the back of her eyelids. As damaged as their relationship was, she'd missed her family.

Elaine moved forward to touch the white blanket surrounding Sophie. "Is this our little Rose Elizabeth?"

The moment of weakness fled. Her mother had insisted Jenna name her baby after two matriarchs of the Carrington family, considering her choice far more fitting than anything Jenna suggested. Elaine had even preenrolled Sophie in an elite private school under that name and against Jenna's wishes.

"Her name is Sophie Joy."

Elaine drew back, startled that her will had been questioned, but as "befitting one of her station," she quickly masked her real feelings.

"Sit down, darling. You look terrible." She glanced at Parm, head of Carrington security for as long as Jenna could remember. "Don't you agree, Parm? She's clearly been ill."

Parm inclined his head, agreeing as always with his employer.

"I've never been healthier, Mother."

"Don't try to hide the truth from me, darling. I know when something's wrong." She tilted Jenna's face upward and studied her as if she were a painting. "If you would only have told your father or me how distraught you were over Derek's death and—well, that other distasteful affair, we would have gotten you the help you needed."

Leave it to mother to consider death and adultery as equally distasteful. "The situation with Derek was only one of the reasons I left. I don't expect you to understand. But I do expect you to get in your car, return to the airport and go home."

"Not without you and my granddaughter." Elaine smoothed

the back of her skirt and reseated herself. "You're ill. You have been for some time."

"You want me to be ill so you can control me. And Sophie."

"Don't be ridiculous. Genevieve, darling, do you have any heart at all? Don't you realize the terror and despair your father and I experienced when we realized you were gone? We thought our worst nightmare had finally come to pass." She paused, pressed a pampered hand to her heart and closed her eyes. "I wept for days, waiting for the ransom call, certain some vicious monster had stolen my only child."

Jenna's conscience pricked. The Carringtons feared kidnapping above all things. "I left a note."

"A note could have easily been forced from you at gunpoint. Even Parm was deeply concerned that something untoward had occurred."

Jenna swallowed. "I'm sorry, Mother. I never meant to worry you."

"Don't you see, darling, your behavior has been unbalanced, a danger to you and my grandchild."

"I'm a good mother."

"Your love is not in question, but your emotional health is. Now that I'm here I see for myself how desperate the situation is. You look dreadful, exhausted, weathered like a common street urchin. And those hands, your once-beautiful hands…" Her mother's voice trailed away as she stared at Jenna's chipped fingernails.

"I work for a living."

Elaine placed the back of her hand against her forehead as if a migraine was coming on. "Clearly another symptom of how ill you are. Our kind do not work for a living. We serve others in charitable duties. Jenna, child, as difficult as it may be for you to think rationally, consider the things you've done. You engaged in an ill-begotten alliance with a golddigging philanderer and got yourself pregnant. That alone shows very poor judgment. Then only days before that baby's birth, you disappeared, putting both your child and yourself in jeopardy. Anything could have happened. Dear heavens above, you gave birth to the Carrington heir on the side of the road. You could have died. Don't you understand how terribly ill you must be to have done such a dangerous thing?"

Jenna's heart sank lower than the Texas sun. She had never looked at the situation quite this way. Was Mother right? Had running away been the sign of a mental illness?

"I'm sorry, Mother," she said again and heard the voice of a little girl who had always apologized and obeyed. Five minutes in the company of her mother and Jenna was a child again. Growing more confused and uncertain by the minute, she felt herself weakening.

Perhaps she should go home. Perhaps she wasn't well. Sophie deserved to grow up in a healthy environment. She reached down to smooth the soft cap of blond curls and stared into her baby's eyes. What was the right thing to do for Sophie?

Elaine touched her shoulder, though Jenna hadn't seen her leave the chair. "Come on, darling. Let's get your things and leave before that cowboy person returns."

Like a remote control doll, Jenna rose, clutching Sophie to her breast. "I have to say goodbye."

Elaine took her elbow. "I don't think that's a good idea. Mr. Coleman was very upset."

She blinked. "He was?"

"There's no predicting what he might do now that he knows you're an heiress. Extortion, blackmail. Anything is possible."

Something clicked inside Jenna's brain. "Dax isn't like that. Dax is—" A flood of emotion rushed through her at the thought of everything she'd shared with the Texas rancher.

Here on the Southpaw with Dax, she'd changed from a frightened runaway to an adult with the strength and good sense to run a household, nurture her child as well as his, and turn a lonely house into a lively, beautiful home filled with love. Thanks to Dax, she'd learned that her value and worth had nothing to do with a trust fund. Here she loved and was loved for who she was inside.

Suddenly she knew her mother was wrong. Neither depressed nor mentally ill, Jenna Garwood had become a woman in control of her own life. And she wanted that life to be here, on the Southpaw with Dax if he'd have her. "I love him."

Elaine's head snapped back. "Don't be a fool again. You know what happened the last time a man discovered your trust fund."

Jenna shook her head slowly from side to side as hope returned, a gentle salve to her wounded soul. "He didn't know. He didn't know and he loves me anyway."

He'd never said as much but she knew now. Dax loved her and Sophie. His love was there in everything he said and did.

She wouldn't go back. She would not allow the Carrington money to ruin Sophie's childhood the way it had ruined hers. She'd run away for Sophie's sake, not to cause her harm, and no amount of psychological manipulation by her mother would change her mind.

Right then, she knew what she had to do.

"Mother, I love and respect you, but I am a grown woman. I am not returning to Pennsylvania." Regardless of what happened with Dax, she could not go home again. "If you wish to be a part of my life and Sophie's, you'll do so under my rules."

Elaine's mouth dropped open. Parm snapped to attention but Jenna knew he wouldn't stop her. He couldn't.

"Now if you will excuse me, Sophie and I have some unfinished business to attend to." With a song in her heart and head held high, she went in search of Dax. Somehow she would make him understand.

CHAPTER SIXTEEN

DAX SAW HER ROUND the corner of the barn and come toward him across the dead grass, purpose in her stride. The hood of her coat had fallen and her hair blew away from her face. The cold air tinged her cheeks with rose, giving her an invigorated, healthy look. She was carrying the baby bundled in a thick blanket. As she drew near, he could see the excitement emanating from her like heat from a summer sidewalk.

He knew. She was coming to tell him goodbye. She was heading back to the fancy life where she belonged.

Dax hurt so bad he didn't have the strength to cuss. He was breaking in half, shattered at the thought of losing this woman that he'd known all along he shouldn't fall for. And yet he had.

When Reba left, he'd been furious and bitter. But with Jenna, he was simply broken. She'd done nothing but make his life better. She'd driven out the bitterness and replaced it with soft smiles, lobster croquettes and Christmas decorations. And the best kisses a man could fantasize about.

Ah, man, he loved her. Maybe if he'd told her and held her and promised her the moon…ah, what was he thinking? She could buy the moon for herself. She didn't need him.

"Dax?" she said, coming to a halt at his side. He should be angry, but he couldn't muster the energy. He looked down into those brown eyes and fell apart. Dropping the wrench he'd been using to hang the metal gate, he pulled her and Sophie gently into his embrace.

"I'll never forget you, Jenna," he said, memorizing the scent and silkiness of her hair and the curve of her body. Long after she was gone from his life, he wanted to remember. "Gavin will miss you. I hope you'll keep in touch. For his sake."

She stilled. "What about you? Will you miss me?"

He squeezed his eyes against the question. Jenna wasn't normally a cruel person.

"Yeah," he answered raggedly. "I'll miss you, too."

Jenna's body began to tremble. Dax held her tighter. Soft weeping filled his ears. Gripping her upper arms, he put her a little away from him. Tears flowed down her face and dripped onto Sophie's blanket.

"What? Why are you crying?"

"Because I think you love me."

So that was it. She knew he'd fallen hard, and tender-hearted Jenna felt bad about hurting him. But Dax refused to lie about something as precious as love.

He tilted her chin. "You stole my heart the day we brought Sophie into this world. And every day since then I've fallen more in love than I ever dreamed possible."

More tears gushed from her eyes, down her cheeks and into the corners of her mouth. It was all he could do not to kiss them away.

"What would a beautiful angel like you want with me? But I don't regret one moment we spent together. And if I could have one wish in this world—" He stopped, too emotional to go on.

Still weeping softly, Jenna turned her face into his palm and kissed him. The sweetness of that act nearly brought him to his knees.

"Tell me your wish."

He shook his head. "No. I won't put any more guilt on you.

Go home with your family and be happy, Jenna. That's what I wish for you."

The baby had grown restless while the adults talked and let out a whimper. Thinking this was the last time he'd get to hold her, Dax took Sophie and rested her against his shoulder. She settled instantly and if possible Dax's heart broke a little more. He'd fallen for this baby girl as surely as he'd fallen for the mother.

Jenna smiled through her tears and gripped the lapel of his work coat.

"I *am* home with my family, Dax."

He wasn't sure he understood. "Aren't you going back East with your mother?"

Her face crumpled again. "Do you want me to?"

"No!" he shouted.

Sophie jumped and started to cry. Dax patted her back and made a shushing sound until she settled again.

"I mean," he said more quietly, "I want you to do what's best for you. I won't stand in your way." Even if it killed him. "But tell me one thing, why weren't honest with me from the start?"

"I'm sorry. I wish I had been." So did he. "But I was so very afraid."

"Of me?"

"Yes, and of my own inadequacies. Mostly I feared being found by my family and having Sophie taken away."

"I don't understand."

"I know you don't. Unless you've lived in a gilded cage, you can't imagine what it's like. All my life, I've been nothing but a trust fund baby, controlled, overprotected, and only accepted for my fortune. The one time I tried to break away, I chose a man who claimed to love me until he had his hands on my money. And then I was nothing. Nothing."

"You thought I'd care about your blasted fortune!" The idea infuriated him.

"Derek did."

"I'm not him."

"Exactly. You didn't know and you loved me anyway. You saw me and accepted me for who I am in here." She tapped her chest. "Do you know what that means to me? For the first time in my life, I'm a normal person, living a free, happy life. That's what I want. That's what Sophie deserves. Don't you see? I could never subject my daughter to that smothering lifestyle where she never really knows someone else's motives. I want her to have confidence that she can do things for herself, that she can earn her own way, that she's beautiful and special for herself, not her money. I want her to grow up where she was born, surrounded by the simple life and good people of Saddleback."

Wonder and hope began to warm his frozen blood. "You want to go on as my housekeeper? You? A woman who could buy this place and hire a dozen servants?"

Her eyes flashed fire. If he'd been kindling, she would have incinerated him.

Hands on hips, she said, "For a smart man, you can sure act dumb. If that's all you want from me, tell me now and I will leave. Because I don't want to be your housekeeper."

"What do you want?"

She slashed at the tears that had begun again. "I want to love you every day of my life. I want to be your partner and your friend and—"

Before she could finish, he used his free hand to yank her against him. His heart banged against his rib cage like hail on a tin roof. "And my lover and my wife?"

She raised her face to his, eyes red-rimmed but glowing with joy. "Yes!"

With a fierce groan of relief, he kissed the lips he craved. For the rest of his life, he'd remember the feel of the December chill seeping through his clothes, the smell of wood smoke in the air, and the taste of her salty tears…mingling with his.

EPILOGUE

CARS LINED THE YARD and driveway of the Southpaw Cattle Company. Jenna's Christmas Eve party was in full swing and she was so excited and happy she could hardly think straight.

The house was full of friends and Dax's family, who'd driven up from Austin for the holiday. She'd been a little nervous about meeting them, but they seemed to like her and were taken captive by Sophie. Even now, the baby, dressed in a red velvet Mrs. Santa suit, was being passed from person to person.

"The house is gorgeous, hon," Crystal said, coming up from behind with a mini quiche in one hand and a glass of wassail in the other.

"So are you." The darkly pretty nurse had chosen a body-skimming dress in Christmas red, a color that suited her perfectly.

"Joe can't keep his hands off me." Crystal giggled and waved at her husband, a quiet guy as blond as Crystal was dark.

"Who can blame him?"

"Same with your man. Look at him over there by the canapés, watching your every move. I think he could gobble you up in one bite."

Jenna blushed, tingling with anticipation at what was to

come before this night was over. Dax had gone cross-eyed when she'd slid into the barely silver one-shouldered dress and strappy stilettos. "I think I just might let him, too."

Crystal's eyes widened and she laughed. A pair of snow-flake earrings danced against her dark skin. "You two are perfect together. I'm thrilled for both of you."

Jenna's heart beat a happy rhythm. "Me, too. The day I crashed my car into Dax's fence, I never dreamed how won-derfully my life would work out."

"You seemed so lost and scared that day, but gritty and de-termined, too. I knew you were gonna make it. But I have to admit things turned out better than I thought." She sipped her steaming wassail and then whispered, "But the Gucci purse should have given me a clue."

"I'm sorry for keeping that from you."

Jenna had shared the truth about her wealthy family with Crystal, but she was still determined to live a normal life and put the trust fund money to use for others less blessed.

"Trust me, girl. I totally understand." She hunched her shoulders and grinned. "Well, sort of. The emotional part anyway, but money and Crystal are soon parted. Oops, I see that hunky husband of mine coming my way. Bet he wants to find a dark corner and make out." She popped the remaining quiche into her cherry-colored lips and waved two fingers. "Ta-ta."

Heart glad, Jenna waved and continued her journey through the partygoers, stopping to chat with first one and then another. Gavin's teacher was there, looking cute and young in a Santa hat. Her little girl was twirling in circles to *The Nutcracker* music playing softly through the sound system.

Talk of the weather and Christmas, politics and children, and lots of laughter mingled with the clink of glasses and the smells of pine and cinnamon. It was a good party. People seemed to be enjoying themselves.

But the best was yet to come.

Gradually, she made her way to Dax's side. He was deep in conversation with another rancher about an upcoming stock show in Fort Worth. As soon as he saw her, Dax said to the other man, "'Scuse me, Jake. There's a beautiful woman wanting my attention."

Jake clapped him on the shoulder. "Talk to you later, then. Great party, ma'am."

Jenna smiled her thanks as he moved away.

Dax slid an arm around her waist and nuzzled her ear. "You smell good. Look good, too."

"Ready for our surprise?"

"Can't wait." He stroked the sensitive flesh on the back of her neck. "I'm sorry your parents chose not to come."

With Dax at her side, she'd talked again with her mother and hammered out a fragile truce. Though Elaine would never fully understand, Jenna hoped to build a workable relationship with her family. She loved them. She just couldn't live with them anymore. When they'd been invited to the wedding, however, they'd refused, certain Jenna was making another mistake. She'd been disappointed, though she'd expected the response.

"Someday, they'll realize. But until they do, I refuse to let them ruin tonight."

"I love you." He kissed her cheek.

"I love you, too."

"Come on, then. Let's find our boy." They glanced around the crowded room and located Gavin easily. Reindeer antlers poked up from his dark head. He'd insisted on wearing a brown suit and antlers in honor of Rudolph who, he was convinced, would be stopping at the house later tonight.

"You painted his nose." Dax said, eyes twinkling.

"He asked."

"I wasn't complaining. I was remembering. You. Me. A lot of sugary frosting." He nuzzled her ear again and whispered.

"Very soon, I'm going to paint you all over, just so I can clean up the mess."

She gave him a sultry look and twitched one eyebrow. "Ready when you are, cowboy."

His pupils dilated until the green irises were but a rim around the edges. "How about now?"

She laughed, feeling beautiful and sexy and desirable. Dax had done that for her, given her the confidence to be a woman. "How about you get the real party started and we'll save the good stuff for later."

"As my lady wishes." He executed an elegant bow and led her to a roped-off area in front of the crackling fireplace. Guests assumed she'd been protecting the white rug, but she and Dax had other plans. Dax's family already knew and when they spotted Dax and Jenna, they moved into action.

Within minutes, the houselights came down and the glow of the tree, the candles and the fireplace filled the vast room with a festive, romantic glow. A hush came over the guests as they turned in curiosity.

Holding Jenna's hand, Dax stood with his back to the stone fireplace, surrounded by flickering candlelight as he spoke. "Friends and family, Jenna and I have a surprise for you tonight. You've come to celebrate Christmas with us, but we also invited you here for another, more personal reason." He glanced her way and she smiled, certain she radiated enough love and joy to light the darkness all by herself. "Jenna Garwood, this gorgeous, classy, incredible woman has agreed to be my wife."

A murmur of excitement rushed through the crowd. Dax held up a hand to quiet them. "And all of you are invited to our wedding which will take place—" he glanced at his watch for effect "—right now."

The excited murmurs started again as the minister from Dax's church stepped forward. Dax's sister had control of the sound system and the music changed to gentle piano by the

O'Neil Brothers. A swish of recorded wind and wind chimes set a mood of peace, and hushed expectation settled on the room. As the minister began to speak and gentle strains of "I Wonder as I Wander" added background, tears filled Jenna's eyes. For indeed, she had wandered a very long distance to find her rightful place.

Dax turned to face her and spoke his words of love and commitment. His voice trembled with emotion that she knew was not nerves but his heart speaking to hers. He slid the diamond band onto her finger and then it was her turn.

She was too full of feelings to tell him everything, but she spoke from her heart, and when a tear slid down her cheek, he bent to kiss it away. A collective sigh went up from the guests.

The ceremony ended and the minister said, "Ladies and gentlemen, I present to you, Mr. and Mrs. Dax Coleman. May they always be as happy and committed as they are this moment."

Applause sounded. The photographer they had hired to capture their party and wedding snapped photo after photo. Gavin, his antlers quivering, pulled away from his grandmother and rushed to hug Dax's legs. "Does this mean Jenna is my mom now?"

Tugging Jenna down with him, Dax crouched to meet his son at eye level. "Yep. What do you think about that?"

Gavin threw his arms around his father's neck. "I think all my Christmas wishes just came true."

As the melody of "I'll be Home for Christmas" began to play, Jenna joined the embrace of her new husband and son, thinking how prophetic both the song and Gavin's words were.

All her Christmas wishes had come true, as well, and she was truly and forever home for Christmas.

* * * * * *

This season we bring you
Christmas Treats
For an early Christmas present Linda Goodnight would like
to share a little treat with you…

Creative Way to Give Money
Teenagers love receiving money as a gift, but let's face it,
handing over an envelope of money is kind of boring. There
are many great ideas for giving money creatively. I stumbled
onto my idea quite by accident. As I browsed the department
store, I spotted a small, inexpensive snow globe that doubled
as a two-sided photo frame, and an idea was born. I inserted
the teen's photo on one side of the globe and a carefully
folded twenty dollar bill on the other side and wrapped the
globe as I would any other gift. When my granddaughter
opened the gift and turned it over, there was Andrew
Jackson's green face smiling through the falling snow. She
loved it, of course, and can reuse the snow globe photo frame
for other pictures. Don't have a photo of the teen? Go to
MySpace or any of the popular online communities. Chances
are you can lift one there as I did.

Edible Craft for Kids
Simple, edible crafts are just the thing to get your child
involved in the Christmas celebration. One tasty and fairly
healthy treat is made with pretzel rods. I've seen a number
of variations, but the simplest one is pretty to look at, very
tasty, and kids can make these themselves with only a little
supervision. Take the fat pretzel rods and dip one end in
melted almond bark/candy melt, the flavor of your choice. (I
like the chocolate best, but the white chocolate and butter-
scotch are good, too.) Let them cool a minute and then roll
in a plate of colored sprinkles, sugars, or crushed candies. The
resulting product looks pretty standing in a festive cup and

your child feels as if she/he has really done something special. These are great for your child to make and take to school parties, too!

Merry Christmas

& A Happy New Year!

Thank you for a wonderful
2013...

A sneaky peek at next month...

By Request

RELIVE THE ROMANCE WITH THE BEST OF THE BEST

My wish list for next month's titles...

In stores from 20th December 2013:

☐ The Snow Bride – Jennie Lucas, Helen Brooks & Anne McAllister

☐ Bedroom Seductions – Nicola Marsh, Anne Oliver & Lucy King

3 stories in each book - only £5.99!

In stores from 3rd January 2014:

☐ Boardroom Kings – Catherine Mann, Emilie Rose & Maya Banks

☐ Playboy Bachelors – Marie Ferrarella

Available at WHSmith, Tesco, Asda, Eason, Amazon and Apple

Just can't wait?

Visit us Online

You can buy our books online a month before they hit the shops! **www.millsandboon.co.uk**

1213/05

Special Offers

Every month we put together collections and longer reads written by your favourite authors.

Here are some of next month's highlights— and don't miss our fabulous discount online!

On sale 3rd January

On sale 3rd January

On sale 20th December

Save 20%
on all Special Releases

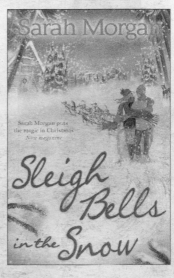

Come in from the cold this Christmas with two of our favourite authors. Whether you're jetting off to Vermont with Sarah Morgan or settling down for Christmas dinner with Fiona Harper, the smiles won't stop this festive season.

Visit:
www.millsandboon.co.uk

Meet The Sullivans...

Over 1 million books sold worldwide!

Stay tuned for more from The Sullivans in 2014

Available from:

www.millsandboon.co.uk